DELIBERATION

Clifton Wilcox

Fredericksburg, Virginia

Print ISBN: 978-1-969770-14-2

EBook ISBN: 978-1-969770-21-0

Published by Windward Publishing LLC., Fredericksburg, Virginia.

The characters and events in this book are fictitious. Any similarity to real persons, living or dead, is coincidental and not intended by the author.

Wilcox, Clifton

Deliberation

Windward Publishing, LLC

2026

DEDICATION

To the thirteenth voice—
the one no one sees,
but everyone eventually hears.

Table of Contents

Books by Clifton Wilcox

Non-Fiction

Scape Goat: Targeted for Blame

Groupthink: An Impediment to Success

Bias: The Unconscious Deceiver

Witch-hunt: The Assignment of Blame

The Fall of the Kingdom of Northumbria

Witch-hunt: The Class of Cultures

Road to War: The Quest for a New World Order

Envy: A Deeper Shade of Green

The Rise of the Nazi SS

The Horrible Void Between the Trenches

Fiction

Cool's Last Stand

Where Despair Comes to Play

The Monuments Must Bleed

Keeper of the Fallen Ages

I, Monster

Harvest of Eyes

The Case Against Jasper

Crimson Plume: The Song of Corvus

Framed in Love

Echoes of the Forgotten

Blacktop Harvest

The Plagiarist Game

The Black Forest Protocol

Outcome without Appeal

Prologue

The room had no memory.

That was the first thing the man noticed.

Not that he knew how he noticed it—only that the feeling pressed against him the moment he stepped inside. The walls were dull gray, the long wooden table scarred with decades of scratches, and twelve chairs sat around it like silent witnesses waiting to be questioned. The air smelled faintly of dust and old paper. Somewhere above, a fluorescent light hummed with the patience of something that had been waiting far longer than it should.

He looked at the clock on the wall.

2:26.

The second hand moved once.

Then it stopped.

The man frowned, unsure why that bothered him so much. Rooms like this existed in every courthouse across the country. Places where strangers were forced together to make impossible decisions about other people's lives. Rooms where opinions hardened into verdicts and verdicts hardened into consequences.

Ordinary rooms.

But this one felt… aware.

The chairs were empty, yet the man could almost feel the shape of people who had sat there before—twelve shadows of arguments that had not quite faded. Voices that had filled the air with certainty, anger, fear. Somewhere in the wood of the table, in the worn grooves of the floor, the room seemed to remember every word ever spoken within it.

Every accusation.

Every denial.

Every verdict.

The man walked slowly around the table. His fingers brushed the back of one chair, then another, counting them without realizing he was counting.

One.

Two.

Three.

By the time he reached the last chair, his hand stopped.

He counted again.

Twelve.

Yet something felt wrong.

He moved to the center of the room and listened. The building beyond the door was silent—too silent for a courthouse that should have been alive with footsteps, murmurs, and the distant echo of gavels striking wood.

No voices.

No movement.

Just the hum of the light and the quiet certainty that the room was waiting.

He looked down at the table.

A single slip of paper lay at the center.

Blank.

No writing. No signature. No decision.

Just a verdict form waiting to be filled.

The man stared at it for a long moment.

Then he whispered the question that every jury eventually asked, though rarely out loud.

"Who decides?"

The room offered no answer.

But somewhere deep inside the walls, something seemed to listen.

And wait.

Chapter 1

The Deliberation Room

The deliberation room smelled faintly of old coffee and furniture polish, the kind of institutional cleanliness that never quite erased the sweat of other people's arguments. Fluorescent lights hummed overhead with a steady, indifferent buzz. A long wooden table dominated the center, surrounded by twelve chairs that had been scuffed by decades of restless shoes. A chalkboard hung on one wall, its tray holding two nubs of chalk and an eraser worn down to gray felt.

One by one, they filed in through the door the bailiff held open, each juror stepping across the threshold as if stepping into a different set of rules.

Juror #1 entered first, not by accident. He walked with the quiet urgency of a man who measured time in quarterly reports and policy compliance. His suit was neat without being flashy, his hair combed flat, his eyes already taking inventory: number of chairs, placement of the water pitcher, whether the blinds were angled evenly. He paused near the head of the table, a natural claim staked by posture alone, and set his briefcase down with care, as if the table were a conference room and he owned the agenda.

Behind him came Juror #2, a woman in a plain cardigan who held her purse tight against her ribs. She looked as though she'd apologized her whole life for taking up space. Her eyes moved from face to face quickly, then away, always away, as if contact might invite confrontation. She chose a chair not at the center of anything, but not quite at the far end either, a compromise between wanting to disappear and fearing what might happen if she did.

Juror #3 filled the doorway next, a man whose anger arrived before he did. He wore a sport coat that no longer fit his shoulders the way it once had, and his jaw worked as if he were chewing something bitter. He didn't greet anyone. He dropped into a chair with a hard exhale and stared down the length of the table, daring someone to contradict him. When his gaze landed briefly on the timid woman, she immediately looked down at her hands.

Juror #4 walked in as if he'd been assigned here by an algorithm. His expression was composed, his movements efficient. He carried a legal pad and a pen already uncapped, and he nodded once in the general direction of the others, a gesture so small it could be mistaken for coincidence. He chose a seat where he could see everyone clearly, then placed his pad squarely in front of him and aligned the edges with the table, as though order itself might keep the room from becoming emotional.

Juror #5 came in with a guarded swagger, a young man with an older man's eyes. His clothes were clean but worn, the kind of wear that came from necessity rather than style. He scanned the room with practiced caution, reading posture and tone the way some people read headlines. When Juror #3's glare touched him, he lifted his chin in response, not challenging, exactly, but refusing to be made small. He sat with his back to the wall, as if he'd learned long ago not to let danger sit behind him.

Juror #6 followed, broader through the chest, hands that looked like they belonged to someone who did things for a living rather than discussed them. He nodded to the bailiff and muttered something that might have been thanks, then took a seat with the blunt finality of a man parking a truck. He stared at the center of the table, his mouth set, his patience already rationed.

Juror #7 entered talking, the words spilling out before the room had even registered, he'd arrived. "Finally," he said, flashing a grin that didn't reach his eyes. "Thought we were going to sit out there until retirement." His tie was loosened, his sleeves slightly rumpled, the uniform of a man who treated obligation like a joke he couldn't get out of telling.

He gave Juror #1 an exaggerated nod, as if they were old colleagues, and dropped into a chair with a flourish that made the table vibrate.

Juror #8 came in quietly.

He looked ordinary enough at first glance, which was perhaps why he was easy to miss. Not tall, not short, not heavy, not thin. His face held the kind of calm that didn't announce itself, it simply refused to be disturbed. He didn't carry a briefcase or a legal pad. He didn't check his watch. He offered a small, polite nod to the group as if they'd met at a bus stop rather than in the wake of a murder trial. Then he chose a seat that was neither prominent nor peripheral, a place where he could listen without being forced to perform.

Juror #9 entered slowly, each step measured. He was elderly, his suit older than some of the others, and he held himself with a careful dignity, like someone used to moving through rooms where people underestimated him. His eyes were sharp despite the faint tremor in his hands. He paused in the doorway to take in the faces, not the furniture, and there was something in his gaze that suggested he was already listening for what wasn't being said.

Juror #10 came in like a storm looking for a place to land. He wore impatience as if it were a right. His mouth curled slightly when he looked around, and his eyes lingered on Juror #11 with a particular kind of appraisal, the kind that reduced a person to a category before they'd spoken a word. He sat heavily, spreading into the space with ownership.

Juror #11 entered with quiet restraint, straight-backed, hands folded briefly in front of him as he stepped inside. His accent had been noticeable in court, and it was still there now, though he spoke little. His clothes were neat, his expression serious in a way that didn't seek approval. He offered a courteous greeting to the room, a simple "Good afternoon," as if civility were a duty, not a preference. He sat near the middle, close enough to be part of the group, but not close enough to invite easy familiarity.

Juror #12 arrived last, checking something on his phone until the bailiff cleared his throat. "Phones," the bailiff reminded, not unkindly.

"Right, right," Juror #12 said, giving it up to the bailiff offering a sheepish smile. He had the polished look of someone used to being seen, hair styled with effort that pretended to be effortless. He carried himself as if life were a series of meetings he could charm his way through. He took the remaining chair and immediately glanced around as if gauging the room's mood, then adjusted his cuff as though that might help.

When the last chair scraped into place, the bailiff stepped inside and closed the door behind him, though not with any special emphasis. "Ladies and gentlemen," he said, voice practiced, "you've been selected to serve on the jury in this matter. Your role now is to deliberate and reach a verdict based solely on the evidence presented in court and the judge's instructions."

He placed a thick manila envelope on the table, along with a stack of exhibits in clear sleeves and a sheaf of paper clipped neatly together. The foreman's badge, a small metal pin, sat on top like a tiny crown.

"You'll select a foreperson," the bailiff continued. "If you need anything, there's a buzzer by the door. The restroom is down the hall, but you'll need to be escorted. Lunch will be arranged. You are not to discuss this case with anyone outside this room, and you are not to use any outside information." His eyes moved over them, a standard sweep, then paused just long enough to make sure they understood the weight of what he was saying. "Once you've reached a verdict, notify me."

Juror #7 raised two fingers, as if he were in a classroom. "How long does it usually take?" he asked, grin returning.

The bailiff did not smile. "As long as it takes."

Juror #3 let out a harsh laugh. "It won't take long."

Juror #1 cleared his throat, already stepping into the space of leadership. "We'll proceed in an orderly manner," he said, as if he were speaking to a team that had missed a deadline. He reached for the foreman's pin but didn't put it on yet, waiting for someone to object.

No one did.

Juror #2 watched him take it, her fingers worrying at the edge of her purse. Juror #10 leaned back and crossed his arms; an expression of bored certainty fixed on his face. Juror #4 opened his pad and wrote something down without looking at the paper first, a motion so automatic it suggested habit rather than thought. Juror #5 tapped his foot lightly under the table, heel hitting the chair rung, a contained energy that didn't know where to go.

Juror #8 sat with his hands loosely folded, eyes moving from person to person, not judging, exactly, but noticing. When Juror #1's gaze swept past him, Juror #8 met it briefly, offering nothing but attention.

The bailiff nodded once. "All right. I'll be outside." He turned, opened the door, and stepped out. The latch clicked shut behind him.

For a moment, no one spoke. The room settled around them, the hum of the lights filling the gap where the courtroom's formalities had been. Here, there were no attorneys performing certainty, no judge guiding the sequence, no gallery murmuring at the edges. Just twelve strangers and the quiet knowledge that a teenage boy's life could be decided by what happened next.

Juror #1 finally pinned the small metal badge to his lapel, a gesture that seemed to please him in a way he didn't admit. "All right," he said, hands flattening on the table as if pressing down on chaos before it started. "Let's begin by making sure everyone understands our responsibilities. Then we'll review the judge's instructions and take an initial vote."

Juror #7 made a soft whistle. "Music to my ears."

Juror #9's gaze drifted toward the chalkboard, as if expecting something to already be written there. Juror #11 sat very still, listening. Juror #12 offered a friendly, empty smile around the table, the kind meant to smooth things over before there was anything to smooth.

Juror #3 leaned forward, elbows on the table. "We already heard the evidence," he said. "The kid did it."

Juror #8 did not react, not outwardly. He only looked at the envelope of exhibits, then at the others, as if measuring the distance between what they thought they knew and what they were willing to examine.

Juror #1 nodded once, the way managers did when letting someone speak before redirecting. "We'll get to that," he said. "But we'll do it properly."

Outside, the courthouse continued its ordinary rhythm: footsteps in corridors, distant doors opening and closing, the muted voice of a clerk calling a name. Inside the deliberation room, the air felt slightly thicker, as if the walls themselves were waiting to hear what these twelve people would decide to live with.

Juror #1 pulled the judge's instructions toward him. "First," he said, "we summarize the case, so we're all on the same page."

And as he began, the others settled into their seats, some eager, some reluctant, some already convinced. The table held their hands, their papers, their assumptions. It held, too, the first faint tremor of something else, something not yet visible, like a crack forming under paint.

Juror #8 listened without interruption, his face calm, his eyes attentive.

As if he had all the time in the world.

Juror #1 cleared his throat again and lifted the judge's instructions like they were meeting minutes. He didn't read them yet. Instead he placed them neatly at the top of his space, squared with the edge of the table, then slid the manila envelope of exhibits closer.

"Before we get into opinions," he said, "we need to be aligned on what the case is and what it isn't.

We're not here to solve a mystery novel. We're here to determine whether the prosecution proved guilt beyond a reasonable doubt, based on the evidence and the law as the judge gave it."

Juror #7 leaned back, hands behind his head. "Translation: don't get cute."

Juror #1 ignored the comment without looking up. "We have one charge. Murder in the first degree. That requires intent and premeditation. The prosecution argues the defendant planned it, waited for his father to come home, and stabbed him repeatedly. The defense argues… what, exactly?"

Juror #12 offered, too quickly, "That the kid snapped. Heat of passion. Or he didn't do it at all."

Juror #4 made a small note on his pad. Juror #3 snorted, a sound like something dragged across concrete.

"The defense argued reasonable doubt," Juror #1 corrected. "They offered alternative explanations and attacked the reliability of the witnesses. They did not provide an alibi that holds up, and they didn't call many witnesses of their own."

Juror #2 nodded faintly, as if relieved someone else was speaking for her.

Juror #1 continued, hands resting flat as though he could keep the room from tipping. "Now. The facts as presented."

He tapped the top exhibit sleeve with a finger.

"The victim is the defendant's father. Forty-six years old. Pronounced dead at the scene. Cause of death: multiple stab wounds to the chest and abdomen. Time of death estimated between ten fifteen and ten forty-five p.m. on the night in question."

Juror #6 shifted in his chair, the wood creaking under him. "That's when they said the neighbors heard yelling, right?"

"Yes," Juror #1 said. "We'll get to that. The defendant is seventeen. Lives in the apartment with the victim. Mother deceased. No siblings in the home."

Juror #9's eyes remained on the table, but his attention was unmistakably sharp. He didn't look like he was remembering the trial so much as weighing the words for hidden seams.

Juror #1 lifted another sleeve. Inside was a photograph, the kind you couldn't look at for long without feeling like you'd been made to participate.

"The weapon," he said, voice staying carefully neutral. "A kitchen knife from the apartment. The prosecution says it matches a missing knife from the set in the defendant's kitchen. The blade length is consistent with the wounds. The knife was recovered two floors down in the building's garbage chute collection area. Partial prints were found on the handle."

Juror #10 made a dismissive sound. "Partial prints, full guilt."

Juror #11's gaze moved briefly to Juror #10, then away again, the look contained but not soft. "The expert said the prints were not sufficient for a definitive match," he said quietly.

Juror #10 rolled his eyes. "Oh, come on."

Juror #1 lifted a hand, not inviting debate yet. "The testimony was that the partials were consistent with the defendant's hand size and pattern, but not conclusive. There was also blood on the blade. The lab testified it matched the victim."

Juror #5 leaned forward, forearms on the table. "They ever say if the kid's blood was on it?"

Juror #1 flipped through his memory with the confidence of someone who trusted his own filing system. "No. Not on that knife. The prosecution emphasized that the victim's blood was on the blade and the defendant had minor superficial cuts on one hand consistent with slippage or a struggle."

Juror #3 slammed his palm lightly, not enough to rattle the exhibits but enough to make a point. "That's it right there. You stab somebody, your hand slips, you cut yourself. Happens in every story."

"Or you handle a broken glass," Juror #8 said mildly.

The room stilled for a beat, surprised more by the calm delivery than by the contradiction. Juror #8 hadn't been silent exactly, but he'd been careful not to insert himself. Now he looked at the photo as if it were simply an object, not a conclusion.

Juror #3 turned toward him, eyes narrowing. "You think he got cut doing dishes after murdering his father?"

"I think cuts happen," Juror #8 replied. "I'm not suggesting a scenario. I'm suggesting we treat it as one data point."

Juror #4's pen paused, then resumed, slower this time.

Juror #1 took the opening as permission to steer them back to the outline. "The defendant was arrested the next morning after the body was discovered. The building superintendent called police after noticing blood in the hallway outside the apartment door."

Juror #2's face tightened at the word blood.

"The apartment itself," Juror #1 went on, "showed signs of a struggle according to the responding officers. An overturned chair, broken lamp, blood spatter in the living room area. The victim was found on his back near the couch."

Juror #7 let out a low whistle, not amused anymore. “Kid did a number.”

Juror #1’s gaze flicked toward him. “We’re not using that language.”

Juror #7 held up his hands. “Right. Sorry, boss.”

Juror #1 continued anyway, as if he hadn’t heard. “Now. The prosecution’s theory of motive. The father was allegedly abusive. There was testimony from a teacher about bruises noticed on the defendant’s arms over the last year. There was testimony from a neighbor about yelling through the walls, threats, things thrown. The prosecution argued the defendant had a longstanding reason to hate his father, and the final argument that night was the trigger.”

Juror #3 leaned back, his jaw working. For a moment his anger didn’t look like certainty. It looked like something else trying to stay hidden.

Juror #9 spoke softly, almost to himself. “A motive doesn’t prove an act.”

Juror #1 nodded once, satisfied with the sentiment because it sounded responsible. “Correct. Which is why they also put on witnesses.”

He turned a page in the packet, the sound crisp in the too-bright room.

“Witness one,” he said. “An elderly woman in the apartment across the hall. She testified that around ten thirty she heard a heated argument. She said she recognized the father’s voice and the defendant’s voice. She heard a loud crash. Then she heard footsteps, the apartment door opening and closing, and someone running down the stairs.”

Juror #6 frowned. “She said she saw him?”

“No,” Juror #1 said. “She did not see a face. She said she looked through the peephole but it was too late, she only saw a shadow moving down the hall.”

Juror #5 muttered, “Convenient.”

Juror #10 scoffed. “Or accurate.”

Juror #1 kept going. “Witness two. A man on the floor below who testified he saw the defendant on the stairs shortly after ten thirty. He said the defendant looked agitated, breathing hard. He also said he noticed what looked like a stain on the sleeve of the defendant’s hoodie.”

Juror #12 asked, “Didn’t the defense bring up that the guy was half asleep? Like he was coming back from work and wasn’t sure of the time?”

Juror #1 nodded. “Yes. The defense attacked his certainty about the exact time and his ability to identify the defendant. But the witness said he’d seen the defendant before in the building and recognized him.”

Juror #11 folded his hands tighter. "Recognition is not the same as certainty."

Juror #10 shot him a look. "Everybody's a philosopher now."

Juror #1 raised his voice just a fraction, the corporate tone that meant the meeting was sliding. "We'll get to evaluating. I'm summarizing."

He tapped the packet again.

"Witness three. The responding officer who testified about the defendant's demeanor when located the next morning. The officer said the defendant appeared calm and did not ask about his father's condition."

Juror #2 swallowed. "People react differently."

Juror #1 glanced at her, acknowledging her existence in a way that was almost kind. "True. But that's what was testified."

Juror #4 finally looked up from his pad. "We should include the defendant's statement," he said.

Juror #1 nodded. "Yes. The defendant's statement. He told police he left the apartment after an argument and stayed out late. He did not say where. He claimed he came back near midnight, found the apartment dark, assumed his father had gone out, and went to his room. He claimed he discovered the body in the morning and panicked."

Juror #7 huffed. "Panicked so hard he didn't call 911."

Juror #8's eyes moved to Juror #7, not accusing, simply attentive. "He was seventeen," Juror #8 said. "His father's dead on the floor. Fear doesn't behave."

Juror #3's chair scraped as he leaned forward again, anger returning to its familiar place. "Or he didn't call because he did it."

Juror #1 held up a finger. "And the prosecution argued exactly that. They argued the defendant hid the knife, cleaned himself up, and tried to act normal. They emphasized there was no credible alternative suspect and no evidence of forced entry."

Juror #5 drummed his fingers once on the table, then stopped when Juror #1 glanced his way. "No forced entry doesn't mean no one else could've been there," Juror #5 said. "People let people in."

"Correct," Juror #1 said, though his tone suggested the word was a concession he didn't enjoy. "But there was no evidence presented that anyone else was in the apartment."

Juror #9's gaze drifted toward the chalkboard again. It was still blank, a dusty rectangle waiting for someone to write something that would stain the room.

Juror #1 reached the end of his summary and exhaled, satisfied he'd restored structure. "That's the case in broad strokes. Now we review the judge's instructions and then we take an initial vote. After that, we discuss."

Juror #7 straightened a little. "Now you're speaking my language."

Juror #1 began to read from the instructions, voice adopting a practiced formal cadence: presumption of innocence, burden of proof, reasonable doubt. The words were familiar, almost comforting in their ritual. They made the room feel like it belonged to the courthouse.

But as Juror #1 read, Juror #8 watched the others more than he watched the paper. The foreman's rigid focus. The timid clerk's clenched hands. The furious father's simmering impatience. The analyst's tidy notes. The slum kid's guarded posture. The working man's blunt frown. The joker's forced ease. The old man's quiet attention. The bigot's contempt. The immigrant's contained dignity. The advertiser's restless charm.

Twelve people in a room, pretending the law could keep their hearts from showing.

When Juror #1 finished, he set the paper down as if he'd put a lid on something volatile.

"All right," he said. "Ballots. We'll do it quickly and then we'll talk."

Juror #8's hands remained folded.

As if the talking had already begun.

Juror #1 slid a stack of small paper slips from the envelope and set them in the center of the table like a dealer about to start a game nobody had agreed to play.

"Write your vote," he said. "Guilty or not guilty. Fold it. Pass it back."

Juror #7 made a show of looking around. "Secret ballot. Very democratic. Love it."

"No commentary," Juror #1 replied, and there was something in the way he said it that suggested he was already tired of being tested.

Juror #12 leaned forward, smiling as if this were a team-building exercise. "Just two words," he said lightly. "Should be easy."

Juror #9 didn't smile back. His eyes rested on the slips, then lifted to each face as if he were trying to memorize them for later, for a time when their expressions would matter more than their words.

Juror #1 pushed the stack toward Juror #2 first, closest to his left. It was a small decision, procedural, but it carried an unspoken message: we will do this in order. We will do it properly. We will do it my way.

Juror #2 took a slip with careful fingers, as if paper could cut. She glanced at the others before looking down, shoulders curling slightly inward. In court she had spoken only when spoken to, nodding at the right moments, eyes fixed on the witness stand or her own lap. Now, with the pencil in her hand, she hesitated the way people did when they were afraid of doing even the simplest thing wrong. Her gaze darted once toward Juror #1, as though searching his face for the correct answer.

Juror #3 didn't need a pencil to know what he would write. His impatience filled the room in short bursts: the scrape of his chair, the hard exhale through his nose, the way his fingers drummed once on the table and stopped, as if even that small noise offended him. He had the look of a man who didn't come here to think. He came here to confirm what he'd already decided.

Across from him, Juror #11 sat very straight, hands relaxed but not loose, the posture of someone who had learned that in certain rooms you survived by controlling your body. He watched the pencil pass from person to person with a quiet attentiveness that didn't ask permission. When his eyes met Juror #10's for a heartbeat, Juror #10 looked away first, pretending he hadn't been staring.

Juror #4 had already written the word in his head before the slip reached him. He didn't speak. He rarely moved his face. His penmanship, when he finally put pencil to paper, was neat and narrow, the kind of writing that made you think of spreadsheets and margins. He folded his slip with a precision that looked like respect for the process but felt more like insulation. If he kept everything orderly, perhaps nothing could get inside.

Juror #5 took his slip and leaned back with it, angling his body away from the center of the table. He wrote quickly, then folded the paper and held it between two fingers without passing it on right away. He glanced at the door, the handle, the small square buzzer beside it. In court, he'd watched the attorneys like they were trying to hustle him, and the witnesses like they were hiding something. In this room, his suspicion didn't evaporate. It simply changed targets.

Juror #6 accepted the pencil and slip like tools handed off on a job site. He wrote with a heavy pressure that left a faint indentation on the paper beneath. His jaw was set. He looked as though he'd spent most of his life swallowing frustration because it didn't pay to spit it out. When he folded his ballot, he creased it sharply, once, twice, as if making sure it stayed shut.

Juror #7 twirled the pencil between his fingers before he wrote, performing ease. In court he'd rolled his eyes at the defense's objections, smirked at the prosecution's dramatic pauses. He'd been the kind of juror attorneys hated and feared: the one who might decide the case based on whether he liked the sound of a voice. But the smile he wore now had a brittle edge to it, as if he knew he was supposed to take this seriously and resented the expectation.

Juror #8 watched all of them.

He didn't watch their hands so much as the small tells that escaped when they thought nobody was looking: Juror #2's thumb worrying the edge of the slip until the paper began to fray; Juror #3's knee bouncing under the table like a piston; Juror #4 aligning his folded ballot with the table's grain before passing it on; Juror #10's constant scanning of faces for someone to agree with him, someone to validate the anger he brought into the room like a personal belonging.

Juror #8's own slip lay untouched in front of him for a moment, as if he were waiting for the room to settle into its shape before he added anything to it. His calm wasn't passive. It was deliberate. He had listened to the judge's instructions as though they were worth hearing, but he had listened to the others as though their silences were the real testimony.

The pencil reached Juror #9. The old man held it for a long moment, not writing, just looking at the blank slip. His hands trembled faintly, not from frailty exactly, but from the quiet energy of thought. He had spoken only a few words so far, but those words had carried weight. A motive doesn't prove an act. He seemed like someone who had lived long enough to understand that certainty was often just impatience wearing a suit.

When he finally wrote, his letters were careful, slightly slanted, as if he were signing his name on something permanent.

Juror #10 took his slip next and wrote with an aggressive speed. He folded it without smoothing it, then slapped it lightly on the table in front of Juror #1 like a receipt. His mouth curled as he did it, satisfaction already blooming. He didn't look at the paper again. He didn't need to. He looked at Juror #11 instead, as if daring him to be different.

Juror #11's turn came. He took the slip, glanced at it, then at Juror #1, then down again. He wrote slowly. Whatever he put on the paper, it cost him something, not because he was uncertain but because he understood the meaning of a vote in a way the others treated as abstract. His expression didn't change when he folded it. He passed it on with a small, polite motion, as if handing over a fragile thing.

Juror #12 received the pencil last. He flashed a grin toward Juror #7, then to Juror #1, the kind of grin that tried to make everyone friends in a room designed for disagreement. "Moment of truth," he said under his breath, though it wasn't quiet enough to be private.

Juror #1's eyes lifted. "No commentary," he repeated.

Juror #12 chuckled as if he'd been caught telling a harmless joke. He wrote quickly, folded his slip, and placed it on the pile forming in front of the foreman.

Now all eyes moved, briefly, to Juror #8.

It was subtle, but it happened. Not everyone stared openly. Juror #2 glanced up and away. Juror #3 stared like he wanted to burn through him. Juror #4's gaze flicked from his pad to Juror #8's hands and back. Juror #9 watched without impatience, the way you watched someone about to do something that mattered.

Juror #8 picked up the pencil.

For a moment, the room's hum seemed louder. The fluorescent lights didn't change, but the air felt tighter, as if the walls were leaning in. The chalkboard remained blank, two nubs of chalk waiting in their tray like unused teeth.

Juror #8 lowered his eyes to the slip and wrote with measured strokes. His handwriting was ordinary, neither careful nor sloppy, as if he didn't believe the aesthetics of a word changed its truth. When he finished, he folded the paper in half and set it down gently on the table before sliding it across to Juror #1.

Juror #1 collected the last ballot and stacked them neatly, tapping the edges against the table to square them. He treated the folded slips with a bureaucratic reverence, as though they were official documents rather than small, private decisions.

"All right," he said, voice firm. He looked around the table, making brief eye contact with each person in turn, like a supervisor taking attendance. "We'll read them aloud. Then we'll discuss."

Juror #3 leaned forward, ready to pounce on whatever dissent might reveal itself. Juror #7 sat up a little straighter, his grin fading into something more alert. Juror #2 clasped her hands together tightly, knuckles pale. Juror #11's gaze settled on Juror #1's hands, calm but intent.

Juror #9 watched the foreman's fingers with the same quiet focus he'd given the witnesses in court, as if he expected something to slip.

Juror #1 placed the stack of ballots in front of him, took the top one, and began to unfold it.

The paper made a soft crackle in the still room, loud enough to sound like the first break in something that had been holding for a long time.

Chapter 2

The First Vote

Juror #1 unfolded the first slip with the careful patience of a man opening a contract.

The pencil mark inside was bold, almost carved through the paper.

“Guilty,” he read aloud.

No one moved. It was as if the word had been said in the courtroom a hundred times already and this was only the echo catching up.

Juror #3’s mouth tightened into something like satisfaction. Juror #7 let out a soft breath that might have been relief. Juror #2’s shoulders loosened by a fraction, as if agreement from someone else meant the room was safer.

Juror #1 placed the ballot to his right, starting a new stack. He reached for the next.

The second slip crackled as he opened it. “Guilty.”

Juror #10's lips curled. He leaned back farther, arms still crossed, the posture of a man watching a predictable outcome unfold. Across from him, Juror #11 did not react at all, but his eyes stayed fixed on the foreman's hands.

Juror #1 unfolded the third ballot. "Guilty."

The word landed with more weight now, not because it had changed, but because repetition had begun to turn it into a current. The room had a direction. It was heading somewhere. A teenage boy's fate was being decided in a sequence of small paper sounds.

Juror #1 kept his expression neutral, but his movements grew subtly quicker, as though he could already see the end of the process and wanted to reach it efficiently.

He opened the fourth. "Guilty."

Juror #4's pen stopped moving for the first time since he'd opened his legal pad. His eyes lifted, measuring the tally without needing it spoken. Four. The analyst in him seemed pleased by consistency. The human part, if it existed on his face at all, stayed hidden behind composure.

Fifth ballot. "Guilty."

Juror #6 exhaled through his nose, a sound of tired inevitability. He stared at the table's surface as if it were a shop floor and this was just another job that had to be finished, whether you liked it or not.

Sixth ballot. “Guilty.”

Juror #5 shifted in his chair, foot tapping once under the table before stilling. His eyes flicked from the growing guilty stack to the faces around him, checking reactions the way he checked exits. He didn’t look triumphant. He looked alert, like someone who’d learned that being on the same side didn’t always keep you safe.

Seventh ballot. Juror #1 opened it and didn’t pause. “Guilty.”

Juror #7’s earlier grin threatened to return, then died halfway there. He drummed his fingertips on the chair arm, not in impatience now but in a kind of restless confirmation. He wanted it done. He wanted the word to become a door back to normal life.

Eighth ballot. “Guilty.”

The fluorescent hum overhead seemed suddenly louder, or maybe the room had simply grown quieter around the tally, everyone listening to the paper, listening to the foreman’s voice, listening to the sound of certainty building.

Juror #2 clasped her hands tighter in her lap. Her eyes had gone glossy, not with tears, but with the strain of holding herself still. In court she had looked at the defendant only in brief glances, like touching something hot. Now she stared at the guilty stack as if it were a verdict already inked, already filed, already irreversible.

Juror #1 reached for the ninth slip.

He unfolded it. “Guilty.”

Nine.

Juror #3 leaned back for the first time since the ballots started. The tension in his shoulders eased into something almost smug. He looked around the table as if he expected to see nods of recognition, a silent agreement that he’d been right from the beginning. When his eyes passed Juror #8, they sharpened, searching for some flicker of resistance.

Juror #8’s face stayed calm. His hands remained folded, resting lightly on the table as if he were waiting for something else to begin.

Tenth ballot. “Guilty.”

Juror #10 made a small sound in his throat, not quite a laugh. “There we go,” he muttered, loud enough to be heard, even if he pretended it wasn’t meant for anyone.

Juror #1 didn’t look at him. He kept his gaze on the ballots, maintaining the pretense of procedure. But his posture had shifted. He sat a little straighter, the way he did when a meeting went according to plan.

Juror #11's eyes moved briefly to Juror #10, then back to the table. His expression remained controlled, but something tightened around his mouth, a quiet restraint that had nothing to do with the evidence and everything to do with the people.

Juror #1's fingers hovered over the next slip.

Eleven ballots were on the table in front of him now, with two still folded in the stack. The guilty pile was thick, squared neatly at the corners from the way he kept aligning it. It looked official already, like an exhibit.

He unfolded the eleventh ballot. "Guilty."

The word came out softer this time, not because Juror #1 meant it to, but because it was harder to keep neutral when the outcome was so close to total. Eleven would be nearly unanimous. Eleven would be decisive. Eleven would mean they were only a breath away from what Juror #3 had promised in the hallway tone of his voice: It won't take long.

Juror #7 shifted, chair creaking. "So," he said, not quite joking now, "that's pretty clear."

Juror #1 held up a hand, silencing him without a glance. "We haven't finished," he said, and the reprimand carried more edge than his earlier no commentary. He wanted the count clean. He wanted the final number before anyone spoke.

Juror #9 watched him with steady attention, the way he had watched witnesses in court, as if the truth was not in the statements but in the pauses. The old man's eyes moved from the guilty stack to the remaining folded ballots. There was no satisfaction on his face. There was, instead, a faint sadness, the kind that came from recognizing how quickly a group could become a single mind.

Across the table, Juror #2 glanced at the last two slips and then quickly away, as if looking at them might invite something to go wrong. Juror #6 rubbed his thumb along the edge of the table. Juror #4's pen began to move again, recording the tally as if it were a statistic.

Juror #3's gaze stayed fixed on the foreman's hands, hungry for the last word.

Juror #5 leaned forward slightly, eyes narrowed, not at the ballots but at the room itself, as though he sensed that the speed of this decision carried its own kind of danger. A quick verdict meant no time for doubts to surface. No time for questions. No time for anyone to change their mind. In the neighborhood he came from, speed was how mistakes got made, and also how bodies got left behind.

Juror #1 took the next ballot.

The room seemed to hold its breath with him. Even Juror #10 stopped shifting, stopped radiating impatience for just a second, waiting for the final confirmation that he'd been right to trust his contempt for nuance.

The foreman unfolded the slip.

For a moment, he didn't read it.

His eyes scanned the word on the paper, and something subtle happened in his face, so small most people would have missed it. A delay. A hesitation. The tiniest break in the smooth rhythm of procedure.

Juror #9 saw it.

Juror #8 saw it too, his gaze steady, unreadable, as if he'd been expecting exactly this pause.

Juror #1's mouth opened, then closed again. He looked down at the slip once more, as though he thought the letters might rearrange themselves into something more convenient.

Juror #7 sat up straighter. "What?" he asked, the impatience in his voice suddenly sharpened by uncertainty.

Juror #3 leaned forward again, anger rising like a reflex. "Just read it."

Juror #1's thumb pressed against the paper, creasing it harder. He lifted his eyes from the ballot and looked around the table, not at everyone, but at faces as if he were taking attendance again, as if he could locate the problem by sight.

The guilty stack sat heavy at his right hand, eleven slips thick and squared.

The remaining folded ballot, the final one, waited beneath his palm like an afterthought.

The room that had felt so certain only seconds ago now felt brittle, the kind of quiet that came before something snapped.

Juror #1 drew in a measured breath.

And then, finally, he spoke.

Juror #1 looked down at the slip again, then lifted his eyes as if the room itself had shifted a fraction off center.

"Not guilty," he said at last.

For a heartbeat the words didn't seem to register. The fluorescent hum filled the silence, steady and stupid. The guilty stack sat to his right like a finished product. Eleven slips, squared and aligned. His left hand still held the last ballot, the paper trembling slightly, though his voice had not.

Then the room reacted all at once, like a body flinching.

"What?" Juror #7 said, the single syllable snapping out of him before his humor could catch it and turn it into a joke.

Juror #3 surged forward in his chair so hard the legs squealed against the tile. “You’ve got to be kidding me.”

Juror #10 let out a bitter laugh. “Here we go.”

Juror #2’s hands went to her mouth, not in shock exactly but in sudden fear, as if dissent were contagious. Juror #12 blinked and glanced around the table with the quick, nervous smile of someone who wanted to smooth a room that had just cracked, only there was nothing to smooth yet, only jagged edges.

Juror #1 set the ballot down slowly, as if placing it too quickly might ignite something. He tapped the top of the guilty stack out of habit, trying to impose order through motion. “All right,” he said, though his voice wasn’t as firm as before. “We have one not guilty.”

Juror #3’s head turned, scanning faces with open accusation. His gaze landed on Juror #9 first, perhaps because the old man had spoken about motive earlier. Juror #9 met the look calmly and shook his head once, small and definite.

Juror #3 swung to Juror #11, lips curling. Juror #11 didn’t flinch, but his eyes hardened. “It is not mine,” he said quietly.

Juror #3's eyes moved to Juror #2, who shrank back so fast her chair scraped. "No," she whispered. "No, I didn't..."

Juror #10 pointed his chin toward Juror #5. "I could see him doing it. Always gotta be difficult."

Juror #5's posture tightened immediately, defensive instinct snapping into place. "Don't look at me," he said. "I'm not here to play games."

Juror #4 lifted his eyes from his legal pad, expression unchanged, but his voice had a controlled edge. "We agreed on a secret ballot for a reason. This isn't productive."

"This isn't productive?" Juror #3 repeated, incredulous. "A kid's going to walk because somebody wants to feel special."

Juror #1 raised a hand, the foreman's reflex, trying to stop the room from becoming a brawl. "We're not accusing anyone. We're discussing the case."

Juror #7 leaned forward, the joker's mask slipping enough to show irritation underneath. "Then let's just find out who it is. No point pretending we don't want to know."

Juror #1 hesitated. The procedure had taken him this far, but it didn't come with a clean script for what to do when the room refused to comply.

Across the table, Juror #8 sat with his hands still loosely folded, his face calm in a way that didn't match the sudden heat. He had not looked surprised when the word not guilty was read. He looked, instead, like someone watching a predictable reaction unfold.

Juror #9's eyes shifted toward him, slow and thoughtful.

Juror #3 followed that movement like a dog catching a scent. "You," he said, voice low with certainty. "It's you."

Juror #8 didn't deny it immediately. He let the accusation land, let the room feel its weight. Then he nodded once. "Yes," he said.

The admission didn't calm them. It sharpened everything.

Juror #10 threw his hands out. "Of course. Of course it's him. Mr. Calm-and-reasonable."

Juror #12 tried again to lighten the moment and failed. "Okay, okay, but that's why we talk, right? That's the whole point. We just… we just talk it out and—"

Juror #3 cut him off. "Talk it out? What is there to talk out? The knife was his. The witnesses heard him. He ran down the stairs. He didn't call the police. He's got cuts on his hand. His father beat him and now he's dead. That's not a puzzle. That's a straight line."

Juror #6 nodded once, a blunt motion of agreement. "Looks straight enough."

Juror #2's voice came thin. "Eleven people heard the same thing and came to the same conclusion."

Juror #8 looked at her, not unkindly. "Eleven people can be wrong."

Juror #3's face reddened. "Oh, come on."

Juror #1 leaned forward, trying to reclaim control from the emotion flooding in. "Juror number eight," he said, formal, as if using the number would make it less personal. "We took an initial vote. Now we discuss. If you have doubts, state them. But understand the burden here. Beyond a reasonable doubt doesn't mean beyond all doubt. It means reasonable."

Juror #8 nodded, as though he'd been waiting for that exact sentence. "I understand the burden," he said. His voice stayed even. "I'm not saying he's innocent. I'm saying we shouldn't kill him without talking first."

The word kill hit the room differently than guilty had.

It made it less like paperwork and more like a body.

Juror #2's eyes filled, quickly blinked away. Juror #12 swallowed and looked down at the table as if he'd suddenly remembered there was a boy attached to all of this, a boy who had sat in court with his hands in his lap and his face carefully blank, as if expression itself could be used against him.

Juror #3 scoffed, but his scoff was strained. "Nobody's killing him," he snapped. "The law is the law."

Juror #8's gaze held steady. "The law doesn't pull the switch or administer the injection. People do."

Juror #10 leaned forward, voice dripping. "So now you're gonna make this about your feelings."

"I'm making it about our responsibility," Juror #8 said.

Juror #4 cleared his throat, precise. "If you have a specific point of doubt, we can examine it systematically."

Juror #8 turned slightly toward him, acknowledging the offer. "I do," he said. "But I want to start with something simpler. We all came in here ready to be done. We're tired. We want to go home. That makes certainty feel good. It doesn't make it true."

Juror #7 snorted. "You don't know what I want."

Juror #8 glanced at him. "You want this to be easy."

Juror #7 opened his mouth, then closed it again, annoyed by how accurate it sounded.

Juror #1 took a measured breath. “All right,” he said. “Then we’ll do this properly. We’ll go through the evidence piece by piece. But I want to make one thing clear. This can’t turn into a philosophical seminar.”

“It already is,” Juror #9 murmured, almost too soft to catch.

Juror #3’s head whipped around. “What was that?”

Juror #9 didn’t back down. “I said it already is. The moment we decide to send a boy to die, it becomes philosophical whether you like the word or not.”

Juror #3 stared at him as if the old man had betrayed the room. “So you voted not guilty too?”

Juror #9 shook his head again. “No.”

Juror #3’s anger re-aimed at Juror #8, easier target, younger face, calmer posture. “Then why are you helping him?”

“I’m not helping him,” Juror #9 said. “I’m helping us. A room that can’t tolerate one dissenting voice is a room that wants permission, not truth.”

Juror #10 made a sound of disgust. “Truth? The truth is the kid did it.”

Juror #11 finally spoke again, voice controlled but firm. "The truth is what we can prove. That is what we promised to do."

Juror #10 turned toward him with immediate hostility. "Oh, spare me. You're always so big on promises."

Juror #11's jaw tightened, but he kept his posture straight. "Yes," he said, the single word weighted.

Juror #1 cut in before the exchange could ignite. "Enough. We're not here to argue with each other about who we are. We're here to evaluate the case."

Juror #5 laughed once, sharp and humorless. "Good luck with that."

Juror #1 ignored him, eyes fixed on Juror #8. "You've made your point about talking. Now talk. What is your doubt?"

Juror #8 shifted slightly in his chair, not retreating, not advancing. He looked at the exhibits in their clear sleeves, then at the faces.

"I want to start with the witness who claimed to see him on the stairs," Juror #8 said. "He said it was shortly after ten thirty. He said the kid was breathing hard. He said there was a stain on his sleeve."

Juror #3 threw up a hand. "Yes. Exactly. End of story."

Juror #8 continued as if he hadn't been interrupted. "But he also admitted he was coming back from a shift. He said he was tired. He wasn't sure of the time until the police suggested it. He didn't describe the defendant's face. He described a hoodie."

Juror #6 frowned. "He said he recognized him."

Juror #8 nodded. "He said he'd seen him around the building. That's not the same as a clear identification in a dim stairwell at night."

Juror #4 tapped his pen once, thoughtful. "Eyewitness confidence is not always correlated with accuracy."

Juror #3 stared at Juror #4 like he'd just switched sides. "Don't start."

"I'm not starting anything," Juror #4 said, voice cool. "I'm stating a fact."

Juror #1's fingers tightened on the edge of the judge's instructions. He could feel the meeting slipping from a tidy agenda into something messier, the kind of mess that took time.

Juror #8's eyes moved to the photograph of the knife. "And the partial prints. Consistent, but not conclusive. That's what the expert said. We all heard it."

Juror #10 scoffed again. “So what? You want a confession?”

“I want us to be honest about what we’re calling proof,” Juror #8 said.

The room went quiet in a different way. Less chaotic. More wary.

Juror #3 leaned forward, voice lowering into something dangerous, like a threat disguised as logic. “What you want is to waste everyone’s time. You want to feel like you’re the only one with a conscience. Meanwhile, that kid sits there pretending he didn’t put a knife in his father.”

Juror #8 met his stare. “And what you want,” he said gently, “is for it to be simple. Because simple doesn’t ask anything of you.”

The sentence hung in the air, and for a moment even Juror #3 seemed unsure what to do with it.

Juror #1 cleared his throat, loudly, reclaiming the room with sound. “We’re going to proceed in order,” he said, forcing the word order like a wedge between them. “We’ll revisit each major piece of evidence. We’ll talk through it. And then we’ll vote again if necessary.”

Juror #7 muttered, “If necessary,” like it tasted bad.

Juror #2's fingers twisted together. "How long is this going to take?"

Juror #8 looked at her, and his expression softened just slightly, not pity, but recognition. "As long as it takes," he said.

It was the bailiff's phrase, but in Juror #8's mouth it sounded less like policy and more like a warning.

Juror #1 slid the exhibits toward the center of the table. The plastic sleeves whispered against wood. The room leaned in, not together, but toward a shared point of focus, like twelve separate minds forced to look at the same blade.

And somewhere beneath the argument, beneath the procedure, beneath the hum of the lights, something else seemed to wake.

Not in the walls, not yet.

In the people.

Juror #1 spread the exhibits so they fanned across the table: the crime scene photos sealed behind glossy plastic, the lab reports clipped and stamped, the transcript pages with highlighted lines from the attorneys. His movements were deliberate, managerial, like arranging a presentation for people who didn't want to be there.

"All right," he said. "We start with the witness on the stairs. Then the neighbor across the hall. Then the physical evidence. We do not jump around."

Juror #3 let out a sound somewhere between a laugh and a growl. "Yeah. Great. Let's pretend we didn't just sit through a whole trial."

Juror #7 tapped two fingers against his chair arm. The rhythm wasn't playful anymore. It was counting time. "Can we just… handle this fast? I got work tomorrow."

Juror #8 didn't answer him. He kept his eyes on the paper in front of Juror #1, the clean lines of procedure being used like sandbags against a flood.

Juror #4 leaned in slightly, pen poised. "Let's restate exactly what the stairwell witness said. No interpretations."

"That's what I'm doing," Juror #1 replied, though his tone sharpened. The badge on his lapel seemed heavier now, not a crown but a target. He flipped through the packet until he found the relevant page. "He testified he saw the defendant on the stairs shortly after ten thirty. He stated the defendant was moving quickly, breathing hard. He noticed a stain on the sleeve. He recognized him from the building."

Juror #6 scratched his jaw. "Seems pretty clear."

Juror #8 nodded once, as if granting the point its due. "It seems clear," he said. "But I want to know what 'recognized' means. Did he say he saw his face? Or did he see a hoodie and a build and fill in the rest?"

Juror #1's eyes flicked over the page. "He said he recognized him."

Juror #8's gaze didn't move. "That's the summary. What were his words?"

The question landed softly, but it landed. It forced Juror #1 to do something he didn't like: slow down.

Juror #12 tried a half smile, the social lubricant he kept reaching for. "He did point at the kid in court though, right?"

"He identified him in court," Juror #1 agreed.

Juror #11 spoke without raising his voice. "In court, the defendant is seated at the defense table. Everyone knows who the defendant is."

Juror #10 snorted. "Here we go."

Juror #11's eyes stayed forward, refusing the bait. "It is not an insult. It is reality. Identification in court is not the same as identification in the moment."

Juror #3 slapped the table lightly, a short impatient hit that made the plastic sleeves jump. "So now witnesses don't count. Great. We can all go home."

Juror #9 watched the small jump of the exhibits and then the way everyone's shoulders tightened afterward, as if the table itself had threatened to split. "Witnesses count," he said. "But so does the fact that people remember what they need to remember."

Juror #2's voice came out thin and apologetic. "He sounded sure."

Juror #8 looked at her, and there was nothing patronizing in his attention, only focus. "He sounded sure," he repeated. "That's important. But the defense also got him to admit he didn't look at a clock until later. That he'd just gotten off a shift. That the stairwell lighting was dim. I'm not saying he lied. I'm saying he might have been wrong."

Juror #6 leaned forward, elbows spreading, taking up space with the bluntness of his certainty. "Why does it matter? If it wasn't him on the stairs, who was it? Some random guy in the building running around after the murder?"

Juror #8 didn't flinch. "Maybe," he said. "Or maybe the time is off. Or maybe the stain he saw wasn't blood. Or maybe he didn't see what he thinks he saw."

"You can maybe anything to death," Juror #10 said, voice loud, contemptuous. "This is exactly what lawyers do."

Juror #4's pen made a small, precise mark. "Lawyers do it for strategy. We do it to avoid error."

Juror #10 turned on him, eyes narrowing. "You on his side now?"

Juror #4 didn't look up. "I'm on the side of coherent reasoning."

Juror #3's laugh came out sharp. "Coherent. That's good. Meanwhile, the kid's father is dead."

The words hung there, raw and heavy. For a moment the room had the weird sensation of the victim entering it, not as a body, not as a photo, but as a fact that demanded to be felt. The prosecution had made them feel it in the courtroom, in a controlled way. Here, it was uncontrolled.

Juror #8 reached toward the transcript page and tapped a line, not dramatic, almost gentle. "He said, 'I saw someone in a dark hoodie,'" Juror #8 read aloud, "and then later he agreed he couldn't be sure it was the defendant until the police showed him a picture."

Juror #1's face tightened. He hated being corrected in front of a group. "All right," he said. "So we have some uncertainty about that witness. What else?"

Juror #7 exhaled loudly, not quite a sigh, more a protest. "We have the neighbor. We have the knife. We have the cuts. We have the kid's story that doesn't make sense. How much uncertainty do you need before you admit what's obvious?"

Juror #8's eyes went to him. "How much certainty do you need before you stop asking questions?"

Juror #7 blinked. The line hit him in a place his humor usually protected. His mouth opened, then he looked away, jaw working.

Juror #12 shifted, rolling his shoulders as if trying to shake off discomfort. "Look," he said, attempting to sound reasonable, "I get it. I do. We should talk. But if this is just going to turn into picking apart every sentence, we'll be here all week."

Juror #9's gaze stayed on the table, on the words sealed under plastic. "A week is not the problem," he said softly. "A mistake is."

Juror #3 leaned back and stared at Juror #8 like he was watching a slow fuse burn toward something explosive. "What's your angle?" he asked. "You got a kid at home? You see yourself in him?"

Juror #8 didn't answer right away. The silence in his pause made the question uglier, as if it had teeth.

"No," Juror #8 said finally. "My angle is that everyone in that courtroom talked like the ending was already written. Like it was inevitable. I don't believe in inevitability."

Juror #2's fingers twisted together so tightly the knuckles looked stiff. "But… we're not writers," she whispered. "We're supposed to decide."

Juror #8 nodded. "Exactly. We decide. Which means we can't hide behind 'it was always going to happen.'"

Juror #1 picked up the next exhibit sleeve with two fingers, as if the plastic might contaminate him. "The neighbor across the hall," he said, tone brisk. "She heard arguing. She recognized both voices. She heard a crash. She heard running. She looked through the peephole and saw a shadow."

Juror #6 frowned. "Why would she lie?"

"She doesn't have to lie to be wrong," Juror #8 said.

Juror #3's patience cracked. "Jesus. You're going to do this with every witness. You're going to take the whole world apart until nothing means anything."

Juror #8 kept his voice level. "No. I'm going to take the evidence apart until we understand what it actually means."

The fluorescent lights buzzed steadily above them, indifferent. Yet the room felt hotter, as if the debate had turned up the temperature by degrees no one could measure. Juror #1 loosened his collar slightly, a tiny gesture he tried to disguise as nothing.

Juror #10 leaned forward, elbows on the table now, voice cutting. "You know what this is? This is one guy deciding he's better than the rest of us. Like the rest of us are itching to fry a kid."

Juror #8 looked at him with calm attention that made the accusation feel like a tantrum. "I didn't say that."

Juror #10 jabbed a finger toward him. "You don't have to say it. You sit there like you're the only one thinking."

Juror #11's voice came out firmer than before. "He is thinking. That is his right."

Juror #10 snapped his head toward Juror #11. "There it is. The choir's joined in."

Juror #11 didn't rise to the insult, but something tightened in his posture, a hardening that made him look less like a quiet man and more like someone who had learned what happens when you let hostility go unanswered. "I am not a choir," he said. "I am a person. Like you. And we are here to follow the law."

Juror #10's mouth curled. "The law. Sure."

Juror #1 raised his voice, not loud enough to shout, but loud enough to reclaim authority. "Enough. Personal comments stop now. We are going to keep this about the evidence."

Juror #5, who had been watching the room more than the paperwork, shifted his chair so it scraped. The sound made everyone glance at him, a quick nervous reaction like the table had bumped. He didn't apologize.

"This is what he wants," Juror #5 said, nodding toward Juror #8 but not with hostility. With something like reluctant respect. "To slow us down. Because if we rush, we'll just go with whatever the loudest guy says."

Juror #3's eyes flared. "Watch your mouth."

Juror #5 met his stare without blinking. "You gonna tell me you don't push people?"

Juror #3's face reddened, anger immediate and physical. "Don't psychoanalyze me."

Juror #9 spoke before it could boil over. "This is the ripple," he said quietly, almost as if narrating. "One stone in the water and suddenly everyone sees the surface moving."

Juror #12 forced a laugh that died halfway. "Can we not do poetry?"

Juror #9 didn't look at him. "It is not poetry. It is what happens when certainty is disturbed."

Juror #2 swallowed hard and looked at the buzzer by the door, then away, as if the small square of plastic was an escape she wasn't allowed to touch. Her chair seemed too close to everyone else's. The air seemed too shared.

Juror #1 gathered the transcript pages and tapped them into alignment again, a nervous habit masked as professionalism. "We're going to do this step by step," he said. "No shouting. No accusing. We'll talk through each piece, and then we'll see where we stand."

Juror #7 stared at the table, jaw tight. "And if we still stand with eleven guilty and one not guilty?"

Juror #8 answered before Juror #1 could. "Then we keep talking," he said.

Juror #3 laughed again, but this time it sounded like disbelief trying to disguise fear. "You can't hold us hostage."

The word hostage made the room go still for a fraction of a second. It was too sharp, too specific, like a thought accidentally spoken aloud.

Juror #1's eyes flicked to the door, then back to the table. "No one is holding anyone hostage," he said, too quickly.

But the ripple had already traveled. It moved through the room in small, involuntary gestures: Juror #2's tighter grip on her purse; Juror #6's restless shift as if testing the weight of his own body; Juror #12's glance toward the blinds, then the ceiling, then the door again. Even Juror #4, so controlled, paused his note-taking and looked up, as if realizing the meeting had become something else.

Juror #8 sat quietly as the discomfort spread, not satisfied, not smug. Simply present.

Juror #1 slid the next exhibit toward the center: the photo of the kitchen knife, the one the prosecution had held up in court with a gloved hand, as if showing a relic.

"All right," he said, voice clipped. "Let's talk about the knife."

And as the photo settled on the table between them, the room's tension didn't ease. It sharpened, concentrating around the blade's image, around the idea that a single object could end an argument and also begin a reckoning.

The water had been disturbed.

Now they had to watch what surfaced.

Chapter 3

Unseen Barriers

Juror #1 left the photograph of the knife in the center of the table as if it were a magnet meant to pull their attention away from each other.

"Let's stick to facts," he said again, though the phrase had begun to sound less like guidance and more like a prayer. "The knife came from the apartment. The defendant had access. The victim's blood was on the blade. The knife was found in the building's garbage collection area. No forced entry. No other suspect. That is the physical evidence."

Juror #3 leaned forward, ready to pounce on the word physical, as if it meant final. "There," he said. "That's it. That's all you need."

Juror #8 looked down at the photo, then at the sleeves of reports. "It's not all," he said. "It's what we have. There's a difference."

Juror #10 barked a laugh. "You hear that? There's a difference. God forbid we use our eyes."

Juror #11's mouth tightened. "Our eyes are not evidence. The exhibits are."

Juror #7 rubbed his palms on his thighs, restless. "Can we at least call for coffee before this turns into an overnight retreat?"

Juror #2 flinched at the word overnight like it had teeth. She glanced toward the door, then quickly back down at her hands. The room seemed smaller than it had ten minutes ago, the air more shared, the walls closer.

Juror #1 nodded, glad for something manageable. "Fine," he said. "We can request coffee. There's no reason to make this harder than it has to be."

He pushed his chair back and stood. The foreman's badge caught the fluorescent light with a dull glint. He walked to the door, the motion purposeful, the way he moved through office hallways with an expectation that doors would open for him.

The buzzer was mounted beside the handle, a small square of plastic that looked out of place against the old wood. Juror #1 pressed it once.

Nothing happened.

He pressed again, longer this time.

Still nothing. No faint bell in the corridor, no answering footsteps, no distant voice of a bailiff calling through.

Juror #7 let out a quiet, humorless sound. “Maybe it’s on mute.”

Juror #1’s jaw tightened. He pressed a third time, hard enough that the button sank flush and stayed there for a moment before springing back out. Still silence.

Across the room, Juror #4 lifted his eyes. “Could be a wiring issue. Older building.”

Juror #1 ignored the analysis. He reached for the handle.

It didn’t turn.

At first it was a simple resistance, the kind you got from a stiff latch. He tried again, more firmly. The handle moved a fraction, then stopped with a solid, unmistakable block.

Juror #1 frowned, irritated now. He pulled, then pushed, as if the door might have changed its mind about which way it wanted to open. It didn’t budge.

Juror #3’s voice rose. “What are you doing?”

“It’s stuck,” Juror #1 said, already annoyed with the implication that he didn’t know how a door worked. He shifted his grip and tried again, twisting harder. The latch rattled in its metal plate, but the door stayed shut.

Juror #6 leaned back in his chair, eyebrows lifting. "You sure it ain't locked?"

Juror #1 paused, then looked at the lock as if seeing it clearly for the first time. It was the standard courthouse lock, nothing dramatic. No heavy bolt. No visible chain. The kind of hardware designed for privacy and control, but also for easy access from the corridor.

"The bailiff has a key," Juror #1 said, as though that answered everything.

He knocked once, sharp and authoritative.

No response.

He knocked again, louder. "Bailiff?"

The word bounced off the door and came back thin. The corridor beyond remained silent. Not even the faint shuffle of shoes.

Juror #2's hands tightened around her purse. "Maybe he stepped away," she whispered.

Juror #12 forced a small laugh, but it came out wrong. "Yeah. Bathroom break. He'll be right back."

Juror #9 watched the door with the steady patience of someone who'd seen enough locked things in his life to know they weren't always accidents.

Juror #1 tried the handle again, not because he expected it to work, but because it was unbearable for it not to. The metal was cool under his palm. The resistance on the other side felt absolute.

Juror #7 sat forward. "Let me," he said, standing too quickly, as if movement itself could make the situation less real.

Juror #1 hesitated, unwilling to surrender control, then stepped aside with a stiff nod.

Juror #7 grabbed the handle and gave it a theatrical twist, then yanked. When it didn't open, his expression flickered, a quick flash of something behind his usual performance.

"Okay," he said, voice lighter than it should've been. "So it's locked."

Juror #3 stood abruptly, chair legs squealing. "This is ridiculous." He strode to the door and shoved his shoulder against it, as if force could resolve what procedure couldn't.

The door didn't move. The impact thudded through the wood and into the room, vibrating faintly through the table. Juror #3 stepped back, red-faced, and hit it again with his shoulder.

Still nothing.

Juror #5 rose more slowly, eyes narrowed. He didn't go to the door right away. He watched Juror

#3 slam into it, watched the way the door held like it was part of the wall, then glanced at the seams around the frame.

"Stop," Juror #5 said, not loud but sharp. "You're wasting energy."

Juror #3 rounded on him. "You got a better idea?"

Juror #5 nodded toward the lock. "Figure out what's actually happening."

Juror #4 stood and moved in, careful, like he expected the situation to turn volatile. He examined the knob and the lock plate. "It's engaged," he said. "Dead latch or some kind of corridor lock. But it's not one we can open from this side."

Juror #2's voice was very small. "But they can't lock us in. That's not… allowed."

"Of course they can't," Juror #1 snapped, too quickly, anger flaring because fear was trying to surface. He rapped his knuckles against the door again. "Bailiff!"

Nothing.

The silence beyond the door felt wrong. Courthouses were never this quiet. Even on slow afternoons there were voices, footsteps, the distant echo of someone calling a case number. Here there was only the fluorescent hum and the sound of their own breathing.

Juror #12 swallowed. His eyes flicked to the ceiling as if he expected a speaker to crackle with an explanation. “Maybe,” he said, carefully, “maybe there’s an emergency drill? Like lockdown? I’ve seen that on the news. Active shooter stuff. They lock doors.”

Juror #11 shook his head once. “There would be an announcement.”

Juror #9 spoke, soft but clear. “And a sense of urgency in the building. We would hear it.”

Juror #6 stood, slower than the others, heavy as a closing door himself. He went to the window and pulled at the blinds. They were angled down, letting in pale daylight through narrow slats. He tilted them open more.

Outside was not the street. The jury room overlooked an interior light well, a narrow shaft of space between courthouse walls. You could see other windows, other blinds, glass reflecting glass. No people. No movement. Just the dull geometry of a building folded in on itself.

Juror #6 let the blinds fall back into place. “Can’t see a damn thing,” he muttered.

Juror #10 stood too, as if the loss of control demanded he occupy more space. He walked to the door and slapped his hand against it, not to open it but to punish it. “This is some bureaucratic crap,” he said. “They forget we’re in here? That’s what happens, you get stuck in a system.”

Juror #8 remained seated. He watched the others gather at the door like iron filings. His face stayed calm, but his eyes had sharpened, attentive to more than the lock.

Juror #1 tried to keep his voice steady, managerial. “All right. No one panic. It’s probably an equipment issue. The buzzer could be dead. The bailiff may be in another room. We’ll knock until someone comes.”

Juror #3 laughed, short and harsh. “Yeah? And if nobody comes?”

Juror #1 glared at him. “Someone will come. This is a courthouse.”

Juror #5 stepped closer to the door and looked down, then up, then at the gap under it. “If it’s just the buzzer,” he said, “we should still hear people in the hallway.”

Juror #2’s breath hitched. “Maybe court recessed.”

“Not that fast,” Juror #4 said. His tone was rational, but the logic couldn’t hide the unease. “We only walked in here minutes ago. There were people outside. I heard them.”

"So did I," Juror #7 said, and the way he said it made the memory feel suddenly unreliable, like something half-dreamed.

Juror #9 moved to the door without hurrying. He didn't touch the handle. He simply placed his palm against the wood as if he were listening through it. For a moment he closed his eyes.

Then he opened them and looked around the room.

"It is not only locked," he said. "It is sealed."

Juror #12 gave another nervous half laugh. "Okay, that's dramatic."

Juror #9 didn't react. "I have lived long enough to know the difference between a door that is stuck and a door that is meant to keep you in."

Juror #10 scoffed. "Meant by who?"

No one answered him, because the obvious answers were too strange to say. The court. The building. Someone in the hallway with a key. Or something less reasonable, something that didn't belong in the clean, bureaucratic world Juror #1 kept trying to enforce.

Juror #1 cleared his throat and knocked again, louder, his knuckles stinging. "Bailiff! We need assistance!"

Silence.

Juror #8 finally spoke, his voice low, even. "When the bailiff closed the door," he said, "did anyone hear it lock?"

The question turned their attention backward in time, to the small click they'd barely noticed. The latch. The ordinary sound of being shut in.

Juror #2's eyes widened. "It just… clicked."

Juror #6 frowned, as if replaying the sound in his mind. "It always clicks."

Juror #8 nodded once. "Yes," he said. "It always does."

Juror #1 turned away from the door, attempting authority through posture, through the simple act of facing the table again. "All right," he said. "We will remain calm. We will continue deliberations. Someone will realize we need to be escorted to the restroom eventually."

His words were practical, but they landed wrong. Continue deliberations. As if they were choosing to stay. As if the locked door were a minor inconvenience.

Juror #3's voice dropped, rough. "You serious? You want to keep arguing about a knife while we're trapped in here?"

Juror #1's eyes flashed. "We're not trapped. We're temporarily delayed."

Juror #5 looked from the door to the buzzer, then to the table with the knife photograph still lying in the center like an accusation. “Feels like trapped,” he said.

Juror #7 returned to his seat, but he didn’t sit comfortably. His leg bounced under the table, faster than before. “Maybe this is what the kid felt like,” he muttered, then seemed surprised at himself for saying it.

Juror #11’s gaze went to him briefly, thoughtful, then back to the door.

Juror #9 sat down slowly, hands folding in front of him. His voice, when it came, was almost conversational. “Perhaps,” he said, “we should stop pretending the room is behaving normally.”

Juror #12 rubbed at his forehead, trying to keep his smile alive and failing. “It’s a door,” he said, as if repetition could shrink it back into an ordinary problem. “It’s a stupid door.”

But the door remained shut. The buzzer remained dead. The courthouse beyond might as well have been another world.

And in the silence that followed, as they settled back into their chairs with forced normalcy, the sound of the fluorescent lights seemed to change. Not in volume, but in character, as if the hum had gained a thin, strained edge.

Juror #1 reached for the exhibits again, determined to put the meeting back on its rails. He slid the knife photograph closer to himself, preparing to continue.

When he glanced up at the clock on the wall out of habit, ready to gauge how long they'd been at this, he paused.

His eyes lingered a fraction too long.

Then his brow furrowed.

The second hand wasn't moving.

Juror #1 stared at the clock as if it had insulted him.

For a full breath he didn't speak, didn't move, only watched the thin second hand suspended between numbers, frozen in a posture of motion without the motion itself. The clock was one of those cheap courthouse fixtures: white face, black plastic rim, blocky black numbers. It had probably hung in a dozen rooms like this, measuring a thousand dull arguments, a thousand coffee breaks, a thousand verdicts reached with boredom and relief.

It should have been measuring them now.

"It's stopped," Juror #1 said finally.

Juror #7 let out a short laugh that didn't carry any humor. "No kidding. It's a clock. That's what stopped looks like."

Juror #1 shot him a look. "I'm aware of what a stopped clock looks like."

Juror #4 had already turned in his chair to get a clear angle on it, eyes narrowed with the focus he reserved for numbers and discrepancies. "What time does it show?"

Juror #1 looked again, as if the time mattered more than the fact it wasn't moving. "Two twenty-six."

Juror #12 glanced at his wrist as if he'd forgotten, for once, that he wasn't supposed to have a phone. The gesture died halfway. His hand hovered awkwardly in midair, then dropped to the table. "But it can't be— we just came in here."

Juror #6 grunted and leaned back, the chair complaining under his weight. "Could've been dead all day."

Juror #9 didn't answer immediately. He watched the clock the way he'd watched the door a moment ago, as if both objects were part of the same decision being made somewhere else. "It was running when we entered," he said at last.

Juror #2's voice was barely above the hum of the lights. "How do you know?"

Juror #9 turned his head slightly toward her. "Because I looked at it." His tone carried no pride, only a simple statement of fact. "Habit. I always look."

Juror #3 scoffed. "So the clock stopped. Big deal. The door's locked. The buzzer's dead. It's a broken room in an old building. What are we doing, inventorying defects?"

Juror #8, still seated, still calm, lifted his eyes from the table to the clock. His gaze held there for a beat longer than the others, as if he were listening for something behind the silence. "It is a big deal," he said quietly.

Juror #10 snorted. "Sure. Now we're haunted by a clock."

Juror #11 spoke with careful restraint. "In court, time is part of control. This room is built to control us. If even the clock is wrong…"

He didn't finish the sentence. He didn't need to. The unfinished thought spread through the room and filled the gaps: then what else is wrong.

Juror #1 stood up abruptly, as if standing could reset the situation through authority alone. He walked to the wall and looked up at the clock from directly beneath it, squinting. The second hand stayed still. He listened, too, as though he expected to hear a ticking that would prove it was working despite the evidence of his eyes.

There was no ticking.

He reached up and touched the clock's rim with his fingertips. The plastic felt warm from the room's heat. The clock didn't shudder, didn't respond. It remained inert, a dead face staring down at them.

Juror #7 leaned toward Juror #12 and muttered, "We break it?"

Juror #12 whispered back, "Don't say that out loud. He'll have a stroke."

Juror #1 heard them anyway. He turned, impatience sharpening his features. "Nobody is breaking courthouse property."

Juror #3 pushed his chair back and stood too, restless energy needing somewhere to go. "Fine. Take it down and check the battery."

Juror #1's jaw tightened. The idea was sensible, and that was what made it difficult. Sensible meant admitting there was a problem he couldn't manage by procedure alone. He looked up again, as if hoping the second hand would start moving out of obedience.

It didn't.

Juror #4 rose, smooth and controlled. "It's mounted on a bracket. It should lift off."

Juror #1 hesitated. Then, with obvious reluctance, he reached up with both hands and lifted the clock. It came away from the wall with a small click, revealing a narrow metal hook and a smudge of dust where it had been undisturbed. He turned it over.

A cheap battery compartment. He slid it open with his thumb.

The battery was there.

He frowned and pressed it, as if pressure could revive it. Then he took it out and held it up, examining the dull copper and silver ends. He looked around, searching for a solution that didn't exist.

"Anybody got a spare?" Juror #7 asked.

Juror #10 barked a laugh. "What, you think we're Boy Scouts? You got a whistle and a compass too?"

Juror #1 ignored him and tried something else: he replaced the battery, snapped the compartment shut, and held the clock upright again. The hands stayed frozen at two twenty-six. He gave it a small shake, then a slightly more aggressive one, as if the mechanism might have gotten stuck.

Still nothing.

Juror #2's eyes were fixed on the clock now, her mouth slightly open, like a child watching a magician fail. "It should… it should do something."

Juror #6 scratched his cheek. "Battery could be dead."

Juror #5, who had been quiet, watching the room as if it might shift under their feet, spoke without looking away from the clock. "If the battery was dead, it would've stopped whenever it stopped. But the old man says it was running when we came in."

Juror #9 didn't react to being called the old man. He only nodded faintly. "It was," he said again, firm enough to be certainty.

Juror #1's grip tightened on the clock. He looked at Juror #9 like he wanted to challenge him, to insist memory could be wrong, but there was something in the old man's steadiness that made argument feel pointless.

Juror #4 stepped closer. "Hold it," he said, and gestured. "Let me see."

Juror #1 handed the clock over, a manager forced to relinquish a tool.

Juror #4 turned it in his hands, opened the compartment, examined the contacts. His face stayed composed, but his eyes moved faster than before, a subtle acceleration that betrayed tension. "No corrosion," he said. "Contacts look fine. The battery might be low, but…"

He trailed off, looking up at the wall where the clock had hung. Then he glanced to the other side of the room.

"Is there another timepiece?" he asked.

Juror #12 made a helpless gesture. "We're not supposed to have phones."

"That's not what I asked," Juror #4 said, sharper than his usual tone. It was the first time he'd sounded irritated, as if a crack had opened in his sterile control.

Juror #1 scanned the room. The deliberation room was plain, designed to be forgettable. Table. Chairs. Chalkboard. Water pitcher. A metal cabinet. A wall calendar with the courthouse logo. The blinds. The locked door. The dead buzzer.

Then Juror #1's eyes landed on the wall calendar.

He crossed to it, as if the date might reassure him. It was one of those large, glossy months with a scenic photo at the top. The courthouse had chosen a local lake, calm water, blue sky, a view that felt like a lie from inside this sealed room. Below, the days were printed in neat squares.

Juror #1 stared at the calendar, then reached up and flipped the bottom edge slightly.

Nothing changed, of course. A calendar didn't move.

Yet the act of looking at it made him look for something else: the thin red line, the small note, the check mark someone might have placed for today.

There was none.

It was blank.

Juror #7's voice came lighter, trying to force normalcy back into place. "Okay, so we know what day it is. It's the day we get trapped in a room with a serial killer clock."

Juror #10 sneered. "You don't know the day if the calendar's blank, genius."

Juror #7's grin twitched, then fell away again. "It's a courthouse calendar. They don't mark stuff."

Juror #11 spoke softly, almost to himself. "In my country, there were times when clocks were stopped on purpose. During raids. During curfews. People stopped keeping time because time stopped meaning anything."

Juror #10 made a dismissive sound. "Here we go with the war stories."

Juror #11's eyes lifted and met his for a brief moment. There was no anger in it, only a hard truth that made Juror #10 look away. "It is not a story," Juror #11 said. "It is what it feels like when the world becomes a room you cannot leave."

Juror #2's breathing had gone shallow. She pressed her hands together on the table, as if praying without admitting it. "Maybe there's another clock in the hallway," she whispered, though the suggestion sounded like a plea. "Maybe someone will come. Maybe we just… wait."

"Wait how long?" Juror #3 snapped. He jabbed a finger toward the blank, inert face in Juror #4's hands. "We don't even know what time it is."

Juror #4 held the clock up as if presenting the corpse of certainty. "We can estimate," he said, too quickly, and then he stopped himself. Estimate. Like the medical examiner's time of death. Ten fifteen to ten forty-five. A range that had seemed reasonable in court and now suddenly felt like a threat. Time, flexible. Time, uncertain. Time, used against you.

Juror #8 watched that realization travel across Juror #4's face. "We all liked the time of death," Juror #8 said, voice quiet, "because it made the story neat. A window. A sequence. A line you could draw from argument to murder to escape."

Juror #3's eyes narrowed. "Don't."

Juror #8 didn't stop. "Now the clock is dead, and we're uncomfortable because we don't have our line anymore."

Juror #1's voice came out strained. "This has nothing to do with the case."

Juror #9's gaze lifted to him. "Doesn't it?" he asked.

The question hung there. Juror #1 opened his mouth, ready to assert control, ready to insist on separation: the room's malfunction and the boy's fate, unrelated. But he didn't speak immediately, because the room was already making connections he couldn't manage.

Juror #5 leaned forward, elbows on the table, eyes sharp. "If somebody locked the door," he said, "they could've stopped the clock too. Somebody could be messing with us."

Juror #12 nodded too quickly, grateful for an explanation that had a human shape. "Yes. Yes, that makes sense. Like a prank. Or some kind of test. Maybe the judge—"

"No judge does this," Juror #1 said, the certainty in his tone sounding thin.

Juror #6 shifted and glanced at the ceiling. "Cameras?" he asked. "There's gotta be cameras in here, right?"

They all looked, instinctive, scanning corners, vents, the fluorescent fixtures. The room offered nothing obvious. Just glare and humming light. No red dots. No black domes.

Juror #2's voice broke slightly. "Why would they do this?"

No one answered her.

Juror #4 lowered the clock and set it carefully on the table, face up, like evidence. The dead hands at two twenty-six stared at them from the wood, a small, silent insistence.

Juror #3 looked at it and then away, as if refusing to give it meaning. “It’s a battery,” he said. “It’s a cheap clock. It stopped. That’s all.”

But even as he said it, he rubbed his palms on his pants, a nervous gesture he didn’t seem to notice.

Juror #1 stared at the clock on the table, and something in his expression shifted. The foreman’s posture, the corporate certainty, the belief that systems worked if you followed them, all of it strained against a simple fact: the room was no longer behaving like a room in a courthouse.

He swallowed and forced his voice into its old managerial cadence. “All right,” he said. “We don’t need the clock to deliberate. We proceed.”

The words landed with a dull thud. Proceed where? Toward a verdict? Toward a locked door? Toward a stopped clock that made minutes feel like a myth?

Juror #8 didn’t argue. He only looked at each face in turn, as if taking attendance again, but for something deeper than bodies in chairs.

Juror #9’s eyes returned to the chalkboard, blank and waiting.

Juror #11’s hands tightened together briefly, then relaxed, as if he’d made a decision not to show fear.

Juror #10 sat down hard, too hard, trying to prove he couldn't be rattled.

Juror #2 stared at the dead clock until her eyes watered.

And beneath it all, beneath the forced normalcy, the room's hum seemed to sharpen again, thin as wire, as if time itself had been pulled taut and might snap.

Juror #1 picked up the knife photograph and slid it toward the center of the table, reclaiming the only script he knew. "We continue with the evidence," he said.

But his gaze flicked once more to the clock lying face up like a witness that refused to speak.

The second hand did not move.

Not even a tremor.

Juror #1 kept the knife photograph in the center of the table as if it were an anchor. The image was familiar now, worn into their minds from the prosecutor's gloved hand and the enlarged projection on the courtroom screen. In the photo, the blade caught a sterile flash of light, the handle dark against the pale tile where it had been found. A kitchen tool made mythic by blood.

"We continue," Juror #1 said again, and tried to make it sound like a decision rather than a refusal to acknowledge what was happening. "We don't need a working clock to do our job."

No one answered right away. Not because they agreed, but because speaking felt like stepping onto thin ice.

Juror #7 shifted and glanced at the dead clock lying on the table, its hands fixed at two twenty-six like a dare. "We don't need time," he said, voice attempting its usual lightness and missing the mark, "but time sure seems to have opinions."

Juror #10 let out a short, irritated breath. "It's a battery. That's what it has. Batteries die."

"And doors lock," Juror #5 muttered, eyes flicking to the handle again. "And buzzers break. All at once. Sure."

Juror #1's jaw flexed. He reached for the lab report sleeve, flipped it, then flipped it back, not actually reading so much as proving his hands were still useful. "We are not going to spiral," he said. "We'll discuss the knife, the prints, the blood. We'll keep it factual."

Juror #2 made a small sound in her throat, like she'd started to speak and swallowed it. Her fingers had gone numb from holding her purse so tight. She released it a fraction, then tightened again as if loosening was dangerous.

Juror #9 looked past the knife photo, past the papers, to the blank chalkboard. His gaze had that same distant focus he'd had when he placed his palm against the sealed door, as if he were listening to the room instead of the people inside it.

The hum of the fluorescent lights continued, steady but wrong. It wasn't louder. It was sharper, like something thin vibrating under tension. Juror #6 rubbed his forearm as if he could feel it on his skin.

Juror #4 leaned forward and read from a line on the report, forcing his voice into a calm, technical lane. "The lab testified the blood on the blade matched the victim. No blood from the defendant. Partial latent prints on the handle inconsistent in quality, inconclusive for positive identification."

"Which doesn't mean anything," Juror #3 snapped. "It means he wiped it. Or it smudged. Or the lab tech was covering their ass. The father's blood is on it."

Juror #11 spoke quietly, careful not to inflame. "The father's blood would be on it if anyone stabbed him with it."

Juror #3 turned on him. "And who else had access? Who else had a reason?"

The air tightened at the word reason. It made the room feel like the courtroom again, like motive could serve as a substitute for certainty.

Juror #8 didn't take the bait. He kept his eyes on the photograph and the report, then lifted them to the faces around the table. "When you say 'who else,'" he said, "you're asking a question we can't answer. We can't invent a suspect. We can only evaluate what was proven."

Juror #10 jabbed a finger toward the center of the table. "That's what was proven. Knife from the apartment. Victim dead. Kid in the apartment. No forced entry."

Juror #12 tried to nod along, but his gaze kept sliding, unbidden, toward the door. It was the kind of glance you made when you expected someone to be standing there. The bailiff. A clerk. Anybody. The door gave them nothing back.

Juror #1 cleared his throat. "We have to keep going," he said, and there was strain under the authority now. "If we sit here and focus on the door and the clock, we'll waste time."

Juror #7 gave a short, humorless laugh. "What time?"

Juror #1's eyes flashed. "Enough."

Silence settled again, heavier this time. Even Juror #3 seemed to feel it, because he stopped moving for a moment, stopped bouncing his knee, stopped looking for a fight, and just listened.

There was nothing to hear beyond them. No courthouse muffled sounds. No distant footsteps. No elevator bell. The building's absence pressed in until the jury room felt less like part of a public place and more like a sealed compartment.

Juror #2's voice came out too thin. "Maybe the power went out somewhere else," she said. "Maybe… maybe they're dealing with something and they forgot."

Juror #9 looked at her, gentle but direct. "People do not forget twelve people," he said.

Her eyes watered, and she blinked fast, as if tears would turn into evidence. "They could," she whispered. "They could forget me."

Juror #8 turned toward her slightly, not crowding, not performing comfort. "No one forgot you," he said. "But something's wrong."

The word wrong landed with more force than locked. It gave shape to what they'd been avoiding.

Juror #6 pushed his chair back a few inches, wood scraping tile. He stared at the ceiling fixtures like he expected to see a camera lens reveal itself. "If this is some kind of test," he said, voice low, "it's not funny."

Juror #12 swallowed. "Courts don't do tests," he said, then added too quickly, "Not like this."

Juror #4's pen hovered above his pad. He had been writing constantly since they sat down, as if the act of recording could keep him anchored in logic. Now the pen tip didn't touch paper. His eyes had gone unfocused in the way of someone whose internal calculations were starting to yield impossible results.

Juror #1 flipped the knife photograph over, then back, the motion sharp. "We're not indulging paranoia."

Juror #5 leaned forward, forearms on the table, voice edged. "This isn't paranoia. This is a locked door."

Juror #3 pointed at Juror #5. "You're enjoying this. You like thinking someone's out to get you."

Juror #5's eyes narrowed. "I like knowing when to watch my back."

Juror #3 pushed his chair back again, standing halfway before sitting again, unable to decide what to do with his body. "We should be banging on the walls," he said. "There's got to be somebody out there."

Juror #9's gaze didn't leave the chalkboard. "If there were," he said, "we would hear them."

The fluorescent hum seemed to fill the space left by everyone's breathing. Juror #2 rubbed her palms against her cardigan as if trying to warm them, but it wasn't cold. That was part of it. The room's temperature didn't match the way her skin felt.

Juror #11 shifted, careful, and spoke as if choosing words from a limited supply. "In the courtroom," he said, "the judge reminds us we must not speak to anyone outside this room about the case. Now we cannot speak to anyone outside this room at all."

Juror #10's mouth curled. "So what, now it's a metaphor?"

Juror #11 met his eyes briefly. "No," he said. "It is a fact. But facts can have shadows."

Juror #7 rubbed the back of his neck. He looked pale under the fluorescent light, the kind of pallor that came not from sickness but from realizing your usual tricks were useless. "I hate this," he admitted, and for once it wasn't a joke.

Juror #12 tried to smile at him and failed. "It's fine," he said, though his voice cracked around the word. "It's… fine. We just keep talking, like the foreman says, and someone will come."

Juror #8 watched Juror #12 for a moment, then let his gaze move around the table. People were changing without noticing they were changing. Shoulders hunched. Hands clenched. Eyes darted to the door and then away, as if looking too long might make it permanent.

Juror #1 pulled the judge's instructions closer and tapped them. "Reasonable doubt," he said, as though reciting it could restore the world. "We apply it to the evidence. Not to our feelings. Not to the fact that the clock stopped."

Juror #4 finally spoke, voice controlled but with a thinness at its edge. "Feelings are data too," he said, and when Juror #1 looked at him sharply, he clarified, as if embarrassed by his own sentence. "Not legally. But… if every variable changes at once, you consider the environment. That's basic analysis."

Juror #3 scoffed. "Now the environment's on trial."

Juror #9's gaze moved from the chalkboard to Juror #3. "Perhaps it is," he said.

The room went quiet again. Not the earlier quiet of bureaucracy, but a hush that felt like waiting for something to happen. Juror #2 held her breath without meaning to. Juror #6's foot began to tap, slow and heavy. Juror #10 cracked his knuckles, the sound too loud.

Juror #1 lifted the knife photo again and forced himself to speak. "If we assume the knife is the murder weapon, which the prosecution argues—"

A faint scrape cut through his sentence.

Not a chair leg. Not a pen. Not paper against plastic.

It sounded like chalk.

Every head turned toward the chalkboard.

It remained blank, a dull green surface with faint ghosts of old writing embedded in it, the residue of arguments from other cases, other lives weighed and decided. The tray beneath held two chalk nubs and the worn eraser. Nothing had moved.

Juror #7 let out a short breath. "Did anyone—"

Another sound, softer this time. Like the dry whisper of chalk dragging lightly, then stopping.

Juror #2's hand flew to her mouth. Juror #12's chair squealed as he pushed back, a startled movement he immediately tried to control. Juror #3 stood fully, eyes wild with anger that didn't know where to go. "Who's doing that?" he barked, looking from face to face as if ready to grab someone.

No one held chalk. No one's hands were near the board.

Juror #8 stayed seated, but his posture changed. His spine straightened, attention sharpening, as if he'd been listening for that exact sound.

Juror #1 stared at the chalkboard, then snapped his gaze to Juror #9. "Did you hear that?"

Juror #9 nodded slowly. He didn't look surprised. He looked grimly confirmed.

Juror #10 forced a laugh that sounded like it hurt. "It's the building," he said, too loud. "Old pipes. Air ducts. The board settling."

Juror #4's pen trembled slightly above the page. He lowered it without writing anything.

Juror #11 rose from his chair, deliberate, and took one step toward the chalkboard. He didn't touch it. He simply stood close enough to see if there were marks, if the surface had changed.

Still blank.

Yet the sense that it should not have been blank crept through the room like a draft.

Juror #2 whispered, "Please don't."

No one answered her. Juror #11 looked over his shoulder, face composed but pale beneath the harsh light. "There is nothing," he said. "No writing."

Juror #7 swallowed. "So we're hearing things now."

Juror #5's eyes went to the dead clock. "Or something's making sure we listen."

Juror #1's voice came out tighter than he intended. "Enough. We are not going to let this derail us."

But the derailment had already happened. It wasn't a single event. It was accumulation. The door that would not open. The buzzer that did nothing. The clock that had died in their presence. The courthouse silence that felt like exile. And now that thin, unmistakable chalk sound, like a message starting and stopping before it could be read.

Juror #8 spoke into the hush, voice low. "We keep trying to treat this like a normal deliberation," he said. "But the room isn't normal."

Juror #3's face twisted. "Don't start with your calm crap."

Juror #8 met his eyes, unflinching. "I'm not calm because I don't care," he said. "I'm calm because panicking won't open the door. And it won't bring back the dead."

The last phrase landed oddly, like it belonged to more than one subject. Juror #2 flinched as if struck. Juror #12's gaze snapped to Juror #8, searching his face for what he meant, for whether it was just about the father in the case.

Juror #9 returned to his seat slowly. His hands folded in front of him again, but they did not stop trembling. "There is a feeling," he said, voice soft, "that we are being watched. Not by cameras. By something that does not need them."

Juror #10 opened his mouth to mock him, then seemed to think better of it, and settled for a scowl.

Juror #1 stared at the center of the table where the knife photograph lay. The plastic sleeve caught the fluorescent glare, making the blade look like it was moving when it wasn't.

He tried to speak, to resume the script, to force the conversation back into evidence and reason. But the words snagged in his throat.

Because beneath the hum of the lights, beneath the controlled breathing and the shifting chairs, the room felt as if it had leaned a fraction closer to them.

As if it were listening.

And somewhere in that listening, the photograph of the knife no longer felt like a picture of something that happened outside this room.

It felt like a promise.

Chapter 4

Challenging the Evidence

For a moment, nobody moved.

The knife photograph lay in its sleeve at the center of the table, glare sliding across the glossy surface as the fluorescent light buzzed overhead. It made the blade seem to shimmer, a trick of reflection that had been harmless in the courtroom and felt obscene in here, in a room with a sealed door and a dead clock and chalk sounds that had no business existing.

Juror #1 swallowed and forced air into his lungs. "All right," he said, voice clipped, managerial. "We are not going to—"

A dry sound interrupted him.

Not the whisper of chalk this time. Not paper. Not the scrape of a chair leg.

A small, heavy thud, like metal meeting wood with no apology.

The plastic sleeve in the center of the table shifted slightly, pushed by something that was suddenly there.

Juror #2 made a strangled noise, half gasp, half sob, and jerked back so hard her chair legs screeched. Juror #12's hand flew up as if to ward off a blow, his body forgetting manners and remembering instinct. Juror #6 stood so abruptly the table shook. Juror #7's mouth fell open, the first honest expression he'd worn all day.

On the table, just above the knife photograph, lay a real knife.

Not a picture. Not an exhibit in a sleeve. A kitchen knife, its handle dark, its blade dull under the room's harsh lights. It wasn't plunged into the wood like a theatrical warning. It simply lay there, flat and casual, angled slightly toward Juror #1 as if it had been placed for him.

Juror #3's face went red in a single surge. "Who did that?" he barked, eyes snapping from one juror to another, hunting for a prankster, a conspirator, an explanation that had hands.

No one's hands were near it.

Juror #5 had pushed back from the table, palms open in front of him, his gaze locked on the knife like it might leap. His streetwise suspicion had found something it couldn't argue with. His voice came out low. "That wasn't there."

Juror #4 stared with an analyst's disbelief, pupils small, mind trying to arrange this into a solvable problem. He looked at the knife photograph, then at the knife itself, as if comparing them might restore physics. "It's… it's the same type," he said, and the words sounded foolish as soon as he said them.

Juror #9 didn't speak. He simply looked at the knife with the tired recognition of someone who had seen impossible things dressed as ordinary objects. His hands trembled on the table edge. Not enough to knock anything over. Enough to show that his body understood danger even if his mind refused superstition.

Juror #11 stood slowly, careful and deliberate, as if sudden movement might set off a trap. His eyes went to the door, then to the ceiling corners, then back to the knife. "We are not alone," he said quietly.

Juror #10 forced a laugh that cracked midway. "Oh, come on. Somebody had it. Somebody brought it in. This is a stunt." He glared around the table, landing on Juror #8 as if blame belonged there by default. "This your thing? Magic tricks to save a murderer?"

Juror #8 remained seated, but even he had gone still in a different way, like a man listening for the second sound after a gunshot. His gaze rested on the knife, then lifted to Juror #1. "No one brought that in," he said.

Juror #1's throat worked. He reached for his authority the way he'd reached for procedure, and found it slipping. "This is highly inappropriate," he said, too loudly, as if volume could turn it back into a normal problem. "Whoever did this, you need to stop now. Immediately."

Juror #3 slammed his palm on the table. The knife jumped slightly, metal ticking against wood. Juror #2 flinched like she'd been hit. "Stop talking like it's a meeting," Juror #3 snarled. "That's a weapon. In a locked room."

Juror #6 took one heavy step forward and then stopped himself, looking from the knife to the others. "Nobody touch it," he said, voice blunt. "Don't put your prints on it. Don't give them anything else to use."

"Them?" Juror #7 echoed, and the single syllable made the room colder.

Juror #12 swallowed hard, eyes bright with panic he was trying to charm away and failing. "Okay," he said, voice shaky, "maybe the bailiff came in while we weren't looking. Maybe there's another door. Maybe—"

"There is no other door," Juror #5 cut in. His eyes never left the knife. "And nobody walked in. We all would've heard it. We hear everything now. That's the problem."

Juror #1 stared at the knife as if staring hard enough could identify a culprit. His foreman's badge seemed ridiculous, a small piece of metal pretending to be power. "We need to notify the bailiff," he said.

Juror #7 gestured sharply toward the dead buzzer. "With what, a prayer?"

Juror #1's jaw tightened. He stood, but he didn't go to the door this time. He stayed close to the table, as if leaving the knife behind him would be more dangerous than facing it. "We can knock," he said.

Juror #9's voice came, soft but firm. "We have knocked."

Juror #1 stopped, trapped between action and the memory of failed action.

Juror #8 leaned forward slightly, not reaching, just closing the distance with his eyes. "Is there blood?" he asked, and his calm made the question worse. It made it practical.

Juror #2 shook her head rapidly, tears finally spilling. "Don't," she whispered. "Please don't."

Juror #4 leaned in a fraction, his rationality latching onto something measurable. "From here, I don't see any visible staining," he said, voice careful. "The blade looks clean."

Juror #3 stared at him with disbelief. "You're inspecting it?"

"I'm not inspecting," Juror #4 snapped, and the flash of irritation startled even him. He inhaled, regained control. "I'm observing from a distance. That's what we do. We observe."

Juror #10 pointed at the knife. His finger shook, though he'd never admit it. "It's a threat," he said. "That's what it is. Somebody's trying to scare us into… into what? Voting not guilty? Is that it? Some psycho defense attorney?"

Juror #11 looked at him. "Do you believe a defense attorney can stop time?"

Juror #10 opened his mouth, then closed it, his contempt scrambling for a footing it couldn't find.

Juror #6 exhaled through his nose, the sound heavy. "We need to move it off the table," he said. "That's where our hands are. Somebody's gonna bump it by accident."

Juror #1 hesitated. "We should not disturb it," he said automatically, the way procedure spoke through him even when procedure had collapsed.

Juror #5 gave a short, sharp laugh. "Disturb it? It disturbed us."

Juror #8's eyes lifted to the dead clock on the table, still face-up like a witness. Two twenty-six.

Frozen. He looked back at the knife. "It wants us to look at it," he said.

Juror #3 whipped his head toward him. "It? What is it?"

Juror #8 didn't answer that directly. He kept his voice low, steady, as if raising it would invite something. "We've been arguing about a knife in a photograph," he said. "About a blade sealed behind plastic in a courtroom where rules keep everyone at a distance. Now it's here. In the room. On the table with us."

Juror #2's hands were pressed to her mouth. Her shoulders shook, small silent sobs she couldn't stop. Juror #12 reached toward her and then pulled his hand back, unsure if touch would help or make it worse.

Juror #9 spoke, and when he did, everyone listened because his voice carried the weight of surviving. "Perhaps," he said, "the room is removing our protections."

Juror #1's eyes snapped to him. "Don't talk like that."

Juror #9 didn't flinch. "We keep saying this is a courthouse," he continued. "We keep saying it will behave like one. But the courthouse is gone. Or we are."

The silence after that felt like the moment after a verdict is read, when you realize the words cannot be put back in a mouth.

Juror #6 moved without asking permission. He walked to the metal cabinet against the wall, yanked open a drawer with a loud scrape, and rummaged. His hands came out with a folded cloth, the kind kept for wiping water spills or cleaning the table. He held it up. “We move it,” he said. “With this.”

Juror #1 started to object and then stopped. He had no better plan.

Juror #6 approached the table. His movements were careful but not delicate, the way a man handled something dangerous at work: not with fear, with respect. He draped the cloth over his hand like a glove and reached toward the knife.

Juror #2 made a small keening sound. Juror #12 whispered, “Easy, easy,” as if talking to a frightened animal.

Juror #6 pinched the knife handle through the cloth and lifted it.

Nothing happened. No jolt. No spark. No cinematic horror.

Just weight.

He set it down at the far end of the table, nearer the chalkboard, away from the center where their papers lay. The blade made a soft click against wood, a sound that seemed to echo longer than it should have.

Juror #4 released a breath he hadn't realized he was holding. He stared at the cloth in Juror #6's hand. "Why would it be clean?" he murmured, more to himself than anyone. "If it's the murder weapon…"

Juror #8's eyes went to the knife photograph still in the center. "In court, the prosecution held up certainty like it was clean," he said. "Maybe this is what certainty looks like when it's brought close."

Juror #3's voice came harsh. "Stop making speeches. Tell me what you think is happening."

Juror #8 finally looked directly at him. "I think," he said, choosing each word, "that we are being forced to deliberate without the distance that makes it easy."

Juror #10 shook his head, angry and frightened in the same breath. "This is insane."

Juror #11's voice was quiet, but it cut through. "It is," he said. "But it is also real."

Juror #1 stared at the knife now resting near the chalkboard, then at the dead clock, then at the locked door. His face had gone pale under the fluorescent light, the skin around his eyes tight. He looked like a man who'd spent his life believing rooms could be controlled with rules, and had just learned some rooms answered to something else.

He sat down slowly, as if sitting was an admission.

"All right," he said, and his voice had changed. Not softer. Less certain. "We continue. We have no other option."

Juror #7 let out a brittle laugh that sounded close to sobbing. "We keep saying that."

Juror #9's gaze drifted again to the chalkboard, as if expecting it to respond now that the knife was close. "And perhaps," he said, "that is the point."

Juror #1 pulled the knife photograph toward himself, but his eyes kept flicking to the real blade at the end of the table, a constant reminder that evidence was no longer confined to reports and testimony.

Juror #8 leaned forward, hands still empty, voice calm as a scalpel. "Then let's challenge it," he said. "Not the room. The evidence. Starting with the knife that everyone thinks ends the argument."

At the far end of the table, the knife lay motionless, clean and ordinary, as if it had always belonged there.

As if it had been waiting.

Juror #1 drew the witness transcript packet toward him as if paper could substitute for authority. The knife at the far end of the table sat in his peripheral vision, a dark handle against wood, too present to ignore and too ordinary to explain. He flattened the packet with both palms, a gesture that was meant to steady himself.

"We've talked about the physical evidence," he said, though it came out like an argument with the room rather than a summary. "Now we revisit the witness testimony. That's what we were doing before… before this happened."

Juror #7 let out a thin sound that might have been agreement if it hadn't been so close to a shake of laughter. "Sure. Back to normal. Just twelve people and a convenient murder weapon that appeared out of thin air."

"Enough," Juror #1 snapped, then softened his tone as if remembering he needed them functional. "We stick to what we can evaluate."

Juror #8 didn't look at the knife. His gaze stayed on the packet. "Let's start with the neighbor across the hall," he said. "She's the only one who claims she recognized voices."

Juror #3 leaned back, arms tight across his chest. His anger had nowhere clean to land anymore, so it settled into his posture. "We already heard her. Old lady heard them fighting, heard the crash, heard the kid run. What else do you want?"

Juror #8 held his eyes on Juror #1, not rising to Juror #3's bait. "Read her words," he said. "Not the summary."

Juror #1's jaw flexed. Being told to read, after he'd already read the whole case into shape, felt like being managed. Still, he flipped to the page, his finger tracking lines as if he didn't trust his own eyes.

"Witness one," he said. "Ms. Harlan. Apartment 4B. She testified she heard yelling around ten thirty p.m."

Juror #4 interjected quietly, "She estimated ten thirty."

Juror #1's eyes flicked up, irritated, then back down. "She said 'about ten thirty.' Fine." He continued. "She heard the victim's voice. She heard the defendant's voice. She heard a crash, then footsteps, then the apartment door, then running."

Juror #2 swallowed, her hands still clasped so tightly her knuckles had lost color. "She sounded sure," she murmured again, as if repeating it could keep the room from coming apart.

Juror #11 sat very still, listening the way he had listened in court. "Sure is a word people use when they need certainty," he said. "It does not always mean they have it."

Juror #10 made a sound of disgust. "So now we don't trust old women either. Great. Who do we trust? Nobody? We just let him go because the world's complicated?"

Juror #9's gaze remained on the papers, but his voice was steady. "We trust what holds up when pressed."

Juror #1 cleared his throat and read again, voice flattening into courtroom cadence. "Defense asked about her hearing. She admitted she wears a hearing aid. Prosecution asked if she had it in that night. She said yes."

Juror #8 nodded. "And defense asked about the apartment walls," he said. "Thin walls. Neighbors hear neighbors. But do they recognize two voices clearly through a wall during yelling?"

Juror #3's eyes narrowed. "You trying to say she made up the whole thing?"

"No," Juror #8 said. "I'm saying we treat it as what it is: a woman hearing noise through a wall. The recognition is the fragile part."

Juror #6 rubbed his palm along his thigh, a slow grounding motion. "I've lived in places with thin walls," he said. "You can tell who's who."

Juror #8 accepted the point with a small nod. "Sometimes. If it's normal talking. But yelling changes a voice. Fear changes a voice. Rage changes a voice." He paused, then added, quieter, "And memory changes it later."

Juror #2 flinched at the word memory, as if it had personal heat.

Juror #1 read further, apparently determined to keep them in the text. "She said she looked through the peephole. She saw a shadow. She could not identify a face. She said the person moved quickly down the hall toward the stairwell."

Juror #5 tapped the table once, not impatient, more like marking a beat. "Shadow," he said. "That's what she really saw."

Juror #12's voice came careful, trying to be helpful in a room where help had become complicated. "But there's also the guy on the stairs. That's not just a shadow."

Juror #8 turned to him. "Let's go there," he said. "The stairwell witness. The one who 'recognized' him."

Juror #1 flipped pages, a little too roughly. The paper rasp sounded louder than it should have in the sealed room. "Mr. Dalca," he said. "Apartment 3C. He testified he saw the defendant on the stairs shortly after ten thirty, moving quickly, breathing hard, and he observed a stain on his sleeve."

Juror #4's pen lifted, then hovered without writing. He seemed to have stopped trusting his own record-keeping, as if notes were only useful in a world where time moved forward.

Juror #8 said, "Read the cross."

Juror #1's eyes tightened, but he found the section. "Defense asked about lighting. He said it was dim. Defense asked if he saw the defendant's face. He said, 'Not clearly.' Defense asked how he knew it was him. He said, 'Same hoodie he always wears. Same kid.'"

Juror #3 slapped his knee, triumphant. "There. Same kid."

Juror #8 didn't shift. "That's not a face," he said. "That's pattern recognition."

Juror #10 leaned forward. "You want facial recognition? He's not a camera. He saw him. He knows him. End of story."

Juror #11's voice stayed level, but there was steel under it. "Knowing someone in a building is not knowing them in a moment of stress. In my life, men were 'recognized' in darkness and then they disappeared." He let the sentence sit. "Recognition can be weaponized by the mind."

Juror #10's nostrils flared. "Always with the speeches."

Juror #9 looked at Juror #10, mild but unblinking. "Some people have earned their speeches."

Juror #1 broke in, not wanting the room to become history and morality when he could still cling to a transcript. "The witness also admitted he was coming home from a late shift. He said he was tired. Defense asked about time. He said he checked his phone later after police asked, and then he estimated."

Juror #8 held up a finger slightly, not to silence, but to isolate the point. "He estimated the time after the police asked," he said. "And the prosecution's story needs that time."

Juror #3's eyes flashed. "The time doesn't matter. He saw him after the fight. After the crash. That's what matters."

Juror #8's gaze went to Juror #3, and his voice stayed quiet, which somehow made it cut cleaner. "Time matters when you're using it to make a chain," he said. "If one link shifts, the whole chain can fall apart."

Juror #2 whispered, "But the chain feels right."

Juror #8 looked at her then, not unkind. "Chains always feel right," he said. "That's why people use them."

Silence followed, the kind that made everyone aware of their own breathing. The fluorescent hum had no variation, no relief. The locked door remained a fact at the edge of their sight, the dead clock a fact on their table. A room that wouldn't let them out had a way of making every word heavier, as if the air saved what was said.

Juror #1 cleared his throat and turned another page. "There was also testimony from the responding officer," he said. "He found the defendant the next morning. Said he was calm. Didn't ask about his father."

Juror #7 muttered, "That part still freaks me out."

Juror #8 nodded once, acknowledging it. "It's unsettling," he said. "But it isn't proof. Some people go numb. Some people go quiet. And some people act calm because they've learned calm keeps them alive."

He didn't look at Juror #3 when he said it, but the sentence found Juror #3 anyway. The furious father's mouth tightened. His eyes went briefly unfocused, as if a different room had appeared behind his gaze, a room that had nothing to do with a courthouse.

Juror #4 spoke, voice precise, trying to build a bridge back to the acceptable. "Demeanor evidence is notoriously unreliable," he said. "It's interpretive. Culturally biased. And it's easily framed by whoever's telling it."

Juror #12 nodded too quickly, as if grateful for something he could agree with without consequence. "Yeah, the cop could just be… reading into it."

Juror #10 scoffed. "Now the cop's wrong too."

Juror #5 leaned forward, eyes narrowed at the papers. "What about the superintendent?" he asked. "The one who saw blood in the hallway. That matters, right? That's not memory through a wall."

Juror #1 flipped again. His fingers were starting to shake, just slightly, but he kept them moving so no one could catch the tremor. "Superintendent testified he noticed blood near the apartment door in the morning. Called police. He did not see the defendant that night."

Juror #8 said, "Exactly. The superintendent proves there was blood. He doesn't prove who put it there. The witnesses give us a narrative, but the narrative depends on their senses and their assumptions."

Juror #3 let out a harsh breath. "So, what do we have then? Nothing? We just sit in here and pick everything apart until we can't convict anyone of anything?"

Juror #8 didn't answer immediately. He glanced down at the transcript page, then at the knife photo, then briefly, without meaning to, toward the real knife near the chalkboard. When he spoke again, his voice was softer.

"We have a story that feels complete," he said. "A father and a son. Abuse. A fight. A crash. Running footsteps. A knife. We all know that story. We've seen it in the news, in movies. It fits the shape we expect. And when something fits, we stop checking the seams."

Juror #9's eyes lifted. "And this room," he said, almost to himself, "is nothing but seams."

Juror #1 bristled. "We are not discussing the room," he said, too sharply.

Juror #8 looked at him steadily. "We can pretend the room doesn't exist," he said. "But it does. And it's doing what witness testimony does. It's putting pressure on us to interpret. To decide what we think is happening."

Juror #1's lips parted, ready to push back, then he stopped. The foreman's badge on his lapel looked suddenly childish, like a sticker someone had given him to keep him busy.

Juror #2's voice rose, thin and strained. "Why are we even doing this?" she asked. "If we can't leave, what does the verdict even mean?"

No one answered right away. Even Juror #3 didn't have a clean retort for that.

Juror #11 spoke quietly, eyes on the papers. "It means what it always meant," he said. "Only now we cannot hide from it."

Juror #8 nodded. "So, we keep going," he said. "We reexamine. We challenge. Not because we like doubt. Because doubt is the only honest place to stand when someone's life is on the line."

At the far end of the table, the knife lay still, and the chalkboard remained blank. But as Juror #1 lowered his gaze back to the transcript, his eyes caught on a line he didn't remember being there, a small detail he was suddenly unsure had been printed when he first opened the packet.

He read it again, then again, his throat tightening.

Juror #4 noticed. "What is it?" he asked.

Juror #1 didn't answer at first. He ran his finger under the sentence like a man trying to prove ink was real. Then, with reluctant care, he read aloud.

"On redirect, the neighbor said, 'I heard him say, I didn't mean to.'"

The room went very still.

Juror #3 stared. "The kid said that?"

Juror #1 swallowed. "She testified she heard someone say it. Through the wall."

Juror #2's eyes widened, wet with fear. "I don't remember that."

Juror #12 shook his head slowly. "I don't either."

Juror #9's gaze moved, not to the transcript, but to the chalkboard, as if expecting it to answer the confusion.

Juror #8's expression didn't change, but his eyes sharpened. "Who did she say it sounded like?" he asked.

Juror #1 flipped the page, faster now, searching. His finger stopped. He read, and the color drained from his face in a way that had nothing to do with fluorescent light.

"She said," Juror #1 began, then paused as if the words were stuck. "She said it sounded like the father."

Juror #3's mouth opened, then closed again. For the first time, his anger looked briefly uncertain, like a weapon that had slipped in his grip.

Juror #10 leaned forward, voice hard. "That's not possible."

Juror #8's voice stayed even. "It's testimony," he said. "And now we have to decide what to do with it."

No one spoke for a moment after Juror #1 read the line again, as if repetition could make it settle into the familiar narrative.

"She said it sounded like the father," Juror #1 repeated, voice flatter this time, and that flatness was its own kind of fear.

Juror #3's stare locked on the transcript, then on Juror #1, as if the foreman had personally inserted the sentence. "That makes no sense," he said, and there was something raw under the anger now. Not outrage. Exposure. "The father's the one who's dead."

Juror #8 didn't argue the obvious. He simply leaned forward a fraction and looked at the page with the kind of calm attention that made other people feel seen. "Read exactly what she said," he told Juror #1. "Not what it means. The exact wording."

Juror #1's fingers tightened on the packet. His impulse was to summarize, to smooth the edges, to keep the meeting in its proper channels. But the room had already stopped obeying channels. He cleared his throat and read.

"On redirect, witness stated she heard someone say, 'I didn't mean to.' Defense asked who it sounded like. Witness replied, 'Him. The father.'"

Juror #2 made a small sound, like air pushed out of a chest too fast. "I don't remember that," she whispered again, and then, as if the admission was dangerous, she added, "I would remember that."

Juror #9's eyes stayed on her, gentle but unyielding. "We remember what fits," he said. "And we forget what doesn't."

Juror #10 leaned forward, palms on the table as if preparing to stand and shove the sentence back into the paper. "Or the old lady's confused," he snapped.

"Hearing aids, thin walls, all that. She mixed up voices. End of it."

Juror #8 nodded once. Not agreement. Permission. "That's one possibility," he said. "So, here's my first question. If she mixed up voices, how reliable is any of her identification? The argument. The recognition. The running."

Juror #3's mouth twisted. "You're doing it again. You find one weird line and suddenly everything else collapses."

Juror #8 didn't look at him. He looked at the table: the stacked exhibits, the dead clock lying face-up, the knife photo, and at the far end, the real knife that should not exist. Then he looked at Juror #3, and his voice stayed level.

"I'm asking what we do with inconsistency," Juror #8 said. "Because inconsistency is what reasonable doubt looks like before you call it reasonable."

Juror #4's pen hovered over his pad, then finally touched paper. He wrote a short note, then paused and looked up. "The prosecution didn't emphasize that line," he said quietly, more to the room than to anyone. "If it was there, it should have mattered."

Juror #7 let out a dry breath. "Maybe that's why I don't remember it. Because they didn't want us to."

Juror #1 snapped his gaze to him. "Nobody is orchestrating what you remember."

Juror #7 held his hands up. "I'm just saying. There's a lot we didn't hold on to."

Juror #11's voice came soft, controlled. "In court, you are told what to notice. Here, we have to choose."

Juror #8 looked at Juror #1 again. "Second question," he said. "When did she say she heard it? Before the crash? After? During?"

Juror #1 flipped pages, faster now. He searched like a man trying to find the terms of a contract he'd already signed. "She said after the crash," he read, then hesitated, scanning the next lines. "She described it as… a moment later. Like the yelling stopped and then she heard that."

Juror #2's hands went to her temples as if holding her head would keep it intact. "If the father said it," she murmured, "what would that even mean?"

Juror #8 didn't answer her directly. He let the question breathe, because it needed air. "It could mean nothing," he said finally. "It could be misheard. Misattributed. It could be the neighbor filling in a blank. Or it could mean something we didn't consider."

Juror #6 rubbed his jaw; eyes fixed on the transcript. "Like what? Like the old man said, the father's dead."

Juror #8's gaze stayed steady. "Like an accident," he said. "Like the father fell. Like the father got hurt without the boy intending it. Like someone else was there. Like the story is not as clean as it felt."

Juror #3's chair scraped. He half rose, then stopped, standing over his own seat like he didn't trust it. "You're trying to downgrade it," he said, voice rising. "You want manslaughter instead of murder, so you can say you saved his life. That's what this is."

Juror #8 didn't flinch. "No," he said. "I want us to decide what the evidence supports. The charge requires premeditation. A planned killing. If a witness hears the father say, 'I didn't mean to,' after the crash, it doesn't sound like a planned killing. It sounds like something went wrong."

Juror #10's laugh was sharp and brittle. "So now the father's apologizing while the kid stabs him? That's your logic?"

Juror #8 turned to him. "My logic is we don't ignore a sentence because it's inconvenient," he said. "We test it."

Juror #4 nodded faintly, as if he hated how much sense that made. "If it's noise," Juror #4 said, "we should be able to see it as noise. If it's signal, it should connect to something else."

Juror #8's eyes flicked to the knife photo and then, unavoidably, to the real knife at the far end of the table. "Third question," he said. "Why would the prosecution leave that hanging? If they believed the neighbor, why not use that line to prove guilt? It's almost like it weakens their narrative."

Juror #1's mouth tightened. "Prosecutors don't present evidence that weakens their narrative."

"And yet it's in the record," Juror #9 said quietly. "So, it existed. It was spoken. Someone heard it, even if imperfectly."

Juror #12 shifted in his chair. He looked like he wanted to be helpful, to perform a quick rescue of normalcy. "Maybe it was a different 'him,'" he said. "Like she meant the kid. Like she just said the wrong word."

Juror #8's eyes moved to him. "Good," he said, and the word startled Juror #12 into stillness. "That's a possibility. So, we ask: did anyone clarify? Did the lawyers ask follow-up? Did they pin her down?"

Juror #1 flipped again, scanning. "No," he said, and his voice came out reluctant. "They didn't. Redirect ended shortly after."

Juror #7's eyebrows lifted. "So, we've got a statement that could change the whole frame, and nobody dug into it."

Juror #1 bristled. "It doesn't change the whole frame."

Juror #8 looked at him, not confrontational, simply refusing to be rushed. "Doesn't it?" he asked. "Fourth question, then. What else did we treat as settled because it felt settled? If this line slipped by, what else did we slide past because we were already leaning guilty?"

Juror #2 stared at the dead clock on the table, as if the frozen hands could tell her whether she'd made a mistake. "I didn't want to lean," she whispered. "I just… it was so much. The photos. The bruises. Everyone saying it's obvious."

Juror #8's voice softened slightly when he spoke to her, but it didn't lose its edge. "I know," he said. "That's why I'm asking questions. Not to torture anyone. To make sure our certainty isn't just exhaustion."

Juror #6 let out a breath. "So, what do you want to do?" he asked, blunt. "We can't call her back in. We can't ask the judge. We can't even hit the damn buzzer."

The room heard itself in that sentence. The sealed door. The silence outside. The knife that had appeared like a dare. Their isolation turned every limitation into pressure.

Juror #8 didn't glance at the door, but everyone else did, as if the room itself had spoken. "We do what we can," he said. "We reconstruct. We slow down. Fifth question. The neighbor said the voices stopped after the crash. The crash matters. What was it?"

Juror #1 frowned. "She said it sounded like furniture," he said, reading again. "A chair or something hitting the wall."

Juror #8 nodded. "And the officers said overturned chair, broken lamp," he said. "So, a crash fits. But if the crash happened before the stabbing, it could have been a struggle. If it happened after, it could have been someone falling. If it happened during, it could have been a knife dropping. The crash is a pivot."

Juror #3's voice came through clenched teeth. "Or it's just a crash during a murder."

"It could be," Juror #8 agreed. "So, we ask: what did the physical evidence say about sequence? Blood spatter. Location. The medical examiner. Did we ever talk about whether the wounds happened where the body was found?"

Juror #4 looked up sharply. "The ME testified the victim likely collapsed near the couch," he said. "Blood pooling was consistent with body position."

Juror #8 held his gaze. "Likely," he repeated. "Not definitively. And 'consistent' isn't 'proved.'"

Juror #10 slapped his palm lightly on the table, a cheap imitation of Juror #3's force. "This is ridiculous," he said. "You can turn anything into doubt if you ask enough questions."

Juror #8's eyes met his. "That's the point of questions," he said. "They reveal what we actually know."

Juror #9 spoke softly, and the room quieted around him. "Questions are how you keep from becoming part of the machine," he said. "And machines are very good at making death feel procedural."

Juror #1 flinched at that, as if it had been aimed directly at him.

Juror #8 didn't let the moment drift into philosophy. He turned it back to the page. "Sixth question," he said, and his voice was calm enough that it sounded like he'd been doing this his whole life. "If the father said, 'I didn't mean to,' who was he speaking to? The boy? Himself? Someone else? And why would that line exist at all if the prosecution's theory is a planned ambush?"

Juror #2 whispered, almost inaudible, "Because maybe he didn't mean to hurt him."

Juror #3's head snapped toward her. "What?"

Juror #2 shrank immediately, but the words had already entered the room. She looked at her hands as if they'd betrayed her. "The father," she said, voice shaking. "If he was abusive and something happened… maybe he did something and then—"

Juror #3 cut her off, harsh. "He didn't mean to, so the kid stabs him seventeen times? Come on."

Juror #8's gaze didn't leave Juror #2. "Let her finish," he said quietly.

Juror #2 swallowed hard. "I don't know," she said. "I'm just saying… the neighbor hearing that makes it feel less simple. Like there was a moment of… regret."

Juror #11's eyes lowered, as if looking at something only he could see. "Regret does not undo harm," he said softly. "But it changes the shape of it."

Juror #12's voice came tight. "This is going nowhere. We're stuck in here, arguing about what a woman maybe heard through a wall."

At the far end of the table, near the chalkboard, the real knife caught the fluorescent light and gave back a dull, indifferent shine.

Juror #8 glanced at it for the first time since he started counting questions, and when he did, his expression didn't change. But the room seemed to lean in, listening.

"It feels like it's going nowhere," Juror #8 said, "because we want a straight line. But cases aren't straight lines. They're knots. We either untie them or we cut them."

He paused, then asked one more, quieter than the rest.

"Seventh question," he said. "Why does this room keep giving us the one thing we tried not to handle: responsibility? The door won't open. Time won't move. Evidence shows up on our table. And now a sentence we don't remember is sitting in front of us like it was placed there."

Juror #1's voice came out strained. "Stop," he said. "Stop talking about the room like it's a person."

Juror #8 looked at him steadily. "Then treat it like a fact," he replied. "Something is controlling what we can do. That's a fact. And it's forcing us to confront what we usually avoid: that a verdict is not just a decision about someone else. It's a decision about who we are when we have power."

Silence thickened, and in it Juror #1's authority seemed to thin, like paint stretched over a crack.

Juror #3 stared at the transcript, jaw clenched, and for the first time his anger didn't look like certainty. It looked like fear of what questions might uncover.

Juror #2 wiped at her face with the back of her hand, embarrassed by tears she could not stop.

Juror #10 sat back, scowling, but his eyes kept flicking to the knife as if it might move again.

Juror #9 watched Juror #8 with the weary recognition of someone who knew a reckoning when he saw one.

Juror #8 placed his hands flat on the table, palms down, an anchoring gesture. "We can't leave," he said. "So, we do the only honest thing left. We keep asking."

At that, a faint sound rose behind them.

Dry. Soft. Familiar now.

Like chalk touching the board.

Chapter 5

Cracks in the Facade

The chalk sound came again, longer this time. Not a single scrape that could be dismissed as settling wood or air in the vents, but the unmistakable drag of something dry across slate.

Juror #1's head snapped toward the board so fast his chair squeaked. Juror #2 made a small, involuntary moan and pressed her palms flat to the table as if bracing for impact. Juror #6's shoulders lifted, readying, while Juror #12 half rose and then froze, caught between flight and the fact that there was nowhere to go.

Juror #11 was already standing. He took two careful steps toward the chalkboard, his hands open at his sides, showing everyone he carried nothing. Juror #9 remained seated, but his eyes tracked the board with the same steady attention he'd given the sealed door.

The chalkboard was no longer blank.

Not completely.

A faint, crooked line sat near the center, too light to be a message, too deliberate to be residue. Like the start of a letter that had been abandoned. Or the first stroke of a tally.

Juror #11 leaned closer, not touching it. His breath fogged nothing; the room was too dry for that. "There," he said, and the quiet certainty in his voice made the room tilt.

Juror #10 barked out a laugh that sounded like it had been forced through clenched teeth. "A line," he said loudly. "Congratulations. It's a chalkboard. It has chalk on it."

"It wasn't there," Juror #12 said, voice sharp with panic. He heard himself and tried to soften it, failed. "It wasn't."

Juror #3 pushed back his chair hard enough that it knocked the leg of the table. The dead clock on the tabletop vibrated and then settled again, hands still accusingly fixed. "Who's doing this?" he demanded, and his eyes swept the room as if he expected to find someone grinning with chalk dust on their fingers. "Which one of you thinks this is funny?"

No one answered him. The silence made his anger search for a new target.

It landed on Juror #8.

Juror #3 jabbed a finger across the table. "You. You've been talking in circles since we walked in here. Asking questions like you're running the show. And now the room's doing magic tricks."

Juror #8 didn't move. His palms remained flat on the table, as if keeping himself anchored in the only thing that was still solid. "I'm not doing anything," he said.

Juror #3's voice rose, filling the sealed space. "Oh, come on. You sit there all calm, like you're not surprised by any of it. Door locks, clock dies, knife appears, chalk starts writing, and you're just… what, taking notes?"

"I'm paying attention," Juror #8 said. His tone stayed even, which only fed the fire.

Juror #3 stepped away from his chair, circling the table a half-step, like a man who needed motion to keep from exploding. "Paying attention," he repeated, mockingly. "Or controlling the narrative."

Juror #1 stood abruptly, pushing his chair back with a sharp scrape. "That's enough," he said, voice loud with a brittle authority. "We are not accusing each other. We don't know what's happening, but we're not turning this into—"

"Into what?" Juror #7 cut in, and the interruption surprised everyone, including him. His usual joking cadence was gone. His face had a strained, pinched look, as if his skin didn't fit right anymore. "Into exactly what it already is?"

Juror #1's jaw tightened. "We're going to remain professional."

Juror #7 gave a short, humorless sound. "Professional. Right. With the ghost chalk."

"Stop calling it that," Juror #10 snapped, as if naming it made it more real.

Juror #5 leaned forward, elbows on the table, eyes darting between faces. The old defensive alertness in him had turned into something sharper. "Does anybody else feel like we're being pushed?" he asked. "Like it doesn't matter what we want, it's gonna keep happening until we... until we do something."

Juror #4's pen lay untouched beside his legal pad. He stared at the faint mark on the chalkboard as if his mind could measure it into normal. "Environmental manipulation," he murmured, almost to himself. "If it's not supernatural, it's engineered. Sound, stress, confinement. It could be a psychological test."

Juror #12 seized on that as if it were a rope. "Yes," he said quickly. "Yes. That's what I said earlier. A test. Somebody watching us. This is like those studies. They lock people in and see what happens."

Juror #9's voice came gently, but it carried. "A test implies a tester," he said. "A human one."

Juror #10 swung his head toward him. "You got a better explanation?"

Juror #9 didn't flinch. "I have lived long enough to know," he said quietly, "that sometimes there is no better explanation. Only the one you can tolerate."

Juror #2 made a small, strangled sound and finally spoke louder than a whisper. "I can't tolerate any of them," she said. Her eyes were red, her cheeks wet, and she looked furious at herself for it. "I want to go home."

Her voice cracked on the word home, and something in the room shifted. The arguments stopped being abstract. The sealed door stopped being a puzzle. It became a wall between them and ordinary life.

Juror #6 looked toward the door, then back at the table. "We all want to go home," he said, blunt. "Yelling at each other won't open it."

Juror #3 rounded on him, and now the anger had somewhere safer to go than fear. "So what, we just sit here and let it happen? Let him"—he gestured again toward Juror #8—"drag us through every little maybe until we lose our minds?"

Juror #8 finally shifted, not back, not away. He leaned forward slightly, his eyes steady. "You keep saying 'let,'" he said. "Like you don't have a choice."

Juror #3's face contorted, the muscles in his jaw working. "My choice is to vote guilty and be done," he snapped. "That's my choice. And you took that away."

"I didn't take anything away," Juror #8 said. "The law requires unanimity."

"The law," Juror #3 spat, and the word sounded like an insult now. "Don't hide behind the law. You said it yourself. People pull the switch."

Juror #1 stepped around the end of the table, trying to insert himself physically between them without making it a confrontation. "Juror number three," he said sharply. "Sit down."

Juror #3 didn't. He stared at the foreman, and the stare carried something old and familiar: a challenge to authority that didn't feel earned. "Make me," he said, and the words came out before he could stop them.

Juror #1 went still. In any other room, in any other day, that would have been unthinkable. In this room, with the door sealed and the clock dead, the normal hierarchies had started to rot.

Juror #11's voice cut in, controlled but firm. "We should not threaten each other."

Juror #10 turned on him immediately, as if he'd been waiting for an opening. "Oh, shut up," he said, loud. "Always with the should. Should this, should that. You think you're better than us because you say the right words."

Juror #11's posture straightened. The air around him seemed to stiffen. "No," he said. "I think we are worse when we abandon them."

Juror #10 stood so fast his chair toppled backward, clattering against the tile. The sound echoed off the walls in a way that made the room feel smaller. "Don't preach to me," he barked. "You don't know me."

Juror #2 flinched at the crash, her hands trembling openly now.

Juror #12 looked from Juror #10 to Juror #11, then to the knife near the chalkboard, and his voice came out sharp with sudden practical terror. "Sit down," he said, too loudly. "Everyone sit down. There's a knife on the table. This is how people get hurt."

The word hurt hung there, because it carried two meanings and both of them felt too close.

Juror #5's gaze fixed on Juror #10's hands, then on Juror #3's, tracking them the way he'd tracked hands in darker places than courthouses. "He's right," Juror #5 said. "Everybody cool it."

Juror #3 gave a harsh laugh. "Cool it? We're trapped in here, the walls are talking, and you want cool?"

Juror #4 finally spoke louder, and the change in volume from him was startling. "Volume isn't the variable that matters," he said, and his voice had an edge, a crack in his usual clinical calm. "It's escalation. Escalation is predictable under confinement. It leads to violence. That's what it does."

Juror #7 stared at him. "So, what, you're diagnosing us now?"

Juror #4's eyes flicked to the faint line on the chalkboard, then to the dead clock, then to the knife. "I'm telling you what comes next if we keep going like this," he said.

Juror #1 clenched his hands at his sides, forcing them not to shake. "Everyone sit," he ordered, louder than before, and the word sit came out like an attempt to nail their bodies back into place.

Juror #10 hesitated, chest heaving. For a moment it looked like he might refuse just to prove he could. Then he yanked his chair upright with a scrape and dropped into it hard, eyes still burning.

Juror #3 remained standing a beat longer, staring at Juror #8 like he wanted to will him out of existence. Then, finally, he sat with a violent shove of his chair.

The room didn't calm. The silence that followed was worse, charged and ugly.

Juror #8 looked past them to the chalkboard. The faint line was still there. Nothing more had been written. No message. No explanation. Just that small beginning, like a finger tapping once on a table to demand attention.

"We're breaking," Juror #2 whispered, and she sounded ashamed of the truth.

Juror #9's hands trembled on the table edge. "No," he said softly. "We are being broken."

Juror #1 stared at the faint chalk mark, then at the knife, then at the dead clock. His voice came out hoarse, and the change in it startled him. "We need to focus," he said, and the words were no longer managerial. They were pleading. "If we don't, we'll tear each other apart."

Juror #3 laughed again, but it was small now, almost a cough. "Maybe that's the point," he muttered.

Nobody asked him what he meant. Nobody wanted to hear it said aloud.

Because in the sealed room, with raised voices still vibrating in the air, it was becoming harder to pretend this was only about a boy on trial somewhere outside these walls. Harder to pretend the pressure in their chests was only frustration.

The chalk line sat on the board like the first crack in glass.

And every one of them could feel the fracture spreading, silent and inevitable, beneath the surface of their composure.

Silence didn't fix anything. It only gave their anger room to reorganize.

Juror #1 remained standing, hands braced on the back of his chair as if he could hold himself upright by force alone. His eyes moved from face to face, searching for a hook he could hang authority on. Nobody offered one. The foreman's badge on his lapel looked like a joke the room refused to laugh at.

Juror #3 sat rigid, shoulders bunched, still vibrating from the confrontation. Juror #10's chair legs were planted wide, his hands gripping the armrests as though the furniture owed him obedience. Juror #2 stared at the tabletop, cheeks wet, blinking hard like she could blink the last five minutes into being a misunderstanding. Juror #7's gaze skittered anywhere but the chalkboard, as if not looking at it could make the faint line disappear.

Juror #8 broke the hush first, but he didn't speak to the men who had been shouting. He spoke to the room.

"We're not going to get out of here by turning on each other," he said.

Juror #3 let out a short laugh that had no humor left. "That's rich," he said. "You've been turning us on each other since the first vote."

Juror #8 didn't bite. "I asked questions about the case."

"No," Juror #3 snapped, leaning forward now, voice sharp but contained, like a blade kept close to the body. "You asked questions about us. Don't pretend you didn't. You look at people when you say things. You pick at them. 'Simple doesn't ask anything of you.' You said that to me."

Juror #8 met his eyes. "Because you were trying to end the discussion by force."

Juror #3's face tightened. "I was trying to end it because it's obvious. The kid did it."

Juror #9 spoke gently, without looking away from Juror #3. "And if it were your son?" he asked.

The question was not loud. It didn't need to be. It slid under the skin.

Juror #3's jaw flexed. "Don't," he said. The word came out like a warning, not to Juror #9 but to the room.

Juror #10 seized it immediately. "Oh, now we've got sacred topics," he said, voice dripping with contempt. He looked around as if taking a poll. "We can send some kid to the chair, but we can't bring up someone's personal life. Convenient."

Juror #11's posture stiffened. "We are not supposed to use our personal lives to decide," he said.

Juror #10 turned toward him with quick, practiced hostility, grateful for a target that wasn't supernatural chalk. "Listen to him," he said to the others, as if Juror #11 were performing. "Always the rules. Always the right way. Like he invented fairness."

Juror #11 didn't raise his voice. That restraint, in this room, sounded like accusation. "I did not invent it," he said. "I only know what happens without it."

Juror #10 leaned forward, eyes narrowed. "You know what happens? You run. That's what you people do. You run from wherever you come from and then you show up here and tell us how to behave."

Juror #2 made a small sound, almost inaudible, like pain swallowed. Juror #12's head jerked up as if he'd been slapped by the ugliness of it.

"Enough," Juror #1 said, but his voice lacked the snap it used to have.

Juror #11 looked at Juror #10 steadily. "You do not know what I did," he said. His accent seemed heavier now, not because it had changed, but because the room was listening for weakness. "And you do not get to use ignorance as a weapon."

Juror #10 scoffed. "Weapon. Everything's a weapon with you."

Juror #5 shifted in his chair, eyes flicking between them. "He didn't say anything crazy," he muttered. "You're just itching to start something."

Juror #10's head snapped toward Juror #5. "And what are you, his backup?" He gestured at Juror #5's clothes, his posture, the defensive way he sat. "You've been glaring at everyone like we're cops. Maybe you should be on trial, not this kid."

Juror #5's mouth tightened. He didn't rise, but his shoulders squared as if preparing for impact. "You don't know me," he said, the same phrase Juror #10 had thrown earlier, only this time it sounded like a fact, not a threat.

Juror #10 smiled thinly. "I know your type. Always one step from trouble and two steps from blaming everyone else for it."

Juror #5's laugh came out sharp. "My type. Yeah. That's convenient too. Put people in boxes, then you don't have to think."

Juror #4 finally looked up from his unused legal pad. His eyes were cold, but something in his composure had frayed. "This is irrelevant," he said. "Personal speculation is noise."

Juror #7 gave a brittle sound. "Noise is kind of all we've got right now."

Juror #4 ignored him, gaze fixed on Juror #10. "We are here to evaluate evidence, not attack each other's character."

Juror #10's grin turned toward Juror #4. "Character," he said, tasting the word. "You want to talk about character? Look at you. You've been sitting there scribbling like a robot, acting like you're above it. Like you're not one of us."

Juror #4's face remained composed, but the skin around his eyes tightened. "I am not above anything. I am trying to be accurate."

Juror #10's voice rose slightly, not into a shout, but into something that filled the room. "Accurate. Sure. That's what guys like you always say when you're cutting corners. Numbers, data, plausible deniability. You hide behind spreadsheets, so you don't have to feel anything."

Juror #4's pen hand twitched as if he meant to write that down, then didn't. "You're projecting," he said, and it was the first time he'd sounded anything like contempt.

Juror #10's eyes flashed. "I'm calling it like I see it."

Juror #8 watched the exchange with a stillness that didn't calm it. It made it worse, like an audience makes a fight more violent.

Juror #3 seized on the new direction, eager to turn attention away from the question Juror #9 had asked. "Yeah," he said, pointing at Juror #4 now. "And you," he added, voice thick with resentment. "You were ready to vote guilty like the rest of us until he started playing philosopher. Don't pretend you care about doubt. You care about being right."

Juror #4's gaze slid toward Juror #3. "I care about coherence," he said.

Juror #3 barked a laugh. "Coherence. Listen to him. Like a verdict is a math problem."

Juror #9's voice came quiet, but it carried into the space Juror #3 had opened. "Sometimes it is," he said. "And sometimes it is a mirror."

Juror #7 flinched at the word mirror as if he'd seen something in it. He rubbed his palms on his thighs again, trying to keep his body from betraying him. "We're really doing this," he muttered. "We're really gonna eat each other."

Juror #12 leaned forward, forcing cheer that sounded cracked. "Okay. Okay, look, can we not? This isn't helping." His eyes darted to Juror #2 like a plea for support, but she didn't look up. "We can be scared without being cruel."

Juror #3 rounded on him, quick and cruel because it was easier than being afraid. “Oh, spare us,” he said. “You’ve been trying to crack jokes since we walked in. Now you want to be the conscience?”

Juror #12’s smile flickered. “I’m just trying to keep us from—”

“From what?” Juror #3 interrupted. “From seeing what we are?”

Juror #12 swallowed. The words stuck. His gaze slid toward the knife near the chalkboard and then away again, like his eyes couldn’t bear to rest on anything sharp for too long.

Juror #2 finally spoke, but her voice was small, shaken. “Please,” she said. “Stop. Please stop.”

The room didn’t stop. Her plea only redirected the current.

Juror #10 leaned back and looked at her with a kind of disgust that pretended to be impatience. “See, this is what happens,” he said to no one in particular. “People get emotional and then everything becomes about their feelings. Crying. Hand-wringing. Meanwhile, a murderer gets a second chance.”

Juror #2’s head jerked up, eyes bright and furious now through the tears. “Don’t,” she said, and there was steel under it that hadn’t been there before.

Juror #10 lifted his eyebrows, amused. "Don't what?"

"Don't talk about me like I'm—" Her voice cracked, and she pressed her lips together hard, forcing it steady. "Like I'm nothing."

Juror #10's smile sharpened. "Then don't act like you're going to faint because someone raised their voice."

Juror #6's chair scraped as he leaned forward, the movement heavy and deliberate. "Back off," he said to Juror #10, blunt as a tool.

Juror #10 glanced at him, dismissive. "What are you gonna do, tough guy?"

Juror #6's eyes were flat. "I'm gonna tell you to shut your mouth before you make this worse."

Juror #1 took a step forward, then stopped. He looked suddenly uncertain where to put himself. In a normal room, he would have called the bailiff. In this room, there was only wood and silence beyond it.

Juror #8 spoke again, not loud. "This is what the room does," he said. "It strips away the roles. Foreman. Analyst. Joker. Working man. It leaves whatever's underneath."

Juror #3's eyes snapped toward him. "Stop talking like you know what's underneath people."

Juror #8 didn't look away. "I know what comes out when people feel trapped," he said.

Juror #3's laugh was harsh. "Oh yeah? From where? What, you've been trapped before?"

For the first time, Juror #8 paused. It was brief, but in this room a brief pause had weight. His face stayed calm, but something behind his eyes shifted, as if Juror #3 had touched a surface that was not meant to be touched yet.

Juror #9 noticed. Juror #4 noticed too, his gaze narrowing, analytical instinct returning.

Juror #8 answered carefully. "We're all trapped in things," he said. "Some are just easier to pretend aren't locked."

Juror #3 leaned forward, hungry now. "There it is," he said. "That's your game. You talk like that and you make everyone else feel dirty, like we're the problem for wanting a verdict."

Juror #8's voice remained level. "Wanting a verdict isn't the problem," he said. "Wanting it fast is."

Juror #3's face reddened again. "Fast," he repeated. "Like you're not enjoying this. Like you don't love being the one man holding the whole room hostage."

The word hostage hung in the air, familiar now, returning like a bruise pressed twice.

Juror #1 flinched. Juror #2's breath caught. Juror #7's eyes darted to the door again, as if expecting it to react to the accusation.

Juror #5 muttered, "Careful with that word."

Juror #3 ignored him. He jabbed a finger at Juror #8. "What do you do, huh?" he demanded. "You never said. Everybody else talked a little. Foreman won't shut up about procedure, big mouth over there won't shut up at all, numbers man's got his pad, joke man's got his jokes. What about you? Who are you, Juror Eight?"

Juror #8 held the stare. "Does it matter?"

"It matters if you're playing us," Juror #3 said. "It matters if you're some activist, some ex-con, some.."

Juror #1 cut in, voice strained. "We are not interrogating each other."

Juror #3 didn't even look at him. "Why not?" he snapped. "We can't interrogate the witnesses again. We can't call the judge. We can't open the door. So, what do we do? Sit here and let him steer us into whatever he wants?"

Juror #7 whispered, almost to himself, "Maybe it's not him steering."

The room heard it anyway.

The fluorescent hum seemed to thin, like a wire pulled tighter. The dead clock lay on the table with its frozen hands, still insisting on two twenty-six. The knife at the far end sat in quiet certainty. And the faint chalk line on the board waited like the beginning of a sentence.

Juror #8 looked past Juror #3 to the chalkboard, then back to the faces. "Personal attacks won't get us out," he said. "They'll only tell us what the room wants."

"And what's that?" Juror #10 demanded, voice harsh.

Juror #8 didn't answer immediately. He seemed to listen, the way he had earlier, for the second sound after the first.

Then, from behind them, the chalk moved again.

Not a scrape this time. A steady, deliberate drag, as if an unseen hand had found its nerve.

Juror #11 turned slowly toward the board, eyes widening despite his effort to stay composed.

Juror #2 let out a small whimper and clutched her purse again, as if it contained something holy.

Juror #1 stood frozen, mouth slightly open.

On the chalkboard, beside the faint first line, a second mark began to form, angling into the beginning of a word.

The room had listened to their cruelty, their accusations, their weak points.

And now it was answering.

The chalk moved with purpose now, not the hesitant scratch of something testing the surface, but a steady drag that made the hairs on Juror #2's arms rise.

Juror #1 was still staring as if his eyes could refuse what they were seeing into being. Juror #11 took another small step closer, careful to keep his hands visible, careful to make it clear he wasn't the one holding the chalk that no one could see.

The second stroke on the board lengthened, angled, then curved into something unmistakably deliberate. A letter. Not a random line.

Juror #12's voice came out thin. "Okay. No. That's… that's a letter."

Juror #10's laugh broke out too quickly and died too fast. "It's somebody messing with us. There's a string, a magnet, some trick. There's always a trick."

"No," Juror #5 said, and the word came from somewhere that didn't entertain tricks anymore. His eyes stayed on the board. "That's handwriting."

The chalk stopped, lifted, then touched down again with a small click that sounded far too close in the sealed room.

Juror #7 swallowed hard. "If it writes my name, I'm quitting jury duty forever."

"You can't quit," Juror #3 snapped automatically, then seemed to hear himself and hate it. The anger in his voice had become a reflex, something he used to avoid the other feeling pressing at the back of his throat. Fear.

The chalk dragged again. Two more letters formed, rough and imperfect, like someone writing with their off hand. The word began to take shape.

J U—

Juror #2 made a sound like a sob caught between teeth. "Please stop," she whispered, but she wasn't speaking to anyone in the room. She was speaking to the board.

Juror #1 found his voice, brittle and loud. "All right. Whoever is responsible for this, you will stop immediately. This is tampering. This is—"

The chalk wrote on, indifferent to his authority.

J U R—

Juror #4's eyes narrowed, tracking it like data. He had stopped pretending it was a prank, but he was still trying to solve it like one. "It's spelling," he said, as if naming the obvious might make it manageable. "It's communicating."

Juror #9's hands trembled on the table edge. "We understood that," he murmured.

The chalk lifted and set down again, finishing the last strokes with a finality that made the word feel less like a message and more like a label applied to a file folder.

JUROR.

The room went silent in the way it did when a verdict was read aloud. Even Juror #10 stopped making noise. Even Juror #3 stopped moving.

Juror #11 stood close enough to see the grainy texture of the chalk. His face was composed, but the muscles around his eyes had tightened. "It says 'juror,'" he said quietly.

Juror #7 let out a breath that sounded like relief and then immediately like regret. "Okay. So it's just… it's just saying what we are."

Juror #8's gaze moved from the board to the table, to the dead clock, to the knife, to the faces. "No," he said softly. "It's telling us what it sees."

Juror #1 opened his mouth to respond, but he never got the words out, because the room answered first.

It started with the lights.

The fluorescent fixtures didn't go out. They changed. The hum that had been thin and strained suddenly deepened, dropping into a lower register that you felt in your teeth more than you heard in your ears. The light shifted almost imperceptibly from harsh white to something flatter and more clinical, as if the room had been scrubbed of warmth it never really had.

Juror #2 flinched and pressed her palms against the table. "Did you— did you feel that?"

Juror #6 looked up at the fixtures, jaw set. "Power surge," he muttered, the words automatic, workmanlike. But he didn't sound convinced.

Then the air changed.

Not temperature, not exactly. It was the smell first: old paper, dust, and something faintly metallic. Like pennies rubbed between fingers. Like blood that had dried a long time ago and been forgotten in the grain of wood.

Juror #12's nose wrinkled. "What is that?"

Juror #5 shifted in his chair, eyes darting to the knife again as if it had released the scent. "That's not the knife," he said, and it wasn't a guess. He sounded like someone who knew what the world smelled like when it turned.

Juror #3 pushed back from the table, the scrape loud in the altered hum. "This is insane," he said, but his voice lacked its earlier bite. It was smaller now, swallowed by the room's new tone.

Juror #1 straightened, trying to reclaim the space with posture. “Everyone stay calm,” he ordered, and the word calm sounded ridiculous against the stale metallic air. “We do not move until we know—”

A soft thud interrupted him.

Not metal on wood this time. Something heavier. Something like a book being set down.

They all looked.

On the table, near the dead clock, a new object sat where nothing had been a moment before: a thick, brown folder, the kind used in offices for personnel files. It was plain except for a white label affixed to the front, and the label looked freshly typed, too crisp to belong in this old room.

Juror #4 leaned forward reflexively, then stopped himself, as if remembering that leaning could become reaching and reaching could become a mistake. “That wasn’t there,” he said, his voice finally betraying him with a slight tremor.

Juror #7 gave a short laugh that sounded like he was trying not to scream. “Okay. So, the room has props now.”

Juror #10 stood halfway, then sat again, as if his body couldn’t decide whether to fight or hide. “No. No. Somebody’s in here. Somebody’s coming in.”

Juror #6's gaze went to the door. The door remained shut, unchanged, solid. The gap beneath it showed nothing but shadow.

Juror #11 spoke without taking his eyes off the folder. "No one came in," he said. "We would hear it."

Juror #2 stared at the folder like it was an animal. "What does it say?"

No one answered immediately, because answering meant looking closely, and looking closely meant admitting it was real.

Juror #8 looked at Juror #1. "Open it," he said.

Juror #1 snapped his head toward him. "Absolutely not."

Juror #8 didn't react to the tone. "It's here," he said. "Whether we want it or not."

Juror #3's laugh came out rough. "Of course you want it opened. Of course you do."

Juror #8's eyes held his for a moment. "I want us to know what's happening," he said.

Juror #9 nodded faintly, as if bracing himself. "If a room wishes to speak," he murmured, "it will keep speaking until you listen."

Juror #1's lips pressed into a hard line. He looked around the table, searching for backup, for someone to agree that rules still mattered. Juror #4 wouldn't meet his eyes. Juror #2 looked like she might be sick.

Juror #12 kept glancing between the folder and the chalkboard as if the two were connected by a wire only he could sense. Juror #10's face had gone pale beneath his anger.

Finally, Juror #1 moved, stiffly, as if forced by something he couldn't name. He didn't reach for the folder with his bare hands. Instead, he grabbed the cloth Juror #6 had used earlier, the one now lying crumpled near the far end of the table like a discarded excuse. He wrapped it around his fingers, then pinched the edge of the folder as if it might bite.

He pulled it toward him.

It slid easily. No resistance. No trick.

The label faced up.

JUROR #1 – FOREMAN

Juror #1 froze.

For one long second, the room felt as if it had inhaled and was waiting to exhale into someone's face.

Juror #7 whispered, almost reverent with fear, "It knows our numbers."

Juror #5's eyes narrowed. "Or it's been watching us since before we sat down."

Juror #1's throat worked. His voice came out thin. "This is… this is harassment," he said, and he sounded like he didn't believe his own word. "This is illegal."

Juror #10 snapped, relief in the aggression because it gave him something to do. "Open it," he said, and the hunger in his voice surprised even him. "If someone's trying to mess with us, we should see what they've got."

Juror #2 shook her head rapidly. "No. No, don't."

Juror #3 leaned forward despite himself, eyes locked on the folder. "What is that?" he demanded. "A file? On him?"

Juror #4's voice was very quiet, and for once it held no clinical distance. "A personnel folder doesn't appear out of nowhere," he said. "But if it did, it would be because someone wanted to change the conversation."

Juror #8's gaze stayed on Juror #1. "The room is changing," he said, as if stating weather. "It's turning from a deliberation into something else."

Juror #1's hands tightened around the cloth. He didn't open the folder, but he didn't push it away either. The moment stretched, and in the stretched moment, other details surfaced, small and wrong.

The table felt different under their forearms. Not rougher, not smoother, just… older. The wood grain seemed darker, the varnish more worn, as if the table had lived through more than one set of jurors and remembered them.

The walls, too. The paint looked less clean than it had ten minutes ago. Near the baseboard, faint scuffs appeared that hadn't been there, marks like shoes had scraped in panic. Juror #12 blinked hard, as if his eyes were playing tricks, but the scuffs stayed.

Juror #2's voice came out as a fragile question. "Is it… is it changing because we're looking?"

Juror #9 answered her, gentle but grim. "Perhaps it is changing because we are not looking away anymore."

The chalkboard remained in the front of the room, with its single word, JUROR, written in uneven strokes. It looked less like a prank now and more like a sign hung in a courtroom.

Juror #11 took a step back from the board, as if the space near it had become charged. His gaze moved to the knife at the far end of the table. "This room is bringing evidence," he said quietly. "Not of the case. Of us."

Juror #3 swallowed, his anger faltering under the weight of the idea. "Us? Why us?"

Juror #8 didn't answer him immediately. He looked at the folder again, then at the locked door, then at the dead clock, frozen at two twenty-six as if time had chosen a moment to trap them in.

"Because," Juror #8 said at last, voice calm enough to be terrifying, "we came in here ready to judge."

Juror #1 stared at the folder with his name on it, the foreman designation typed like a title on a charge sheet. His jaw worked as if he were chewing on words he couldn't swallow. "This is nonsense," he said, but the protest had no strength. "We don't have files. We're jurors."

The fluorescent hum deepened again, a low vibration that seemed to run through the table and into their bones.

Juror #10's voice came sharp. "Open it."

Juror #2 whispered, "Don't."

Juror #3 said nothing, but his eyes were fixed on Juror #1's hands, waiting to see whether authority would break.

Juror #9 watched with a kind of weary sorrow.

Juror #8 sat perfectly still, as if he already knew what was inside and was waiting for the rest of them to catch up.

Juror #1's fingers slipped under the folder's flap.

The cloth crinkled, loud in the sealed air.

He hesitated, one last moment balanced on the edge of denial.

Then he opened it.

Chapter 6

The First Secret Revealed

The folder opened with the soft, dry sound of paper separating, a noise so ordinary it felt obscene in a room that had stopped obeying ordinary rules.

Juror #1 kept the cloth between his fingers and the folder, as if fabric could protect him from whatever waited inside. He lifted the cover slowly. For a fraction of a second he saw nothing but cream-colored sheets and the corner of a stapled packet, the kind of packet he'd signed off on a thousand times in conference rooms.

Then he saw the first page.

It wasn't court paper. It wasn't a transcript.

At the top, in clean, typed text, it read: SUMMARY.

Below it, a name.

Not the boy's. Not the father's.

His.

Juror #1's mouth went dry. He tried to swallow and found there was nothing to swallow. His eyes moved down the page with the forced steadiness of a man determined to keep his hands from shaking.

Across the table, Juror #3 leaned forward like a predator that had smelled blood. "What is it?" he demanded. "Read it."

Juror #2 made a small sound, barely a voice at all. "Please don't."

Juror #10 had gone quiet in a way that was almost worse than his shouting. His eyes were fixed on the folder, wide and hungry, as if he wanted it to be anything other than what it looked like.

Juror #4 didn't speak. His gaze tracked Juror #1's face instead of the pages, watching for the first crack.

Juror #7's hands hovered near his knees, uncertain what to do with themselves. He looked like he was waiting for a punchline he knew wasn't coming.

Juror #9's eyes were sad and steady.

Juror #8 remained still, his attention anchored on Juror #1 with the quiet patience of someone who didn't need to force the moment.

Juror #1's lips parted. For a moment, everyone thought he might read it aloud, like he'd read the transcript, like the words on paper could be made harmless by being performed.

Instead, he shut the folder halfway, instinctive, protective.

Juror #3's voice shot up. "No. Don't you close that. You opened it."

Juror #1's head snapped up. "This is not evidence," he said, too sharply. "This is not part of our deliberation."

Juror #5's voice came low. "Neither was the knife."

That landed. Juror #1's eyes flicked, unwillingly, toward the far end of the table where the real blade lay near the chalkboard. It hadn't moved. It didn't need to. Its presence did the work without effort.

Juror #1 tried to regain his tone, tried to sound like a man who could call for order and get it. "We don't know where this came from. We don't know who made it. It could be—"

"A prank?" Juror #7 offered, but his voice was hollow. "Somebody's really committed to the bit."

Juror #11 shook his head slowly. "A prank does not lock doors from the outside," he said. "A prank does not stop time."

Juror #10 barked, sudden and furious, as if anger could put him back in control. "Stop talking like it's a damn spirit," he said. "It's a person. It has to be a person. And if it's a person, then it's a crime. It's intimidation."

Juror #9 looked at him. "And if it is not a person?"

Juror #10's jaw clenched. "Then we're all losing our minds."

Juror #2's shoulders shook. She pressed her fingertips into her temples again, as if holding her head would keep it from splitting open. "What does it say?" she whispered, and there was something different in her whisper now. Not only fear. A desperate need to know what shape the danger had taken.

Juror #1 stared down at the folder again. The cloth in his hand felt damp, though his palms were cold. He opened the folder a second time, slower, resigned in the way a man is resigned when his options have collapsed into a single path.

His eyes returned to the page.

The room seemed to lean in.

The fluorescent hum had deepened into something that vibrated in the table. The dead clock sat between them like a joke with no punchline, hands still nailed to two twenty-six. On the chalkboard, the word JUROR stared back at them in smeared white strokes, labeling them the way a tag labels a toe.

Juror #1's throat tightened. He didn't want to read. Reading would make it real. Reading would turn it into a proceeding. And he could feel, in the marrow behind his sternum, that whatever this was had been waiting for him to treat it like that.

He forced his eyes to the next lines.

There were bullet points. Dates. Locations. The language was blunt, almost clinical, the way an internal report is blunt when it assumes it will never be seen outside the company.

Then a line that struck him with such force his vision briefly narrowed.

FATALITIES: 3.

Juror #1's grip on the folder spasmed. The top page crinkled. The cloth slipped slightly, and for the first time his bare thumb brushed paper.

His breath came in shallow. He felt suddenly, absurdly, like a boy caught cheating. Like a man whose entire identity had been built on being the one who signs off, the one who approves, the one who keeps the machine running.

Juror #4 saw the change and leaned forward. "What are you looking at?" he asked, quiet.

Juror #1 didn't answer.

Juror #3's chair scraped as he rose halfway. "Read it," he insisted. "You're foreman. You wanted procedure. So do it. Put it on the table."

Juror #1's eyes flicked up, and for an instant his expression was naked. Not anger. Not authority. Something else, something that didn't belong on his face.

Guilt, before it turned itself into denial.

He lowered his gaze again. The words on the paper blurred and then snapped back into focus.

Juror #2's whisper turned into a plea. "Please," she said, and no one could tell whether she was pleading with Juror #1 or with whatever had placed that folder in front of them.

Juror #6 spoke for the first time in minutes, voice blunt, the way it always was when he didn't know how to be anything else. "It's about you, isn't it?"

Juror #1's lips moved soundlessly. He licked them once. His mouth tasted like metal, like old pennies, the same smell that had seeped into the room when the folder appeared.

Juror #10 leaned in, eyes narrowed. "What is it? What did you do?" His voice sharpened on the last word, and it sounded too eager, as if he needed someone else to be guilty so his own fear could find a target.

Juror #1's chest rose and fell. He could feel all of them watching him, measuring him, waiting. Twelve bodies in a room that would not open, staring at the man who'd tried to keep them working like a committee.

Juror #8's voice cut through the tightness, low and even. "You don't have to read it if you can't," he said. "But you can't pretend it isn't there."

Juror #1 looked up at him, and something in the look was almost hatred. Not because Juror #8 had put the folder there, but because Juror #8 had always been the one to insist on looking.

Juror #1 swallowed again. His eyes dropped. His finger moved down the page, tracing without touching, as if he could keep the words from sinking into his skin if he didn't press too hard.

Then his voice came out.

It wasn't the voice he'd used in the courtroom, or at the start of deliberations. It wasn't even the voice he'd used when he snapped at Juror #7 or ordered Juror #3 to sit down.

It was smaller. Stripped.

"It's not… it's not about the case," he said.

Juror #3 laughed once, harsh. "No kidding. What is it?"

Juror #1's gaze stayed on the paper. His lips barely moved as he spoke again, and the sound that came out was closer to a confession than a statement. It didn't feel like something he chose to say. It felt like something pulled out of him by the room itself, the way the chalk had been pulled across slate.

"It says three people died," he whispered.

The room went very still.

Juror #2's hand rose to her mouth. Juror #12's eyes widened, and his face lost the last trace of forced cheer. Juror #7's jaw worked as if he were chewing on panic.

Juror #10's voice came too fast. "Three people? Where? How? What are you talking about?"

Juror #1 didn't look up. His focus remained locked on the page like it was the only thing keeping him from falling. "It's… it's a report," he whispered. "An internal report."

Juror #4's tone changed, sharp with sudden understanding. "A workplace incident."

Juror #1 flinched at the precision, the way he'd flinched earlier when the transcript produced a line none of them remembered. He gave a tiny nod, almost imperceptible.

Juror #9 spoke, voice gentle and unforgiving at the same time. “Not an accident,” he said. “A decision.”

Juror #1’s breathing hitched. He finally looked up, and his eyes were wet, though no tears had fallen. The sight of that, on a face built to intimidate conference rooms into silence, was more frightening than if he’d shouted.

“I didn’t mean—” he began, and the phrase stopped in his throat as if the room itself had recognized it. I didn’t mean to. The line the neighbor had heard through the wall. The line that had twisted their neat story into a knot.

Juror #1’s voice dropped even lower, a raw whisper that sounded like it had been scraped out of him.

“I knew,” he said.

It didn’t sound like a confession of a crime. It sounded like the admission of a sin.

Juror #2’s breath came out in a thin sob. Juror #6 stared hard at the tabletop. Juror #5’s eyes narrowed as if he were looking at a man he’d misjudged, and that realization angered him.

Juror #3 spoke slowly now, each word measured. “You knew what?”

Juror #1's hands tightened on the folder until the paper bent under his grip. His foreman badge glinted dully on his lapel, a piece of metal insisting on authority in a room that had begun to trade authority for truth.

"I knew it wasn't safe," he whispered. "And I signed anyway."

No one spoke after that. The silence wasn't empty. It was heavy, packed tight with the sudden understanding that the folder wasn't random, and the room wasn't playing games.

It was choosing, carefully, where to begin.

On the chalkboard, the word JUROR remained, but it didn't feel like a label anymore.

It felt like an accusation.

Juror #8's gaze didn't leave Juror #1. His voice, when it came, was almost quiet enough to miss. "How many?" he asked.

Juror #1 swallowed. The muscles in his face worked like he was trying to keep something back.

Then, with the same stripped whisper, he answered.

"Three," he said. "Three workers."

Juror #9 closed his eyes briefly, as if in mourning.

Juror #10 exhaled, a hard sound, and for once it wasn't contempt. It was fear finding its first proof.

Juror #3 sat down slowly, like his legs had stopped trusting him.

Juror #2 stared at the folder as if it had teeth.

And Juror #1, still holding the papers that had turned him from foreman into something smaller and more human, lowered his gaze again and began to read, because the room had taken away his distance and left him only one option.

To tell them what he had done.

Juror #1's eyes tracked the page as if reading fast enough could turn it back into a private document, the kind meant to be filed away and forgotten. His voice, when it came, was uneven at first, the syllables snagging on something deeper than shame.

"Facility: North River Packaging. Incident date…" He swallowed. "Two years, four months ago."

Juror #7 made a soft sound, somewhere between a sigh and a flinch. "Jesus."

Juror #1 continued anyway, because stopping felt worse. The room didn't demand volume or drama. It demanded plainness.

"Summary: During the overnight shift, a conveyor housing panel failed. The safety guard had been removed. Worker one was pulled into the mechanism. Worker two attempted to intervene and was struck. Worker three…" His throat tightened. He blinked hard and looked down again. "Worker three was crushed when the support frame collapsed."

The words were so clean they felt vicious. No names. No faces. Only functions and outcomes.

Juror #2's hand trembled against her mouth. Her eyes darted to the knife on the far end of the table, then to the dead clock. Two twenty-six. Frozen as if the room had chosen a moment for them to live in until they understood it.

Juror #6's jaw worked. "That ain't a freak accident," he muttered, more to himself than anyone. "That's a chain."

Juror #4 leaned forward, elbows near his pad without touching it, his analytical calm now sharpened into something prosecutorial. "Read the cause section."

Juror #1's lips tightened. He didn't like being directed. Not now, not with his insides exposed. But he did it. He turned the page with the cloth still between his fingers and the paper, a pointless barrier he couldn't abandon.

"Contributing factors," he read. "Repeated maintenance requests regarding panel integrity were logged and deferred. Safety guard removal was noted in prior inspection. Corrective action was not implemented due to production targets."

Juror #10 let out a short, ugly laugh. "Production targets." He shook his head as if the phrase was obscene. "That's what you call bodies when they're in the way."

Juror #1's eyes flashed up, but the anger didn't hold. It collapsed under the simple fact that the page agreed with Juror #10 more than it protected him.

Juror #9 spoke quietly. "And your part."

The sentence wasn't a question, exactly. It was an instruction the way the room had instructed them with chalk and objects and silence.

Juror #1's gaze dropped again. His thumb had left a faint bend in the corner of the page, proof his hand was not as steady as he needed it to be.

"Approval," he read, voice thinning. "Deferred maintenance authorized by operations management pending end-of-quarter review."

Juror #3 leaned forward slowly, eyes narrowed, voice low. "That's you."

Juror #1 stared at the word management as if it had been typed by an enemy. "Yes," he said, and the word felt scraped out of him. "That's me."

Juror #12 shook his head, the motion small and helpless. "But… you didn't take the guard off yourself."

Juror #1's mouth twitched, almost grateful for the life raft. For a second he looked like he might climb onto it. Then he looked at the label on the folder again, as if the room wouldn't let him lie by omission.

"No," he said. "I didn't take it off."

Juror #8's gaze stayed on him, steady and unblinking, a presence that didn't accuse so much as refuse to let the moment become convenient. "Did you know it was off?"

Juror #1's breath hitched. He glanced at the door, a reflex he couldn't control, like someone expecting an exit to appear if he looked hard enough. The door remained shut, its handle indifferent.

"I knew," Juror #1 said, and now his voice had lost its pretense of reading. "I knew they were bypassing guards. I knew the panel was failing. I knew the requests. I knew what it meant."

Juror #2's eyes squeezed shut. A tear slipped down the side of her nose. She wiped it quickly, ashamed to be seen reacting, as if emotion itself was evidence.

Juror #4 spoke again, clipped. "Why didn't you shut the line down?"

Juror #1's shoulders rose and fell, a shallow breath. "Because it was always a 'temporary' risk," he said, and the defensiveness in his voice sounded rehearsed, like something he'd told himself for years. "Because the maintenance team said they could nurse it to quarter's end. Because corporate was on us. Because every time we stopped production, there were consequences."

Juror #5 made a quiet sound of disbelief. "Consequences," he echoed. "Like what, you'd miss a bonus?"

Juror #1 flinched as if the word bonus had struck him. His eyes moved to the table, to the exhibits that had started as someone else's tragedy. "You think I did it for money," he said, voice rising a notch, and then he caught himself. The room didn't reward volume. It rewarded honesty.

He swallowed and lowered his tone again. "It wasn't just money. It was the whole structure. If I shut the line down without clearance, I'd be written up. If I got written up, I'd be replaced. If I was replaced, it wouldn't change anything. They'd put someone in who'd say yes faster than I did."

Juror #9 looked at him steadily. "So, you said yes," he murmured.

Juror #1's jaw clenched. "I thought I was protecting my people," he said, and now he sounded like he almost believed it. "I thought if I kept the plant running, at least they'd keep their jobs. At least the overtime would come through. At least… at least—"

"At least you'd keep yours," Juror #10 cut in, and his voice had the sharp satisfaction of a man who finally saw someone else bleed.

Juror #6 shot him a look. "Shut it," he said, not gentle. "Let him talk."

Juror #10 leaned back, lips curling, but he held his tongue. For now.

Juror #1 stared down at the folder again. The typed words were still there, indifferent to his explanations. He turned another page.

"This section lists notifications," he said, and his voice had gone hollow. "Emails. Meeting minutes." He stopped, eyes fixed on something. His throat bobbed.

Juror #7 shifted, face pale. "What is it?"

Juror #1's lips moved without sound for a moment, then he forced the words out. "There was a meeting," he said. "Two weeks before the incident. Safety brought photos."

Juror #3's voice was low and relentless. "And you were there."

"Yes," Juror #1 whispered.

Juror #8 didn't move. "What did the photos show?"

Juror #1's eyes flickered, and for the first time the corporate manager disguise cracked enough to show something childlike underneath: the memory of looking at a warning and choosing not to feel it.

"The panel," he said. "Hairline fractures. Rusted bolts. And the guard… removed. They said it was only off during maintenance, but we all knew. We all knew it was off during production too."

Juror #2's whisper slipped out before she could stop it. "Then why didn't you stop it?"

Juror #1 looked at her, and his expression softened in a way that made him look older. "Because I didn't believe it would happen that night," he said. "Or the next. Or ever. I believed in probability. I believed if it hadn't happened yet, it wouldn't happen on my watch."

Juror #4's eyes narrowed. "You treated the risk like a statistic."

Juror #1 nodded, once, a small broken motion. "Yes."

The fluorescent hum deepened for a moment, subtle but present, as if the room approved of the clarity. The chalkboard still read JUROR in uneven letters. The knife lay near it like an exclamation point no one wanted.

Juror #9's voice was gentle, but it carried weight. "Did you go to the families?"

Juror #1's eyes dropped. "There was a statement," he said. "Corporate sent someone. HR. A grief counselor." His lips tightened. "I didn't go."

Juror #7 let out a breath that sounded like a laugh but wasn't. "Of course you didn't."

Juror #1's gaze snapped up, and for a second the manager returned, defensive and sharp. "What was I supposed to do?" he demanded. "Show up and what, make it better? Stand in a kitchen with a widow and say, 'Sorry I signed a paper'? It wouldn't bring them back."

"No," Juror #8 said quietly. "But it would make it harder to pretend it wasn't you."

The room went still again. Even Juror #3 didn't jump in. The sentence had landed too neatly, like a gavel.

Juror #1's shoulders sagged. The anger drained out of him the way heat drains when a door opens. Except the door hadn't opened. Only something inside him had.

He looked down at the folder. His voice, when it came, was smaller than before.

"There's a line at the end," he said. "Recommendations. Corrective action." He stared at the typed words, then read them as if reading them now might count as doing them then. "Install new guard. Replace panel. Retrain staff. Audit management approvals."

He stopped. A humorless sound escaped him, half breath, half sob. "Audit management approvals," he repeated, and his eyes went wet again.

Juror #6 stared at the tabletop, knuckles white. "Three men went to work and didn't come home," he said, bluntly. "Because paperwork beat sense."

Juror #1 nodded faintly, unable to argue. The cloth was crumpled in his fist now, damp with sweat.

Juror #2 lowered her hands from her face. She looked at him with frightened sympathy, like she was seeing a man trapped in a confession he couldn't survive. "Do you… do you think you killed them?" she asked.

Juror #1's throat worked. He looked at the dead clock, then at the knife, then at the chalkboard, as if the room had become a jury and the objects were its exhibits.

He didn't answer right away. The silence stretched. The hum pressed into their teeth.

Then he gave the only answer the room would accept.

"I signed," he whispered. "I knew. And they died."

He lifted his gaze, and for a moment it seemed like he was waiting for a judge to speak, for a bailiff to open the door, for a rule to rescue him from what the truth meant.

Nothing happened.

Only the presence of the other jurors, their faces tightened with their own thoughts, their own memories shifting uneasily as if something inside each of them had just been tapped.

Juror #9's hands trembled, but his voice remained steady. "The first file," he said softly. "It began with the foreman."

Juror #8 looked around the table, not triumphant, not cruel. Simply aware.

"Because he wanted procedure," Juror #8 said. "And procedure is how we learn to live with what we've done."

Juror #1 stared down at his folder as if it might now contain an escape clause. It didn't. It only contained the neat, typed record of three deaths and one signature.

At the far end of the table, the knife remained motionless.

But in the hush that followed, it felt less like a threat aimed at them and more like a reminder.

This room wasn't interested in what they could prove in court.

It was interested in what they already knew.

For a moment, no one spoke, as if speech itself had become a kind of consent.

Juror #1 sat with the folder open in front of him, shoulders rounded, his foreman's badge catching the flat fluorescent light like a stain that wouldn't wash out. He had read the words aloud, and now that the words were in the air, they felt heavier than the paper. Three workers. A guard removed. Deferred maintenance. A signature.

Across the table, Juror #3 stared at him with a look that shifted between disgust and recognition, like he'd just discovered the foreman was capable of violence and hated himself for not being surprised.

Juror #2's hands hovered over her lap, trembling. She kept looking at Juror #1's mouth, as if waiting for him to say it wasn't true. That it was a mistake. That there was a second page that changed everything.

Juror #10 broke first, because silence always seemed to make him frantic.

"So you killed three people," he said, blunt and loud, the way a man says something cruel when he can't bear to feel afraid. "That's what we're doing now? We're just saying it?"

Juror #1 flinched, a reflexive recoil. "I didn't—" he began, then stopped. The room didn't accept half-sentences. It had already stripped the comfortable language away. Accident. Unfortunate. Oversight.

Juror #6 leaned forward, forearms on the table, voice low. "He already said it," he muttered. "He signed. He knew. They died. That's enough talk."

"It's not enough," Juror #10 snapped. "It matters what you call it. It matters what it is. Murder? Manslaughter? Negligence? Because if we're calling everything killing, then none of it means anything."

Juror #4's gaze had hardened into something sharp and impersonal, but there was strain under it, like steel flexing. "He authorized a known hazard," he said. "The outcome was predictable. You can argue classification all day. The causality is clear."

Juror #7 gave a small, brittle laugh. "Listen to us. We're back to legal definitions. Like that's gonna open the door."

Juror #9 looked at the folder, then at the chalkboard where JUROR still sat in uneven white strokes. His voice came softly, almost kindly. "We want definitions because they keep guilt in its proper box," he said. "If we name it correctly, we think it will stay contained."

Juror #12 swallowed, Adam's apple bobbing hard. "This isn't… this isn't part of deliberations," he said, not with conviction, but with desperation. "This can't be. There are rules. You can't just… pull someone's private life into—"

He stopped when his eyes flicked to the knife near the chalkboard. The knife didn't move, but it didn't need to. It was a reminder that rules were no longer in charge.

Juror #11's hands were clasped so tightly his knuckles had gone pale. He stared at Juror #1, and when he spoke, his voice was steady, controlled. "In the courtroom, you tried to make everything clean," he said. "Facts. Procedure. A system. But people died inside your system."

Juror #1's jaw tightened, a brief return of his old corporate posture. "You think I don't know that?" he said, and the harshness of it sounded like a plea in disguise.

Juror #5 leaned back in his chair, eyes narrowed, the set of his mouth hardening as he put pieces together. "You weren't some kid on the line," he said. "You weren't the guy who didn't know. You were the guy who got paid to know."

Juror #1's gaze dropped to the folder again, as if the typed bullet points could defend him better than he could. "I was trying to keep the place open," he said, and the words came out like a justification he'd rehearsed for himself in the dark. "It wasn't just my job. It was hundreds of jobs."

Juror #5 stared at him. "And it cost three," he said flatly.

Juror #2 made a small sound, caught between sobbing and speaking. "Were they… were they young?" she asked, and the question made her look ashamed, as if she'd asked the wrong kind of detail.

Juror #1 blinked, confusion flickering. "I don't know," he whispered.

The admission was worse than any anger. It meant the deaths had been real enough to haunt him, but not real enough for him to learn the names.

Juror #7's laugh came out again, softer this time, and it broke at the end. "Of course you don't," he said. "Of course it's a file and not a face."

Juror #3 slammed his palm against the table, not hard enough to rattle the knife but hard enough to puncture the paralysis. "So what now?" he demanded. His eyes were bloodshot, his voice rough. "We sit here and confess? That what this is? A therapy circle?"

Juror #8 finally spoke again, and the calm in his tone made Juror #3's anger look clumsy. "Not therapy," Juror #8 said. "Accountability."

Juror #3's head snapped toward him. "Oh, spare me. You're enjoying this. You sit there like you've got all day."

"No," Juror #8 said quietly. "I sit here because we don't have anywhere else to sit."

Juror #10 pointed at Juror #8, eager for a different target. "And what about you?" he barked. "You keep asking questions like you're above it. Like you're the only clean one in the room."

Juror #8 didn't answer, not immediately. He just looked at Juror #10 until Juror #10's eyes flicked away, irritated by being held in silence.

Juror #4's voice cut in, precise. "We should consider the possibility that the foreman's file is not isolated," he said. He gestured toward the folder without touching it. "It was labeled. It appeared intentionally. That implies sequence."

Juror #12's breath came shallow. "Sequence," he repeated. "Like… like we're next."

Juror #2 shook her head rapidly. "No," she whispered. "No. That's not… that's not possible."

But her eyes betrayed her. They flicked to the brown folder as if it were a mouth that might open again on its own.

Juror #6 looked around the table, his bluntness suddenly careful. "If it's doing this," he said, "it's got something on all of us."

Juror #9's gaze remained gentle, but the truth in it was uncompromising. "Or it believes it does," he said. "And belief can be enough to break a man."

Juror #1 pushed the folder away a few inches, as if distance might restore dignity. The cloth he'd used to open it lay crumpled in his fist. He stared at his hands like they weren't his. "We can't do this," he said, voice hoarse. "We can't sit here and—"

"And what?" Juror #11 asked softly. "Judge a boy while pretending we have no blood on our own hands?"

Juror #1 jerked his head up. His eyes were wet again, but now there was anger too, the anger of a man cornered by truth. "This has nothing to do with the case," he snapped. "It's a distraction."

Juror #8's voice was even. "It has everything to do with the case," he said. "Because the case is about deciding who deserves punishment. And the room is asking whether we understand what punishment actually is."

Juror #3 let out a harsh breath, somewhere between a laugh and a growl. "So what, the room's the judge now?"

Juror #7 whispered, "Feels like it."

No one mocked him. Not this time.

A low vibration ran through the fluorescent hum, subtle but present, like the room acknowledging it had been named. Juror #2's eyes darted to the fixtures. Juror #12 pressed his palms flat on the table, as if grounding himself would keep the walls from shifting again.

Juror #4's gaze slid toward the chalkboard. "It wrote 'juror' first," he said, almost to himself. "Not 'defendant.' Not 'guilty.' It labeled us."

Juror #5 rubbed his hands together once, a nervous habit sharpened by street instincts. "Then it drops a file," he said. "On the foreman. On the guy in charge."

Juror #6 nodded slowly. "Take out the boss first," he muttered.

Juror #1 stiffened at the phrase, but there was no authority left to bristle with. The room had already reduced him to a man with a signature.

Juror #2's voice rose, thin and shaking. "Why?" she asked. "Why are we being punished? We didn't ask for this. We were called. We showed up. We did what they told us."

Juror #9 looked at her with a sadness that felt older than the courthouse. "Many people have said that," he murmured. "And many people have used it as a shield."

Juror #2's lips parted as if she wanted to argue, then closed. Her eyes glistened, and she looked down quickly, ashamed of something she didn't yet understand.

Juror #10 pushed his chair back a fraction, restless. "This is insane," he said. "We should be banging on the door. Breaking the window. Something."

"There's no street window," Juror #6 reminded him, blunt. "It's a light well. And the door didn't move when three went at it."

Juror #12's gaze darted to the gap beneath the door again. The shadow there looked the same as it always had. And somehow that sameness felt like cruelty.

Juror #3 stared at the folder as if it were a threat with a readable shape. "If it's a sequence," he said slowly, "then what, it's gonna go around the table?"

Juror #4's voice went quieter. "Unless it chooses based on reaction," he said. "Unless it escalates where there is pressure."

Juror #7 looked at the dead clock, then away fast. "Pressure's everywhere," he muttered.

Juror #1 finally spoke again, and this time he wasn't trying to manage. He sounded afraid. "If there are… if there are files," he said, "we shouldn't open any more."

Juror #10 scoffed. "Yeah, easy for you to say now. You already got yours."

Juror #1's face tightened as if struck, but he didn't defend himself. Defending himself would mean claiming innocence in a room that had just made innocence feel like a costume.

Juror #8's gaze moved around the table, taking them in. Not like a foreman taking attendance. Like something weighing a roomful of souls. "We're already in it," he said quietly. "Whether we open them or not."

Juror #2's breath hitched. "I can't," she whispered, and the words sounded less like fear of the room and more like fear of herself.

Juror #9's hands trembled again on the table edge. He stared at the chalkboard as if expecting the next word to appear. "It began with procedure," he said softly. "And now it will move to whatever we hide behind next."

The room seemed to hold its breath with him.

Then, without any scrape of chalk this time, without any warning sound at all, a second thick brown folder appeared on the table with a dull, heavy thud, closer to the other end, as if the room had chosen a new seat.

Juror #2 gasped. Juror #12 jerked back so hard his chair legs squealed. Juror #10's eyes went wide, and for once his mouth didn't have a ready cruelty to fill the air.

A white label on the front faced upward, crisp and typed like an indictment.

JUROR #2 – CLERK

Juror #2 stared at it, frozen.

Her lips parted. No sound came out at first. Just breath, thin and fast.

Juror #1's folder lay open in front of him like a wound that wouldn't close.

The knife waited near the chalkboard, clean and patient.

The clock stayed dead at two twenty-six.

And Juror #2, hands trembling in her lap, looked at the new folder as if it were already reading her.

Chapter 7

Ghosts of Guilt

Juror #2 didn't touch the folder.

It sat in front of her like a thing alive, heavy and brown and ordinary in the way coffins were ordinary. The label faced up, crisp and merciless.

JUROR #2 – CLERK.

Her fingers curled into the fabric of her skirt until her knuckles whitened. She kept staring at the typed words as if, with enough staring, they would rearrange themselves into someone else's name.

Juror #10 recovered first, because he always did. Panic had nowhere to go in him except outward. "Well?" he demanded, voice too loud in the sealed room. "Open it. Let's see what the room thinks you did."

Juror #2 flinched at the word did. Her breath went fast and shallow, a bird trapped behind ribs.

"No," Juror #1 said abruptly, and the firmness surprised everyone, including him. The foreman's folder was still open in front of him, pages bent where his hands had gripped too hard. His face looked hollowed out, but something stubborn still lived in his posture. “We don’t have to play along.”

Juror #7 gave a quiet, broken snort. “We’re way past ‘have to,’ aren’t we?”

Juror #6 leaned forward, forearms on the table, his gaze fixed on the new folder. “Nobody’s making her,” he said, blunt but not unkind. “Not like that.”

Juror #2 swallowed. Her throat made a small clicking sound, as if even her body was trying to stay quiet.

Juror #8 didn’t speak. He watched her the way he’d watched Juror #1, not hungry for spectacle, not merciful enough to look away. There was a patience in his attention that felt like pressure.

Juror #4’s eyes moved between the label and Juror #2’s face, calculating. “It chose you next,” he said softly, as if saying it differently might make it less true. “Not randomly.”

Juror #9 nodded once, slow, the motion heavy with recognition. “The timid,” he murmured. “The easy one to overlook. The one people think cannot do harm.”

Juror #2’s eyes snapped to him. For a moment indignation sparked a tiny ember. Then it died beneath the weight of the folder. “I didn’t—” she began, and her voice collapsed. She tried again, and this time it came out as a whisper. “I didn’t kill anyone.”

The room held that sentence carefully, the way you hold something fragile and sharp at the same time.

Juror #10 leaned back, lips curling. “That’s what they all say.”

Juror #11’s gaze settled on Juror #10 like a hand on a shoulder that could also become a grip. “Do not,” he said quietly.

Juror #10 rolled his eyes, but he didn’t push it further. Not yet.

Juror #2 stared at the folder until her eyes stung. The metallic smell in the air seemed stronger when she breathed in, as if the room knew exactly what it was feeding her.

“I can’t,” she whispered.

“You can,” Juror #8 said, and his voice was gentle in a way that didn’t soothe. “Or you can sit with it. But it won’t disappear.”

Juror #2’s chest rose, fell, rose again. She looked toward the door without meaning to, a reflexive search for anyone in authority. The door remained shut. No footsteps. No voices. Nothing but the low hum in the lights and the dead, accusatory clock on the table.

Her gaze drifted to Juror #1's open folder. The typed bullet points. The word fatalities. The number three.

It had happened to him. It could happen to her.

Juror #2 made a small sound, as if her body had decided to cry and her mind had denied permission. Her hand lifted, trembling, and hovered over the folder without touching it.

Juror #12 spoke, voice thin with fear and a strained attempt at kindness. "You don't have to read it out loud," he said. "We could… we could just, I don't know, close it. Push it away. We could vote and… and—"

"And what?" Juror #7 asked softly. He wasn't joking now. He sounded tired. "And pretend we didn't see the room hand her a file?"

Juror #2's fingertips finally touched the folder's edge.

The contact was nothing. Paper. Cardboard. Normal texture.

But her hand jerked as if it had burned.

She pulled it back, pressed it to her mouth, and let out a small, strangled sob.

"I can't," she said again, louder this time, and the words shook. "I can't do this."

Juror #1 reached for what was left of his authority and found a different kind. "We don't force her," he said. His voice was hoarse, but it had spine. "We are still people."

Juror #9 looked at him with something like pity. "People force each other every day," he said. "Sometimes with words. Sometimes with silence."

Juror #2's eyes flicked to the chalkboard. JUROR. The word looked older now, like it had always been there under the paint.

"I don't want you to hate me," she whispered.

The sentence landed strangely. Not I'm innocent. Not it's a mistake. Not this is illegal.

I don't want you to hate me.

Juror #5 shifted in his chair, discomfort tightening his shoulders. "Nobody's talking about hate," he muttered, but it sounded like a lie told for his own comfort.

Juror #2's gaze darted to him, then away again, as if she couldn't bear to be seen being seen.

Juror #8 leaned forward slightly. His hands stayed flat on the table. "Open it," he said, not as an order, but as an invitation to end the suspense that was already poisoning them.

Juror #2 stared at the folder. Her breath hitched once, twice. Then she reached again, slower, as if approaching an animal that might bite.

She lifted the flap.

The folder opened with the same dry, obscene sound as the foreman's. Paper separating. Ordinary. Administrative. The sound of something being processed.

Juror #2's eyes moved across the top page, and whatever color had returned to her cheeks drained away again.

She didn't read aloud. She couldn't.

Juror #10 leaned forward, hungry. "What is it? What does it say?"

Juror #2 shook her head rapidly, tears spilling again. "No," she whispered, and her voice broke on the word. "No, no, no."

Juror #4's tone was precise, but his eyes were too sharp. "Is it medical?"

Juror #2's head jerked up, startled, as if he'd reached into the folder without touching it. "How—"

"You work as a clerk," Juror #4 said. "The label didn't say where. But the room chose that title, not 'assistant' or 'secretary.' 'Clerk' is specific. It suggests documentation. Records."

Juror #2's lips trembled. She looked down again, and her shoulders caved, as if her body had been holding itself upright on denial and denial had just been removed.

Juror #11 spoke softly. "You do not have to perform your shame," he said. "But you cannot keep it secret in a room that has decided secrets are evidence."

Juror #2 made a sound like a laugh, but it was a sob in disguise. "I didn't think it was…" She shook her head. "I didn't think it would matter."

Juror #1's fingers tightened on the edge of his own folder; the cloth crumpled beside it. "Tell us," he said, and the words came out raw. He sounded less like a manager now and more like a man who had just learned what confession costs. "If it's going to come out anyway… tell us yourself."

Juror #2's mouth opened, closed. She tried to breathe and couldn't get enough air. Juror #6 pushed his chair back a fraction, giving her space without standing, the way a big man tries not to intimidate.

"It was years ago," she whispered. Her eyes stayed on the page as if the page was safer than faces. "I worked in a clinic. Not a hospital. A… a private place. Lots of patients. Lots of forms."

Juror #7 said nothing, but his gaze fixed on her with an intensity that felt like apology for everything he'd ever joked about.

Juror #2 swallowed again, hard. "I wasn't a nurse," she continued. "I didn't touch anyone. I just… I filed. I checked boxes. I made sure the paperwork matched what the doctor wanted. That was my job."

Juror #10's voice cut in, impatient. "And?"

Juror #11's head turned slightly toward Juror #10. The warning in his eyes was quiet, but it was there.

Juror #2's voice rose a notch, thin with panic. "There was a patient," she said. "A woman. Her name was…" She stopped, and her throat worked, and when she spoke again her voice had changed. Smaller. "Her name was Elise."

Saying it made it real.

Juror #9's eyes closed briefly, as if the name had weight.

Juror #2's hands shook as she held the folder open, her thumb smudging the edge of the page. "She came in with chest pain," she whispered. "She was scared. She kept saying she thought it was her heart. The doctor said it was anxiety. He said she was dramatic. He… he didn't like her."

Juror #5's brow furrowed. "So you wrote what he told you."

Juror #2 nodded quickly, grateful for the simplification and immediately horrified by it. "Yes," she said. "I wrote what he told me. But that wasn't the… that wasn't the worst part."

Juror #4's voice stayed measured. "What was the form?" he asked.

Juror #2 stared at the paper as if it might blur into something else. "A referral," she whispered. "A referral request for a cardiology consult. She wanted it. She begged for it. The doctor refused. He said no. But later… later he changed his mind."

Juror #12 let out a shaky breath. "That sounds like a good thing."

Juror #2's eyes filled again. She looked up, finally, and the shame in her face made her look younger than she was. "He changed his mind because the clinic was audited," she said. "He didn't want a complaint. So, he told me to submit the referral."

Juror #10's voice sharpened. "And you didn't."

"I did," Juror #2 said, and the words came out fast, desperate. "I did submit it. But I…" She shook her head, and the motion was small, like a child refusing a nightmare. "I altered the date."

The room went still in a new way.

Juror #1 stared at her. Juror #6's jaw tightened. Juror #7's face went pale. Even Juror #10 quieted, as if he hadn't expected the harm to be so small and so devastating.

Juror #8's voice was gentle, but it didn't let her slip away. "Why?" he asked.

Juror #2's eyes darted to the folder again. Her breath came in short bursts. "Because the insurance," she whispered. "It was stupid. It was so stupid. The referral needed to be within a certain window from her first visit, or it would be denied without extra approval. The doctor didn't want extra paperwork. He told me to 'make it work.' Those were his words. Make it work."

Juror #9 spoke softly, as if speaking to himself. "Paperwork kills," he murmured.

Juror #2 flinched at the phrase, like it had struck her.

"I changed the date," she said, and now her voice sounded flat, emptied out. "I made it look like the doctor had ordered it earlier. So it would go through. So it would be easier."

Juror #4's gaze sharpened. "That would speed it up," he said.

Juror #2 shook her head, and a sob escaped. "No," she whispered. "It didn't speed it up. It did the opposite."

Juror #6 frowned. “How?”

Juror #2 swallowed, and the confession finally broke all the way open. “Because it went into the system wrong,” she said. “The date triggered a different queue. A routine queue. Not urgent. It flagged her as… as already evaluated. Like she’d been waiting, not like she was… like she needed help.”

Her hands clenched around the folder. “They scheduled her weeks out,” she whispered. “And I saw it. I saw the appointment date pop up. And I thought… I thought it was fine. I thought she’d be fine. She was young. She looked healthy. She was anxious.”

Juror #1’s voice came out rough. “And she wasn’t.”

Juror #2’s eyes squeezed shut, and when she opened them the tears were streaming freely. “She died,” she whispered. “Before the appointment. She collapsed at home. Her husband called an ambulance. She was gone before they got there.”

The words hung in the sealed air. Not dramatic. Not cinematic.

Administrative tragedy. A date changed. A queue selected. A woman dead.

Juror #12 stared at her as if he couldn't reconcile the scale of it. "Did anyone know?" he asked, voice barely above a whisper.

Juror #2 shook her head, frantic. "No," she said. "They blamed genetics. Stress. Bad luck. The doctor said, 'See? Anxiety can do that.' And I…" Her voice broke. "I said nothing."

Juror #8's eyes didn't leave her. "Why didn't you correct it?" he asked.

Juror #2 gave a small, terrible laugh. "Because I was scared," she whispered. "Because if I admitted I'd falsified it, I'd lose my job. And the doctor would say he never told me. And the clinic would say it was my fault. And it would be my fault."

She looked down at the page again, and her voice dropped into something almost inaudible. "It was my fault."

Juror #9's hands trembled on the table edge, but his voice stayed calm. "You did not stab her," he said gently. "You did not push her. But you moved a piece of paper and a life fell through the gap."

Juror #2's face crumpled. She pressed her palm to her mouth again, as if she could force the confession back inside.

Juror #10 finally found his voice, but it was thinner than usual. "So you're saying you killed her with a form."

Juror #11's eyes turned on him, cold. "Do not make it smaller," he said. "That is how people survive what they should not survive."

Juror #6 stared at Juror #2, something like understanding tightening his expression. "You didn't mean to," he muttered.

Juror #2 jerked at the phrase, as if it had been slapped onto her skin.

"I didn't mean to," she whispered, and the room seemed to recognize the words again. The line from the transcript. The father's voice through the wall. The phrase that had cracked their certainty.

Juror #2 looked up, eyes wild. "I didn't mean to," she said louder, as if volume could make it an alibi. "I didn't. I thought I was helping. I thought I was… making it work."

Juror #8's voice was quiet, almost kind. "And then you didn't say anything," he said.

Juror #2's shoulders shook. "I couldn't," she whispered. "I couldn't live in a world where I was the reason she died. So, I acted like I wasn't."

The fluorescent hum seemed to deepen, and for a moment the metallic smell in the air sharpened, like the room had leaned closer to listen.

Juror #1 stared at his own hands, as if seeing in them the same kind of clean violence. Juror #4's face had tightened into a mask of controlled calculation that didn't fully hide the discomfort in his eyes. Juror #5 looked away, jaw clenched, like the story had hooked something personal. Juror #7 sat very still, his usual motionless humor finally gone. Juror #12 looked sick.

Juror #3 hadn't spoken since she said the woman's name.

Now he shifted, just slightly, as if the confession had nudged something loose in him that had been packed down for years. His eyes weren't on Juror #2 anymore. They stared past her, unfocused, as if another room had opened behind his gaze.

Juror #2 wiped her face with the back of her hand, leaving a wet streak. She looked at the folder again and gave a tiny nod, as if acknowledging a verdict she could no longer fight.

"It's all there," she whispered. "The form. The audit. The time stamp. The… the death certificate." She let out a broken breath. "I didn't even know her last name until after. I looked it up."

Juror #9's voice came softly. "A file and not a face," he murmured, echoing Juror #7's earlier cruelty back into something like mourning.

Juror #2's head bowed. "I'm sorry," she whispered, and the apology didn't feel aimed at the room. It felt aimed at a kitchen floor, a man holding a phone, an ambulance too late.

For a moment no one moved. The door remained locked. The clock remained dead. The knife remained clean and waiting at the far end of the table.

And then Juror #3 made a sound.

Not a word. Not a shout.

A low, involuntary noise, like breath being forced through teeth.

All eyes turned toward him.

His hands were clenched on the chair arms, white-knuckled, and his face had gone a color that wasn't anger anymore. It was something deeper, something that had been hiding behind anger like a shield.

"Stop," he said, but he didn't

"Stop," he said, but he didn't sound like he was talking to Juror #2.

He sounded like he was talking to the room.

His hands were still clenched on the chair arms, knuckles pale, the tendons in his forearms standing out as if his body had decided to hold him in place. The color in his face had drained in a way that didn't match his earlier rage. That rage had been heat. This was cold.

Juror #2 flinched, still hunched over her folder, tears wet on her cheeks. She seemed ready to apologize again, as if his distress was just another thing she'd caused by existing.

Juror #10 leaned forward, scenting weakness the way he always did. "Stop what?" he demanded. "We're just getting to the good part, right? Everybody's got a little file now; everybody's got a little sob story—"

"Shut up," Juror #6 said, low and heavy. It wasn't a shout. It was worse. It was a warning.

Juror #10's mouth opened, then closed, surprised into silence for once.

Juror #3's eyes were fixed on nothing in front of him. Past the table. Past the knife. Past the chalkboard that still read JUROR like a label on a drawer. His pupils looked too wide under the flat fluorescent light, as if his mind had backed away from the room and left his body behind.

Juror #8 watched him carefully. "Juror Three," he said, voice steady. "What's happening?"

Juror #3 blinked like he'd forgotten how. His breath came in shallow pulls. Then, abruptly, he stood.

The chair legs scraped against the tile, loud in the sealed space. The sound made Juror #2 jerk, made Juror #12's shoulders rise, made Juror #1's gaze snap up from the folders as if he'd been slapped awake. Juror #3 didn't seem to register any of it.

He took a step away from the table, then another, moving without direction toward the wall near the door. His hand lifted, not to the handle, but to the painted surface beside it, as if he needed something solid that wasn't wood and paper and the low hum vibrating through the room.

"Stop," he said again, and this time the word broke. The second half of it dissolved into breath.

Juror #9's voice came softly, not pushing. "It's your turn," he said. It wasn't a threat. It sounded like a fact he didn't enjoy saying.

Juror #3's head snapped toward him, and for a heartbeat the old anger flashed in his eyes, reflexive and familiar. "Don't you start," he said hoarsely. "Don't you look at me like that."

"I'm not looking at you like anything," Juror #9 replied. "I'm looking at you like a man who's running out of places to hide."

Juror #3's jaw worked. He pressed his palm harder against the wall until his fingers splayed, as if he could push through it. "I didn't kill anyone," he said. The words came out fast, too fast, as if speed could turn them into truth. "I didn't."

Juror #4 tilted his head slightly, cold logic trying to map the moment. "You haven't been accused," he said.

"Yes, I have," Juror #3 snapped, and the sudden volume made Juror #2 flinch again. "You all have. That's what this is. That's what it wants. It wants us to say it. It wants us to… to—" He stopped. His throat bobbed. The muscles around his mouth trembled like they were fighting to keep it closed.

Juror #7 spoke carefully, almost gently. "Hey," he said, and it was the first time his voice had sounded like it belonged to an actual person in the last ten minutes. "Nobody's making you say anything."

Juror #3 let out a short laugh that turned immediately into something wet. He wiped at his face with the back of his hand, furious at the moisture as if it were an insult. "You think I care what you make me do?" he said. "You think I'm scared of you?"

He wasn't looking at them now. He was looking at the floor, at the baseboard scuffs that hadn't been there before, marks like someone's shoes had scraped in panic. Marks like the room remembered other people breaking.

Juror #1 shifted, the foreman reflex rising despite the hollowness in him. "Everyone needs to sit down," he said, and even he sounded like he knew how pointless it was.

Juror #3 rounded on him. "Don't," he spat, and the word carried a different kind of violence than earlier. Earlier it had been dominance. Now it was desperation. "Don't tell me what to do."

Juror #1 fell silent, shrinking back into his chair as if his authority had been physically removed and set on the table next to the knife.

Juror #8 didn't move. He didn't raise his voice. "No one's forcing you," he said. "But the room has a way of taking what we don't say and saying it for us."

At that, Juror #3 went still.

A tremor ran through him, subtle but visible in his shoulders. He stared at Juror #8 as if he hated him for being calm, hated him for being right, hated him for being the one person in the room who didn't look surprised by the idea of confession.

Juror #3's mouth opened. For a moment it seemed like he might shout again, fling some accusation, make the room an enemy so he didn't have to be one.

Instead he whispered, "My son's dead."

Silence slammed down, thick and instant.

Even Juror #10 didn't fill it.

Juror #2's sobbing quieted into a stunned stillness. Juror #12 stared as if he hadn't heard correctly. Juror #5's eyes narrowed, not with suspicion now but with recognition of a type of pain that didn't come with clean edges.

Juror #9 didn't react. He simply nodded once, as if he'd known it was there behind the rage all along.

Juror #3 swallowed hard. "He's dead," he repeated, and the repetition wasn't for them. It was for him, like he needed to say it twice to make it feel real enough to hurt. "So don't you—" His voice rose, cracked, dropped again. "Don't you put that on me."

Juror #11 spoke softly. "We did not," he said. "You did."

The words weren't cruel. They were precise. They landed with the weight of a door closing.

Juror #3's breath came jagged. He looked down at his own hands like they belonged to someone else, then back at the table where Juror #2's folder lay open, where Juror #1's pages still showed typed bullet points and deferred decisions. Evidence of guilt that wasn't a knife in the back but a choice made in an office, a date changed on a form.

"I didn't kill him," Juror #3 said, louder. "I didn't touch him. I didn't—" He stopped, and his eyes squeezed shut as if something inside had finally pushed up against the last thing he could deny.

Juror #8's voice came, quiet. "How did he die?"

Juror #3's eyes snapped open. "Don't ask me that," he said, and the plea in it was naked.

Juror #8 didn't flinch. "You asked us to convict a boy quickly," he said. "You asked for death without questions. I'm asking one."

Juror #3's lips pulled back, almost a snarl, but it collapsed as soon as it formed. His shoulders shook once, a single violent tremor, then another.

"He hung himself," he whispered.

The room seemed to tilt, just slightly, as if the air itself needed to adjust around the fact of it.

Juror #2 made a small sound, hand flying to her mouth again. Juror #12 stared at the tabletop like it had become unsafe to look at faces.

Juror #3 pressed his palm against the wall again, hard. "In a garage," he said, voice hollow. "A rope. A stupid rope. And I…" He swallowed. "And I found him."

Juror #7's face tightened. His usual instinct to make it lighter looked like it had finally died in him. He said nothing.

Juror #3 drew in a breath that whistled faintly between his teeth. "So don't tell me I killed someone," he said, and the sentence sounded like it was built on splinters. "Don't tell me I did. I already live with it."

Juror #9's voice came, gentle and merciless. "You live with what you allow yourself to name," he said. "And you refuse to name the part that is yours."

Juror #3 turned his head sharply. "You don't know anything about me."

Juror #9 held his gaze. "Then tell us," he said.

Juror #3 laughed once, a short jagged sound, then choked on it. His eyes went bright, furious with tears. "He was weak," he said, and the old cruelty in the word was automatic. It came from deep habit. Then he flinched, as if the word had burned his tongue. "No. That's what I said. That's what I always said. He wasn't weak. He was… he was a kid."

Juror #8's voice was steady. "What did you do to him?" he asked.

Juror #3's jaw clenched. "I raised him," he snapped.

Juror #11's eyes narrowed slightly. "That is not an answer," he said.

Juror #3's breathing grew fast again. He looked like a man being cornered by a memory he'd kept locked in a room of his own.

"I pushed," he said suddenly, and the word came out raw. "I pushed because that's what my father did to me. You think I had a choice? You think I woke up and decided I wanted to be a monster?"

Juror #6 spoke, voice low. "Everybody's got a choice," he said. Not accusing. Not absolving. Just stating the thing nobody wanted to hear.

Juror #3's eyes flashed to him. "You ever have a son?" he demanded.

Juror #6 didn't answer right away. His jaw tightened. "I've had people depend on me," he said finally. "That's enough."

Juror #3's laugh broke again. "Depend on me," he repeated, and the bitterness in it was sharp. "He depended on me and I made him…" He stopped, shaking his head hard. "I made him tough. That's what I told myself."

Juror #8 watched him without blinking. "And what did it actually make him?" he asked.

Juror #3's throat worked. His gaze dropped to the floor, then lifted again, unfocused. "Quiet," he whispered. "It made him quiet. He used to talk all the time when he was little. About stupid things. Games. Space. Bugs he found in the yard. And then one day he stopped. He'd come home and go straight to his room and close the door. And I…" His voice cracked. "And I thought that meant it was working."

Juror #2's eyes were wide, wet, fixed on him. She looked like she wanted to say something kind and couldn't find permission in the air.

Juror #3's face twisted, grief and rage battling over the same territory. "He got older," he said. "He started… he started cutting school. Getting into trouble. Drugs, maybe, I don't know. He wouldn't tell me anything. And I made it worse. Every time he looked at me like he needed something, I gave him… punishment. Rules. Yelling." He swallowed hard. "I told him he was nothing if he didn't straighten up. I told him I'd throw him out."

Juror #9's voice came soft. "Did you mean it?" he asked.

Juror #3 shut his eyes. A tear finally slipped free and tracked down the side of his nose. He wiped it away violently, like it offended him. "No," he whispered. "I didn't mean to."

The phrase hung there, joining the others like a refrain the room collected. The father in the transcript. The clerk at the clinic. Now the furious father in the jury room, broken open by the same helpless words.

Juror #3's voice rose suddenly, desperate. "I didn't mean it," he said. "I just wanted him to stop scaring me. You understand? He scared me. He looked at me like I'd already lost. Like he knew something I didn't. And I couldn't… I couldn't stand it."

Juror #8 didn't move. "So you tried to control him," he said.

Juror #3 opened his eyes and stared at him with hatred and relief tangled together. “Yes,” he said. “Yes. Because if I couldn’t control him, then what was I? What was I for?”

Juror #1 flinched at that, as if it had found him too.

Juror #3 pushed off the wall and took one step back toward the table, but it wasn’t an approach. It was a drift, like gravity had changed.

“He left,” he said, voice quieter now, wrecked. “He left at eighteen. Told me he was done. Said he couldn’t breathe in the house. His mother cried, begged him to stay, and I…” His mouth twisted. “And I told her to let him go. Told her he’d come crawling back.”

Juror #12 whispered, “Oh God,” barely audible.

Juror #3’s face tightened, eyes shining. “He didn’t come back,” he said. “Not like that.” He swallowed. “He called once. One time. I was at work. I saw his name on the phone. And I didn’t pick up.”

The admission dropped into the room like a stone into a well.

Juror #5 exhaled slowly, eyes narrowing. “Why?” he asked, not unkind, but sharp with disbelief.

Juror #3’s mouth trembled. “Because I was mad,” he whispered. “Because I wanted him to feel it. I wanted him to know what it was like to be ignored.”

He swallowed hard, and his voice turned thin. “And then there was another call, a week later, from a number I didn’t know. A cop. He said they found him. And all I could think was… I should’ve answered. I should’ve answered.”

Juror #3’s knees seemed to soften. He grabbed the back of his chair as if it were the only thing holding him up. His head bowed.

“I didn’t hang him,” he whispered. “But I built the room he died in. I built it piece by piece.”

No one spoke. The fluorescent hum pressed into the silence. The dead clock stayed fixed at two twenty-six, as if the room insisted on keeping them all in the same frozen moment of consequence.

Juror #8’s voice came softly. “That’s what killing can look like,” he said. “Not a knife. Not a gun. A slow narrowing until there’s no air left.”

Juror #3 lifted his head, and his eyes were red, raw. “So, what do you want me to say?” he asked, and there was nothing aggressive left in him now. Only a terrible sincerity. “You want me to say I killed him? Fine.” His voice broke. “Fine. I killed him.”

The last word came out like something torn loose.

Juror #2 sobbed quietly, not for herself now. Juror #12 pressed his lips together, fighting the urge to speak and finding nothing useful.

Juror #9 closed his eyes briefly, as if in prayer or grief.

Juror #3 stood there trembling, hands gripping the chair, his confession hanging in the air like smoke that wouldn't clear.

And in the hush that followed, as if the room had been waiting for that exact sentence, a faint dry scrape rose behind them again.

Chalk on slate, patient and ready to write the next name.

The chalk scraped again, slow and deliberate, like a match being dragged across a box without striking. No one turned right away. They all knew what they would see. Knowing didn't make it easier.

Juror #3 stood trembling, hands still clamped around the back of his chair as if he might fall through the floor if he let go. His confession hung in the air, raw and newly spoken, and the room treated it the way it treated everything lately: as material.

Juror #2's quiet sobbing had changed pitch, thinner now, like a leak that wouldn't stop. Juror #1 stared at the open folder in front of him but didn't seem to be reading it anymore. The typed words had stopped being information and become a mirror.

Juror #8 watched the chalkboard without moving, the same stillness he'd worn since the first vote. Not relaxed. Not indifferent. Intent.

Juror #11 was the one who finally turned first. He did it the way he did everything: carefully, as if sudden motion might be interpreted as guilt.

The chalkboard had been waiting.

Beneath the word JUROR, new marks had appeared. Not letters yet. Just lines, drawn down the slate in uneven strokes.

One line.

Then a second, beside it.

Not quite a tally. Not quite a sentence.

Juror #7 let out a breath that sounded like it scraped on his teeth. "It's counting," he said, and tried to make it sound like a joke and failed.

Juror #9's eyes narrowed slightly, studying the spacing. "Or it is keeping record," he murmured.

Juror #10 pushed his chair back an inch, then another, as if distance from the table might protect him from the board. "Record of what? Confessions? Entertainment?" His voice tried to climb into anger and couldn't find the rung. "This is sick."

Juror #6's gaze stayed on Juror #3, not the board. He looked like he wanted to say something practical and couldn't find a practical shape for grief. "Sit down," he muttered finally, but it wasn't an order. It was a plea disguised as one. "You're gonna drop."

Juror #3 didn't sit. He stood there, breathing hard, eyes red and unfocused, as if he expected someone to contradict him. To say it didn't count. To say words couldn't kill.

Nobody did.

The room held him in the silence it preferred, the silence where memory could seep up through the seams.

Juror #12 swallowed and rubbed his palms against his thighs, a repetitive motion like he was trying to erase something. "We should… we should stop talking," he said. "We should stop feeding it. It's reacting to us. Every time we say something—"

The chalk scraped again, louder this time. A longer stroke.

Juror #12 flinched and fell quiet.

Juror #5 leaned forward, elbows on the table, gaze sharp. "It ain't reacting," he said. "It's leading."

Juror #4 hadn't spoken since Juror #3 broke. He sat very still with his legal pad untouched, his pen lying beside it like an instrument abandoned mid-operation. His eyes tracked the board's marks with a kind of cold attention, but his face had lost some of its earlier composure. Not fear exactly. Something like an unwanted calculation happening behind his eyes.

Juror #8's voice came softly, but it found everyone. "When he said it," he murmured. "Did anyone else feel it?"

Juror #1 looked up, blinking. "Feel what?"

Juror #8 didn't take his eyes off the board. "The room shift," he said. "Like it recognized the sentence."

Juror #2 wiped at her face with shaking fingers. "I didn't mean to," she whispered, almost to herself, and then pressed her lips together hard as if she'd spoken the room's name by accident.

Juror #9 nodded, a slow, weary motion. "Certain phrases are keys," he said. "They open things we keep locked."

Juror #10 scoffed, but the sound came out thin. "Here we go," he muttered. "Now we're doing poetry."

Juror #11's eyes flicked to him. "No," he said, quiet and firm. "We are doing consequences."

The word sat in the air, heavy enough to silence even Juror #10 for a beat.

And in that beat, the memories began to move.

It happened without warning and without drama, the way a smell can put you back in a year you thought you'd buried. The metallic scent in the air, pennies and old blood, thickened for a moment and then seemed to pass through the jurors rather than around them, as if the room exhaled it directly into their lungs.

Juror #1's gaze dropped to his hands. His fingers flexed slightly, like he could still feel the weight of a pen, the clean pressure of signing. A conveyor housing panel. Deferred maintenance. He looked as if he'd like to argue with the paper again, to insist that a system had done it, not him. But he didn't. The argument had worn out.

Juror #2 stared at the open folder in front of her, but her eyes weren't seeing the typed lines now. They were seeing a clinic hallway, fluorescent lights that hummed in a different building, a woman in a chair pressing a hand to her chest, the impatience in a doctor's voice. She mouthed something without sound. When she blinked, tears slid down again as if the memory had opened a tap.

Juror #7 stared at the knife near the chalkboard. For the first time since it appeared, he didn't look at it like a prop. He looked at it like a decision. His mouth worked as if he wanted to say something clever and couldn't. The humor that had been armor all day hung off him like wet clothes.

Juror #6's jaw clenched. His eyes shifted toward Juror #1's folder, then Juror #2's, then away fast. He pressed his tongue to the inside of his cheek, a tic of restraint, as if something inside him wanted to speak and he was keeping it pinned down. His hands were big and steady on the table, but his knuckles had gone pale.

Juror #5 sat back slightly, his gaze darting to the locked door, then to the gap beneath it. His foot tapped once, twice, then stopped. He looked like he was listening for something that wasn't sound. Sirens, maybe. Footsteps running away. He swallowed hard, throat working like he was trying to force down a memory that had come up too fast.

Juror #12, who had been pleading for cheer and normal rules, stared at the chalkboard marks and whispered, "This is like… like when you see a commercial and it's not selling you anything, it's just reminding you of something you did." He stopped, as if realizing what he'd said. His eyes widened, guilty at his own metaphor.

Juror #3 finally let go of his chair. His hands dropped to his sides with a helplessness that looked unfamiliar on him. He stared at the board's marks as if expecting it to write his son's name. When it didn't, when it only kept its silent record, his shoulders sagged in a way that made him look suddenly older.

Juror #9 watched them all with a kind of sad attention, as if he could see the private rooms opening behind each face. "It doesn't just want confession," he murmured. "It wants recall. It wants us to feel the weight, not just name it."

Juror #10 shifted, restless. "This is ridiculous," he said again, but his voice had lost its edge. He looked around the table like a man checking exits in a burning building. "We're letting it get in our heads."

"It's already in there," Juror #8 said, and his calm made the statement worse. "It didn't bring these memories. It just stopped us from outrunning them."

Juror #4's fingers moved toward his pen, then stopped. He stared at the chalkboard marks as if they were data points that refused to organize. His throat bobbed once.

Juror #8's gaze slid to him, the shift small but unmistakable. "You've been quiet," he said.

Juror #4's lips tightened. "I'm thinking."

Juror #8 nodded, as if granting him that. "About the boy?" he asked.

Juror #4 hesitated just long enough to give himself away. "About causality," he said.

Juror #7 let out a low breath. "Always causality."

Juror #4's eyes flicked to Juror #7, irritation flashing, then away. "If this room is presenting information," he said, "it's doing it in a sequence that escalates. It began with physical evidence, then the board, then the file. Now it's pushing confession. That suggests—"

"A plan," Juror #1 whispered.

Juror #4 didn't respond to the foreman directly. He looked at the dead clock on the table. Two twenty-six. The frozen hands stared up like a fixed accusation. "A controlled environment," he said. "A closed system."

Juror #9's voice came gentle. "Closed systems break when pressure builds," he said. "And pressure always finds the weak seam."

Juror #4's gaze returned to the chalkboard. His face went very still. "If it is identifying weak seams," he said quietly, "it will not stop with emotion. It will move toward whatever we rely on most."

Juror #12 licked his lips. "And what do you rely on most?" he asked, voice thin.

Juror #4 didn't answer. He didn't need to.

The table made a soft, heavy sound.

Not chalk. Not paper.

A thud like a book being set down with intention.

Everyone's heads snapped toward it at once, the movement almost synchronized now, trained by fear.

A third brown folder sat on the tabletop near Juror #4's unused legal pad. It hadn't been there a second earlier. The label was crisp, typed in the same merciless font as the others.

JUROR #4 – ANALYST

Juror #4 stared at it without blinking.

Juror #7 whispered, "There it is."

Juror #2 made a small, broken noise in her throat, a sound of recognition that was also warning.

Juror #10 leaned forward, hungry again because hunger was easier than dread. "Open it," he said, but his voice wasn't triumphant this time. It was strained. "Let's see what the numbers guy's got."

Juror #4 didn't move.

His eyes stayed on the folder as if he could will it into being harmless by refusing to touch it. The fluorescent hum pressed into the silence. The metallic smell lingered. The knife lay clean at the far end of the table, waiting like a period at the end of a sentence.

On the chalkboard, beneath JUROR and beside the new uneven marks, the chalk made one last short stroke, and stopped.

As if the room had finished selecting its next witness.

Juror #8 watched Juror #4 with the same patient attention he'd given the others. "Memories surface," he said quietly, almost to himself. "Whether we invite them or not."

Juror #4's hand finally lifted, slow and reluctant, hovering over the folder's flap.

And no one in the room breathed like they believed they would ever be clean again.

Chapter 8

Haunted by the Past

Juror #4's fingers hovered over the folder as if the air above it had become hot.

He didn't look at anyone. He didn't need to. He could feel the gaze of the room fixed on him, eleven pairs of eyes trying to turn his stillness into an answer. The brown folder sat beside his legal pad like an accusation wearing office stationery. The label was clean, typed, as crisp as the ones that had broken Juror #1 and Juror #2.

JUROR #4 – ANALYST.

Juror #4's hand dropped to the table without opening it. The soft thump of his knuckles against wood sounded louder than it should have.

"This is absurd," he said. His voice was controlled, precise. It was the voice of a man who believed control could still function as a kind of exit. "We have no way to verify the origin of these documents. They could be fabricated."

Juror #10 leaned forward, elbows on the table, eyes bright with a hunger that had nothing to do with truth. "Yeah?" he said. "Then open it. Prove it's fake."

Juror #4 didn't flinch. "That's not how verification works," he replied, as if he were correcting a junior employee. "Opening a document doesn't authenticate it."

Juror #7 let out a dry, humorless breath. "In this room, opening it seems to do something."

Juror #1 sat with his own folder still open, as if closing it would be admitting he hoped to forget. He looked at Juror #4 with a hollow exhaustion. "Just… read it," he said. "Whatever it is, it's not going away."

Juror #2 kept her eyes down, fingers twisted together in her lap until they looked painful. She hadn't shut her folder either. She sat like someone afraid of sudden movement, as if the room punished gestures.

Juror #3 had finally lowered himself into his chair, but his body still trembled faintly, as if the confession had left an electrical current running through him. He stared at the new folder with a kind of grim expectation, like a man watching someone else approach a cliff he'd already fallen off.

Juror #8 said nothing. He only watched.

Juror #4's gaze flicked once to the chalkboard. JUROR. Beneath it, the uneven marks that had begun like a count, like a record. They looked like someone had started keeping track of something and didn't intend to stop.

He reached for the folder at last, not with trembling fingers like Juror #2, not with the reluctant shame of Juror #1. He did it like a procedure.

He lifted the flap.

The paper inside was ordinary. Cream-colored. Typed. The kind of paper that had built his whole sense of safety: clean fonts, sharp margins, a world that pretended consequences could be contained by formatting.

He read the top line in silence.

His face didn't change much. That was his gift, his armor. But the room had learned to read the smaller indicators: the slight tightening at the corners of his eyes, the way his throat moved when he swallowed, the tiny pause before breath continued.

Juror #10 couldn't bear that silence. "Well?" he demanded. "What's it say? Who'd you kill with a calculator?"

Juror #4 looked up slowly. "No one died," he said.

The room seemed to hold very still around the sentence, not because it believed him, but because it recognized the shape of the lie. It was a familiar shape now. Not I'm innocent. Not it's wrong.

No one died.

Juror #9's voice came soft, almost kind. "That is what you tell yourself," he said. "Not what is true."

Juror #4's jaw tightened. "You don't know what you're talking about."

Juror #6 leaned forward, forearms heavy on the table. "Then tell us," he said. "What's in there."

Juror #4's gaze dropped back to the page. He didn't want to read it aloud. Reading it would turn it into a hearing. Reading it would put him in the same posture he'd wanted for the boy: accountable to a room.

But the folder was there. And his eyes had already absorbed the words.

He drew in a breath. When he spoke, it was clipped, stripped of unnecessary detail the way a report is stripped when it expects compliance, not empathy.

"It's... a compliance summary," he said. "Financial. Investment reporting."

Juror #12's voice came thin. "Like pensions?"

Juror #4's eyes lifted briefly, a flicker of annoyance that someone else had found the right category. "Yes," he said. "A fund."

Juror #5's gaze sharpened. He sat back slightly, watching Juror #4 the way he watched people on the street: not listening just to what was said, but to what was avoided. "So, it's money," he muttered. "It's always money."

Juror #4 ignored him and stared down again. "It says," he continued, and now his voice had a faint tension beneath its smoothness, "that performance data was adjusted to meet reporting targets. That risk exposure was… misrepresented."

Juror #7's laugh came out once, low. "Misrepresented," he repeated, tasting the corporate antiseptic on it. "That's a nice word."

Juror #4's eyes flicked up. "Language matters," he said sharply. "It's not antiseptic. It's accurate."

Juror #10 scoffed. "Accurate my ass. Say what you did."

Juror #11's posture straightened. "Let him speak," he said, his voice steady and cold. "And do not rush him to the easiest version."

The easiest version. The room seemed to like that phrase. Juror #4's mouth tightened as if he'd been struck, not by an insult, but by recognition.

He looked back at the folder. His thumb pressed the edge of the page and left a slight bend in it, a human flaw in a clean stack of paper.

"The fund managers relied on my analysis," he said. "My models. My recommendations."

Juror #9 nodded once. "People relied on you," he murmured, and the words carried the echo of Juror #6's earlier confession: I've had people depend on me.

Juror #4 continued, still trying to keep it clinical. "There was a downturn. The portfolio was exposed in a way it shouldn't have been. If the truth had been reported when it should have been, investors could have withdrawn, rebalanced, mitigated losses."

Juror #12 blinked hard. "But you didn't report it."

Juror #4's eyes lifted again. His gaze was cold, but the coldness now looked like fear carefully arranged. "The situation was temporary," he said. "Market volatility. Liquidity constraints. There was a strategy to recover."

Juror #5 let out a sharp breath. "You gambled with people's retirement," he said, and his voice was flat with disgust.

Juror #4's head snapped toward him. "That's simplistic."

"Is it?" Juror #5 asked. "Or you just like words that make it feel less ugly?"

Juror #4 turned back to the folder as if the paper could rescue him from the mess of human voices.

"The document claims," he said, emphasizing claims like a lawyer, "that I changed classification codes. That I moved assets into a lower-risk category on quarterly statements."

Juror #1 stared at him, the corporate manager in him recognizing the maneuver with a sick familiarity. "So, on paper it looked safe," he said quietly.

Juror #4 didn't answer immediately.

Juror #8 spoke for the first time since the folder appeared. "Did you do it?" he asked, simple.

Juror #4's eyes met his, and for a moment the analyst's composure held. "It wasn't illegal," Juror #4 said. "That's the point. It was within discretion. There are guidelines. Interpretations. Materiality thresholds."

Juror #10 laughed, loud and ugly. "Oh, here we go. He didn't kill anybody. He just used 'thresholds.'"

Juror #6 shot Juror #10 a look that cut him off, then stared back at Juror #4. "Answer the question," he said. "Did you do it?"

Juror #4's nostrils flared once. He was losing the ability to control the frame, and that, more than guilt, disturbed him. "I followed standard practice," he said. "The fund was under pressure. The firm was under pressure. If we'd disclosed the full exposure immediately, it would have triggered a run. Panic. Collapse. People would have lost everything."

Juror #9's voice came soft. "And instead," he said, "they lost it slowly. Quietly. Without knowing why."

Juror #4's jaw tightened. "We recovered partially," he said. "Some losses were mitigated. The outcome wasn't as catastrophic as it could have been."

Juror #2 made a small, involuntary sound, a strangled exhale that might have been a laugh in another room. Her eyes lifted to him, wet and shining, and the shame in her face sharpened into something like anger. "That's what I told myself," she whispered. "That it could have been worse. That it was fine."

Juror #4 looked at her, and for the first time there was something human in his expression: irritation mixed with discomfort, as if her comparison had forced him to see himself reflected in someone he'd categorized as weak.

Juror #8's voice remained steady. "The file isn't asking whether you broke a law," he said. "It's asking what your choice did to people."

Juror #4's hand slid to the next page as if speed could protect him. He scanned, then froze.

Juror #11 saw the pause. "What is it?" he asked.

Juror #4's lips parted, then pressed together. He looked suddenly like a man encountering a number he couldn't explain.

Juror #7 leaned forward slightly. "Oh no," he murmured. "There's a number, isn't there."

Juror #4 swallowed. "There are… testimonies," he said, and his voice had changed. Not softer. Just altered, as if the air had gotten thinner. "Statements from beneficiaries."

Juror #12's brow furrowed. "People who lost their pensions."

Juror #4 nodded once, minimal. "A teacher," he said. "A maintenance worker. A widow."

Juror #1 stared at the table like he couldn't bear another list of ordinary lives.

Juror #4's eyes moved down the page and he read, but the words weren't his. They were the raw edges the reports usually sanded down before the boardroom saw them.

"She wrote," Juror #4 said, voice tight, "'We sold the house.'"

Juror #2's hand rose to her mouth again. Juror #3 stared at Juror #4 with the same haunted distance he'd worn when he talked about his son's last call.

Juror #4 kept reading, and it sounded like punishment precisely because he was so good at reading aloud without emotion.

"'My husband worked thirty-four years,'" he continued. "'He died two years before retirement. I thought at least I would be safe.'" His eyes flicked again, and his throat bobbed. "'I take half a dose of insulin to make it last.'"

The room went very quiet.

The fluorescent hum seemed to press into their teeth. The metallic smell returned, sharper, like old pennies warmed by a hand.

Juror #10 didn't speak. His mouth was open slightly, but no cruelty came out.

Juror #5's gaze hardened into something dangerous. "You did that," he said softly, and his softness made it worse.

Juror #4's head snapped up. "No," he said, too fast. "No. That's not how causality works. Markets move. Policies change. Individuals make decisions."

Juror #9's voice came gentle and brutal. "And you moved numbers," he said. "And you chose what they would see. You chose what they would believe."

Juror #4 stared at him, and something in his eyes began to fracture. "I didn't put a rope in anyone's garage," he said. His voice rose slightly on the word rope, a flare of defense that grabbed at Juror #3's pain like a shield. "I didn't alter a medical form. I didn't sign off on a broken machine."

Juror #8 didn't flinch. "Then what did you do?" he asked.

Juror #4's breath came shallow. He looked down at the folder again, and when he spoke, it sounded like he was forcing himself through a narrow gap.

"I lied," he said.

The room tightened around the sentence.

Juror #4's mouth worked, as if the words were too big to fit. "I told them it was stable," he continued. "I told them the risk was contained. I told them to stay in, to hold, to trust the model. I told them they were safe because the numbers said they were safe."

Juror #11's eyes narrowed. "And you knew it was not true."

Juror #4's gaze flicked to the dead clock, frozen at two twenty-six, as if time itself might offer him a loophole. It didn't.

"Yes," he whispered.

Juror #1 closed his eyes briefly, like a man hearing a verdict read for a crime he recognizes.

Juror #2's shoulders shook once, but she didn't cry loudly now. She looked at Juror #4 like she was seeing him clearly for the first time, and that clarity scared her.

Juror #3 sat very still, grief and rage quieted into something exhausted.

Juror #5 leaned forward, voice low. “People died?” he asked, and the question wasn’t accusation. It was the terrible curiosity of a man who already knows the answer.

Juror #4 hesitated, and that hesitation was its own confession.

“I don’t know,” he said finally, and the words sounded like poison. “I don’t have… that data.”

Juror #9’s voice came like a sigh. “A file and not a face,” he murmured again, and this time it didn’t sound like cruelty. It sounded like the core of the room’s lesson.

Juror #4’s face tightened, and for the first time his composure cracked enough to show something raw underneath: not tears, not remorse performed for forgiveness, but fear of the moral arithmetic he could no longer avoid.

“I told myself,” he said, and the phrase was almost identical to Juror #2’s earlier confession, “that I was preventing a worse collapse. That I was buying time. That I was protecting people from panic.”

Juror #8's voice was quiet. "Were you protecting them," he asked, "or protecting your performance report?"

Juror #4's eyes flashed, offended by the precision. Then the flash died, because precision was his language, and he couldn't argue with it without betraying himself.

He looked down at the folder again. His fingers trembled, just slightly, the first visible tremor the room had managed to extract from him.

"I protected my position," he admitted. "I protected the firm. I protected my reputation. And I used the word 'stability' like it was a promise."

Juror #6's voice came low. "And somebody paid for it," he said.

Juror #4 nodded once, a small broken motion that looked nothing like a corporate presentation. "Yes," he said. "Somebody always does."

The chalkboard scraped behind them, a short, dry stroke. Not a word, not a sentence. Another mark added beneath JUROR, as if the room had recorded Juror #4's admission the way a clerk records a plea.

Juror #7 stared at the board, pale. "It's keeping score," he whispered.

Juror #9 corrected him softly. "It is keeping truth."

Juror #4 sat very still with the open folder in front of him, the neat pages now contaminated by the lives they described. His legal pad remained untouched. His pen lay beside it, useless. He had tried to make the room accept definitions. Classifications. Thresholds. Discretion. He had tried to argue that what couldn't be proven in court shouldn't count as killing.

And the room had answered in the only language it seemed to trust.

Not law.

Consequences.

Juror #8 looked around the table once, slow. His gaze passed over the broken foreman, the trembling clerk, the furious father drained of fury, the analyst emptied of logic's protection. It paused on Juror #5, whose posture had tightened as if the room's attention had finally found the seam in him.

Another folder had not appeared yet.

But the air in the sealed room felt like it was turning, preparing the next exhibit.

And Juror #5, eyes narrowed and jaw clenched, stared at the knife near the chalkboard like he already knew what his file would smell like when it landed. Juror #5 kept his eyes on the knife, because looking at the knife felt safer than looking at the others. A blade was simple. A blade didn't pretend to be paperwork or discretion or a bad day. A blade cut. It drew a line you couldn't reclassify. .He realized, with a jolt of irritation that tasted like fear, that he was doing the same thing Juror #4 had just done. He was trying to control the shape of guilt by choosing the object that defined it.

Across the table, Juror #4 sat motionless with the folder open, pages splayed like an autopsy report. Juror #1's shoulders had collapsed inward, as if each new confession folded him smaller. Juror #2's face was still wet, but she wasn't sobbing now. She looked hollowed out; eyes fixed on nothing. Juror #3 stared at the tabletop with the stunned absence of a man who had emptied his worst memory onto the floor and was waiting to see if the floor would swallow it.

Juror #8's gaze passed over them, slow, and paused on Juror #5 with the same patient pressure it had used on the others. Juror #5 bristled. He shifted in his chair, planting his feet, trying to remind his body that he was not cornered. He'd been cornered before. He'd learned how to survive it.

The room made that soft, heavy sound again. A dull thud, like a book set down with care.

Juror #12 jerked, half rising. "No," he breathed, as if refusal could undo physics.

The folder sat on the table directly in front of Juror #5, placed so neatly it felt insulting. Thick brown cardstock. White typed label. No smudge, no crease, no sign of human hands.

JUROR #5 – SLUMS.

The word slums hit him first, harder than any accusation of killing. It was a label people used when they wanted to feel clean. Like the place he'd grown up was a disease you could catch from contact. Like it explained everything about him so nobody had to ask questions. His throat tightened. He didn't realize he'd clenched his jaw until his teeth ached.

Juror #10 let out a low whistle, then tried to turn it into a sneer. "Well, isn't that something," he said. "They're really being honest with the titles now."

Juror #6 shot him a look that could have snapped bone. "Don't," he said.

Juror #10 held up his hands, mock-innocent. "What? I'm just reading the label. That's what we do in here."

Juror #5 didn't look at Juror #10. He kept staring at the label, feeling heat crawl up his neck. The room's metallic smell thickened, pennies warmed in a palm. Blood memory.

Juror #9 spoke softly. "It does not call him 'kid,'" he observed. "It calls him what the world called him."

Juror #7's voice came out rough, stripped of humor. "That's… messed up."

Juror #5 swallowed. His hands were on the table now, palms flat, as if he could steady the folder by pinning it to wood. The paper looked ordinary. It was always ordinary. That was the point, wasn't it? Ordinary objects that carried extraordinary weight.

"You don't have to open it," Juror #1 said, but the words sounded like a man offering mercy he knew wouldn't be accepted. "Not if you can tell us."

Juror #5 laughed once, sharp, defensive. "Tell you what?" He heard his own voice and didn't like how thin it sounded. "Tell you I stole a car? Tell you I got into fights? That what you want? Something that fits the label?"

Juror #8 didn't react to the edge in him. "I want the truth," he said simply.

Juror #5's gaze snapped to Juror #8. There was something infuriating about that calm, like it assumed everyone had the luxury of truth. Like truth didn't get you hurt where he came from. He looked down again at the folder, and in the stillness he felt his body remembering before his mind did. His stomach tightened. His hands went cold at the fingertips.

"I'm not doing this," he muttered.

The fluorescent hum deepened a fraction, a low vibration that seemed to run through the table into his wrists. Not a threat exactly. Not a voice.

A pressure.

Juror #12 whispered, “It’s making us.”

Juror #11’s face was tense, but his voice stayed controlled. “It is not making us,” he said. “It is removing the lies we hide behind.”

Juror #5’s fingers moved to the flap.

He told himself he was doing it because he refused to be defined by a label. He told himself he’d open it and laugh, prove it was wrong, prove it didn’t know him. His fingers lifted the flap anyway. The folder opened with that dry administrative sound, paper sliding against paper. The same obscene normality. His eyes dropped to the first page and froze.

He didn’t have to read long. The room didn’t waste words. It never did. Bullet points. A date. A location that wasn’t a courthouse or a clinic or a boardroom. An alley off a street he hadn’t said out loud in years. His throat worked. He tasted metal.

Juror #10 leaned forward, hungry again. “Well? What’d you do? You mug somebody? Stick ‘em? Come on, don’t be shy.”

Juror #5’s grip tightened on the folder. The paper crinkled under his fingers.

Juror #6’s voice came low, warning. “Back off.”

Juror #5 lifted his eyes, scanning faces. He expected judgment, disgust, the look people gave him when they decided his past was all he was. What he saw instead made his chest tighten: fear. Recognition. The same quiet dread that had passed through them each time a folder landed. They weren’t afraid of him. They were afraid of what the room was doing to all of them.

He forced his gaze back down. His voice came out rough. “It’s not… it’s not what you think.”

Juror #7 let out a breath. “That’s never a good start.”

Juror #5’s eyes flicked up again, irritated at the attempt to lighten it. “Shut up,” he said, then immediately hated himself for it. Old reflex. Hardness as armor.

Juror #7 didn’t respond. He just nodded faintly, chastened, and looked away.

Juror #9 spoke quietly. “Then tell us what it is,” he said. “Before the room tells it for you.”

Juror #5’s jaw clenched. He looked at the typed page again, and a name stared back at him. Not his. Someone else’s. His friend’s. The letters seemed too clean to hold the sound of that voice, the way it had cracked when it asked for help. The way it had used Juror #5’s childhood nickname like a rope.

Juror #5 inhaled, and the air felt thick, tainted. "It says," he began, then stopped. His throat tightened. He swallowed hard, trying to force words through a narrow passage. "It says I left him," he said finally.

The room went still.

Juror #12's mouth parted. Juror #2's eyes squeezed shut, as if she couldn't bear another story where someone didn't pick up a phone, didn't fix a form, didn't shut down a line, didn't do the one thing that might have changed the ending.

Juror #4 stared at Juror #5 with a sharpness that wasn't judgment as much as analysis. Like he was trying to see how a single decision could curve into a death.

Juror #10's voice rose, eager and cruel to cover his own discomfort. "Left him where?"

Juror #11's gaze cut to Juror #10. "Be silent," he said. Not loud. Just absolute.

For once, Juror #10 didn't argue.

Juror #5 stared at the folder until his eyes burned. He could feel sweat gathering at his hairline, cold and sticky. His fingers shook, just slightly, and he hated that too.

"It was a fight," he said. His voice sounded distant to his own ears. "Not like… not like in a bar. Not like a stupid punch-up. It was… neighborhood. People you know. People you don't want to know."

Juror #6's face tightened. He didn't speak, but he watched with a focus that felt practical, like he'd seen the aftermath of violence enough to recognize the shape of it.

Juror #5 continued, words forced out one by one. "We were kids," he said. "Me and… him. We were dumb. We thought being tough was the only thing that mattered."

Juror #3's eyes flicked up at that, then away again, as if the sentence had scraped against his own confession.

Juror #5's hands tightened on the folder. "We got jumped," he said. "Or we jumped them. It doesn't matter. It was chaos. Knives came out."

Juror #2 made a small noise, hand rising to her mouth. Her eyes darted to the knife on the table, and the symmetry of it made her look sick.

Juror #5's voice dropped. "He got cut," he said. "Bad. In the side. He fell."

The memory rose so fast his vision narrowed, as if the room had pulled him by the collar back into the alley. The smell of garbage, wet concrete, the distant laughter from somewhere people weren't bleeding. His friend on the ground, eyes wide with shock more than pain, hands red and slippery.

"I remember," Juror #5 said, and his voice cracked on the word. He swallowed and pushed through. "I remember him looking at me like he didn't understand. Like it didn't make sense. Like he thought the world had rules."

Juror #9's voice came softly. "And you?"

Juror #5's jaw trembled. He clenched it harder, forcing it steady. "And I heard sirens," he said. "Far away. Not even close. But in my head they were already right there."

Juror #6 nodded once, slow. "You panicked," he said.

Juror #5 laughed, harsh. "Yeah," he said. "I panicked. Because I'd been in trouble before. Because I'd been stopped. Because I'd been searched. Because I knew how it goes when you're the one standing over a bleeding body and you look like you belong in the report."

The word report tasted bitter now, connecting him to Juror #1's internal incident summary, Juror #2's time stamp, Juror #4's statements from beneficiaries. Different worlds, same paper trail.

Juror #8's voice was quiet. "What did he say?" he asked.

Juror #5's eyes flicked up, furious at the precision of the question. Furious because it went for the throat of the memory, not the facts.

He looked back down at the folder. There it was, typed out in merciless simplicity.

"He said my name," Juror #5 whispered. "He said, 'Don't leave me.'"

Juror #12 sucked in a breath, sharp, like pain.

Juror #5 squeezed his eyes shut for a second, and when he opened them the room looked flatter, more clinical, like the lights had stripped away the last warmth from everything.

"I told him I was gonna get help," he said. "I told him to hold on. And then I ran." He heard his own words echo in the sealed room and felt something inside him fold inward.

Juror #3 whispered, almost inaudible, "You didn't come back."

Juror #5's head snapped toward him, anger flaring. "You don't get to—"

Then he stopped. Because Juror #3 wasn't accusing him. Juror #3's face was empty with recognition. Another call not answered. Another person left alone with their last minutes.

Juror #5 looked down again. "I didn't come back," he said, quieter. "I went home. I washed my hands until my skin hurt. I sat on my bed and listened to sirens later and told myself they weren't for him."

Juror #9's hands trembled on the table edge. "Did he die?" he asked, and the gentleness in the question made it worse.

Juror #5 swallowed. He nodded once, sharp. "Yeah," he said. "He died."

Juror #2's eyes filled again, but she didn't make a sound. She just bowed her head like someone at a funeral where the body is not present.

Juror #10 shook his head slowly, trying to build contempt and failing. "So you left a guy bleeding," he said, and his voice sounded smaller than he wanted. "To save your own skin."

Juror #5's gaze lifted, and there was something dangerous in his eyes now, not violence, but raw truth. "Yeah," he said. "That's exactly what I did."

Juror #11's voice came softly, almost like a prayer. "Cowardice kills too," he said.

Juror #5 flinched, not because it was cruel, but because it was accurate. He stared at the folder, at the clean typed lines that had reduced an alley and a death into bullet points. The room's metallic smell seemed to thicken again, pennies and old blood, as if it approved of the clarity.

"I told myself," Juror #5 said, and his voice went flat with self-disgust, "that if I stayed, I'd be the one in cuffs. That I'd go away. That my life would be over."

Juror #8's voice was steady. "And his life?" he asked.

Juror #5's throat tightened. He couldn't answer immediately. The question was too clean, too sharp.

Finally, he whispered, "I didn't think about it." That was the betrayal, sharper than the running. The moment of choosing his own future so completely that his friend's became background noise.

Juror #7's voice came out ragged. "How old were you?"

"Seventeen," Juror #5 said. He hated the number because people used it like a balm. Like youth excused everything. Like it turned betrayal into a mistake.

Juror #6 stared at him, expression hard but not unkind. "And you never told anyone," he said.

Juror #5 shook his head. "No," he whispered. "I told myself he was already gone when I ran. I told myself it wouldn't have mattered. I told myself… I didn't mean to."

The phrase landed in the room like a familiar coin dropped on a table. Juror #1 had said it. Juror #2 had said it. Juror #3 had said it. Now Juror #5 said it, and it sounded less like an excuse and more like a curse they all shared.

The chalkboard scraped behind them.

A short, dry stroke. Another mark added beneath the word JUROR, as if the room had taken Juror #5's confession and filed it in the same ledger as the others.

Juror #12 stared at the marks, pale. "It's counting us down," he whispered.

Juror #9 corrected him, voice tired. "It is counting us in."

Juror #5 sat back in his chair, the folder still open in front of him. His hands lay on either side of it, palms down, as if he was afraid his fingers might reach out and try to shove the truth away.

The knife sat near the chalkboard, unchanged.

The clock stayed dead at two twenty-six.

The door remained locked.

And the room, having pulled betrayal into the light, felt quieter for a moment, like a thing that had been fed and was deciding what it wanted next. For a few breaths, the room stayed still, as if it needed to digest what had just been placed on the table.

Juror #5 sat back with the folder open in front of him, eyes fixed on nothing. His confession had left a residue in the air, the way smoke lingers after a fire is put out. Nobody reached for water. Nobody suggested voting again. Even Juror #10, usually eager to turn someone else's pain into a spectacle, was quiet, his mouth set as if he'd bitten down on something bitter.

The chalkboard held its uneven ledger beneath the word JUROR. Another mark had been added. Another truth recorded. The room's fluorescent hum pressed low and steady, like a hand on the back of their necks.

Juror #6 looked at the marks and then away, the motion abrupt. He stared at the tabletop, at the grain of the wood, as if he could find an exit between the lines. His posture was heavy, squared off, the kind of stance built by years of lifting things too large for one person and learning not to complain about it.

Juror #7 noticed him. He shifted in his chair, restless, and tried to speak lightly, failed, and settled for honesty. "You're quiet," he said.

Juror #6 didn't look up. "Ain't much to say."

Juror #9's gaze rested on him with the same patient attention he'd given the others. "Sometimes," he murmured, "silence is where the worst things live."

Juror #6's jaw tightened. A muscle jumped in his cheek. He kept his eyes on the table. "Don't start."

Juror #1 exhaled slowly, as if breathing hurt. He glanced at Juror #6 like he was seeing him properly for the first time, not as a steady voice of practicality but as another man in a sealed room with no escape.

"He's not starting," the foreman said hoarsely. "He's… he's pointing."

Juror #6's hands were on the table, broad and callused. The knuckles were pale, as if he'd been gripping something invisible.

Juror #12 swallowed. "Is it going to do this to all of us?" he asked, not to anyone in particular. He sounded like a man asking if a storm had plans.

The lights didn't flicker. The door didn't rattle. The room didn't need theatrics anymore. It had learned their rhythm.

A dull thud landed on the tabletop.

They all turned at once.

A fourth thick brown folder sat near Juror #6's elbow, placed with the same careful neatness as the others, as if whatever was placing them took pride in order. The white label was crisp, typed in that merciless font.

JUROR #6 – WORKING MAN.

Juror #6 stared at it without moving. The words seemed to offend him more than JUROR #5 – SLUMS had offended Juror #5. Not because of shame, but because it was a costume he'd worn his whole life without asking anyone's permission, and now the room was using it like a category in a file cabinet.

Juror #10 let out a thin laugh that didn't reach his eyes. "Here we go," he said. "Mr. Common Sense. Mr. Straight Talk. What's yours, huh? You push somebody off scaffolding?"

Juror #11's head turned toward Juror #10. "If you cannot be decent," he said quietly, "be silent."

Juror #10 lifted his hands as if surrendering, but his mouth stayed twisted. He didn't add anything. The room had made him careful, if it hadn't made him kind.

Juror #6 kept staring at the folder. His breathing was steady, but there was a slight tremor in his nostrils, like a suppressed reaction. He looked down at his hands as if checking whether they would betray him.

Juror #8 spoke gently, the way he had each time, never hurrying, never letting anyone pretend the object wasn't there. "You don't have to open it," he said. "But if you don't, it will still sit in front of you. And the room will still know."

Juror #6 lifted his eyes to Juror #8, and something hard lived there. Not rage. Something like resentment. "You talk like you know what it's like," he said.

Juror #8 held the look. "I know what it's like to carry something you don't name," he replied.

Juror #6's mouth tightened as if he wanted to argue and couldn't find the right angle.

Juror #9's voice came soft. "Open it," he said, not as an order, but as a weary request. "If you are going to bleed, do not make us guess where."

Juror #6 stared at the folder again. His fingers moved, slow and reluctant, to the flap. He didn't use a cloth. He didn't flinch at the paper. He opened it the way a man opens a toolbox: resigned to what it contains. The dry sound of paper separating felt louder than it should have. His eyes dropped to the first page, and for a long moment he didn't speak. His face stayed blunt, practical, but his throat worked once in a way that betrayed him.

Juror #7 leaned forward slightly. "What is it?" he asked, quieter than he usually managed.

Juror #6's voice came out low. "It's… a report," he said. The word landed with a bitter echo in the room. Reports. Summaries. Time stamps. Statements. Clean language for messy damage. "Worksite."

Juror #1's eyes closed for a second, as if the category alone hurt. Juror #4 stared at Juror #6 with that analytical attention he couldn't turn off even now, as if trying to map the mechanics of guilt the way he mapped data.

Juror #6 swallowed and read without lifting the page, eyes tracking lines. "Accident investigation," he said. "Warehouse. Loading dock."

Juror #12 whispered, "Oh no," like a child recognizing a sound before the impact.

Juror #6's lips pressed together. He wasn't trembling. Not yet. He looked like he was holding himself in place by force.

Juror #10 leaned forward, unable to resist. "So you dropped something," he said. "You screwed up at work. That's not killing."

Juror #6's eyes snapped up, and his stare shut Juror #10's mouth like a slammed door. "You don't get to tell me what it is," Juror #6 said, quiet and dangerous.

Juror #10 leaned back, muttering, but he didn't push it.

Juror #6 looked down again. His voice grew flatter, like he was trying to turn the story into facts so it couldn't hurt. "We were moving pallets," he said. "Forklift. Tight space. People everywhere because management wanted it done fast."

Juror #1 flinched at the familiar shape of it: production targets, speed, consequences that always landed on bodies.

Juror #6 continued. “There was a guy on foot. New. Temp worker. Didn’t know the layout.” He paused. His jaw worked. “His name’s in here.”

He didn’t say the name.

Juror #9’s eyes softened with something like grief. “A file and not a face,” he murmured, and this time it sounded like a lament, not a lesson.

Juror #6’s fingers tightened on the page until the paper bowed slightly. “I was on the forklift,” he admitted. “I was tired. Double shift. Somebody called from behind me. I turned my head for half a second.”

Juror #2 made a small noise, almost inaudible, the kind of sound that meant she was already imagining the moment.

Juror #6’s voice went rough. “Half a second,” he repeated, like he was still bargaining with time.

The dead clock sat between them, hands fixed at two twenty-six, mocking the idea that half a second could be returned.

“I rolled,” Juror #6 said, and the word came out like metal. “I rolled forward, and he… he stepped where he shouldn’t have. Or I went where I shouldn’t have. Doesn’t matter. The forks caught his leg. Dragged him down.”

Juror #12's face went pale. He brought a hand up to his mouth as if to hold something back.

Juror #6 stared at the page like it could absorb the horror for him. "He hit the concrete. His head," he said, then stopped. He inhaled through his nose. "He didn't get up."

Silence thickened. The fluorescent hum seemed to press deeper into their teeth. The metallic smell in the air sharpened, pennies rubbed warm.

Juror #5's eyes were narrowed now, not judging, just listening like someone who knew what it meant to watch a body stop moving.

Juror #6's shoulders lifted slightly with a breath he couldn't control. "They called an ambulance. They did CPR. Like in the videos. Like it works if you do it right." His mouth twisted. "It didn't work."

Juror #7 whispered, "Jesus."

Juror #6 swallowed. "He died at the hospital," he said.

Juror #10, quieter now, tried anyway, because he couldn't stand the implication settling on the table. "Accidents happen," he muttered. "That's why they call 'em accidents."

Juror #6 looked up slowly. His eyes were flat, but there was something underneath, something raw and ashamed. "Yeah," he said. "Accidents happen."

Juror #8's voice was gentle, precise. "The folder isn't here because of the accident," he said. "It's here because of what you did after."

Juror #6 went still.

Juror #4's eyes narrowed, the analyst in him recognizing a pattern. "Liability," he said softly. "Blame assignment. Documentation."

Juror #6's jaw clenched hard enough to show muscle. "They asked questions," he said. His voice had that worksite bluntness, the language of men who know how to describe damage without sounding like they feel it. "Safety guy. Supervisor. HR. They asked if I'd been trained, if I was on break, if I was on my phone."

He shook his head once, sharp. "And I saw my supervisor's face," he said. "Not worry. Not grief. Calculation. Like he was already figuring out how to keep it from landing on the company."

Juror #1 stared at him, expression hollow, recognizing that face because he'd worn versions of it.

Juror #6 continued, quieter. "They wanted a clean story. A reason. Someone to point at so the rest of the system could keep moving."

Juror #11's voice came soft. "And you gave them one."

Juror #6's eyes flicked to Juror #11, then dropped. "There was another guy," he said. "Older. Worked there a long time. He'd been complaining about the temp workers. Said they were careless. Said somebody was gonna get hurt."

Juror #2's eyes widened. She whispered, "You blamed him."

Juror #6's mouth tightened. He nodded once, barely. "Not straight out," he said, and the defense in the phrase sounded pathetic even to him. "I didn't say, He did it. I just… I said he'd been in the area. I said he'd been directing foot traffic. I said he'd waved me through."

Juror #9 closed his eyes briefly, as if the moment was painful to watch.

Juror #6's voice cracked, just once, like a board splintering under weight. "He hadn't," Juror #6 admitted. "He was on the other side. I knew that. I knew it right when I said it."

Juror #5 stared at him. "Why?" he asked, not unkind, just stunned by the familiar shape of it. Run. Save yourself. Leave someone else holding the blood.

Juror #6's breathing grew heavier. He looked at the folder and then, for the first time, at the others, as if he couldn't keep the truth contained in paper anymore.

"Because I've got kids," he said. The words came out fast. "Because I've got a mortgage. Because if they pinned it on me, I'd be done. Fired. Maybe sued. Maybe worse. And he… he was older. Close to retirement. They could call it negligence, write him up, push him out. They could make it look like it was his attitude, his complaints, his fault."

Juror #8's voice was quiet. "So you sacrificed him."

Juror #6 flinched. His eyes went bright with anger that was really shame. "I didn't push him in front of a forklift," he snapped.

Juror #8 didn't move. "No," he said. "You pushed him under it afterward."

The sentence hung like a gavel strike.

Juror #6's shoulders sagged. He stared down at his hands, and his voice dropped. "They wrote him up," he whispered. "They cut his hours. They made him the problem. And when the family of the guy who died asked questions, it was all clean. A temp worker didn't follow protocol. A veteran employee misdirected traffic. A tragedy. Nobody's fault, really, if you say it the right way."

Juror #1 let out a broken sound, half breath, half grief, as if hearing the system speak in another man's mouth was unbearable.

Juror #6 swallowed hard. "That older guy," he said, and now his voice sounded raw, stripped. "He came to me in the break room a week later. He asked me why I said what I said. He didn't yell. He just looked tired. Like somebody had scooped the life out of him."

Juror #6 closed his eyes for a second, and when he opened them his gaze was wet, though no tears fell. "And I told him I didn't know what he was talking about," he whispered.

Juror #2 made a small sobbing noise. Juror #3 stared at the table like he couldn't bear one more moment of cowardice wearing a reasonable face.

Juror #6's voice dropped even lower. "He retired early," he said. "Lost money. Lost insurance. His wife got sick after. I heard. Somebody said he was doing deliveries to make up the difference." He shook his head slowly. "All because I couldn't stand to be the one who did it."

Juror #9's voice came soft, relentless. "And the man who died," he said. "Do you tell his family the truth?"

Juror #6's mouth twisted. "No," he whispered. "I didn't. I went to the memorial at the warehouse. Stood there with my hard hat in my hands and listened to them say it was a terrible accident. And I nodded like I was innocent."

The room felt tighter after that, as if the confession had thickened the air instead of clearing it.

Juror #6 stared at the folder as if it might contain a different ending on the next page. It didn't. It only contained what the room had already dragged out of him: not a moment of inattention, not even the death itself, but the choice afterward. He looked up finally, eyes moving across the faces, and his voice came out like something torn loose.

"I did it," he said. "I blamed him. I let them bury it on somebody else. I let a dead man stay dead and a living man get punished so I could keep my job." He swallowed, jaw trembling once. "I didn't mean to," he whispered, and the phrase sounded like ash now, a common language in a room that had collected it from them one by one.

Behind them, the chalk scraped.

A short stroke. Another mark added beneath JUROR, the room's ledger acknowledging the confession with the indifferent precision of a clerk stamping a form.

Juror #12 stared at the chalkboard marks, eyes wide and wet. "How many is that now?" he whispered, as if counting might help him understand what was happening.

Juror #9 answered without looking. “Enough,” he said softly. “Enough to know it will not stop.”

Juror #6 sat back slowly, as if his bones had become heavier. The folder lay open in front of him, the typed lines neat and unforgiving. The knife at the far end of the table remained still, clean, patient. The clock stayed frozen at two twenty-six.

And for the first time since the first vote, Juror #6 looked less like the practical man who kept the others grounded and more like everyone else in the room: another juror stripped down to the part that couldn’t be managed, documented, or safely blamed on someone else.

Chapter 9

The Room on Trial

For a moment after Juror #6's last words, the room seemed to settle into a heavy pause, like a machine cycling down after a surge. No one reached for the exhibits anymore. No one asked about the boy. Their chairs had become confession booths, and the table had become an altar for paper.

Juror #7 shifted first.

He had been quiet through the last confession, his usual twitchy energy replaced by a stillness that didn't fit him. Now he cleared his throat and let out a laugh that sounded like it had been squeezed out of the wrong part of his body.

"Well," he said, voice light on the surface, too light. "This is going great. Everybody's having a really healthy day."

No one joined in.

Juror #7's smile held for a beat, then tightened when it didn't find company. He glanced around the table as if searching for someone to throw him a rope, some familiar rhythm of eye-rolls and snorts and a shared sense that he was harmless.

Juror #3 stared at nothing, hollowed out.

Juror #2's hands stayed folded tight in her lap like she didn't trust them not to change another date.

Juror #5 looked down at the open folder in front of him as if he expected blood to seep through the paper.

Juror #6 sat with his shoulders slumped, gaze fixed on his own hands, the place where he had once thought truth could be kept by not speaking.

Juror #1's foreman posture had collapsed into something smaller, the badge on his lapel now only a reminder of how little authority meant in this sealed room.

Juror #4 stared at the chalkboard marks the way he used to stare at charts, trying to discover a logic that would make it tolerable.

Juror #10 watched everyone else, angry in the way a man gets when he realizes he can't bully his way out of fear.

Juror #11 sat upright, jaw set, eyes dark and steady.

Juror #9 looked tired, ancient, like he'd seen a thousand rooms where people pretended they hadn't done what they'd done.

Only Juror #8 looked the same as he always had: attentive, calm, inexhaustible.

Juror #7's laugh faded completely. The smile fell off his face as if it had finally gotten too heavy to hold.

"Okay," he muttered. "Okay. Tough crowd."

The fluorescent hum pressed down into the silence. The metallic smell lingered, faint but persistent, like a reminder that something in the room had been cut open and wasn't closing again.

Then the table made that sound they all had come to dread: a soft, decisive thud, like an office file placed neatly at the point of no return.

Juror #7 froze.

The folder sat directly in front of him, aligned with the edge of the table as if someone had measured it. Thick brown cardstock. White label. Crisp typed letters.

JUROR #7 – JOKER.

The word made his throat tighten in a way he didn't expect. It wasn't an insult. It was an identity, the one he'd relied on since he walked into the jury room and decided the easiest way to survive civic duty was to treat it like a sitcom. His fingers hovered above the folder without touching it, as if the air itself had become sensitive.

Juror #10 let out a short, ugly sound. "Oh, that's perfect," he said, and there was relief in his cruelty.

Someone else was on the hook. "The clown's up next."

Juror #11's gaze snapped to him. "If you cannot stop yourself," he said quietly, "then at least do not enjoy it."

Juror #10 leaned back, lips curling. "I'm not enjoying anything. I'm just saying, if this room wants to do a show, let's see the showman."

Juror #7 attempted a grin. It came out crooked.

"Yeah," he said, too quickly. "Sure. Great. My turn. What, did I kill someone with a bad pun? Death by dad joke?" His voice echoed oddly against the sealed walls. The humor didn't land. It slid off the table and fell to the floor, dead weight.

Juror #8 watched him steadily. "You don't have to be funny," he said.

Juror #7 blinked at him, startled by the softness. He opened his mouth as if to snap back, then shut it again. He stared at the folder.

"I mean," he said, quieter, "this is insane. Right? We all agree this is insane."

Juror #9 spoke gently. "Insane things still happen," he said. "And sane people still do terrible acts."

Juror #7 swallowed. His Adam's apple bobbed hard. "I didn't… I didn't kill anyone," he said, and the way he said it sounded less like a claim and more like a prayer he didn't fully believe.

Juror #6 finally lifted his eyes. "Just open it," he said, voice low. He didn't sound angry. He sounded like a man who had discovered the only way through was straight.

Juror #7 stared at him, then at the folder again. His hands were trembling slightly now, just enough that he tucked them under the edge of the table for a second, trying to hide it.

He pulled them back out anyway. Denial was pointless in a room that placed names in front of you.

With a shaky breath, he lifted the flap.

The paper inside was the same as the others. Cream-colored. Typed. Margins clean enough to feel cruel.

He looked down and went very still.

It wasn't the dramatic kind of stillness Juror #3 had carried before breaking. It was the kind that happens when the air gets sucked out of a place and your body forgets what to do without it.

Juror #12 whispered, barely audible, "What is it?"

Juror #7 didn't answer. His eyes moved across the first lines like he was reading something written in a language he'd once known and tried to forget.

Juror #10 leaned forward. "Come on," he said. "Read it. Tell us. What's the gag?"

Juror #7's lips parted. He wet them once. His voice came out hoarse, stripped of performance. "It's… it's a police report," he said.

Juror #2 made a small sound in her throat. Juror #1's gaze dropped as if he could already see where this went. There were only so many kinds of paper that carried death.

Juror #7 continued, eyes locked on the page. "Traffic collision," he whispered. "Two decades ago."

Juror #9 closed his eyes briefly, as if the time span didn't soften anything, only proved how long a man could carry something without letting it show.

Juror #7's fingers tightened around the edge of the folder. "I was… I was driving," he said.

Juror #10 scoffed, too fast, trying to make it small. "Everybody drives."

Juror #11 looked at him, and the chill in his gaze could have quieted a courtroom. Juror #10 subsided, but the contempt stayed on his face like a stain.

Juror #7 swallowed again. "It says… it says I was intoxicated."

The word intoxicated sat in the air like a chemical spill.

Juror #7's laugh tried to return, a reflex. It showed up as a short exhale that didn't become sound. His eyes stayed on the paper. "I don't even drink anymore," he said, and the sentence sounded pathetic the moment it left him.

Juror #8's voice was steady. "Tell us what happened," he said, as if the room demanded sequence, not excuses.

Juror #7 nodded faintly, as if agreeing with a judge. He looked down again.

"It was after a wedding," he said. "My buddy's wedding. I was… I was the funny guy. The guy everybody kept buying drinks for. Because I made them laugh. Because it was a celebration. Because it was… you know." He shook his head, as if the past was something he could physically dislodge.

His eyes flicked up, quick and panicked. "I wasn't falling-down drunk," he said. "I could walk. I could talk. I thought I was fine."

Juror #4's voice came quiet, almost automatic. "That's what everyone says," he murmured, like a statistic he'd seen too many times.

Juror #7 looked down again, jaw tightening. "I got in the car," he said. "I drove. It was late. Roads empty. I thought that made it safer." He let out a breath that trembled. "I turned onto this street. There was a crosswalk. I remember the streetlights, the way they made everything look… washed out."

His eyes lost focus for a second, as if the room had pulled him back into the windshield view.

"I saw him too late," he whispered. "He was crossing. Just walking. Like he had the right to." His throat worked. "I hit him."

Juror #12's face went pale. Juror #2's hand rose to her mouth. Juror #5 stared at Juror #7 with a hard, familiar look: the look of someone who knows how fast a body becomes an object when fear takes over.

Juror #7's voice cracked. "He went up," he said, and winced as if the words themselves were impact. "And then… down." He swallowed hard. "I stopped. I swear to God I stopped."

Juror #9's eyes opened. "And?" he asked softly, as if the next part mattered more than the collision.

Juror #7's fingers clenched around the folder so hard the paper bent. "I got out," he said. "I ran to him. People came out of a house. Someone screamed. Someone called an ambulance." His eyes were shining now, but he didn't let tears fall. He looked like he was fighting them out of habit. "He was breathing. He was making this sound, like he was trying to talk through water."

Juror #6 stared at the table, jaw flexing, as if he could hear the sound too.

Juror #7 whispered, "I kept saying, 'I'm sorry.' Like that meant anything. Like it was a magic word."

Juror #8 didn't interrupt. His stillness was a kind of pressure that didn't allow Juror #7 to exit into vagueness.

Juror #7's eyes dropped again to the folder. "It says he died at the hospital," he said. "Internal injuries." He blinked hard. "It says my blood alcohol was above the limit."

Juror #10 exhaled through his nose, contempt trying to return because contempt felt safer than recognizing himself in the story. "So you went to jail," he said.

Juror #7's mouth twisted. His laugh returned for a moment, and it was the ugliest sound in the room, because it wasn't humor. It was self-loathing wearing a grin.

"No," he said.

The single word cut the air.

Juror #1's head lifted sharply. Juror #4's eyes narrowed. Juror #11's jaw clenched. Juror #9 looked at Juror #7 with a sadness that seemed to deepen.

Juror #7 swallowed and spoke again, voice low. "I didn't go to jail," he said. "Not really. I got… probation. A reduced charge. Reckless. Not DUI manslaughter." He shook his head, eyes wide and bright now. "My uncle knew someone. A lawyer. He handled it. He told me to keep my mouth shut. To say as little as possible. He said it was tragic, but the judge would be sympathetic. First offense. Good kid. Bright future." His voice cracked on bright future, as if the phrase had been used to pave over blood.

Juror #8's voice came quiet. "And you let him," he said. Not a question.

Juror #7 nodded once. The motion was small, almost childlike. "I let him," he whispered. "Because I was scared."

Juror #5's eyes narrowed. "Did you ever talk to the family?" he asked, and the question had the rough edge of his own story: someone left behind to carry the weight alone.

Juror #7 stared at the folder. "No," he said. "My lawyer told me not to. He said it would be admitting liability. I listened. I listened to everything he said because I wanted it to go away." He inhaled sharply. "I told myself I'd make it right by never drinking again. Like that was a trade. Like that balanced anything."

Juror #9's voice was soft. "You made a vow," he said, "and called it a payment."

Juror #7's face crumpled for a second before he forced it back into something composed. "I became the funny guy harder," he admitted. "I made jokes. I kept people laughing. I kept myself laughing." His eyes flicked to the knife near the chalkboard, then away. "Because if I stopped, I'd see it. The streetlights. The crosswalk. His face when he looked up."

Juror #2 whispered, "Did he have a name?"

Juror #7's breath hitched. He looked down, scanning the page as if he'd never dared to memorize it. "Yeah," he said. "He had a name." He said it then, quietly, and the room absorbed it like a bruise forming.

The fluorescent hum deepened, subtle but unmistakable, as if the room approved of the detail becoming human.

On the chalkboard, beneath JUROR and its growing ledger of marks, the chalk made a short, dry stroke by itself.

Another line.

Another truth recorded.

Juror #7's shoulders sagged. The folder lay open, and his hands rested on either side of it like he was afraid it might float away and take his confession with it. He looked up at the others, and for the first time since he'd entered the room cracking jokes, his face held no performance at all.

"I thought," he said, voice barely above a whisper, "that because it was an accident, it didn't count the same."

Juror #8 held his gaze. "And now?" he asked.

Juror #7 swallowed. His eyes shone, and this time a tear slipped free and ran down the side of his face without him wiping it away.

"Now it feels the same," he said. "Now it feels like the only difference is the story I told myself so I could sleep." He breathed in, shaky and thin. "I killed him," he whispered.

No one spoke. Not even Juror #10. The silence that followed wasn't mercy. It was recognition.

Juror #7 stared at the chalkboard marks, at the knife, at the dead clock fixed forever at two twenty-six, as if the room had chosen that time to represent all the moments they had wished they could rewind. And whatever laughter had once lived in him was gone, not taken by force, but dissolved by truth until there was nothing left to hide behind.

The silence after Juror #7's whisper didn't feel empty. It felt occupied, crowded with the image of a crosswalk under streetlights and a man's body turning into an object the second impact made it undeniable.

Juror #7 sat with his shoulders sagged, staring at the open folder as if it might close itself and swallow what he'd said. The tear line on his cheek had dried into a thin track, evidence like everything else in this room: small, human, impossible to argue with.

Across the table, Juror #10 looked down at his own hands, jaw working, as if he were chewing on anger and finding it tasteless. Juror #12's lips moved without sound, a silent count or prayer. Juror #2 kept her gaze fixed on the tabletop, eyes glassy, like she didn't trust herself to look at anyone without breaking again. Juror #1's foreman badge caught the fluorescent light when he shifted; it looked less like authority now and more like a tag.

The chalkboard held the word JUROR above its growing tally of short, dry strokes. Each confession had earned one. The board didn't write names. It didn't need to. They were sitting in order.

The room smelled faintly of pennies. The hum in the lights pressed into their teeth.

Juror #9, who had watched every confession like he was witnessing a ritual he'd hoped never to see again, folded his hands on the table edge. His fingers trembled, not with panic the way Juror #2's had, not with restrained violence the way Juror #3's had, but with age and something older than age: the subtle shake of a man who has been holding a single memory in the same position for decades. He had spoken in observations so far. He had offered phrases that landed like verdicts. He had been the one to say a file and not a face, and each time it had cut deeper. Now he stared at the chalkboard ledger as if it were familiar.

Juror #8's eyes were on him. Calm, attentive, patient. The same gaze that had waited out every denial until the truth surfaced like a body. Juror #9 noticed, and his mouth twitched once. Not a smile. Something like resignation.

"You're looking at me," he said quietly.

Juror #8 didn't pretend otherwise. "You've been looking at everyone," he replied. "Now it's your turn to be seen."

Juror #9's throat moved. He didn't reach for the water pitcher. He didn't look at the locked door. He didn't glance at the knife. His attention stayed on the chalkboard, then drifted to the dead clock fixed at two twenty-six.

"It chose a time," he murmured.

Juror #4's eyes narrowed. "Or it's not time at all," he said. "It's a marker. A condition."

Juror #9 nodded faintly. "In some places," he said, "time stops when you do something you cannot undo."

Juror #7 flinched as if the sentence had pulled him back toward the crosswalk. Juror #6 stared at the table, face stiff, like he didn't want another man's guilt to add weight to his own.

Then the table made its soft, decisive sound.

A thud, measured and careful, like a file placed down in a quiet office where the only noise is the turning of pages.

Juror #12 jerked as if struck. Juror #2 sucked in a breath. Juror #10's eyes snapped up, immediate, hungry, then caught on the label and stalled, as if even his appetite had limits.

The folder sat in front of Juror #9. Thick brown cardstock. A white typed label, crisp as an indictment.

JUROR #9 – OLD MAN.

Juror #9 stared at it without moving.

Juror #10 made a short sound that tried to become a laugh and failed. "Old man, huh," he said, too loud, then quieter, like the room had adjusted his volume for him. "What's yours? You run over somebody with a walker?"

Juror #11 turned his head and looked at Juror #10 for a long, cold beat. Juror #10's mouth tightened and he said nothing else.

Juror #9 didn't react to the insult. The label didn't offend him the way it had offended Juror #5. It didn't reduce him; he had already been reduced by time, by his own body, by the world that looked at him and saw fragility. He placed his fingertips on the folder. They trembled against the cardboard.

"I've been waiting," he said.

Juror #1 blinked. "For this?"

"For my life to be weighed by people who don't know it," Juror #9 replied, and there was no bitterness in the words. Just fact. "I didn't think it would happen in a jury room."

Juror #8 said, "Open it."

Juror #9 didn't argue. He lifted the flap with slow care, as if the paper inside might crumble to dust. The folder opened with the same dry, administrative sound, obscene in its ordinariness. He stared at the first page. His eyes moved across it. He didn't inhale sharply. He didn't gasp. His reaction was quieter than that, and worse: his shoulders sank as if the words had been a weight he recognized instantly. He spoke without looking up. "They got it right," he said.

Juror #12 whispered, "What is it?"

Juror #9's voice remained soft. "A report," he said. Then he paused, as if tasting the word. "Not a police report. Not exactly. A record."

Juror #4 leaned forward slightly. "Government?"

Juror #9 nodded once. "Yes."

Juror #2's hands tightened together in her lap. "What did you do?" she whispered, and the question sounded like fear wearing a polite voice.

Juror #9 turned the page. The paper made a small, controlled sound, the way paper does when you handle it properly. He had always handled his past properly. Kept it filed.

"It was during the war," he said.

Juror #3's eyes lifted, slow and wary. "What war?"

Juror #9's gaze stayed on the folder. "Not the one you're thinking of," he said. "Not the one that makes it easy to pick sides from a distance. It was a war of uniforms and lists. A war of neighbors and accusations. A war where survival could be traded for silence."

Juror #1's mouth went dry. "Where?" he asked.

Juror #9's eyes flickered up for the first time, and the look in them made the room feel smaller. "In the country I left," he said. "The one I don't talk about because people like tidy stories of immigration. Hard work. Fresh start. They don't like the part where you carry what you did across an ocean and pretend it sank."

Juror #11's posture changed, subtle and alert. He didn't speak, but his gaze sharpened with recognition of the theme if not the details.

Juror #9 looked down again. "We lived in an apartment building," he said. "Concrete. Thin walls. You knew when your neighbor coughed. You knew when their child cried. And you knew who went out and didn't come back."

Juror #6 swallowed. Juror #7 stared at the ledger marks like he could see where this would land.

Juror #9 continued, the words coming steadily now, as if he'd said them many times in his head and the room had finally removed the lock. "There was a man on the third floor. A tailor. Quiet. Married. No children. He kept a little radio that he wasn't supposed to keep. He listened at night with the volume low, ear pressed close like it was prayer."

Juror #8 asked, gentle but unyielding, "What was his name?"

Juror #9's fingers tightened on the page. He glanced at it as if reading the name required permission. "Marek," he said. Saying it changed the air. A file and not a face. This time Juror #9 gave them a face.

Juror #2 made a small sound, grief in her throat before she knew why.

Juror #9's voice remained even. "They came to our building more than once," he said. "Men in uniforms. They asked questions. They took notes.

They smiled like they were doing you a favor by letting you answer."

Juror #4 murmured, almost to himself, "Information gathering."

Juror #9 nodded. "Yes. And people learned that if you gave them a name, they would leave you alone for a while." His eyes lifted again, and his expression was not pleading. It was condemning himself without performance. "You could buy a week. A month. Sometimes more."

Juror #10 scoffed, trying to build distance. "So you ratted somebody out."

Juror #11's gaze snapped toward him like a blade. "Be careful," Juror #11 said quietly. It wasn't a threat. It was a warning born of knowing how quickly judgment turns into cruelty when it's safe.

Juror #9 did not defend himself. He didn't soften the language. He didn't reach for context the way Juror #4 had reached for thresholds, the way Juror #1 had reached for corporate pressure.

"Yes," Juror #9 said. "I did."

The room went still in a new way.

Juror #9 turned another page. His fingers shook more now, the tremor no longer only age. "They came again," he said. "One night. Very late. They knocked on doors with the butts of their rifles, not their hands. They asked my name. My papers. They asked what I did for work. They asked if I'd seen anyone suspicious." He swallowed. "They asked if anyone in the building was disloyal."

Juror #1's hands curled slightly on the table, as if he could feel the knock through his own door.

Juror #9 stared at the folder as if it were a mirror that refused to blur. "I had my wife behind me," he said. "She was holding our baby. She didn't cry, because she had learned not to." His voice thinned briefly. "She was so small then. My daughter. I could feel her breathing through the blanket."

Juror #3's face tightened. The mention of a child in danger moved something in him. He didn't interrupt.

Juror #9's lips pressed together. "The officer looked past me into the apartment like he was taking inventory," he said. "He asked again. Names."

Juror #8's voice was low. "And you gave him Marek."

Juror #9 nodded once. "I did," he said.

Juror #2 whispered, "Why?"

Juror #9's eyes closed briefly, then opened. "Because I was afraid," he said, and the simplicity of it was almost unbearable. "Because I wanted them to leave. Because I told myself that Marek was already on a list, that it didn't matter if I spoke. Because I told myself I was not killing him. I was only saying a name." He looked up at them, and for the first time his voice carried a tremor that wasn't physical. "And because," he admitted, "part of me resented him."

Juror #6 frowned. "Resented him?"

Juror #9's mouth twisted. "He was brave in the way I was not," he said. "He listened to forbidden broadcasts. He believed something could change. He still acted like the world had rules. People like that make cowards feel exposed."

Juror #8 held his gaze. "What happened to him?"

Juror #9's fingers tightened on the page until the paper bowed. "They took him," he said. "Not that night. Two days later. They came in the morning. His wife screamed. Someone tried to close a door. The officer hit him in the mouth. There was blood on the stairwell." His voice stayed controlled, but his eyes shone. "They dragged Marek down the stairs like a sack. He looked up once. He looked at all the doors. All the neighbors who didn't open them."

Juror #7's face went pale. Juror #12's eyes filled, and he blinked hard as if he could blink the image away.

Juror #9 whispered, "He looked at my door."

No one spoke.

Juror #9 kept going, because stopping would be mercy and the room did not offer it. "His wife came to me later," he said. "She asked if I'd seen anything. She asked if I'd heard anything. She asked if I knew where they took him."

Juror #2 let out a tiny sob, helpless.

Juror #9's expression tightened, and the tremor in his hands became more pronounced. "And I lied," he said. "I told her no. I told her I was asleep. I told her I didn't know. I told her it was probably a mistake."

Juror #8 asked, "Did you know what would happen to him?"

Juror #9's eyes lifted. There was no escape in them now. "Yes," he said. The single syllable landed like a gavel. "I knew," Juror #9 repeated. "Not the exact place. Not the exact method. But I knew he would disappear. That's what we called it. Disappear. A word that makes murder sound like weather."

Juror #11's jaw clenched. His eyes stayed on Juror #9 with something like sorrow rather than judgment, as if he recognized the shape of that word from his own past.

Juror #9's voice dropped further. "I have lived a long time," he said. "Long enough to forget many things I wish I could remember. And I have never forgotten his face at the bottom of those stairs." He looked down at the folder again. "The record," he said, tapping the page with one trembling finger, "says I made a statement. It says I cooperated. It says I was thanked for my civic responsibility." The phrase civic responsibility echoed against the walls, mocking. This room had begun with civic responsibility.

Juror #1 let out a strained breath. Juror #4 stared at the page as if the cruelty of bureaucratic language was the only part he could bear to focus on.

Juror #9 lifted his gaze to the chalkboard ledger, then to Juror #8. "Is this what you want?" he asked softly. "The sentence?"

Juror #8's voice was quiet. "What do you call it?" he asked.

Juror #9's throat worked. The fluorescent hum pressed down, patient. The door stayed locked. The clock stayed dead. The knife stayed clean. Juror #9 swallowed once, and when he spoke, the words came out like something he'd been choking on for decades.

"I killed him," he said.

The chalk scraped behind them, short and dry, and another mark appeared beneath JUROR as if the room had stamped the confession into its record. Juror #9 didn't flinch at the sound. He watched the new line settle into place. Then he closed the folder carefully, like the act of closing it could honor the man whose name had been used as currency.

"I told myself," he murmured, almost inaudible, "that I did it for my family." He looked around the table, eyes wet, voice still controlled. "Maybe I did," he said. "And maybe that is what makes it unforgivable. Because I can understand it. Because I can justify it. Because I can make it sound like love instead of cowardice."

No one interrupted. Even Juror #10 sat silent, his usual certainty stripped away by the recognition that the room did not care how old the sin was or how necessary it had once felt.

Juror #8's gaze stayed on Juror #9, steady as ever. "When you picture him now," he asked, "is he still at the bottom of the stairs?"

Juror #9's mouth trembled once. He nodded. "Yes," he whispered. "Always waiting for someone to open a door."

The room held that image, and in the hush that followed, it felt less like they were jurors in a deliberation and more like they were the accused, seated in order, watching the room decide who would be called next.

The silence that followed Juror #9's confession did not loosen the room. It tightened it.

Juror #9 sat with the closed folder in front of him, fingertips resting on the cardboard as if he could keep the past from rising again if he held it down. His eyes were wet, but his face stayed composed in the way of a man who had learned to survive by never giving anyone the satisfaction of seeing him break.

Around the table, no one seemed to know where to look. Every gaze felt like trespassing now. They had come in to measure a boy's guilt and had instead become a row of open files, waiting for the next stamp.

On the chalkboard, beneath the smeared word JUROR, the ledger of marks stood like a crude tally. Eight short strokes now, uneven and blunt. Eight acknowledgments. Eight truths dragged into air that did not circulate.

Juror #12 stared at the marks with the desperate focus of someone trying to count their way out of a nightmare. His lips moved silently. When he finished the count, he swallowed hard and didn't look relieved.

Juror #7 rubbed at his cheek where the tear had dried, as if the friction could erase it. Juror #6 sat heavy in his chair, his big hands clasped and unclasped once as though testing whether his own fingers still belonged to him. Juror #5's gaze stayed low, jaw set, eyes sharp with a kind of exhausted vigilance.

Juror #1, the foreman who had once demanded procedure like a shield, seemed unable to find it anywhere. His badge still caught the light, but it looked meaningless, a scrap of metal in a room that had stopped recognizing official roles.

Juror #10 shifted in his chair, restless, and the motion drew eyes the way a sudden sound draws heads in a quiet building. His usual contempt had gone brittle. He looked around at the sealed door and the dead clock and the knife, and his expression carried the dawning understanding that the room wasn't doing this to random people. It was doing it to the ones who had assumed they would be judging, not judged.

Juror #8 remained calm, hands still, gaze attentive. It wasn't comfort. It was control without force, which somehow felt worse.

Juror #2 spoke first, voice small, like she was afraid the room would hear her and answer. "If it's… if it's keeping record," she whispered, eyes flicking to the chalkboard, "what happens when it finishes?"

No one answered.

They all heard it then, faint at first, like a sound traveling through walls from another room. A single, sharp knock.

Not on the door. Not from the hallway.

From inside the room.

Juror #12 flinched so hard his chair legs squealed. Juror #7's head snapped toward the sound, eyes wide. Juror #6's posture changed, shoulders squaring, as if his body had decided on instinct that sound meant threat.

Knock. Knock.

Two precise raps, measured. The kind of sound used to call a courtroom to order.

Juror #1 turned toward the table as if expecting to see a gavel, and in a sick twist, he almost did. Not a gavel, but the water pitcher near the center of the table, its base set down just slightly off from where it had been a moment before. It hadn't fallen. It hadn't been bumped. It had simply… adjusted, as if something invisible had made a minor correction for symmetry.

Juror #4's eyes narrowed, tracking details because he couldn't help it. "Did anyone touch that?" he asked.

No one answered, because no one could answer honestly without sounding insane.

The fluorescent hum deepened, not louder but lower, vibrating through the table legs into the floor. The air turned cold in a way that didn't feel like an HVAC issue. It felt like the room was clearing its throat.

On the chalkboard, the chalk moved without a hand.

Not a long scrape this time. A firm, deliberate stroke.

The word JUROR remained at the top, but beneath the ledger marks, a new line appeared. Letters formed slowly, the chalk pausing between strokes as if it wanted them to watch each one land.

COURT IS NOW IN SESSION.

Juror #12 made a soft sound of panic, an almost laugh that died in his throat. Juror #2 pressed her fingertips to her lips again, eyes shining. Juror #3 sat very still, face hollow, as if he'd been bracing for exactly this without knowing it.

Juror #10 scoffed reflexively, but the sound came out thin. "Oh, come on," he said. "This is… this is theatrics."

Knock. Knock.

Again, two raps. A warning. A call for silence.

Juror #10's mouth closed, not because he'd decided to be respectful, but because some part of him understood that the room didn't need his consent.

The chairs shifted.

Not dramatically, not sliding across the floor all at once. Subtle changes, like a dream rearranging itself while you watch. Juror #12 felt his chair edge tug against the tile, a slow, steady pull that made his stomach lurch. He grabbed the table automatically, knuckles whitening. Across from him, Juror #7's chair angled a few degrees inward. Juror #6's chair moved back a fraction, as if pushed into a straighter line.

The jurors looked at each other, alarmed, hands tightening on wood and fabric.

The table did not move. The folders did not scatter. The knife stayed at the far end, clean and patient.

But the seating was changing into something else. The loose circle of deliberation was being corrected into rows.

Juror #1's eyes darted to the door, then back to the chalkboard, as if searching for a clerk, a bailiff, anyone official enough to make this real in a way that could be appealed.

Juror #11 spoke quietly, voice strained but controlled. "It is arranging us," he said.

Juror #9's gaze stayed on the chalkboard. His hands trembled on the edge of the table. "Like defendants," he murmured.

That word landed in the room with a weight the earlier confessions hadn't carried. They had said killed. They had said lied. They had said left him. But defendant was a legal category, a role in a room they all understood.

Juror #1 swallowed. "We're the jury," he said, and the insistence sounded childish now.

Juror #8 looked at him with a steady patience. "We were," he said.

The lights flickered once, not the weak flutter of a bulb failing, but a deliberate blink. When they steadied again, the room looked the same and also not the same, as if the angles had sharpened.

The deliberation table suddenly felt less like a table and more like a barrier.

Juror #12 whispered, "I don't like this," and the sentence was so obvious it almost sounded like prayer.

On the chalkboard, a new line began to form beneath the declaration. Chalk moved in precise strokes, handwriting that wasn't handwriting, because it held no personality. It was the room's voice translated into letters.

CASE: THE PEOPLE VS. THE JURY.

Juror #2 let out a small sob she couldn't swallow in time.

Juror #10's chair creaked as he leaned back hard. "No," he said. "No, no, no. That's not a case. That's not a thing."

Juror #4 stared at the chalkboard, lips slightly parted. "It's framing," he murmured, more to himself than anyone. "It's converting the environment into an adversarial proceeding."

Juror #7 gave a strained, humorless breath. "You mean it's making us the bad guys."

Juror #6's gaze went to the knife again, then to the dead clock. "Or it's making us honest," he muttered.

Juror #1's voice rose, the last scraps of his old authority scraping for air. "We need to remain calm," he said. "We need to document what's happening. We need to—"

Knock. Knock.

A sharper rap this time, like a judge irritated by talking over the bench.

Juror #1 went silent. The humiliation in that silence hit him visibly, because he was a man who had spent his life being obeyed when he spoke with certainty.

Juror #8 turned his head slightly, taking them in. "Listen," he said. His voice was not loud, but it carried in the sealed room. "This place is using our language. Files. Records. Procedure. It's turning what we recognize against us."

Juror #3 stared at the chalkboard, face drawn tight. "So what's the sentence?" he whispered. "What does it want?"

Juror #9 answered without looking away. "It wants us to convict," he said, voice soft with dread. "Only not the boy."

Juror #12 shook his head rapidly. "I didn't sign up for this," he whispered.

Juror #11's eyes narrowed. "No one signs up for consequences," he said. "They arrive anyway."

A low sound rose then, not from the lights, not from the ventilation. From the walls themselves. A faint murmur, like many voices speaking at once on the other side of plaster. Too indistinct to understand, but unmistakably human in texture. It reminded Juror #2 of the clinic's waiting room, of hushed complaints and whispered names. It reminded Juror #1 of the factory floor, of men talking under machines, unheard by the people above them. It reminded Juror #7 of hospital corridors and families pleading behind closed doors.

Juror #12 pressed his palms hard to his ears. "Stop," he whispered, but it didn't stop.

Juror #5 leaned forward slightly, eyes narrowing as if trying to catch a word. "You hear that?" he asked.

Juror #6 nodded once, grim. “Yeah,” he said. “Sounds like… people.”

The murmurs swelled for a moment, then organized into something colder. A single phrase rose above the rest, not spoken clearly by any one mouth, but shaped by the room itself, as if the air had learned to form syllables.

“Guilty.”

Juror #2’s breath hitched. Juror #7’s eyes widened. Juror #1’s face went pale.

Juror #10 shot to his feet, chair scraping loud. “No!” he shouted, and the sound cracked against the walls. “You don’t get to do that. You don’t get to—”

Knock. Knock.

The two raps cut through him. He froze mid-breath, eyes wild, looking suddenly less like a bully and more like a man who had been reminded of something he couldn’t outrun.

On the chalkboard, chalk began to write again.

ORDER OF TESTIMONY.

Beneath it, the room drew a simple line, then another, forming a list. Not names yet. Just positions. As if it didn’t need to introduce them to themselves.

Juror #8’s gaze slid to that new heading, and for the first time, something like anticipation touched his expression. Not pleasure. Not cruelty. The certainty of a process continuing.

Juror #1's voice dropped to a hoarse whisper. "This isn't a courtroom," he said, as if saying it softly might make it true.

Juror #8 looked at him. "It is now," he replied.

The murmurs behind the walls quieted into a waiting hush, like an audience that had settled after the judge entered. The dead clock still read two twenty-six, but it no longer felt like a broken object. It felt like a ruling: time for deliberation was over, and time for judgment had begun.

Juror #9's hands trembled on the table edge as he stared at the chalkboard list. "It will call the next one," he said softly, and his voice carried the weary certainty of a man who had watched people disappear after their names were spoken aloud.

Juror #12's eyes darted toward the locked door again, as if hoping it might finally open out of mercy. It didn't.

The knife remained near the chalkboard, untouched, its stillness now less like a threat and more like a symbol. Not how guilt happened, but how cleanly it could be presented when someone needed an exhibit.

A courtroom had emerged around them without a judge in sight. The bench was invisible, but the authority was absolute. The prosecution was absent, but the accusations had never been clearer. And the jury, seated in their corrected rows, understood with a dawning horror that they were no longer deciding a verdict.

They were waiting to hear one.

Chapter 10

Descent into Paranoia

Juror #10 stayed on his feet, chest heaving, as if standing could keep the room from arranging him too.

The chalkboard held its new heading, ORDER OF TESTIMONY, with two blank lines beneath it like a mouth that hadn't decided which name to bite first.

No one spoke for a beat. The murmurs behind the walls had gone quiet, but the quiet wasn't relief. It was the kind of hush that makes you hear your own pulse and wonder if it's loud enough to be used against you.

Juror #1 cleared his throat, then stopped as if the sound might draw those two sharp knocks again. When he tried again, his voice came out hoarse. "We need to… we need to think." The sentence sounded ridiculous the moment he said it. Thinking had been their trap. Procedure had been their bait.

Juror #7 gave a small, brittle laugh that didn't become humor. "Yeah. Think. Great. Maybe we can think the door open."

Juror #12 had his hands on the table, fingers spread like he was bracing against an impact only he could see. "It's making a list," he said. His eyes kept flicking to the chalkboard. "Like… like a roll call."

Juror #9 didn't move. He looked smaller than before, not in body but in presence, as if saying Marek's name had taken something essential out of him. "That is what it is," he murmured. "A roll call."

Juror #4's gaze stayed fixed on the board, pupils tight, mind still trying to map this into something solvable. "If it's an adversarial proceeding," he said, "then it needs a structure. It needs a sequence of testimony. It needs escalation."

Juror #5's mouth twisted. "You keep saying it like it's a meeting," he muttered. "Like we can follow the agenda and then go home."

Juror #4 looked at him sharply. "I'm saying the order matters," he replied. "If we can predict it, we can—"

"Control it?" Juror #6 said, and the bluntness in his voice was a dull hammer. "You think you can control this?"

Juror #4 hesitated, and in that hesitation the others saw the same instinct they'd all had since the first vote: if you can name the rules, you can hide in them.

Juror #10 slammed his palm on the table. The folders jumped slightly, paper edges whispering.

"We're not doing this," he snapped. "We're not lining up to confess like it's some church. This is a courtroom. Real courtrooms have judges, bailiffs, records. This is—" He gestured at the walls, at the dead clock, at the knife sitting clean and gleaming near the chalkboard like an exhibit that had been waiting its whole life to be used. "This is a sick trick."

Juror #11's voice cut in, quiet and controlled. "You are shouting because you are afraid," he said. "Sit down."

Juror #10 turned on him immediately, the way a man turns toward the closest thing he can fight. "Don't tell me to sit down," he barked. "You don't get to be the moral authority in here. Not you. You're all acting like you're saints because you cried a little and said you're sorry."

Juror #2 flinched at the word cried, and her fingers twisted tighter in her lap. Juror #3's eyes lifted, red-rimmed and dull, as if he'd forgotten anger was still available to him.

Juror #7 spoke softly, the closest he'd come to gentle all day. "He's right about one thing," he said, voice thin. "We're not saints."

Juror #10 pointed at him, triumphant for a second, then his face twisted. "And you," he said, venom returning because it was familiar. "You killed a man and you got away with it. Don't sit there looking like some wounded puppy."

Juror #7's jaw tightened. He didn't argue. The absence of defense made Juror #10's anger flicker, searching for new fuel.

His finger swung toward Juror #9. "And you," he said. "You call it war, you call it survival, but you sold someone out. You're all the same. You just dress it up."

Juror #9 looked at him with a tired steadiness. "Yes," he said. "We are the same. That is the point."

Juror #10's nostrils flared. "No," he spat. "No. Don't lump me in with you. At least you admit what you did. At least you wear your guilt like a medal."

Juror #1's voice rose, thin and strained, trying to force a meeting tone into a room that no longer respected it. "Enough," he said. "We need to stop attacking each other. We need to focus on the situation."

Juror #5 let out a harsh breath. "What situation?" he asked. "The boy? Or us?"

The question landed like a slap. For a moment it yanked them back toward the reason they'd walked into this building at all: a teenage boy, a dead father, a knife, testimony.

Juror #2 whispered, almost reflexively, "The boy is still on trial."

Juror #8 spoke for the first time in several minutes. "Is he?" His voice was calm, and the calm made it feel like a trapdoor opening under them.

Juror #10's head snapped toward him, eyes narrowing as if he'd finally located the quiet center of the storm and decided to blame it for the weather. "Don't start," Juror #10 said. "Don't you start with your little questions."

Juror #8 didn't flinch. "It's a question worth asking," he replied. "If the room is prosecuting us, what happens to the boy?"

Juror #12 stared at him, fear sharpening into something like suspicion. "Maybe the boy was never real," he whispered.

Juror #2 jerked her head up. "Of course he's real," she said, too quickly. "We saw him. We heard him."

Juror #4's eyes shifted, calculating. "We heard testimony," he said. "We saw a defendant. But we also saw a knife appear on this table. We saw written words appear on that board. We saw files appear with our names. Reality in this room is… compromised."

Juror #3's voice came out rough. "Don't," he said. "Don't tell me my son was compromised. Don't tell me that was a trick."

Juror #4's gaze flicked to him, then away. "I'm not," he said. "I'm saying the environment is capable of manipulating perception. That has implications."

Juror #6 leaned forward, forearms on the table, posture heavy. "Here's an implication," he said. "Somebody in here knows more than they're saying."

He looked at Juror #8 when he said it.

The shift was subtle, but it was there, like the whole room's attention angling toward the same point.

Juror #8 met his gaze without surprise. "Why do you think that?" he asked.

Juror #6's jaw worked. "Because you're too calm," he said. "Because you keep nudging people to open folders like you're… like you're running it."

Juror #12 nodded quickly, desperate to grab onto an explanation that wasn't supernatural. "Yes," he blurted. "Yes, I've been thinking that. You're always ready. You knew what to say to get him to talk, and her, and him." He pointed clumsily around the table, finger shaking. "You knew the questions."

Juror #5's eyes narrowed, suspicion sliding in because it felt safer than helplessness. "You brought that knife in," he said suddenly, voice sharp. "Didn't you? You could've. Nobody checked us like they should've."

Juror #1 shook his head, but it was too slow, too uncertain. “They did check—”

“Did they?” Juror #5 cut in. “Or did we just assume they did because that’s how it’s supposed to go?”

Juror #10 seized the momentum like a man grabbing a weapon off the ground. “Finally,” he said, voice bright with ugly relief. “Finally somebody’s saying it. This guy,” he jabbed a finger toward Juror #8, “has been playing conductor since we got in here. Mr. I-just-want-to-talk. Mr. Mercy. Meanwhile the door locks the second he doesn’t get his way. The clock stops. The room starts handing out confession folders like party favors.”

Juror #11’s eyes went to Juror #8, then to the others, as if measuring how quickly fear could turn into a mob. “Careful,” he said. “Accusing him will not unlock the door.”

Juror #7’s voice was small, almost ashamed. “But it feels like it might,” he admitted. “That’s the problem.”

Juror #2 looked between them, tears gathered but not falling. “He’s been the only one trying to be fair,” she whispered, and then her face tightened as if she’d just realized fairness could be another kind of weapon.

Juror #9 watched Juror #8 with a distant, thoughtful look. “In every courtroom,” he said softly, “there is someone who believes the procedure will save them. And someone who knows it will not.”

Juror #10 sneered. “Which one is he?” he demanded.

Juror #6’s voice went lower. “Tell us,” he said to Juror #8. “What’s your file say?”

The room went still around that sentence.

Juror #8 didn’t glance at the chalkboard. He didn’t look for a folder. He didn’t pretend not to understand. He simply held Juror #6’s gaze, and for the first time his calm looked less like patience and more like restraint.

“There hasn’t been a file for me,” he said.

Juror #12 shook his head hard. “No,” he whispered. “No, that can’t be right. Everybody gets one.”

Juror #8 nodded once, slow. “Everybody,” he repeated. “So far.”

Juror #10’s eyes widened slightly, and his face shifted with a new kind of excitement, mean and fearful at the same time. “Because you don’t have one,” he said. “Because you’re not one of us.”

Juror #2’s breath hitched.

Juror #1 stared at Juror #8 as if seeing him for the first time, not as Juror Eight, not as a man with a quiet voice and a stubborn conscience, but as an unknown quantity seated among them like an unlisted item in an inventory.

Juror #5's chair scraped back half an inch. His hand moved unconsciously toward the edge of the table, not reaching for the knife, but acknowledging it.

Juror #7 swallowed hard. "Are you… are you doing this?" he asked, and the question sounded like a child asking if the monster under the bed is real.

Juror #8's expression didn't change, but something in his eyes sharpened. "No," he said.

Juror #6 stared at him. "Then what are you?"

Juror #8 didn't answer immediately. Not because he didn't have one, but because the room seemed to enjoy the silence, the way suspicion grew legs and started pacing.

Juror #10 took a step closer, looming over the table. "He's a plant," he said, voice rising. "He's an actor. He's—"

Knock. Knock.

Two raps, crisp and authoritative, cut through Juror #10's escalation like a blade through thread. Juror #10 froze mid-word, jaw clenched.

On the chalkboard, beneath ORDER OF TESTIMONY, the first blank line filled in.

JUROR #10.

The letters formed slowly, deliberately, as if written by a hand that enjoyed watching fear redirect itself into the correct channel.

Juror #10 stared at his own number on the board. For a moment his face went slack, and the room saw what had been underneath his loudness all along: a man who believed he could always talk his way into being the one who points, never the one who is pointed at. Then his expression snapped back into anger, brighter than before because it had nowhere else to go.

"No," he said, but the word came out smaller than he wanted. "No, no. I'm not doing this. I'm not playing along."

Juror #9's voice was soft, exhausted. "It is not asking," he said.

Juror #11 watched Juror #10 with a grim steadiness. "Sit," he said again, and this time it wasn't instruction. It was inevitability.

Juror #10 didn't sit.

His eyes darted around the room, wild, and he looked at Juror #8 as if the accusation could still be rerouted. "This is you," he said, voice cracking with rage. "You set me up."

Juror #8 held his gaze. "You don't need me to set you up," he replied quietly. "You brought your own rope."

Juror #10 flinched at the word rope, as if the room had learned to use their language against them.

The chalkboard stayed still now, as if it had done its job and would wait for the next sound: paper opening, a voice breaking, a truth dragged into the air. And around Juror #10, paranoia tightened like a noose, because every juror in the room understood the most dangerous part of accusation. It didn't have to be true to be useful. It only had to keep the spotlight off you for one more minute.

Juror #10 stared at the chalkboard as if the letters might crawl off it if he refused to read them.

JUROR #10.

His name in that stark, typed imitation of chalk looked wrong, too official for something that wasn't supposed to be real. He stood at the end of the table with both hands planted on the wood, shoulders high, jaw clenched so tight the muscle twitched.

"No," he said again, but the word had lost its volume. It was not defiance anymore. It was bargaining.

No one moved to comfort him. Comfort had become dangerous in this room, a gesture that could be interpreted as complicity. Even sympathy had started to look like strategy.

Juror #1's eyes flicked from the board to the locked door and back, searching for procedure like a man patting his pockets for keys he no longer owned. "We need to keep order," he rasped, and it sounded like he knew how absurd it was as he said it.

Juror #6 shifted his weight, heavy forearms still on the table, eyes fixed on Juror #10. "Sit down," he said, the same blunt instruction he'd given before. Not kindness. Not cruelty. Just the closest thing to stability he had left.

Juror #10's gaze darted to him. "You don't tell me what to do."

Juror #6 didn't blink. "I'm not telling you," he said. "I'm saying you're gonna fall over if you don't."

That was the first small alliance of the moment: not between friends, not between moral equals, but between men who recognized the shape of panic and what it did to the body.

Juror #10's hands flexed against the table edge. For a second it looked like he might shove it, tip the folders, scatter the paper evidence like confetti and force the room to chase it. But the room had already proven it could replace anything it wanted. He seemed to realize that too, because his shoulders sagged a fraction.

Juror #12 swallowed loudly in the hush. He hadn't stopped watching the chalkboard since the name appeared, eyes wide and wet, like he was waiting for the next line to fill in with his own. "Maybe we shouldn't… maybe we shouldn't make it easy," he whispered, and the idea was half-formed, a child's attempt to delay the inevitable by not looking at it.

Juror #4 turned his head slowly toward Juror #12. His face was composed, but something in his eyes had sharpened in the last few minutes: calculation migrating into fear. "If it's a sequence," he said, "resisting may change nothing. But it may change how it escalates."

Juror #7 gave a thin sound, almost a laugh. "Great. So we can choose between bad and worse."

Juror #2 flinched at his voice even when he wasn't joking. She sat small in her chair, hands clasped, gaze darting from Juror #10 to Juror #8 like she was watching a fight begin and trying to predict where the blows would land.

Juror #5 leaned back, arms crossed tight over his chest, posture defensive. He looked at Juror #10 with a wary hostility that hadn't been there before, the kind that comes when you've given up your own secret and you resent anyone still trying to keep theirs. "You been real loud about everybody else," he muttered. "Guess it's your turn."

Juror #10 snapped his head toward Juror #5. "Don't you start acting righteous," he spat. "You left your friend bleeding in an alley."

Juror #5's eyes narrowed, and for a second the room felt like it might become physical. His hands flexed at his biceps as if remembering what fists were for. "Yeah," he said, voice low. "And I said it. I didn't stand there pretending I'm better than everybody."

Juror #10's mouth twisted. "You're all enjoying this. You're all sitting there feeling lighter because you dumped your garbage on the table."

Juror #9's voice came quiet from his seat, tired as old paper. "No one is lighter," he said. "Some of us are just no longer pretending the weight is not there."

Juror #10 laughed once, harsh. "Oh, listen to him. The philosopher." His eyes slid toward Juror #9 with something like contempt, but it faltered before it could settle. There was a limit to what he could weaponize now without the room turning on him harder.

Because the room had turned. Not toward justice. Toward survival.

Juror #12's gaze flicked to Juror #1, then to Juror #11, then back to Juror #8. He looked like he was trying to decide who would keep him safest if the room called his name next. The truth, unstated, was that safety had become a social problem. Not whether you were innocent, but whether you were aligned.

Juror #1 cleared his throat again. "We need to stop attacking each other," he said, and his voice cracked slightly on the word stop. He tried to straighten his shoulders, to look like a foreman again. "Whatever this is, it's trying to divide us."

Juror #7's eyes flicked to the chalkboard. "We're doing a great job without help," he murmured.

Juror #11 spoke, and when he did, the room's attention shifted toward him with relief. He had become, in the last hour, something like a spine in the chaos: not comforting, but steady. "We are divided already," he said. "By what we have done. By what we have admitted. By what we still refuse to admit."

Juror #10 jerked his head toward Juror #11 as if grateful to have an enemy with a calm voice. "And you," he said, voice rising again, "you're gonna sit there acting like you're above it? Like you're the judge?"

Juror #11's eyes didn't widen. He didn't flinch. "No," he said. "I am not above it. That is why I do not shout."

Juror #10's nostrils flared. "You think shouting makes you guilty?"

Juror #11's voice stayed level. "I think shouting is what people do when they are trying to make others smaller so they do not have to be seen."

Juror #10 froze for a beat, as if the sentence had landed too close to something he kept sealed.

Juror #2's lips parted. For a moment she looked like she might speak, then she glanced at Juror #10's face and swallowed the words. Her silence was its own shift, her instinct to appease now redirected into self-protection.

Juror #8 sat with his hands flat on the table, gaze steady. He was watching Juror #10, but not the way a rival watches. The way a witness watches. Patient. Unavoidable.

Juror #10 seemed to feel that gaze like heat. He turned abruptly toward Juror #8. "You," he said, and the word was thick with accusation. "You're loving this."

Juror #8 didn't answer immediately. He let the silence stretch just long enough for it to feel like the room itself was listening.

"I'm not," he said finally. "But I'm not surprised."

Juror #10's laugh came out jagged. "Of course you're not surprised. Because you're behind it."

Juror #6 shifted, attention snapping back to Juror #8 for the first time since the chalkboard named Juror #10. Suspicion had been planted earlier; now it sprouted again because fear needed somewhere to go. "He ain't got a folder," Juror #6 said, not loudly, but enough to pull the room toward the idea again. "Still."

Juror #12 nodded too fast. "That's what I keep thinking," he whispered. "Everybody else has one."

Juror #2 shook her head, but weakly. "Maybe his is last."

Juror #4 spoke with an odd precision, like he was forcing himself not to sound afraid. "Or he's not part of the set," he said. "If the system is selecting participants, anomalies matter."

Juror #7's mouth tightened. "The set," he repeated, as if they were actors now, trapped in a script.

Juror #5's eyes narrowed at Juror #8. "Who are you?" he asked, voice hard. "Because I'm done getting surprised."

Juror #8 met his gaze. "I'm here," he said. "Like you are."

"That ain't an answer," Juror #5 snapped.

Juror #9 raised a trembling hand slightly, not to interrupt but to calm. "Do not let it redirect you," he murmured. “A courtroom always wants a spectacle. If you give it the wrong one, you still feed it.”

Juror #10 seized on that. “Listen to him,” he said quickly, eager. “He’s telling you. The old man knows. This is all a trick, and he’s in on it with him.” He pointed between Juror #9 and Juror #8 as if connecting dots on a paranoid map. “You two, whispering like priests.”

Juror #9’s eyes lifted slowly to Juror #10, and for the first time there was something hard in his expression. Not anger. Not fear. Disgust, quiet and absolute. “I would rather be a priest than a man who needs someone else to be guilty so he can breathe,” he said.

Juror #10’s face reddened. He looked around the table, searching for allies, and that was where the real shift happened. In the searching.

Juror #12 looked away first, eyes dropping to the table, refusing the invitation.

Juror #2 stared at her hands.

Juror #7’s gaze stayed on the chalkboard, as if the board were safer than choosing sides.

Juror #4 watched Juror #10 with cold assessment, the way he might once have watched a colleague unravel in a meeting: not intervening, just noting.

Juror #5 didn't look away. He held Juror #10's stare and gave a tiny shake of his head, almost a warning: not me.

Juror #6's expression was grim and closed. He wasn't aligning with anyone now. He was bracing.

Only Juror #1 shifted, the old reflex to manage people surfacing again. "We can't turn on each other," he said, voice strained. "If we do that, we're finished."

Juror #10 latched onto him immediately, relief flashing in his eyes. "Exactly," he said. "Tell them. Tell them we're not doing this."

Juror #1 hesitated, and the hesitation betrayed him. His gaze flicked, involuntarily, to the chalkboard. To JUROR #10 written under ORDER OF TESTIMONY. To the idea that the room had chosen its next target and that any defense of that target might be interpreted as obstruction.

Juror #10 saw the flicker and stiffened. "Don't," he hissed. "Don't you start backing away."

Juror #1's mouth opened, then closed. He looked suddenly exhausted, as if leadership had become a liability. "I'm not backing away," he said, but it sounded like he was trying to convince himself.

Juror #11 spoke quietly, and the sentence cut cleanly through the shifting loyalties. "In a jury room, alliances form around certainty," he said.

"And certainty has been taken from us. So now we will form alliances around fear."

The words landed, and everyone knew they were true.

Juror #10's breathing quickened. He looked at the table as if expecting the folder to appear in front of him any second, expecting the room to produce his name in paper the way it had produced everyone else's. His hands twitched, wanting something to hold, something to tear, something to throw.

Juror #8 watched him steadily. "Sit down," he said, not as a command, but as a simple statement of what had to happen if Juror #10 wanted to remain upright through what was coming.

Juror #10's eyes flashed. "You don't get to tell me to sit," he snapped.

"I'm not telling you," Juror #8 replied. "I'm telling you what you already know."

Juror #10's gaze swept the table one last time, hunting for someone to stand with him. The room gave him only faces, each one turned slightly away, each one calculating the cost of closeness.

That was the shift: the quiet understanding that standing beside someone could make you next.

Juror #10's knees bent as if his body had decided before his pride could. He lowered himself into his chair with a stiff, resentful motion, hands gripping the seat edges. The chair's legs scraped the tile, loud in the hush.

The scrape sounded, for a moment, like the opening of a file.

No one spoke.

The fluorescent hum pressed down. The metallic smell lingered, faint and patient. The chalkboard waited with Juror #10's name fixed in place, as if the room had pinned him there. And around him, the jurors settled into new, unstable configurations: not friends, not enemies, but clusters of avoidance and fragile trust, each person trying to decide who would matter when the next name appeared.

In the stillness, Juror #12 leaned slightly toward Juror #2 without looking at her, a tiny unconscious reach for human contact. Juror #2 didn't pull away, but she didn't lean back either. Juror #6's gaze stayed forward, refusing to align. Juror #5 sat rigid, jaw clenched, eyes alert for motion. Juror #11 remained upright, alone in his steadiness. Juror #1 looked smaller than before, caught between leadership and self-preservation.

Juror #8 remained exactly where he'd been, quiet and centered, as if the room's rearranging of loyalties was just another form of testimony.

The chalk did not move.

Not yet.

But the alliances had shifted, and the room, which understood pressure better than any of them, seemed to lean into the new weakness they'd created: the fact that they were no longer twelve people trapped together.

They were twelve people trapped together and afraid of each other.

Juror #10 sat rigidly in his chair, hands gripping the seat edges as if he could anchor himself to the only object in the room that still obeyed physics. His eyes stayed fixed on the chalkboard where his number had been written under ORDER OF TESTIMONY, and every few seconds his gaze flicked to the sealed door as if he expected it to swing open and prove this was all some elaborate mistake.

No one spoke.

The silence was not peace. It was a collective decision to stop offering each other anything that could be used. Even breathing felt like information.

Juror #12's small lean toward Juror #2 remained suspended between them, a gesture that had not been accepted or rejected, just left hanging like a hand held out in the dark. Juror #2 stared at her lap, fingers laced so tightly the skin around her knuckles had gone pale. She did not look at Juror #10, not because she didn't care, but because looking at him felt like stepping into the path of a moving blade.

Juror #1 cleared his throat, then seemed to regret the sound. His foreman instincts kept reaching for procedure and finding only emptiness. The badge on his suit caught the fluorescent light when he shifted, and the flash looked like a signal in a place that punished being noticed.

Juror #7's eyes were on the table edge, tracking its grain as if it contained a map. He had stopped trying to make jokes. Without that habit, his face looked strangely blank, like a man who had spent so long wearing a mask he'd forgotten what his features did without it.

Juror #4 watched everyone the way he watched data: searching for the rule beneath the chaos. But his gaze kept circling back to Juror #8, then away again, as if the anomaly at the center of the room had become a variable he couldn't model.

Juror #6 stared straight ahead, jaw set, shoulders heavy. His body looked ready to do something practical, anything practical, and the room offered nothing to lift, nothing to fix, nothing to blame on a broken part. Only words. Only choices.

Juror #5 sat with his arms crossed tight, but his eyes never stopped moving. They slid from Juror #10 to Juror #8, from the chalkboard to the knife near it, from the dead clock to the seam beneath the door. He didn't trust stillness anymore. Stillness was when the room moved.

Juror #9's hands trembled as they rested on the folder he'd closed so carefully. His gaze was lowered, but his attention felt wide, like an old animal listening for the sound that precedes a trap.

Juror #11 sat upright, spine straight, expression controlled. He looked less afraid than the others, not because he had less to fear, but because fear had stopped being new to him a long time ago. In him, it had turned into discipline.

Only Juror #8 remained unchanged. He did not shift or fidget. His hands lay flat on the table. His eyes moved slowly, taking them in one by one, not lingering in comfort or accusation, just bearing witness.

Juror #10's voice finally broke the silence, and it came out rougher than he intended. "So that's it?" He gave a short, bitter laugh that didn't carry. "Everybody's just going to sit there?"

No one answered.

He leaned forward slightly, and the legs of his chair squealed faintly against the tile. The sound made Juror #12 flinch, shoulders rising as if expecting a slap.

Juror #10 looked around, hunting for a face that would meet his. "You," he said, pointing at Juror #1 with an accusing certainty that felt rehearsed. "You're the foreman. Do something."

Juror #1's mouth opened. He seemed to consider three different tones: managerial authority, human sympathy, raw panic. None of them worked in his throat. "I don't know what to do," he admitted, and the honesty stripped the last illusion from the badge on his lapel.

Juror #10's expression twisted. "Of course you don't," he snapped, then swung his gaze toward Juror #11 as if searching for a new target. "And you. Mister Justice. Mister Rules. Say something."

Juror #11 looked at him steadily. "What do you want me to say?" he asked. His voice was quiet, but it carried. "That you are not next? You are."

Juror #10's jaw clenched. "You don't know that."

Juror #11 tilted his head slightly, almost sad. "It wrote your number," he said. "It does not write in order to negotiate."

That landed, and the room seemed to tighten around it. The fluorescent hum deepened a fraction, the way it did when a confession approached, like the lights were leaning closer.

Juror #10's eyes flicked to the table in front of him, expecting the brown folder to appear with that soft thud, expecting the label to turn him into a category.

Nothing appeared.

The absence was worse.

Juror #4 noticed it too. His gaze sharpened, and his voice came out controlled. "It's delaying," he said quietly. "It wants him to sit with anticipation."

Juror #7 swallowed, throat bobbing. "Or it wants us to," he murmured.

Juror #2's breath hitched softly as if she'd been holding it too long. Her eyes drifted to the chalkboard and the ledger of marks beneath JUROR. Eight lines. Eight admissions. The chalk had always moved after truth. What happened when truth was withheld?

Juror #5 shifted, a small adjustment, but it created distance. He angled his chair a few degrees away from Juror #10, an instinctive motion like stepping back from someone about to fall. Juror #12 saw it and did the same, though more subtly, pulling his knees in and turning his torso toward Juror #2 without looking at her.

The room registered the movement.

A faint sound rose behind the walls again, that indistinct murmur like a crowd beyond plaster. It wasn't loud. It didn't need to be. It threaded through the silence and made it feel occupied, as if they were no longer alone. As if an unseen gallery had settled in to watch.

Juror #10's eyes widened. He turned his head sharply, searching for a speaker, a vent, a crack. "You hear that?" he demanded.

Juror #6 nodded once, grim. "Yeah."

Juror #10's voice went higher, edged with anger that couldn't find a place to land. "So why aren't you doing anything? You're a big guy. Break the damn door down."

Juror #6's stare hardened. "I tried the handle," he said. "It didn't move. You want me to throw my shoulder into it and crack my collarbone for nothing?"

"For nothing?" Juror #10 barked. "It's not nothing. It's—" He stopped, because he couldn't say it without making it real.

Juror #8 spoke softly, and the calm in his voice made Juror #10 turn on him immediately. "Isolation works when people believe they are alone," Juror #8 said, looking around the table, not just at Juror #10. "We're not alone in here. But it wants us to feel like we are."

Juror #4's gaze flicked to him. "Who's 'it'?" he asked, and there was a sharpness to the question that hadn't been there earlier. "The room? The court? You?"

Juror #8 met his eyes without flinching. "Call it whatever helps you sleep," he said. "But it's using the same method every time. Separate. Pressure. Confession."

Juror #9's voice came low, exhausted. "That is how governments do it," he murmured. "That is how interrogations do it. You remove community. You make the accused believe no one will stand beside them."

Juror #10 snapped, "I'm not accused of anything."

The words came out too fast, too loud, and the murmur behind the walls changed.

For a moment, it seemed to organize around him. Not into words he could clearly understand, but into a directed attention. Juror #10's head jerked slightly, as if a sound had reached him that hadn't reached the others.

He blinked hard. "Stop," he muttered, then louder, "Stop it."

Juror #12 stared at him, eyes wide. "What?" he whispered.

Juror #10 didn't answer immediately. His gaze darted. His throat worked. "I heard…" He stopped, lips thinning. "Nothing."

Juror #11 watched him closely. "You heard something," he said.

Juror #10's face flushed. "No I didn't."

Juror #11 didn't look away. "This room does not only move chalk," he said quietly. "It moves inside people too."

Juror #10's hands tightened on the chair edges again. He looked around the table, and the paranoia that had been a general fog became something more focused: he began to measure the distance between himself and everyone else.

They had all shifted away. Not dramatically. Not with overt cruelty. But enough.

Enough that he could feel it.

Juror #10's gaze landed on Juror #1. "You," he said, voice lower now, sharpened. "You're all waiting for me to go down so you can feel better."

Juror #1 flinched. "That's not—"

"It is," Juror #10 cut in. "You all confessed, and now you're sitting there like you're cleansed. Like you paid your fee. And I'm the last bad one who makes you look good."

Juror #2 whispered, barely audible, "No one looks good."

Juror #10's head snapped toward her. "You shut up," he said, and the reflexive cruelty came out like a knife flicking open. "You killed someone with paperwork and you want to whisper about morals?"

Juror #2 recoiled as if struck. Juror #12's body tightened, and for the first time his half-reach toward her became protective; he leaned a fraction closer, shoulders angling toward Juror #10. It was a small alliance, fragile and instinctive, and it made Juror #10's eyes narrow.

"There," Juror #10 said, almost triumphant. "You see? You're picking sides."

Juror #5's voice came low and flat. "We're not picking sides," he said. "We're backing away from you."

The sentence landed with a dull finality. It was not meant to be a wound, but it became one.

Juror #10 stared at Juror #5 as if he couldn't believe the honesty. Then he looked at Juror #6, then Juror #7, then Juror #4. None of them offered him anything. Not even anger. Especially not solidarity.

The room seemed to reward the fracture.

The air temperature shifted, subtly but unmistakably, as if a vent had changed setting. Cold brushed the back of Juror #10's neck, making the hairs rise. At the same time, the space around him felt a fraction larger, like the room had created an invisible perimeter. Not walls, not barriers, just an absence of human closeness that suddenly had weight.

Juror #10 swallowed hard. “You’re doing this,” he said, but the accusation no longer had a clear target. He gestured vaguely, encompassing the table, the chalkboard, the walls. “You’re all doing this to me.”

Juror #9’s voice came soft, and there was no comfort in it. “No,” he said. “You are doing what you have always done. You are making enemies so you do not have to face yourself.”

Juror #10’s lips curled. “And what do you know about facing yourself?”

Juror #9 didn’t blink. “I know what it costs,” he replied.

Another sound rose then, small and distinct: the faint click of chalk being set down.

All heads turned toward the chalkboard.

Nothing new had been written. ORDER OF TESTIMONY remained. JUROR #10 sat there like a finger pointing.

But on the ledge beneath the board, a single piece of chalk lay now, bright white against the dark tray. A second piece rested beside it, as if someone had placed tools within reach.

Juror #1 stared. “It wants us to write,” he whispered.

Juror #4's face tightened. "No," he said quietly. "It wants someone to."

Juror #10 looked at the chalk as if it were a weapon offered to him. His breathing quickened. He glanced around, and the distance between chairs felt wider than before. It wasn't just that they'd shifted away. It was that the room had made space for his fear to echo.

Juror #8's voice came gently, and for the first time it sounded almost like pity, though it carried no softness of outcome. "This is the part where you feel alone," he said. "And you decide what you are willing to say to stop feeling it."

Juror #10's eyes flicked to him, hatred and desperation mingled. "I'm not giving it anything," he hissed. "I'm not confessing to something I didn't do."

Juror #11's gaze stayed steady. "Then tell the truth of what you did," he said. "Or the room will tell it for you."

Juror #10's mouth opened to spit back an insult, but the murmur behind the walls swelled again, and this time it seemed to shape itself closer to language. Not a full sentence. Not yet. Just fragments, like the beginning of testimony being read aloud.

A name he didn't want to hear.

A place he didn't want to remember.

Juror #10 jerked as if the sound had touched his skin. His hands left the chair edges and flew to the table, palms splayed. He looked around wildly, and for a moment the mask of loud certainty fell away completely, revealing something small and terrified beneath.

"No," he whispered, and the word was not defiance now. It was a plea.

No one moved closer.

No one reached out.

Whatever alliances had existed were gone, replaced by the simplest survival instinct the room had successfully planted in them: stay distant, or be pulled in.

Juror #10 sat in that widened space at the table, isolated not by physical walls but by the collective recoil of people who had learned how dangerous proximity could be.

The chalkboard did not write his folder into existence. It didn't need to.

It had written his number.

And now it waited, patient as a judge, for the sound of him breaking.

Chapter 11

Justice or Punishment?

Juror #10 sat hunched forward, palms spread on the table, eyes fixed on the two pieces of chalk on the tray like they were a dare. The murmur behind the walls thickened and thinned in slow waves, as if the room were breathing through other people's mouths. It wasn't a language the others could understand, not fully. But everyone could feel its intent: it wanted something spoken.

Juror #12 kept his shoulders angled toward Juror #2, not touching her, but close enough that the gesture meant what it meant. Juror #2's lips were pressed so tightly together the skin around them had gone white.

Juror #8 broke the silence without raising his voice. "What do you think this is?" he asked, gaze traveling the table. "Justice?"

Juror #4's eyes snapped to him, then to the chalkboard. ORDER OF TESTIMONY. JUROR #10. "It's coercion," he said. "It's not due process. There's no counsel, no evidence standards, no ability to challenge the record. It's extracting confessions under pressure."

Juror #9 gave a quiet, rasping breath. "And yet," he said, "we are speaking truths we have never spoken."

Juror #6 shifted in his chair, heavy and wary. "Truth don't make it justice," he muttered. "Truth can be a beating too."

Juror #7 stared at his hands, as if checking they were still his. "Maybe that's the whole point," he said. "Maybe justice feels like a beating when you deserve it."

Juror #1 lifted his head at that, the foreman in him flaring weakly. "No one deserves this," he said. The words sounded like policy, like a sign on a wall. "This is… abnormal. Unlawful. We are being detained."

Juror #5 let out a low laugh with no humor in it. "Unlawful," he echoed. "That word still matter in here?"

Juror #11's voice came calm but taut, like rope pulled tight. "In my country," he said, "the law was whatever men with rifles said it was. In this country, the law is written on paper and pretends it is separate from power." His eyes flicked to the folders stacked in front of some of them, to the clean margins. "Both can be used to hide a knife."

The knife near the chalkboard sat untouched, a dark gleam in fluorescent light. It felt less like a weapon and more like a reminder of the boy's trial, the one they had abandoned without meaning to. The case that had brought them here. The father's body. The story the state had told.

Juror #8's gaze settled on the knife for a moment, then returned to the group. "Justice is supposed to be impartial," he said. "It's supposed to be measured. It's supposed to be about what happened, and what can be proved, not what a person feels they deserve."

Juror #4 nodded sharply, grateful for anything that resembled structure. "Exactly. Punishment without process is just violence with a narrative."

Juror #9's fingers tightened on the edge of his closed folder. "And process without truth is violence with paperwork," he said softly.

That stopped Juror #4 for a beat. The analyst's mouth opened, then shut. He looked at the chalkboard tally beneath JUROR, the uneven marks that had become their real ledger. Eight. The room had not cared about titles or education or how well someone could argue. It had cared about consequences.

Juror #2 finally spoke, voice small but clear enough to cut. "Is it… punishment then?" Her eyes were on Juror #10, but she did not look directly at his face, as if seeing his fear too clearly might make it contagious. "Is it punishing us for what we did?"

Juror #6 rubbed a hand over his jaw. "Feels like it," he said. "Feels like somebody decided we don't get to move on."

Juror #7's throat bobbed as he swallowed. "Maybe we don't," he whispered.

Juror #1's hands clenched on the tabletop. "We're not criminals," he insisted, but the word sounded thin. His badge glinted when he shifted, a flash that felt like mockery. "Some of these things… they weren't crimes."

Juror #5 turned toward him with a tired, sharp look. "You keep saying that like it's magic," he said. "Like if it ain't on a charge sheet, it don't count."

Juror #1's jaw tightened. "It matters," he said. "It has to matter. Otherwise we're living in—" he gestured at the room, the locked door, the stopped clock, "this."

Juror #9 answered him gently, and that gentleness was its own kind of cruelty. "Perhaps we have always lived in this," he said. "Only the walls were not visible."

The murmur behind the plaster rose, then settled. Juror #10 flinched as if the sound had teeth. His eyes darted to the corners of the room, to the vents, searching for the source like a man searching for the face of a judge who refuses to appear.

Juror #11 watched him with something like grim recognition. "The question," Juror #11 said, "is not what this is called. The question is whether it is deserved."

Juror #12 made a small sound in his throat, a half-laugh of disbelief that died immediately. "Deserved?" he repeated. "No. No, I don't… I don't believe in that." He looked at Juror #2 as if she might lend him certainty. "People make mistakes."

Juror #2 did not answer. She had said that once, in another life, in another room, and a patient had died anyway.

Juror #8's eyes moved slowly across them. "If a person deserves punishment," he asked, "who decides? A court? A room? The people they harmed? The people who lived?"

Juror #4's voice snapped back into its preferred register, controlled and crisp. "The state decides, through a process. Anything else is vigilantism."

Juror #5 leaned forward, elbows on the table, expression hard. "The state decided my friend didn't matter," he said. The words came out flat, like a fact he'd carried too long. "State decided he was just another body on another street. Nobody came asking me questions. Nobody cared I ran. Nobody cared he bled out." He looked around, eyes shining with anger that wasn't aimed at any one person. "So don't talk to me like the process is holy."

Juror #6 nodded once, slow, as if he couldn't deny that. "Process cared enough to cover for me," he said. "Process cared enough to write a story that saved the company. That's what it does. It makes it neat."

Juror #7's voice was small. "My process was my uncle's friend," he murmured. "It was a lawyer who told me which words to swallow and which ones to say." He touched his mouth, as if he could still taste the lies.

Juror #1 looked as if someone had hollowed him out. "So what," he said, "we just accept this? We accept being… tried by a room? By chalk and folders?"

Juror #9's gaze lifted, weary and ancient. "You accepted a boy being tried by strangers," he said. "By evidence you did not gather. By a knife you did not hold. By testimony filtered through your own prejudices and impatience." He paused, then added softly, "We all did."

Juror #3, who had been quiet for too long, finally spoke. His voice was rough, like it had been scraped against something. "My son deserved something," he said. Everyone turned toward him. His eyes were unfocused, staring past the table, past the walls. "He deserved a father who didn't make him feel like the world was a trap."

No one answered that. There were no arguments left that didn't feel obscene.

Juror #11 broke the silence that followed. "Justice," he said carefully, "is not the same as revenge. But people confuse them when pain is involved." His eyes flicked toward the chalkboard and its tally. "And when the people who caused pain are never made to look at it, they begin to believe they are exempt."

Juror #4's gaze narrowed. "So you think this is justice," he said, and there was accusation in it, as if agreeing would make Juror #11 complicit with the room.

Juror #11 did not flinch. "I think it is judgment," he replied. "I do not know if it is justice."

Juror #12 shook his head rapidly, as if the motion could dislodge the idea. "But judgment without mercy is just cruelty," he said. "Isn't it?"

Juror #9's mouth trembled. "Mercy," he echoed. "A beautiful word. It is the word we wish someone had used on us." He looked down at his closed folder, at the name Marek that had lived inside it. "But mercy is also the word we used to excuse ourselves."

Juror #8 leaned back slightly, the first visible shift in him in a while. "Maybe that's why it feels wrong," he said. "Because it's stripping away the mercy we granted ourselves."

Juror #1's breath hitched. "We're not monsters," he said, but there was no conviction left in it. "We're… people."

Juror #5 gave him a long look. "People kill," he said. "That's what we learned in here."

The murmur rose again, and this time several of them heard something inside it that wasn't just sound. A wordless pressure, a suggestion of names, of moments. Juror #10's face tightened, and he squeezed his eyes shut as if to stop images from arriving.

Juror #8 watched him, then spoke to the table at large. "If this is punishment," he said, "what is it trying to punish? The act? The lie? The fact that we never paid for it?"

Juror #6's voice came low. "Maybe it's punishing the dodge," he said. "The way we all found a way to live with it. Blame somebody else. Hide behind a form. Call it an accident. Call it war. Call it business."

Juror #4's eyes flashed. "You're making everything the same," he said. "They're not the same."

Juror #9 looked up. "Do you want them to be different because that is true," he asked, "or because difference is a ladder you can climb to feel higher than the rest of us?"

Juror #4 went still. The question landed in the space where his categories used to protect him.

Juror #2's voice shook. "If we deserve anything," she whispered, "is it this? Fear? Shame? A room that won't let us leave until we say it?"

Juror #11 answered her, quiet. "Perhaps what we deserve is not decided by us," he said. "That is why justice exists. Because people cannot be trusted to weigh their own sins."

Juror #7 let out a thin breath. "And what if justice doesn't exist?" he asked. "What if all there is, is… this room?"

The fluorescent hum seemed to deepen in response, like the room acknowledging being named.

Juror #8's gaze moved again to the chalk pieces waiting on the tray. "Whatever this is," he said, "it keeps pushing toward the same end. Admission. Ownership. A verdict."

Juror #1 swallowed hard. "A verdict on what?" he whispered.

Juror #9's eyes lifted to the chalkboard tally, the blunt marks that had replaced their civic purpose. "On whether we think guilt is a legal category," he said softly, "or a human one."

Juror #10 made a strangled sound, sudden and involuntary, like someone being pulled underwater. His hands clawed at the table edge. He stared at the air in front of him, pupils blown wide.

Juror #12's voice came out in a whisper. "He's hearing it again."

Juror #11's jaw tightened. "It is not waiting anymore," he said.

Juror #8 didn't move toward Juror #10. He didn't touch him. He only spoke, and his voice was steady in a way that made the words feel inevitable. "This is the debate," he said to the room, not just to the man breaking. "Justice or punishment. Deserved fate or random cruelty." His eyes held on Juror #10's face, then lifted to the others. "But the moment it writes your number, the debate becomes a mirror. You stop arguing philosophy and start bargaining for yourself."

The murmur behind the walls tightened into something almost articulate, and Juror #10 squeezed his eyes shut as if the sound had become a blade pressing at his ear.

"No," he whispered, voice cracking. "No, I didn't… I didn't…"

Juror #6's hands flexed against the table, but he stayed seated. Juror #5's jaw clenched. Juror #2 made a small, broken sound and covered her mouth.

Juror #1 stared, unable to decide whether looking away was cowardice or self-preservation.

Juror #9 spoke softly, not to accuse, but to name what all of them felt in their bones now. "It is not asking whether we believe in deserved fate," he said. "It is making us live inside the question until we cannot breathe around it."

Juror #10's eyes snapped open, wild with terror and rage. He looked at the chalk on the tray, then at the chalkboard, then at the faces turned away from him.

And in the widened space of his isolation, with the room holding its breath like a judge waiting for an answer, the question of justice stopped being abstract.

It became immediate.

What happens to a person when the world finally decides they deserve to pay?

Juror #10's eyes darted from the chalk on the tray to the chalkboard and back again, as if the objects had swapped meaning while he wasn't looking. His mouth moved without sound. His palms were slick on the tabletop.

The murmur behind the walls had tightened into something with edges. Not words, not quite. More like the beginning of words, the way a thought forms before you decide to say it.

He pressed his hands harder against the wood, as if the table could ground him. "No," he said again, but it wasn't aimed at the room or the others. It was aimed at whatever had begun crawling up from inside him.

Juror #8 watched him steadily. "You can keep fighting the moment," he said, voice even, "or you can name it."

Juror #10's head snapped toward him. Rage flared, quick and familiar, the old reflex that had always saved him from looking too long at himself. "Name what?" he barked. "You want a story? You want me to cry? You want me to say I'm sorry so you all feel better?"

No one answered. The silence was not agreement or refusal. It was waiting.

The fluorescent hum seemed to shift lower, as if the lights had leaned in.

Juror #10's gaze flicked toward the others, searching again for an ally, for any face that would mirror his outrage and turn this back into a fight. He found only distance. The small protective angle of Juror #12's shoulders toward Juror #2. Juror #5's hard, watchful stare. Juror #6's grim stillness. Juror #1's exhausted uncertainty. Juror #4's cold attention, like a lens.

Juror #11 sat upright, hands folded, eyes fixed on Juror #10 without hatred. That, more than anything, made Juror #10's skin crawl. He preferred hatred. Hatred meant the other person was guilty too.

Juror #10's breath hitched. "Stop looking at me like that," he snapped at Juror #11.

Juror #11 didn't blink. "Like what?" he asked quietly.

"Like I'm…" Juror #10's voice faltered. He swallowed and tried again, louder. "Like I'm the worst thing in here."

Juror #9's voice came soft, weary. "No," he said. "Only like you are next."

Juror #10 flinched as if the word next had physical force.

Then the table made its sound.

Not loud. Not dramatic. A soft, deliberate thud placed directly in front of Juror #10, as if someone had set down a file at the exact center of his fear.

The brown folder sat perfectly aligned with the table edge.

JUROR #10 – BIGOT.

The label was simple. Too simple. It didn't accuse him of a specific act. It didn't need to. It named the thing he'd always tried to disguise as blunt honesty, as common sense, as "just telling it like it is."

Juror #10 stared at the folder as if it might bite him.

Juror #7 let out a thin, involuntary breath. Not a laugh. Not a joke. Just the sound of a man watching a trap finally close.

Juror #12 whispered, "Oh God."

Juror #10's fingers hovered above the flap. He didn't touch it. He looked around, eyes bright with a frantic kind of logic. "That's not evidence," he said, voice cracking at the edges. "That's a label. Anyone can write a label."

Juror #4's mouth tightened. "Open it," he said. His voice held no sympathy, but it held something else: the sterile recognition of a procedure that would happen whether they wanted it to or not.

Juror #10 shook his head hard. "No. No, I'm not—" He swallowed. The murmur behind the walls rose slightly, like a crowd sensing hesitation and leaning forward. Juror #10 pressed his palms against his ears for a second, then dropped them as if the act had shamed him.

Juror #8 didn't raise his voice. "You've demanded everyone else speak plainly," he said. "Now you can do the same."

Juror #10's eyes flashed. "Don't you quote me," he hissed.

Juror #8 only held the gaze. "Then don't become the kind of man who needs quotes to hide behind," he replied.

Juror #10's jaw worked. His hand jerked toward the folder, then stopped. He looked at it again, breathing fast. The word BIGOT seemed to pulse with the fluorescent light.

He seized the flap and yanked it open.

Paper rasped. Cream-colored. Typed. The same clean margins that had turned all of them into case studies.

Juror #10's eyes moved across the first lines.

His face changed in slow increments. First anger, then confusion, then the sudden loss of color that comes when a person recognizes a name they've tried not to carry.

Juror #2's voice came out small. "What is it?"

Juror #10 swallowed. His throat bobbed once, hard. "It's… a statement," he said. His voice was lower now, stripped of performance. "A witness statement."

Juror #9's eyes narrowed slightly. "For what case?"

Juror #10's gaze stayed fixed on the page, as if looking up would let the room see the exact moment the lie had been built. “Years ago,” he whispered. “Not… not that long. Ten, maybe.”

Juror #6’s voice came blunt. “Read it.”

Juror #10’s lips peeled back in a grimace. “No.”

The murmur behind the walls tightened again, and this time Juror #10 jerked as if he’d been struck by a sound only he could hear. He blinked rapidly, breath stuttering.

Juror #11 watched him, expression unchanged. “It will not stop,” Juror #11 said quietly. “Not until you stop fighting the truth with noise.”

Juror #10’s head snapped up. “You don’t get to talk,” he spat, and the old poison in his voice flared like a match. “Not you.”

Juror #11’s eyes did not harden. They stayed steady. “I am not talking,” he said. “I am listening.”

That made Juror #10’s hands tremble against the folder. He looked down again.

The paper was merciless. Not because it was cruel, but because it was exact.

Juror #10’s voice came out uneven. “It says I identified him,” he whispered.

Juror #12 frowned. “Identified who?”

Juror #10 swallowed again. “A man,” he said. “A guy from a lineup.”

Juror #7's face tightened. "A crime," he murmured.

Juror #10's eyes flicked along the lines like they were pulling him forward by force. "A robbery," he said. "Outside a store. A woman got hurt. It was on the news. Everybody was talking about it."

Juror #1 leaned forward slightly, foreman instincts trying to parse facts. "You were a witness."

Juror #10's mouth twisted. "Yeah," he said, and then the word fell apart under its own weight. "Yeah, I was a witness."

Juror #9's voice came soft. "And?"

Juror #10's fingers tightened on the folder. The paper bent under them. "And they had a suspect," he said. "An immigrant. New in town. Wrong place, wrong time, whatever. He fit the… he fit what people said it would be."

Juror #2's eyes widened. "You didn't see him," she whispered.

Juror #10's head snapped up, furious. "I saw someone," he barked. "I saw a guy run. I saw a jacket. A hood. I saw—"

Juror #8's voice cut through the flailing. "You saw enough to be useful," he said. "Not enough to be certain."

Juror #10's gaze darted back to the page. His voice dropped, cracked. "They asked me questions," he said. "The cops. They said, 'You saw him, right?' They said, 'You can help us put him away.' They told me he'd done things before. They said people like him don't stop unless you make them stop."

Juror #6's jaw tightened. "And you believed them."

Juror #10 shook his head once, a sharp denial that didn't convince anyone. "I wanted it to be him," he whispered.

The sentence landed heavily, because it was the first truly honest thing he'd said.

Juror #7 stared at him, horrified. Juror #12's mouth parted, and no sound came out.

Juror #4 leaned forward slightly, voice precise. "You gave a false identification," he said.

Juror #10 looked up, eyes wild. "I didn't think it was false," he said too fast. "I thought… I thought I was helping. I thought I was doing what you're supposed to do. I thought I was keeping my neighborhood safe."

Juror #9's voice came, gentle and brutal. "And when you were told you were wrong?"

Juror #10 froze.

The room waited in that freeze. Even the murmur behind the walls seemed to pause, like it wanted to hear this part in his own words.

Juror #10's eyes slid back to the paper. His lips moved silently as he read a line he didn't want to say out loud.

Juror #8 spoke softly. "When did you know?"

Juror #10's shoulders rose and fell in a shallow breath. "Later," he whispered. "Months later. His lawyer came around asking questions. Somebody showed me a picture. They said another guy confessed to something similar in another county. They said the timeline didn't match."

Juror #2's hand flew to her mouth. "You could've fixed it," she breathed, as if the idea itself hurt.

Juror #10's voice turned raw, defensive. "You don't just 'fix' it," he snapped, then faltered. His eyes glistened, and it wasn't remorse yet. It was fear of being seen clearly. "I'd already signed it. I'd already said it in court."

Juror #1's face drained. "You testified," he said.

Juror #10 nodded once, small and sick. "I pointed at him," he whispered. "I sat there and I pointed, and everybody watched me like I was doing a good thing."

Juror #9's eyes closed briefly. "And when you realized you may have condemned an innocent man—"

"I didn't do anything," Juror #10 said, and the words came out like a confession dragged through broken teeth. "I didn't go back. I didn't call anyone. I didn't tell the lawyer who came to my door. I told him I didn't want to get involved."

Juror #6's voice was low. "Because you were involved."

Juror #10's face twisted. "Because I didn't want to be wrong," he whispered. He looked down at the folder again as if it contained a different version of him. It didn't. "Because if I admitted it, then I was the one who did it. I was the one who—" His voice caught. He swallowed hard, eyes shining now. "I was the one who put him there."

Juror #11's expression shifted by a fraction, the first visible reaction he'd shown. Not triumph. Pain, controlled.

Juror #8's voice stayed even. "How long did he serve?" he asked.

Juror #10 stared at the page. His lips moved. Then he spoke, and the number came out flat, like a sentence. "Seven years," he whispered.

Juror #12 made a small choking sound.

Juror #2's eyes brimmed. "Seven years," she echoed, and the repetition was pure horror.

Juror #10 lifted his head, suddenly desperate. "I didn't put handcuffs on him," he said. "I didn't sentence him. I didn't—"

Juror #9 cut in softly. "You gave them what they needed," he said. "A clean story. A finger pointing the right way. You gave the room permission to stop looking."

Juror #10's mouth trembled. "He wasn't from here," he whispered, and the ugliness of the phrase showed him even as he said it. "People already hated him. They wanted a reason. I gave them one."

The air felt colder around the table, not because the vent had changed, but because a different kind of truth had entered: not an accident, not a mistake, not a moment of panic, but a choice built from contempt.

Juror #5's eyes were hard. "So that's your safety," he said. "You made somebody else pay so you could feel like you belonged."

Juror #10's face contorted. "I thought he was guilty," he whispered.

Juror #8 didn't raise his voice. "And when you knew he might not be?"

Juror #10's eyes slid toward Juror #11, and for a second the hatred tried to rise again and couldn't find oxygen. What surfaced instead was shame so sharp it looked like anger.

“I let him stay,” Juror #10 whispered. “Because it was easier than admitting what I am.”

The chalk scraped behind them.

One short, dry stroke added beneath JUROR on the tally board. Another truth recorded. Another mark that did not differentiate between kinds of killing, only that a life had been ruined and the ruin had been allowed.

Juror #10 stared at the new mark as if it had carved itself into his skin. His breath came in shallow pulls. “This isn’t justice,” he said hoarsely. “This is… humiliation.”

Juror #9 looked at him with tired clarity. “Humiliation is what pride calls consequence,” he murmured.

Juror #11’s hands tightened together once, then relaxed. He spoke without heat, and the lack of heat made the words heavier. “Do you remember his name?” he asked.

Juror #10 blinked rapidly. His mouth opened. Closed. His gaze dropped to the page again, and his lips moved as he searched the typed lines for the one detail that would make it human.

When he said the name aloud, it was quiet, almost swallowed, as if he hoped the sound would disappear before it touched anyone.

Juror #11's eyes closed for a moment. When he opened them again, his gaze remained fixed on Juror #10, steady and wounded.

On the chalkboard, beneath ORDER OF TESTIMONY, the second blank line filled in with slow certainty.

JUROR #11.

Juror #12 made a soft sound of dread.

Juror #10 didn't look at the board. He sat staring at the open folder, breathing hard, his downfall complete not because he had been forced to speak, but because the room had made him speak plainly enough that even he could hear himself.

Juror #8's gaze shifted from Juror #10 to Juror #11. "It's your turn," he said quietly.

Juror #11 did not move. He only looked at the chalkboard where his number now waited, and the steadiness in him tightened into something else: the posture of a man who knows the room is about to ask him for the one thing he has survived by refusing to give.

Not a defense.

A truth.

Juror #11 did not move.

The room held its breath around him, as if waiting to see whether steadiness could survive being named.

On the chalkboard, beneath ORDER OF TESTIMONY, the words JUROR #11 sat like a summons. Juror #10 was still staring at his open folder, the label BIGOT turned toward him like a mirror he could not shatter. The new tally mark beneath JUROR looked fresh, almost wet, though it was only chalk.

Juror #11's hands rested on the table, fingers interlaced, knuckles pale. His posture remained upright, but something in his face had tightened, as if he were holding back a physical reaction. His eyes were fixed on the board, not blinking.

Juror #12 whispered, "He hasn't even gotten a folder yet," and immediately regretted speaking, shrinking back into his chair as if sound itself might be punished.

Juror #4 leaned forward slightly, the analyst's need for sequence scraping against fear. "It always provides documentation," he murmured. "It will."

Juror #9's voice came low, a tired warning. "Sometimes," he said, "the paper is only there to make the confession feel official."

Juror #8 watched Juror #11 with patient attention. "You don't have to wait for it," he said softly. "You can speak without being forced."

Juror #11's gaze shifted at last. It moved from the chalkboard to Juror #8, then to the others, as if taking inventory of witnesses. When he spoke, his voice was calm, but the calm was thin, stretched tight over something deeper.

"You want to know what I am ashamed of," he said. It was not a question.

Juror #6 shifted, heavy in his chair. "Room wants it," he muttered. "Ain't about what we want anymore."

Juror #11 nodded once, minimal. "Yes," he said. "It wants the part we keep hidden even from ourselves."

The murmur behind the walls stirred, a soft movement like bodies settling in seats. It did not become words. It did not need to. It felt like expectation.

Then the table made its familiar sound.

A soft, precise thud, placed with care.

The brown folder appeared in front of Juror #11, aligned neatly with the edge of the table as if measured. The label was crisp, typed in the same merciless font.

JUROR #11 – IMMIGRANT.

The word should have been neutral, a fact, a biography. In the sealed room it landed like a verdict, reducing him to the thing everyone in the courthouse would notice first, the thing they would use to decide whether his voice belonged here.

Juror #11 looked at the label for a long moment. His expression did not change, but his throat moved as he swallowed.

Juror #10 let out a strained, bitter sound, somewhere between a laugh and a cough. “Of course,” he muttered, staring at his own hands now as if they no longer felt like his. “Of course that’s what it calls you.”

Juror #11 did not look at him. His fingertips touched the folder lightly, like checking whether something was real.

Juror #2 spoke before she could stop herself, voice small. “Are you… are you going to open it?”

Juror #11’s eyes lifted to her for the first time. There was no cruelty in his gaze. Only a quiet exhaustion, as if he had been opening this folder in his head for years.

“I already have,” he said.

He opened the flap with slow care. The dry sound of paper sliding against paper made Juror #12 flinch.

Juror #7's eyes fixed on the page as if he could read the words from across the table and spare himself the waiting.

Juror #11 stared down at the first sheet. His eyes moved across the lines, and for a second the fluorescent hum seemed to deepen, pressing into the silence as if the room were leaning closer to listen.

When he began to speak, his voice remained controlled, but the words were stripped of ornament. He spoke like someone reciting facts that could not be softened without turning them into lies.

"It is not about coming here," he said. "Not the paperwork. Not the border. Not the job I took when no one else would hire me." He paused, eyes still on the page. "It is about leaving."

Juror #9's hands trembled on the table edge. He did not interrupt. He understood the weight of that verb.

Juror #11 continued. "There was a war," he said, and the sentence did not ask for sympathy. It offered context the way a file offers a date. "Not the same as his," he nodded once toward Juror #9 without looking up, "but the same in what it does to people. It turns ordinary choices into life and death, and then it tells you later that you were always what you became."

Juror #6's jaw tightened. Juror #5 sat very still, eyes narrowed, listening with the sharpness of someone who had learned that the worst parts of a story are often spoken quietly.

Juror #11's finger traced a line on the paper as if anchoring himself to it. "I had a brother," he said. "Older. He was brave. He thought bravery was a duty. He thought if you did not stand, you were already dead."

Juror #7 swallowed. His hands tightened on the table edge. He looked like a man watching a door open onto a memory he did not want.

Juror #11's voice remained even, but something in it began to thin, like a fabric wearing through. "We had a plan," he said. "To get out. To cross into another country. There were routes, people who could guide you. It was dangerous, but staying was dangerous too." He paused. "I did not go alone."

Juror #2's eyes glistened. She was staring at him now, fully, as if afraid that looking away would be another kind of abandonment.

Juror #11 lifted his eyes from the paper for a moment. "My brother brought his wife," he said. "And their children. Two. One was a girl who carried a stuffed animal that was missing an eye. She kept asking whether the bear would need papers." His mouth twitched once, not humor, something broken by tenderness. "We told her no."

The room felt colder, as if the story itself lowered the temperature.

Juror #11 looked down again. "We traveled at night," he said. "We avoided roads. We hid in a barn once, under hay, while men with dogs walked outside. We could hear the dogs breathing. The children did not cry. Their mother covered their mouths when they trembled."

Juror #12's lips parted. He did not speak. His eyes were wide and wet.

Juror #11's voice tightened slightly on the next words. "We reached a river," he said. "Not wide, but fast. There were stones you could step on if you knew where they were. The guide pointed, told us to follow exactly. No lights. No talking."

Juror #9 closed his eyes briefly, like he was seeing another stairwell, another disappearing.

Juror #11 swallowed. "Halfway across," he said, "the dogs began barking behind us."

The murmur behind the walls swelled, not into words, but into a pressure that seemed to lean over their shoulders, urging the story forward.

Juror #11 continued, and now the control in his voice sounded less like composure and more like a man forcing himself not to run from his own sentence. "The guide said hurry," he said. "My brother picked up the little boy. His wife held the girl's hand. The water was up to their knees, then their thighs. The stones were slippery."

He paused. His fingers tightened on the page until the paper bent.

"Someone fell," he said.

Juror #6 exhaled through his nose, slow and heavy. Juror #5's jaw clenched as if bracing for impact.

Juror #11's eyes did not lift. "It was the wife," he said. "She slipped. The current pulled her sideways. She grabbed for my brother. The girl screamed then, just once, a sharp sound like a bird's cry. My brother tried to hold both the child and his wife, and the water took them."

Juror #2 made a small, strangled sound and pressed her knuckles to her lips.

Juror #11's voice went quieter, not softer. Quieter in the way a room goes quiet when someone dies and everyone waits to see who will speak first.

"My brother shouted my name," he said. "He told me to take the boy. He shoved the child toward me."

Juror #8 did not move. He watched with the same still attention he had given every confession, but his eyes seemed darker now, as if he knew what the next choice would be before it was spoken.

Juror #11's throat worked. "I grabbed him," he said. "The boy. He was soaked. He was heavy in my arms. He was reaching backward, crying for his mother."

Juror #12 whispered, "Did you save him?"

Juror #11's head lifted slightly at that, and the look he gave Juror #12 was not anger. It was something like sorrow aimed at innocence.

"I saved myself," he said.

The sentence hit the room like a blunt object.

Juror #10 let out a short breath and covered his mouth with his hand, as if hearing someone else say it made his own confession burn again.

Juror #11 stared down at the paper, but his eyes looked unfocused now, as if the typed words had ceased to matter because the image had taken over. "The dogs were close," he said. "Men were shouting. The guide was already across, pulling someone else. My brother was in the water with one arm around his wife, the other reaching for me. His face..." He stopped. Swallowed. "His face was not begging. It was commanding. Like an older brother. Like a man who still believed he could order the world."

Juror #9's voice came faint. "And you?"

Juror #11 closed his eyes for a moment. When he opened them, the steadiness was still there, but now it looked like a cage. "I let the boy go," he said.

Juror #2 inhaled sharply, a sound of pure horror.

Juror #11's voice did not rise. It stayed level, which made it worse. "I pushed him back toward my brother," he said. "I told myself my brother could hold him. I told myself two hands were better than one. I told myself the guide would reach them. I told myself…" His mouth tightened. "I told myself many things in the time it took me to step onto the next stone."

The fluorescent hum pressed down. The dead clock stayed fixed at two twenty-six, indifferent.

Juror #11 went on. "I crossed," he said. "I ran into the trees. The guide pulled me, whispered that if I stopped I would bring them to everyone." His fingers shook on the paper now. "Behind me I heard the water. I heard shouting. I heard the little girl screaming again, and then I did not."

Juror #12's shoulders shook once. Juror #7 stared at the table, eyes bright, like he couldn't stand to picture a child's hand slipping free.

Juror #11 lifted his gaze to the table at large, and for the first time his composure looked like it might fracture, not into tears, but into something harsher:

the naked exposure of a man who has finally said aloud the exact shape of his shame.

"I did not go back," he said. "I did not wait. I did not ask the guide to stop. I did not even turn around. I kept running because I wanted to live."

Juror #6's mouth tightened. "What happened to them?" he asked, though the question already carried its own answer.

Juror #11's jaw flexed. "I never saw them again," he said. "Maybe they drowned. Maybe they were taken. Maybe my brother held them up long enough for someone else to save them." His eyes flicked down to the folder again. "But the folder," he said, voice sharpening, "does not allow maybe."

He read one line, quiet, as if the words burned his tongue. "Recovered bodies downstream," he said. "Two days later."

Juror #2 covered her mouth fully now. A muffled sob escaped between her fingers.

Juror #9's eyes were wet, and his hands trembled more openly now. He did not speak. He had no phrase sharp enough to hold that kind of loss.

Juror #11 stared at the paper as if it were a photograph. "When I came here," he said, "I told people I lost my family in the war." His voice stayed even, but the evenness was cracking at the edges. "I let them assume it was something done to me. Something taken from me."

He looked up, and his gaze swept over the jury as if daring them to look away. "I did not say I was the one who left them in the water," he said.

Juror #8's voice was quiet, almost gentle. "You were trying to survive," he said.

Juror #11's eyes snapped to him. For the first time, heat entered his expression. Not anger at accusation, but anger at mercy offered too easily.

"Do not make it noble," he said, and the sharpness of it cut cleanly through the room. "Do not turn my cowardice into a story you can live with. I did not sacrifice myself for anyone. I did not stand. I did not carry them." His voice tightened. "I ran."

The murmur behind the walls rose again, a low tide of sound.

Juror #11's breath came in controlled pulls. "In this country," he said, voice lower now, "people tell me I should be grateful. They tell me I am lucky. They tell me I escaped."

He looked down at the label on the folder again. IMMIGRANT.

"Yes," he whispered. "I escaped."

The chalk scraped behind them.

One short, dry stroke added beneath JUROR.

Juror #12 flinched as if the sound had struck his spine.

Juror #11 closed the folder with careful hands, as if closing it could keep the river from flowing into the room. When he lifted his eyes again, the steadiness had returned, but it looked different now. Not pride. Not moral certainty. The discipline of a man who has finally stopped pretending he is only what happened after.

Juror #10 spoke hoarsely from his seat, voice stripped down to something almost human. "So what," he muttered, "you're telling me you killed them."

Juror #11 looked at him for a long moment. His expression did not condemn. It did not forgive. It simply acknowledged the shared geometry of guilt.

"Yes," he said. "With my feet. With my silence. With the choice to keep moving."

The room was very still after that.

On the chalkboard, ORDER OF TESTIMONY now held two completed names: JUROR #10 and JUROR #11. The list looked less like a process now and more like a countdown.

Juror #8's gaze moved to the board, then back to the table, as if measuring what remained. His voice, when it came, was soft but absolute.

"It's not finished," he said.

And in the hush that followed, the jurors felt it: the room had taken two more truths and added them to its ledger, feeding the courtroom it had built out of their lives.

Somewhere behind the walls, the unseen gallery seemed to settle again, waiting for the next name to be written.

Chapter 12

Truth on the Chalkboard

No one spoke after Juror #11's last sentence.

The air felt heavier now, not with anger but with saturation, as if the room had absorbed so many admissions it was starting to sweat them back out. Juror #11 sat with his hands on the closed folder, the word IMMIGRANT still facing him like a category the room had chosen to use as a knife. Juror #10 stared at the table, his face rigid, as if the only way to keep his confession from changing him further was to freeze.

ORDER OF TESTIMONY on the chalkboard held two completed lines: JUROR #10. JUROR #11.

Beneath that, nothing. No new number. No new folder.

Just waiting.

Juror #12 made a small sound in his throat, the kind that wasn't meant to be heard. He had been trembling for a while now, not always visibly, but in the way his posture never quite settled. "It's… it's going to write the next one," he whispered.

Juror #6 didn't look up. "Let it," he muttered, though his hands flexed once on the table as if his body still believed in doing something with force.

Juror #1, who had been shrinking in his own suit for the last hour, swallowed hard. "We're not even… we're not even talking about the case anymore," he said, and there was a pleading edge to it. Like if he could drag them back to the boy, back to evidence and procedure, he could make the room forget what it had become.

Juror #4's eyes stayed on the chalkboard. "Maybe that's exactly why it will," he said quietly.

Juror #7 lifted his gaze, hollow-eyed. "Why it will what?"

Juror #4 didn't answer immediately. He seemed to weigh his words, as if choosing the wrong one would be noticed. "Why it will return to the original frame," he said. "It's a trial. It began with a trial. The room is using the boy's case as a vessel. If it wants a verdict, it needs to keep reminding us what we thought we came here to decide."

Juror #9's hands trembled on the tabletop. He looked at the dead clock, then at the knife near the board, then back at the ledger of chalk marks beneath

JUROR. “A vessel,” he repeated softly. “Yes. A story you can pour guilt into until it overflows.”

Juror #2’s voice came out thin. “But the boy is real,” she said. It sounded like she was trying to anchor something that had started drifting. “We saw him. We heard him. He’s sitting out there right now, waiting for us.”

Juror #8 watched her for a moment, and his gaze was not unkind. “We heard what the court allowed us to hear,” he said. “We saw what the court showed us. That’s always been the arrangement.”

Juror #3’s eyes snapped toward him, sudden and sharp. The furious father had been quiet, but quiet didn’t mean empty. “Don’t do that,” he said. His voice was rough. “Don’t turn him into an idea.”

“I’m not,” Juror #8 replied. “I’m saying we never really heard him.”

The fluorescent hum deepened, barely perceptible, but the shift pressed into their teeth. The room seemed to lean toward that sentence as if it had been waiting for it.

Juror #12 flinched. “What does that mean?”

Before anyone could answer, the chalk made its first sound.

Not the short, dry tally stroke. Not the measured, deliberate writing of headings. This was a long scrape, slow and continuous, the sound of someone dragging a truth across a surface that could not absorb it fast enough.

Every head turned.

The chalkboard, already crowded with its declarations and ledgers, began to fill again. The piece of chalk on the tray lifted as if pulled by a string. It rose to the board and paused, hovering just long enough for them to realize it was choosing where to begin.

Then it wrote.

Not ORDER OF TESTIMONY. Not a juror number.

A sentence.

I DIDN'T MEAN TO.

The words appeared in blunt capitals; each letter pressed into the black slate as if the room wanted the message to bruise.

Juror #2's breath caught. She stared at the sentence as though it had been spoken directly into her ear.

Juror #1 stood halfway out of his chair without noticing he was moving. "That's…" he began, then stopped. He couldn't decide whether to call it impossible or familiar.

Juror #7 whispered, "That's the kid."

Juror #9 nodded faintly. “Yes,” he said, voice low. “That is the voice we did not listen to.”

The chalk moved again, faster now, as if once it began it couldn’t tolerate stopping.

HE WAS COMING AT ME.

Juror #3’s face tightened. His eyes darted to the knife near the board, then away, like his mind couldn’t help assembling the scene the prosecution had fed them: a father, a blade, a boy backed into a corner.

Juror #6 shifted in his chair, shoulders squaring. “That’s what the defense said,” he muttered. “Self-defense.”

Juror #4’s voice came tight. “No,” he said. “The defense implied it. The boy never said those exact words on the stand.”

They looked at him.

Juror #4’s jaw flexed. He hated being the one who remembered phrasing, but that was his nature. “He said he was scared,” Juror #4 continued. “He said his father was angry. He said he didn’t remember the knife going in. But he did not say ‘coming at me.’ Not in those words.”

Juror #8’s gaze stayed on the board. “So this isn’t the courtroom,” he said quietly. “This is him.”

The chalk paused, then began again, and now it wrote with an unsettling rhythm, as if transcribing spoken testimony.

THEY KEEP SAYING I HATED HIM.

Juror #12's eyes filled. He brought a hand to his mouth, as if that would keep the sentence from entering him.

Juror #2 whispered, "He didn't say that either."

Juror #8 turned his head slightly. "No," he said. "They said it for him."

The chalk made another long line of words, and this time the sentence was longer, the letters crowding together as if the room had too much to fit inside the board and was forcing it anyway.

I DIDN'T WANT HIM DEAD. I WANTED HIM TO STOP.

Juror #3 squeezed his eyes shut for a second. When he opened them, his face looked like it had been carved down to something raw.

Juror #1's voice cracked. "This is contamination," he said, though the word sounded like something he'd borrowed from a safety manual. "This is… this is not evidence."

Juror #9 spoke without looking away from the board. "Neither were our folders," he said. "And yet you felt them."

The chalk continued, and now the sentences began to shift. Not just recounting the alleged night, but something else. Something layered beneath it.

IF YOU SEND ME TO DIE, DO YOU THINK YOU GET TO GO HOME CLEAN?

The room went very still.

Juror #6 stared at that sentence like it had been slapped onto the board with a wet hand.

Juror #5 leaned forward, elbows on the table, eyes narrowed. “That ain’t… that ain’t from the trial,” he said. His voice was low, almost respectful, as if he didn’t want to offend the thing writing.

Juror #4’s mouth was slightly open. He looked momentarily unmoored. “That’s not testimony,” he said. “That’s accusation.”

Juror #8 didn’t blink. “It’s question,” he corrected.

Juror #10 gave a short, harsh laugh, the sound scraping his throat raw. “What, the kid’s judging us now?” he muttered, but the bravado was gone. He didn’t look at anyone when he said it. He didn’t dare.

Juror #11’s eyes stayed on the chalkboard, dark and steady. “Maybe it is not the boy,” he said quietly.

Juror #2 turned toward him, startled. “Then who is it?”

Juror #11's jaw tightened. "A voice that knows how to use a boy's mouth," he said.

The chalk kept moving, relentless.

YOU ALL LOOKED AT ME LIKE I WAS EASY.

Juror #12 made a small, broken sound, his shoulders curling inward. Juror #7's hands clenched on the table edge, knuckles whitening.

Juror #1's face pinched. "We didn't," he said automatically. "We hadn't even—"

The chalk wrote over him, as if it had heard his denial and found it boring.

YOU VOTED BEFORE YOU TALKED.

Juror #1 went silent, his throat working. The sentence was true, and the room had a way of making truth feel like a hand around the neck.

Juror #8's voice came calm, but it carried weight now, as if the room had tuned itself to him. "It's not just replaying him," he said. "It's answering us. It heard everything we said about justice and punishment, and it's responding in his language."

Juror #4's eyes flicked to Juror #8. "Or in yours," he said, and the suspicion was back, not loud but persistent. "This is awfully convenient."

Juror #8 didn't look at him. "Convenience is what got us here," he said.

The chalk paused, then began again, and now the letters came slower, more deliberate, as if the next line mattered more than the others.

HE HIT HER FIRST.

Juror #2's face went pale.

Juror #3's eyes snapped open wider, suddenly alert, as if the sentence had dragged a new image into the room. "Who?" he asked, and his voice was a rasp.

Juror #6 frowned. "He had a sister," he said, trying to remember the testimony. "Or the mother? There was—"

Juror #4 shook his head slowly. "No," he said. "No mention of a female victim. Not in the charges. Not in the direct testimony. The state kept it clean. Father and son. Knife. Motive."

Juror #9's voice came soft. "They always keep it clean," he murmured. "They remove the parts that would make you hesitate."

Juror #2 stared at the sentence, eyes shining. "If that's true," she whispered, "then this isn't an open-and-shut case."

Juror #5 gave a short, bitter breath. "Was it ever?" he muttered.

The chalk moved again.

I DIDN'T CALL THE POLICE BEFORE. I DIDN'T THINK THEY'D HELP.

Juror #11's expression tightened at that, something pained flickering behind his eyes. Juror #10 shifted in his chair, uncomfortable in a way that had nothing to do with the room's temperature.

Juror #8 watched the words appear, and for the first time in a long while, his calm looked less like control and more like something else: recognition. Not of a detail, but of a mechanism. A boy trying to speak in a system that only hears what it expects.

Juror #1 swallowed hard. "So what is this?" he asked, voice hoarse. "Is it… is it the truth? Is this what he really said somewhere? Is there a transcript?"

Juror #4's voice was tight. "If there was, it would be in evidence," he said, but the sentence sounded like a wish.

The chalk answered by writing a line that turned the room colder than any confession had.

YOU DON'T GET TO HIDE BEHIND ME.

Juror #10 jerked his head up as if struck.

Juror #12 whispered, "Who's it talking to?"

The chalk, indifferent to their confusion, wrote the next sentence as if it had been waiting to say it since the first vote.

IF YOU WANT A VERDICT, LOOK AT YOUR HANDS.

No one moved. It was as though the sentence had rewritten gravity.

Juror #6 stared down at his palms, broad and scarred, as if he might find the shape of his old accident there, the moment he'd blamed someone else to keep his job. Juror #2's fingers twitched in her lap as if they still held a pen. Juror #7's hands hovered near his face, remembering a steering wheel. Juror #9's hands trembled, remembering a door that stayed closed. Juror #11's hands were steady now only through effort, remembering a child's wet weight and the choice to keep moving.

Juror #1 looked at his hands too, and the foreman badge on his chest seemed suddenly absurd, a tiny piece of metal trying to stand in for innocence.

Juror #8 did not look down.

He kept his eyes on the chalkboard, as if he were waiting for the room to reveal what it had been building toward all along.

The chalk wrote one final line, smaller than the rest, pressed into a corner of the board beneath the larger sentences like an afterthought that wasn't an afterthought at all.

WHO IS THE FATHER NOW?

The question hung in the sealed air.

No one answered, because any answer would have been a confession of what the room was implying: that the boy's case was not only about a dead man and a knife, but about inheritance. About harm passed down and repeated. About who becomes the thing they fear. About who deserves to be called monstrous.

The chalk dropped to the tray with a soft click.

The fluorescent hum steadied.

ORDER OF TESTIMONY remained with two names filled in, but the board was no longer just a list and a ledger. It had become a mouth.

And whatever voice had used it had just done something worse than accuse them.

It had brought the boy into the room at last, not as a defendant behind a rail, not as a summary in a foreman's voice, but as words that did not ask permission to be heard.

Juror #2's voice broke the silence, barely more than air. "If that's what he's been trying to say," she whispered, "then we never tried him. We tried the version that made it easy."

Juror #9 didn't look away from the chalkboard. "Easy verdict," he murmured, and the phrase sounded like a curse now.

Juror #8 finally spoke again, and in the stillness, his calm voice felt like the only thing in the room that wasn't shaking. "This is why it brought us here," he said. "Not to decide what a boy deserves." He paused, letting the words on the board hold them. "But to show us what we do when someone else's life makes a convenient container for our own guilt."

Juror #8's last sentence settled in the room like dust in still air. No one moved to brush it away.

Across the table, Juror #12 stared at the chalkboard, at the boy's words pressed into slate as if they'd been carved there with a nail. His fingers had gone numb somewhere around the line YOU DON'T GET TO HIDE BEHIND ME, and now they tingled painfully, waking up in the wrong place.

He cleared his throat. The sound came out thin, too bright in the sealed room.

"This is… this is a trick," he said, and hated himself for how childish it sounded. He tried again, like a man rewriting copy that won't land. "This is psychological. That's all. Group pressure. Suggestion. We've all been sitting in here too long."

Juror #7 gave him a tired look. "Yeah," he murmured. "That's been working great."

Juror #12 forced a laugh. It didn't arrive as humor; it arrived as a reflex, the same reflex that had carried him through client meetings and crisis calls. Keep it light. Keep it moving. Don't let the room feel what it's feeling.

"We're literally staring at floating chalk," Juror #5 said, voice flat. "How long you want to keep calling it suggestion?"

Juror #12's eyes flicked to the tray beneath the chalkboard. Two pieces of chalk lay there, ordinary and bright. Tools waiting to be used. His gaze dropped quickly to the tabletop again, to his hands, to the lines in his palms that suddenly looked like something that could be read.

Juror #1 spoke quietly, almost to himself. "It's picking at what we call reasonable," he said. "It's stripping it down."

Juror #4's attention stayed locked on the board, on the boy's final question. WHO IS THE FATHER NOW? His voice came out clipped. "It's not random," he said. "It's constructing a narrative. It wrote the boy's words to reframe the original case. Next it will…"

"Next it will pick another one," Juror #2 whispered.

The silence that followed made her whisper louder than a shout.

Juror #12 felt the room shift in that strange way it did when something had been named correctly. The fluorescent hum didn't change volume, but it thickened, pressing into his skull. The air took on that faint metallic edge again, pennies and cold rails. He tried to swallow. His mouth was dry. His tongue felt like paper.

Juror #11 sat with his closed folder in front of him, hands resting on it as if it were a grave marker. His gaze lifted slowly, not to the chalkboard this time, but to Juror #12. There was no accusation in the look. Only the steady awareness that a turn had been taken and could not be untaken.

Juror #12 bristled under it. "What?" he snapped, too quick. Then, softer, because he heard the fear underneath his own tone: "What are you looking at me for?"

Juror #11 didn't answer. He didn't have to. The room had trained them now: you didn't look at someone like that unless you suspected a folder was about to land.

Juror #12's gaze jumped to Juror #8, searching for the calm that had been steady while everything else broke. "You said it brought us here," he said, voice pitching into complaint. "You keep saying it like you know. Like you've got the outline."

Juror #8 met his eyes without flinching. "I'm listening," he said. "That's all."

"That's not all," Juror #12 said, and hated how pleading it sounded. He wanted to be indignant. He wanted to be outraged. Outrage was a shield. But the room had made shields feel transparent. “You sit there like this is… like this is what you expected.”

Juror #8 didn’t deny it. “Expected isn’t the same as wanted,” he said.

Juror #12 opened his mouth to press harder, to drag the suspicion back where it felt safer, onto the only man without a folder. Then the table made its sound.

A soft, decisive thud.

The folder appeared directly in front of Juror #12, perfectly aligned. Thick brown cardstock. White label. Crisp typed letters that made his stomach drop as if the chair had vanished beneath him.

JUROR #12 – ADVERTISER.

His first reaction was a flash of offended relief. Not bigot. Not liar. Not killer. Not even a description that sounded like a crime.

Just what he did for a living.

He almost laughed again, because the room had chosen the smallest, safest word it could have used for him.

Then he remembered what the room did with small safe words.

He stared at the label until the letters seemed to separate from their meaning and become shape.

ADVERTISER. A role. A mask. A person who could make anything sound like something else.

Juror #7's voice came quiet. "That's you," he said, and there was no bite in it. Just recognition.

Juror #12 lifted his hands slowly and placed them on either side of the folder without touching it, like it might shock him. "This is ridiculous," he said. He tried to smile. It wobbled. "I didn't… I didn't stab anyone. I didn't run anyone over. I didn't—"

Juror #9 spoke, weary and gentle. "Open it," he said. "We have learned it doesn't care what instrument you used."

Juror #12 looked around the table, searching for a face that would say no, don't, stop, we've had enough. Even Juror #1, who had once tried to force order into everything, only watched him with hollow attention. The foreman's badge glinted when he shifted, an old symbol of authority now reduced to a shiny object catching light.

Juror #12's fingers slid under the flap. He opened the folder.

The paper inside was cream-colored, typed in clean margins that made it look official even before he read a word. The familiarity of that formatting was its own kind of nausea. He'd spent years living in documents like this: briefs, brand decks, compliance memos, market research. Paper as permission. Paper as distance.

His eyes moved across the first page.

He went very still.

Juror #2 leaned forward slightly, voice fragile. "What is it?"

Juror #12's mouth opened. Closed. He wet his lips. "It's… it's a campaign file," he said finally, voice hoarse. "A product."

Juror #6 grunted. "What kind of product?"

Juror #12's throat worked. His eyes dropped back to the page as if reading could delay speaking. "A drug," he whispered.

The word drug landed and didn't leave. It hung there, heavy with everything it could mean: prescriptions and ambulances, dependence and overdoses, clean labels hiding dirty outcomes.

Juror #4's gaze sharpened. "Pharmaceutical advertising," he said, like placing a pin on a map.

Juror #12 nodded once, small. "Yes."

Juror #5 leaned back in his chair, arms crossed, eyes hard. "So what," he said. "You made commercials. People make commercials."

Juror #12 tried to grab onto that. "Exactly," he said too quickly. "That's exactly what—"

The chalkboard made a small sound behind them. Not writing, not scraping. Just the faint tap of chalk shifting on the tray, as if impatient.

Juror #12 flinched and kept reading.

"There were warnings," he said, and his voice broke on were. He cleared his throat violently. "Side effects. Internal reports. A risk profile." He shook his head, eyes fixed on the paper. "Not unusual. Everything has risk."

Juror #9's voice came soft. "And you made it sound like it didn't."

Juror #12 jerked his head up, offended reflex trying to return. "I didn't write the science," he snapped, then immediately heard the emptiness in his own defense. He looked down again, voice dropping. "I wrote the story."

Juror #7 whispered, almost to himself, "Oh."

Because everyone in that room understood story. The prosecution's story. The defense's story. The story they'd told themselves so they could sleep. And now a new story, clean and persuasive, had been dragged into the light.

Juror #12's eyes burned. "It was supposed to help people," he said, and hated how desperate he sounded. "Pain management. Quality of life. It wasn't… it wasn't illegal. It was approved."

Juror #4's mouth tightened. "Approval isn't innocence," he said. His gaze flicked to Juror #1 as if to remind him of factories and paperwork and signatures.

Juror #12 swallowed hard. "We did focus groups," he said, voice thin. "We tested language. We tested colors. We tested how quickly the disclaimer could be read before people tuned out." His hands tightened on the edges of the paper until it bent slightly. "We had a phrase. A line. It says it here."

Juror #2's eyes widened. "What line?"

Juror #12 stared at the page. His voice came out small, stripped. "It was three words," he said. "Simple. Comforting." He shut his eyes briefly, as if bracing to say it aloud. "Back to normal."

The phrase sounded harmless in the air, almost kind. That was the horror of it.

Juror #6 exhaled slowly through his nose. "Back to normal," he repeated, disgust starting to edge his voice. "For who?"

Juror #12's chest rose and fell too fast. "People in pain," he said. "People who wanted their lives back." His eyes flashed up, wild. "You think I was sitting in a room saying, 'Let's kill people'? That's not what it was. It was meetings. Decks. Deadlines. Everyone nodding at the same slide like it meant certainty."

Juror #9 murmured, “Like a jury vote.”

Juror #12 flinched.

He looked down again, and the paper refused to soften. It did what paper always did: it stayed.

“It says… it says the adverse events began climbing,” he whispered. “Calls. ER visits. Dependency.” He swallowed hard, fingers trembling now. “It says the sales climbed too.”

Juror #1’s voice came out hoarse. “Did you know?” he asked, and it wasn’t judgment. It was the exhausted question of a man who had watched the same decision wear different faces.

Juror #12’s eyes filled, but the tears didn’t fall. “We got memos,” he said. “We got risk language that legal told us to include, and then told us how to bury.” His mouth trembled. “We adjusted the message. We didn’t stop the campaign. We polished it.”

Juror #11 spoke quietly, and the words felt like a knife used carefully. “You made harm sound like hope.”

Juror #12’s breath hitched. “I didn’t make it,” he whispered. “I… I packaged it.”

Juror #5 leaned forward slightly, voice low. “And people bought it,” he said.

Juror #12 nodded once, miserably. “Doctors prescribed it more,” he said. “Patients asked for it by name.” His voice cracked. “Families stocked it in bathroom cabinets like it was safety.”

The murmur behind the walls returned, faint but present, like a crowd remembering its own losses.

Juror #12 squeezed his eyes shut. When he opened them again, he looked older than he had that morning. “There’s a section here,” he whispered, staring at the page. “A projection. They estimated… a number.” He shook his head, not wanting to say it. “Not in deaths. They didn’t write deaths. They wrote ‘impact.’”

Juror #9’s voice was tired. “Say it.”

Juror #12 stared at the typed line until it blurred. “Thousands,” he said finally, barely audible. “They estimated the potential for… thousands of severe outcomes.”

Juror #2 made a small sound like she’d been punched.

Juror #7 stared at him, hollow-eyed. “And you kept going,” he whispered.

Juror #12’s shoulders sagged. He didn’t argue. He couldn’t. “I told myself,” he said, voice breaking, “that my job was just words. That I wasn’t the one swallowing pills. That I wasn’t the one writing prescriptions. That I wasn’t the one who—”

He stopped. He looked down at his hands.

He remembered the chalkboard's instruction: IF YOU WANT A VERDICT, LOOK AT YOUR HANDS.

"My hands were clean," he whispered. "That's what I told myself."

Juror #8 watched him steadily. "Were they?" he asked, gently, and the gentleness did not feel like mercy. It felt like accuracy.

Juror #12's throat worked. His eyes were wet now. "No," he said, and the word came out like surrender. "They weren't."

Behind them, the chalk scraped once, short and dry.

Another tally mark appeared beneath JUROR.

Juror #12 flinched at the sound, as if the room had tapped him on the shoulder to claim him.

He stared at the new mark, then at the boy's sentences still crowding the board. He felt, for the first time, the full shape of what Juror #8 had meant. A boy's life as container. A verdict as a lid.

He closed the folder slowly, carefully, as if he could prevent anything else from spilling out. When he looked up, his face had lost its superficial brightness, the polished ease of someone who knew how to sell reassurance. What remained was a man stripped down to the simplest truth he'd avoided naming because it ruined the narrative.

"I didn't stab anyone," he whispered.

He swallowed hard and looked around the table, meeting eyes that had all learned what killing could look like without a weapon.

"But I helped," he said. "I helped it happen. I helped it spread. And I told myself it was just business."

The room held him in silence.

Then, on the chalkboard, one of the boy's lines seemed to burn brighter simply by being there: YOU DON'T GET TO HIDE BEHIND ME.

Juror #12's voice broke on his next breath. "We used people," he whispered, and the confession felt like stepping off a ledge. "We used their pain. We used their hope. And we called it persuasion."

Juror #8's gaze stayed on him, steady as a record. "Do you think you killed someone?" he asked, not harshly, not theatrically. The question was simple, and that simplicity made it brutal.

Juror #12 stared down at his hands again, at the fingers that had typed slogans, approved storyboards, signed off on messaging meant to bypass fear.

He nodded once.

"Yes," he said, and the word came out clean at last, because there was no marketing language left that could soften it. "I did."

The murmurs behind the walls swelled as if an unseen gallery had shifted in its seats, satisfied with another truth entered into evidence.

On the chalkboard, the boy's question remained: WHO IS THE FATHER NOW?

And in the silence after Juror #12's confession, it felt less like a metaphor and more like an accusation aimed at all of them. Because they had all, in their own way, built something that hurt people and then demanded the world call it normal.

The room did not celebrate Juror #12's admission.

It did not soften, or loosen its grip, or offer the smallest reward for honesty. The fluorescent hum stayed low and steady. The dead clock stayed fixed at two twenty-six. The knife near the chalkboard remained clean, as if it had never belonged to anyone's hand.

Juror #12 sat with the folder closed in front of him, his palms resting on the cardboard as though he could keep it from opening again and spilling the numbers back into the air. His eyes kept returning to the chalkboard, to the boy's sentences that still crowded the slate.

YOU DON'T GET TO HIDE BEHIND ME.

IF YOU WANT A VERDICT, LOOK AT YOUR HANDS.

WHO IS THE FATHER NOW?

He swallowed, throat working, then looked down at his hands again as if the lines in his palms might have rearranged themselves into something readable.

Across the table, Juror #1's foreman badge caught the light when he shifted. The tiny flash felt obscene now. He'd worn it like a shield. In here it looked like a tag.

Juror #2 sat with her shoulders drawn inward, the posture of someone bracing for impact that never arrives all at once. Her eyes were fixed on the chalkboard, wide and wet. She kept mouthing the words without sound, as if repeating them might change what they meant.

Juror #3 stared hard at the line HE HIT HER FIRST, jaw clenched so tight the muscle jumped. His hands were flat on the table, fingers splayed, like he was holding himself in place. There was a new kind of anger in him, no longer loud, no longer aimed outward. It was the anger of recognition, and it had nowhere to go.

Juror #4's gaze tracked the board like data in motion. He looked for patterns, for intention, for the point in the story where the author revealed their hand. But the board did not offer him a structure he could argue with. It offered him a voice.

Juror #5 leaned forward, elbows on the table. His eyes didn't leave the slate. He looked like he was listening for a sound beneath the words, something he'd heard before on a street corner or in a stairwell: a kid trying to explain himself to someone who had already decided.

Juror #6 sat heavy in his chair, expression grim. He looked toward the door, then the chalkboard, then his hands, as if the room had given him only three objects and demanded he pick which one would save him.

Juror #7's face was blank in a way that made him look younger, like he'd shed years of practiced expression and been left with whatever was underneath. He stared at the question WHO IS THE FATHER NOW? as if it had reached into him and pulled something out that he couldn't name.

Juror #9's trembling hands rested on his closed folder. He did not look at the chalkboard anymore. He looked past it, eyes distant, as if the slate had become a stairwell and the sentences had become a door that stayed shut.

Juror #10 kept his gaze down. He looked like a man trying to make his body smaller, as if shrinking could make a past act harder to find.

Juror #11 sat upright, but his composure had taken on a different texture. It no longer looked like strength. It looked like discipline forced into place to keep grief from becoming something that tore him apart. His eyes were fixed on nothing and everything, the way they had been when he spoke about the river. He listened without moving.

Only Juror #8 seemed to hold the room in the same steady way he always had, but even that steadiness felt altered. Not softer. Sharper. Like a blade that had finally stopped pretending it was just metal.

The chalkboard made a faint, dry sound.

Not writing. Not scraping.

A whisper of chalk against slate, so light it could have been imagined.

Every head turned at once.

For a moment, nothing changed on the board. The boy's words remained. ORDER OF TESTIMONY remained with JUROR #10 and JUROR #11 filled in, a list that now looked almost quaint beside the crowded confessions and the tally marks beneath JUROR.

Then, from somewhere behind the walls, the murmuring began again.

It was softer than before, but more organized, as if whatever unseen gallery had been listening had learned how to speak in a way the room could carry. The sound moved like breath through vents, like a voice heard through an apartment wall. It made the skin along Juror #2's forearms rise.

Juror #12's lips parted. "Do you hear that?" he whispered.

Juror #6 nodded once, slow. "Yeah," he said.

Juror #5's eyes narrowed. "It's the same voice," he murmured. "The one from the board."

Juror #4's jaw tightened. "Or it wants us to think it is," he said, but his voice lacked conviction. In this room, skepticism had become a habit without power.

The murmur swelled, then thinned, then shaped itself into something that pushed through the air like a hand.

"I didn't mean to."

The words weren't written. They weren't on the slate. They were spoken into the room in a voice that sounded young and tired at the same time, as if the boy had been forced to repeat himself too often. The sentence hung in the air after it was said, vibrating lightly against the sealed walls.

Juror #2 made a small sound, involuntary, like a sob swallowed too quickly. Her hands rose to her mouth.

Juror #1 pushed back in his chair a fraction, the movement small but sharp. "That's not…" he began, then stopped. He didn't know what to say. It wasn't evidence. It wasn't procedure. It wasn't anything he could sign off on.

"I wanted him to stop," the voice said, softer now, as if speaking to someone who wouldn't hear unless the tone was right.

Juror #3's head jerked up. "Stop," he said, but the command wasn't aimed at the voice. It was aimed at himself, at his own mind assembling an image of a teenager with a knife and nowhere to put his fear.

Juror #8 did not speak. He watched the others the way a witness watches a jury when the testimony finally lands.

The murmur returned, and now it sounded less like a single voice and more like the room itself learning to mimic one.

"They keep saying I hated him."

Juror #7's throat bobbed. His voice came out faint. "He didn't," he whispered, and the sentence sounded like guilt disguised as defense.

Juror #9's eyes lifted, slow. "No," he agreed quietly. "We did."

Juror #4 turned his head toward Juror #9, irritation flaring as if he could still win an argument. "We didn't say that," he started.

"You did in your head," Juror #9 replied, not looking at him. "And you voted from your head."

Juror #4's mouth tightened. The room had made thoughts feel like acts, and he hated it for that.

The voice shifted again. "You voted before you talked."

Juror #1 flinched. The sentence had been written earlier, but hearing it spoken made it sharper. He looked down at the table, at the papers they had neglected, at the exhibits that no longer felt like the center of anything. His foreman instincts tried to rise, to reassert authority, but the room had already declared a different case.

Juror #12's hands tightened on his folder. "We didn't know," he whispered, and the defense sounded like a marketing line. We didn't know. We couldn't have known. We did our best with the information provided.

Juror #8's gaze moved to him. "You say that a lot," he said softly. "It doesn't change what happens to the person underneath."

Juror #12 swallowed hard and looked away.

The murmur swelled, and for a moment it wasn't the boy's voice at all. It was many voices, layered, too faint to separate. A crowd in a hallway. A waiting room. A line outside a courthouse. Sound without faces, faces without names.

Then the boy's voice returned, closer than before, as if the room had placed it directly behind them.

"If you send me to die," it said, "do you think you get to go home clean?"

Juror #6's hands curled into fists on the table, knuckles whitening. "He's not wrong," he muttered, and the admission came out rough, as if he hated giving it air.

Juror #10 jerked in his chair as if the words had struck him physically. His eyes snapped toward the chalkboard, then the locked door, then Juror #8, as if searching for someone to blame for the voice finding the exact spot it needed.

Juror #11 closed his eyes briefly. When he opened them, his expression held an exhausted clarity. "That is what it has been doing," he said. "Using him to ask what we refused to ask ourselves."

Juror #2 whispered, "But what if he was telling the truth?"

Juror #4's head turned sharply toward her. "About what?" he demanded, too quick, his mind already assembling the implications like dominoes. "The self-defense? The abuse? The line about her?"

Juror #3's voice was low and dangerous. "He hit her first," he repeated, as if saying it aloud could make it real enough to punish. "Who is 'her'?"

No one answered, because the answer wasn't in their notes. It wasn't in the evidence they'd been handed. It was in the blank spaces the state had left clean so the story would stay simple.

The murmur behind the walls thickened, as if pleased by the question. Then it offered something in return.

A sound, not words. A soft thump, like a fist against wood. A door being hit. A body being shoved into a wall. The noise was faint and distant, like it came from memory rather than the hallway.

Juror #2 gasped and pressed her palms to her ears, but the sound slipped through anyway. Juror #12's face drained of color. Juror #7 stared at the floor as if he could see the shadow of a child there.

Juror #1 stood abruptly, chair legs scraping tile. "Stop it!" he shouted, and the volume cracked against the sealed walls.

Knock. Knock.

Two precise raps sounded from inside the room, not the door. The sound cut through Juror #1's shout with contemptuous ease.

Juror #1 froze, mouth open, eyes wide with the humiliation of being silenced by something that couldn't be appealed.

The chalkboard did not write. It didn't need to. The voice continued, softer now, as if it had gotten what it wanted.

"I didn't call the police before," it said. "I didn't think they'd help."

Juror #11's jaw tightened. Juror #10's eyes flicked toward him, then away, as if even now he couldn't bear the mirror.

Juror #5 leaned in, voice low. "That part," he said, "I believe."

Juror #4's expression sharpened. "Belief isn't the standard," he snapped, but the snap lacked its earlier force. The room had made standards feel like decorations.

Juror #8 finally shifted, just slightly, hands still flat on the table. "This is what you wanted to avoid," he said, and his voice was calm enough to feel cruel. "Nuance. Context. A story that doesn't fit a clean verdict."

Juror #1 swallowed hard. "We can't fix this," he whispered, and the words sounded like surrender rather than fact. "Even if it's true, we can't… we can't go back out there and—"

"Yes, you can," Juror #8 said, and every eye turned toward him. He did not raise his voice. He didn't need to. "You can ask for clarification. You can request to review the full record. You can refuse to deliver a verdict until you understand what you're doing."

Juror #12 stared at him, disbelieving. "The door is locked," he said, as if the physical fact was the only argument left that mattered.

Juror #8's gaze slid to the door, then back to the chalkboard. "Then maybe the room isn't keeping us in," he said quietly. "Maybe it's keeping something out."

The sentence made the air feel different. Juror #2 shivered. Juror #6's eyes narrowed. Juror #9's trembling hands stilled for a moment, as if he'd heard something he recognized.

"What?" Juror #7 whispered. "Like what?"

Juror #8 didn't answer immediately. His eyes rested on the boy's question still written on the slate.

WHO IS THE FATHER NOW?

Then, without chalk moving, without the murmur rising, the boy's voice spoke again, so close it felt like breath on the back of their necks.

"Look at your hands."

One by one, as if pulled by string, the jurors looked down.

Even Juror #8 glanced at his own palms at last.

The room was silent except for breathing and the low hum of fluorescent lights.

Then Juror #3's voice broke, cracked and raw. "If he's telling the truth," he said, staring at his hands as if they belonged to someone else, "then we were ready to kill a kid because it was easier than hearing what he lived through."

No one contradicted him.

The voice behind the walls did not answer with comfort. It answered with repetition, as if echo was all the mercy the room could offer.

"I wanted him to stop," it said again.

"I didn't mean to."

And in the space between those two sentences, the jurors felt what the room had been building all along: the way an easy verdict is not only a decision about a defendant.

It is a decision about the people who get to leave afterward and tell themselves they did their duty.

The chalk on the tray made a faint click, shifting as if nudged by an unseen hand.

Juror #2 lifted her gaze to the slate, eyes shining. “How many of us left someone asking us to stop?” she whispered.

The question hung there, and no one answered it out loud.

But the room, which had become a mouth, seemed to echo the question in the only way it knew how: by making their silence feel like testimony.

And beneath the boy’s words, beneath the tally marks, beneath the headings that had turned their deliberation into a trial, one truth pressed down on all of them with growing weight.

They had thought the boy was the one on trial.

But his voice, echoing through the room without permission, made it impossible to pretend that anymore.

Chapter 13

The Final Secrets

The room stayed very still after Juror #2's question.

"How many of us left someone asking us to stop?"

No one answered, because every answer would have required a name. A place. A moment where someone's voice had been reduced to noise, something inconvenient that could be ignored if you just kept moving.

The fluorescent hum made the silence feel occupied. The dead clock remained fixed at two twenty-six, a time that had stopped meaning anything except that the room did not intend to let time save them. The knife by the chalkboard sat where it always sat now, clean, patient, like a prop that had outlived the story it was supposed to tell.

Juror #8 looked around the table once, slow and deliberate. Not like a man counting allies. Like a man counting witnesses.

The chalk on the tray shifted with a faint click.

All of them turned.

The board did not write the boy's words again. It did not need to. Those sentences already lived in the room like a smell.

Instead, the chalk lifted and began to move with a steadiness that felt less like haunting and more like procedure.

FINAL STATEMENTS, it wrote.

Then, beneath it, as if the room had decided mercy was no longer useful:

SAY IT WITHOUT THE STORY.

Juror #1 made a sound that might have been a laugh if it hadn't been so full of airless dread. "That's not how anything works," he whispered, staring at the words like they were a new kind of law.

Juror #9's hands trembled on his folder, but his eyes were clear. "It is how it works when the story has been the lie," he said.

Juror #4's jaw tightened. "This is coercion," he said again, but the repetition sounded tired now, like he'd been reading from a manual that no longer applied.

Juror #6 didn't look at the board. He looked down at his hands. "Without the story," he muttered. "Just the part you can't scrub off."

The chalk moved again and drew a line beneath FINAL STATEMENTS, as if dividing the room into before and after.

Then it wrote one word, centered and blunt:

FOREMAN.

Juror #1 flinched as if someone had called his name in a hallway.

His badge caught the light when he shifted. The tiny glint felt like mockery.

"I already told you," he said, voice hoarse. "I already said what I did."

The chalk did not move. The room did not argue. It simply waited, the way it had learned to wait, until resistance began to feel like a childish performance.

Juror #1 swallowed hard. His hands slid flat on the table, palms down, as if he needed to prove he was still solid.

"I signed the approval," he said. The words came out stiff, corporate, still trying to hide behind vocabulary. He cleared his throat, and when he spoke again, the language had been stripped. "I knew people could die."

Juror #2 made a small sound in her throat, not surprise but recognition. Knowing and continuing. The room's favorite kind of sin.

Juror #1's face tightened. "There was a report," he continued, eyes fixed on the wood grain as if it could hold him steady. "It wasn't vague. It wasn't a maybe. It said ventilation failures, chemical exposure, a probability of… of fatalities."

He swallowed again. "I told myself it was temporary. I told myself it would be fixed next quarter. I told myself if I didn't sign, someone else would. I told myself a lot of things."

Juror #9's voice was soft. "And three men died."

Juror #1's breath shuddered. "Yes," he said. "And I went to one funeral."

The admission landed like a new weight. Not the deaths. The funeral. The proof that he had looked straight at consequence and still chosen to keep the machine running.

"I stood in the back," Juror #1 whispered, and his voice cracked on back. "I didn't speak to the widow. I didn't tell anyone why I was there. I left early because I had a meeting."

Juror #7's mouth tightened. For once there was no joke waiting behind his teeth.

Juror #1 lifted his eyes at last, and they were wet, furious with himself for being wet. "Without the story," he repeated, almost tasting the instruction like poison. "Fine."

He inhaled, shallow.

"I killed them," he said.

The chalk made a short, dry mark beneath the tally. Another line on the ledger that did not care about intent.

Then the chalk wrote another word:

CLERK.

Juror #2's shoulders rose as if she were bracing for impact. Her hands were clasped so tightly her knuckles looked scrubbed of blood.

"I confessed," she whispered. "I told you I falsified the paperwork."

Juror #11's gaze stayed on her, steady, not forgiving, not cruel. Just witness.

Juror #2 closed her eyes, and when she opened them, something in her expression had shifted from shame to something sharper: the knowledge that she was about to say the part she had tried to bury even inside her confession.

"It wasn't just a form," she said.

Juror #4's eyes narrowed. "What do you mean?"

"I mean…" Juror #2's voice shook. "They told me the patient would be denied coverage if the coding didn't match. They told me the doctor was tired of fighting insurers. They told me it was routine." Her mouth trembled. "But I knew the allergy was real. I saw it in the old chart. I saw it in the notes. And I changed it anyway."

Juror #6 exhaled slowly through his nose, the sound heavy and ugly.

Juror #2 blinked hard. "Because if I didn't, I'd be the problem. I'd be the one slowing things down. I'd be the one making it difficult." She looked down at her hands as if she expected to see ink there. "They gave her medication she shouldn't have had. And when she crashed, everyone moved fast. They moved like it was an accident. They moved like it was no one's fault." Her voice dropped to a whisper. "I watched them work on her like they were trying to erase what we'd done."

Juror #8 did not speak. He didn't need to.

Juror #2 swallowed and lifted her head, eyes wide with an almost childlike horror at her own sentence.

"I killed her," she said.

The chalk marked the tally again.

Then:

FATHER.

Juror #3 went very still. The furious father had been quiet since the boy's words appeared, and the quiet in him had not been peace. It had been containment. "I didn't kill him with my hands," Juror #3 said, voice low. "That's the story I tell myself."

The chalk did not move. The room did not accept stories.

Juror #3's jaw worked. His eyes were red-rimmed and hard. "He used to say 'Stop,'" he whispered, and the word stop sounded like it cut his throat on the way out. "Not when I hit him. He didn't say it then. He said it when I talked."

Juror #12 stared at him. "Talked?"

"When I told him what he was," Juror #3 said. "Weak. Soft. A disappointment. When I told him he didn't get to feel sorry for himself. When I told him he was making me do it."

Juror #9's eyes closed briefly, as if he could hear the echo of a different war, the same tactic: make the victim responsible for the harm.

Juror #3's voice broke, then hardened again. "The last time he tried to leave the house after we fought, I locked the door," he said. "I told him if he walked out, he could stay out. I watched him stand on the porch in the cold. I watched him knock. I watched him put his forehead against the glass."

Juror #2's hand flew to her mouth.

Juror #3 stared at the table as if it were the glass. "He didn't ask for much," he whispered. "He just asked to be let back in." His breath shuddered. "And I didn't." The room was silent in a way that felt like a held breath. Then Juror #3 lifted his head, and his eyes were full of something worse than anger: understanding. "I killed my son," he said.

The chalk marked the tally again.

The chalk wrote again, faster now, as if the room had decided to stop savoring.

ANALYST.

Juror #4's posture stiffened. "I admitted my part," he said, clipped. "I—"

"Without the story," Juror #6 muttered, and there was no malice in it. Just exhaustion.

Juror #4's eyes flashed, then dimmed. He stared at his hands as if seeing them for the first time, as if numbers could leave fingerprints. "I changed the data," he said. "Not by mistake. Not because I misread. Because the truth would have cost money, and the lie would have made me valuable." He swallowed. "People lost everything. Some died after. Heart attacks. Strokes. A man jumped from a balcony. That's what the report said later, when it was too late and everyone was careful about language." He forced the next words out as if dragging them from a place he had locked. "I killed them," he said. "With numbers."

The chalk marked the tally.

Then the chalk wrote:

SLUMS.

Juror #5 flinched, then sat forward, elbows on the table like he was bracing for a punch he'd been waiting for his whole life. "I left him," he said immediately, as if speed could make it hurt less. "That's it. That's the whole thing. I left him."

Juror #7's eyes tightened. Juror #6 stared down. They had all heard the first version, the gang fight, the blood, the fear of police.

Juror #5's voice dropped. "He was still talking," he added, and that detail changed the air. "He wasn't dead yet. He was cussing me out. He was telling me I was a coward. He was telling me to call somebody." Juror #5's hands curled into fists. "And I looked at the alley like it was a trap and decided he was the price of me getting out." He breathed hard through his nose. "I heard him behind me for a few seconds. Then I didn't." He looked up, eyes bright with rage that had nowhere to go but inward. "I killed my friend," he said.

The chalk marked the tally again.

The chalk wrote:

WORKING MAN.

Juror #6's jaw clenched. "I blamed him," he said, voice flat. "I blamed the guy who got hurt." He swallowed. “I pulled the guard off the machine. It kept jamming. It was slowing the line. I told myself it was temporary. I told myself I’d put it back.” He shook his head once, small. “He got pulled in. He screamed. I still hear it.”

Juror #2 made a small broken sound, and Juror #12’s eyes squeezed shut as if the scream could travel through words.

Juror #6’s voice went lower. “And I signed the incident report like it was his fault,” he said. “Like he was careless. Like he deserved it.” He looked down at his hands, broad and scarred. “I killed him,” he said.

The chalk marked the tally again.

The chalk wrote:

JOKER.

Juror #7’s mouth twitched like it was searching for the old escape hatch. Nothing came. “I didn’t even stop,” he said. The words were blunt, stripped of story so thoroughly they sounded like they belonged to someone else. “I hit him. I felt it. I kept going because I was drunk and I didn’t want to lose my life over his.” He swallowed hard. “I told myself it was an animal. I told myself I didn’t know. I told myself the world was full of people in the road.” His eyes were wet now, and he looked furious about it. “I killed him,” he said.

The chalk marked the tally again.

The chalk wrote:

OLD MAN.

Juror #9's hands trembled more openly. He didn't resist. He looked at the board like a man looking at weather he cannot change. "I said his name," he whispered. "I wrote it down. I knew what it meant." He closed his eyes. "I told myself it was for the greater good. I told myself it was survival. I told myself if I didn't, someone would say mine." His eyes opened, glassy. "I killed him," he said. "By pointing."

The chalk marked the tally again.

The board did not write BIGOT, IMMIGRANT, or ADVERTISER again. Those truths were still warm in the air. The room didn't need repetition. It needed completion. When the chalk stopped moving, the silence that followed felt structured, like the end of testimony in a courtroom where everyone is waiting for the next witness to be called.

Juror #1's breathing was ragged. Juror #2's shoulders shook quietly. Juror #3 stared at nothing. Juror #4 sat rigid as if he could still turn feeling into math. Juror #5's fists remained clenched. Juror #6 looked hollow. Juror #7 stared at his hands like they belonged to a stranger. Juror #9 looked older than he had any right to. Juror #10 and Juror #11 sat with their folders closed like gravestones. Juror #12's face was drained of every polished thing he'd ever sold.

All of them, now, had said it without the story.

All of them, now, had spoken the simplest sentence the room demanded.

I killed.

Only one voice remained unaccounted for.

Slowly, as if the room itself were turning its head, their attention shifted toward Juror #8.

He sat as he had always sat, hands flat on the table, posture calm, eyes steady. He did not look away from the chalkboard, but it was clear he wasn't reading it anymore. He was waiting.

Juror #4 spoke first, voice tight. "It didn't write your number."

Juror #6's gaze fixed on him, hard. "Say yours," he said. Not angry. Not pleading. A demand for symmetry. For fairness. For the one thing Juror #8 had kept insisting mattered.

Juror #2's voice trembled. "Please," she whispered, and it wasn't about curiosity. It was about not being alone in the kind of nakedness the room had forced on them.

Juror #9 watched Juror #8 with a quiet, exhausted intensity. "If this is a courtroom," he murmured, "then everyone speaks."

Juror #8 finally turned his head and looked at them one by one. There was no triumph in his face. No satisfaction. Only a stillness that felt, suddenly, like it had always belonged here more than any of theirs.

The chalk did not move.

The room did not help.

It simply waited, as if the last confession was not something it could write into existence.

It had to be offered. And the fact that it wasn't being offered, that the one man who had guided them through everyone else's truth had not placed his own on the table, began to do what the room had always done best.

It turned silence into suspicion.

It made the absence of a story feel like the most dangerous story of all.

Juror #8 held their eyes one by one, and in that slow sweep of attention something turned inside the room.

Not the air. Not the lights. Them.

Because everyone else had spoken the simplest sentence the room demanded, and the fact that he had not made his silence louder than any confession.

Juror #6's hands spread on the table, heavy palms like weights. "Say it," he repeated, and the steadiness in his voice carried an edge now. Not anger exactly. The instinct that fairness is the only thing standing between you and being singled out.

Juror #4 leaned forward a fraction. His face was controlled, but his eyes were too bright. "You've pushed for due process," he said. "You've insisted on evidence. You've insisted we don't vote without talking. If you believe any of that, then you don't get to sit there exempt."

Juror #2's fingers twisted together until her knuckles whitened. "I can't," she whispered. "I can't be the only one who still has to wonder what you're hiding."

Juror #7 made a thin sound, half breath, half laugh, like his body trying to remember how to deflect. "Maybe he doesn't have anything," he said, but it didn't come out as defense. It came out as a test. "Maybe he's the one clean guy in the room."

Juror #5's stare was sharp as broken glass. "Nobody's clean," he said. "Not in here."

Juror #9 didn't raise his voice, but the room seemed to listen when he spoke. "In every confession there is a bargain," he murmured. "We confessed because we hoped it would change something. You watched us make that bargain. Now you ask us to believe you do not have one of your own."

Juror #10 shifted in his chair, shoulders hunched as if he expected another label to land on his back. "This is what he does," he muttered, voice hoarse. "He sits quiet and lets everyone else hang themselves. That's his thing. He's been doing it since the first vote."

Juror #11's gaze stayed on Juror #8, steady and dark. "Silence can be courage," he said, and then, after a pause, "or it can be concealment."

The words landed without malice, and that made them harder to ignore.

Juror #1's voice came out strained, the last vestige of foreman authority trying to hold shape. "If this room is demanding a final statement," he said, "then it demands it from all of us. That's the only way it's been working." He swallowed. "And I don't think it likes exceptions."

The chalkboard stood still. FINAL STATEMENTS. SAY IT WITHOUT THE STORY. The ledger of marks beneath JUROR looked like a spine. No new word appeared. No new name.

The room did not accuse Juror #8.

It waited.

That was what made it worse.

Juror #8 did not look at the chalkboard. His eyes stayed on them, and the stillness in his face had none of the relief that came with confession. It looked like something he had chosen long before today, like a posture practiced in other rooms.

Juror #6's patience snapped, not into shouting, but into a hard, flat line. "You're not better than us," he said. "You hear me? Don't sit there like you're the judge."

Juror #8's expression didn't change. "I'm not the judge," he said quietly.

Juror #5 leaned in. "Then what are you?"

The question moved through the table like a draft.

Juror #8 let a beat pass. Not a dramatic pause. A measured one, like he was refusing to be rushed into giving them a version they could use.

"I don't know what you want me to say," he said.

Juror #4's mouth tightened. "The truth," he snapped.

Juror #8's gaze moved to him. "I've been asking for the truth since we walked in," he said. "From the case. From the witnesses. From each other."

"And from yourself?" Juror #2 asked, the words trembling. "Or just from us?"

Juror #8 looked at her, and for the first time there was something like fatigue in his eyes. Not guilt. Not fear. Weariness at being asked to produce something that would satisfy them.

"You think if I confess," he said, "this ends."

No one answered, because none of them believed it anymore, and yet all of them needed to.

Juror #7 licked his lips. "It has to," he whispered. "That's the whole… that's the whole point. Confess and we get out."

Juror #9's voice came soft, as if spoken to himself. "Or confess and we become something that can be filed and stamped," he murmured. "A completed set."

Juror #12's shoulders shook once. "Please," he said, and the word came out raw, stripped of polish. "Just say whatever it wants. I don't care if it's embarrassing. I don't care if it's ugly. I just want it to stop."

Juror #8 held his gaze on Juror #12 for a moment. "You think words are the cost," he said. "But the cost is what the words do to you once they're said."

Juror #10 barked a bitter laugh. "Oh, come on," he muttered. "Don't turn this into a sermon. You've been playing saint all day. Just say what you did."

Juror #11's eyes narrowed slightly. "Enough," he said to Juror #10, but the instruction sounded more like an attempt to prevent a fire than to keep decorum.

Juror #3, who had been staring at the table as if it were glass and he could see his son's face through it, lifted his head. His voice was low, rough, and it carried a simple brutality that none of the others could manage.

"Maybe he doesn't have one," Juror #3 said, looking at Juror #8. "Maybe he's the only one who didn't kill."

Juror #8 didn't flinch. He didn't seize the opportunity.

He simply said, "If you believe that, then you haven't been listening."

The sentence chilled the room more than the stopped clock ever had.

Juror #4's brow furrowed. "So you did," he said. "You did kill someone."

Juror #8's eyes moved across the table again. "You want a clean sentence," he said. "You want the kind you can tally. I killed him. I killed her. I killed them. That's what it asked for."

The chalkboard remained still.

Juror #8's hands were still flat on the table. His palms looked ordinary. No ink. No blood. No proof.

Juror #6 leaned forward, voice low. "Say it," he repeated, and the repetition was no longer about justice. It was about forcing the world to be symmetrical again.

Juror #8's gaze shifted to Juror #6. "And if I don't?"

Juror #6's jaw flexed. "Then I think you're full of it," he said. "Then I think you've been guiding us because you're hiding."

Juror #5 nodded once, slow. "Or you're the one making the folders," he said, and the accusation came back like an old reflex, safer than helplessness. "You're the one moving the chalk. You're the one making the room talk."

Juror #2 shook her head quickly, but it wasn't certainty. It was panic at how easily the room's paranoia could change targets. "No," she whispered. "No, he can't be. He can't be—"

Juror #1's voice cracked. "He doesn't have a file," he said, and the words sounded like they'd been rotting in his throat. "He said it earlier. There hasn't been a file for him."

Juror #4's eyes snapped to Juror #1. "And you believed him?"

Juror #1 went still, trapped. "I didn't know what to believe," he said.

Juror #9 looked at Juror #8 with a quiet dread that had nothing to do with supernatural tricks. "A missing file," he murmured. "A missing record."

Juror #7 swallowed hard. "It never called him," he said, staring at the board as if the absence of his number were the most important thing written there. "It called everybody else. It wrote FOREMAN, CLERK, FATHER. It called us by what we are. But not him."

The room seemed to listen to that observation.

The fluorescent hum deepened slightly, just enough to make their teeth ache.

Juror #12's voice came quick, almost frantic. "Maybe it's saving him for last," he said. "Maybe that's what it does. Maybe the last one is the worst one."

Juror #10's head jerked up. For the first time since his own folder, his fear sharpened into something like fascination. "Yeah," he said softly. "Maybe he's the main act."

Juror #11's voice cut through the rising speculation. "Or," he said, "maybe he is not part of the jury."

Silence fell hard, as if the room had dropped a weight on the table.

Juror #1 stared at Juror #11. "What?"

Juror #11 didn't look away from Juror #8. "In some places," he said carefully, "men enter rooms like this without being invited. They sit and listen. They ask questions that sound harmless. They let you speak until you cannot take your words back." His jaw tightened. "Then they leave you with what you said."

Juror #2's breath caught. "You think he's… what, a cop?"

Juror #11's mouth twisted. "No," he said. "Not that. Something else."

Juror #5's chair scraped as he shifted, not standing but creating distance. "Who are you?" he demanded again, louder now.

Juror #6's hands moved unconsciously toward the knife's direction, not reaching for it, but acknowledging its existence, the way the body acknowledges an exit it might need.

Juror #8 watched all of it without flinching. And in that moment, his calm stopped looking like composure and started looking like inevitability. He spoke, and his voice was quieter than theirs, which forced the room to bend toward it.

"I'm not here to give you a story," he said. "You've had stories. The court gave you one. You gave yourselves others. You wrapped your hands around them until they felt like truth."

Juror #4's face tightened. "Answer the question."

Juror #8's gaze moved to the chalkboard, to the instruction written there: SAY IT WITHOUT THE STORY.

Then he looked back at them.

"I can't say it the way you want," he said.

Juror #2's eyes filled. "Why not?"

Juror #8 held her gaze, and something in his expression sharpened, not cruel, not kind. Exact.

"Because if I say it," he said, "you'll use it."

Juror #10 laughed again, jagged. "Use it for what?"

Juror #8's eyes flicked to the tally marks. To the folders. To the way confession had become currency in a room that did not accept payment.

"To buy your way out," he said.

The words landed like a slap because everyone in the room had felt that hope, that private bargain: If I give it what it wants, I get to leave.

Juror #9 whispered, "And can we?"

Juror #8 did not answer.

His silence stretched, and the room leaned into it, hungry for any sign that they were still in control of something.

Juror #6's voice went hard. "So what," he said, "you're not going to confess because you think we don't deserve relief?"

Juror #8 looked at him steadily. "Relief isn't the same as absolution," he said.

Juror #3's voice came low, dangerous again. "You're dodging," he said. "That's what my son used to call it. Dodging. Using big words so you don't have to say the thing."

Juror #8's eyes shifted to Juror #3, and for a brief moment something moved across his face. Not guilt. Not pity. Recognition so brief it could have been imagined.

Then it was gone.

"I'm not dodging," he said quietly. "I'm refusing."

The murmur behind the walls returned, a low swell like an audience sensing conflict and leaning forward.

The chalk on the tray made a small click, as if nudged.

Juror #1 stared at the board, waiting for it to write JUROR #8 at last, to restore the order of things, to call him the way it had called them.

But the chalk did not move.

The room did not call him.

And that refusal, that unnatural lack of procedure, did what the room had always done with silence.

It made them turn on each other.

Because if the room wouldn't name Juror #8, then someone else would have to.

Juror #5's voice went low. "Maybe we should make him talk," he said.

Juror #2 gasped. "No."

Juror #6 didn't look at her. He kept his eyes on Juror #8. "Nobody touches anybody," he said, but the words had less authority than he wanted. "We're not animals."

Juror #10's mouth curled. "Aren't we?" he muttered. "We killed. We lied. We blamed. We sold people out. But sure, let's draw the line at grabbing the quiet guy."

Juror #11's voice came tight. "Stop," he said, and for the first time his steadiness sounded strained. "This is what it wants."

Juror #8 watched them argue around him without moving, like a stone in a river that forces the water to break into dangerous currents.

Juror #9's trembling hands finally lifted from his folder. He looked at Juror #8 with a weary, pleading clarity. "If you are one of us," he said softly, "then speak like one of us. Say the sentence."

Juror #8 held his gaze.

Then he did something small, almost invisible.

He turned his palms upward on the tabletop, exposing them to the room like evidence.

He looked down at them for a long moment, as if reading something that wasn't written there.

When he looked back up, his voice was quiet enough that they had to strain to hear it.

"You want me to say I killed," he said. "But the truth is, I don't think you understand what you're asking."

Juror #4's eyes narrowed. "Then explain."

Juror #8 shook his head once, slow. "No," he said. "You've already explained it to yourselves. You just don't like what it makes you."

And with that, he fell silent again.

Not the silence of fear.

The silence of a locked door.

And the room, which had tolerated confession and punished denial, seemed to shift its weight onto that silence, pressing down until it began to feel like the most dangerous thing in the room. Because nothing fractures a group faster than the suspicion that one person has been playing a different game all along.

For a moment after Juror #8 fell silent, no one moved. It was as if the room had been trained to expect the next sound, the chalk's scrape, the soft thud of a folder, the murmur behind the walls shaping itself into accusation. Instead there was only the fluorescent hum and twelve people trying not to be the one who broke first.

Juror #10 did.

He pushed his chair back just enough to make the legs squeal. The sound cut into the hush like an insult. "This is insane," he said, voice rough. "You hear him? He's refusing. Like he's got the right."

Juror #11's jaw tightened. "Sit," he said, and it wasn't a plea.

Juror #10 ignored him. "He's playing us," he snapped, eyes fixed on Juror #8. "All day he's been playing us. He gets everyone else to bleed onto the table and then he folds his hands like he's above it."

"I'm not above anything," Juror #8 said quietly.

The fact that he answered at all made Juror #10's face brighten with a vicious kind of relief, like finally finding a seam in armor. "There," he said. "There he is. Mr. Calm. Mr. Reasonable. You're not above it, you're just not in it."

Juror #4 leaned forward, hands flat, as if he could press the conversation into something measurable. "We need to establish what's true," he said, but his voice carried no authority. It was the voice of a man used to meetings, speaking into a room that had stopped respecting consensus. "He has no folder. The room hasn't written his name. Those are facts."

Juror #5 gave a short, humorless laugh. "Facts," he echoed. "In a room with floating chalk."

Juror #4's eyes flashed. "We still have to operate on something," he snapped. "Otherwise we're just reacting."

Juror #6's gaze stayed on Juror #8. "What I'm reacting to," he said, slow and heavy, "is that this thing made every one of us say it. Without the story. And he's the only one who gets to keep his mouth shut."

Juror #2's voice came small from beside Juror #12, as if she'd been hiding in the angle of his shoulder. "Maybe it can't make him," she whispered. "Maybe… maybe he's not—"

"Don't say it," Juror #1 said, and his voice cracked with strain. The foreman's badge on his chest caught the light when he shifted, a pointless glint in a room that had already stripped his title down to a word on slate. "Don't turn this into a witch hunt."

"A witch hunt?" Juror #7 repeated, and the old habit of humor twitched in his throat and died. "What are we hunting, exactly? Ghosts? Demons? Accounting errors?"

Juror #9 lifted his head slowly. His eyes looked dull with fatigue, but clear in a way that made him dangerous to ignore. "We are hunting a way out," he said.

No one contradicted him.

Juror #12 rubbed his palms against his trousers, as if he could wipe off what he'd admitted. "He said we'd use his confession," he murmured, voice tight and bitter. "Use it to buy our way out. Like that's what we're doing."

Juror #3, who had been staring at his hands as if they belonged to someone else, finally looked up. His voice came out low, stripped raw. "Isn't it?" he asked. The question wasn't aimed at Juror #12. It was aimed at all of them. "You think saying it made it right? You think saying it buys you the right to walk out and pretend you're different?"

Juror #2 flinched at the word pretend. Juror #1 looked as if he'd been slapped.

Juror #6 leaned forward, forearms on the table, heavy and practical. "Nobody's pretending anything," he said. "We're trying to survive."

Juror #9's mouth trembled slightly. "Survive what?" he asked. "Our guilt? Or the room?"

The murmur behind the walls rose at that, faint but present, like an unseen gallery reacting to a line it liked. Juror #2's shoulders tightened; Juror #12's eyes darted to the seams in the walls as if the sound might leak through.

Juror #10 pointed at Juror #8 again, the gesture too sharp to be only anger. It was fear looking for a shape. "Him," he said. "Survive him. Because if he's behind it, then we're just rats in a box."

Juror #11 spoke without raising his voice. "Accusing him is easier than looking at what you did," he said.

Juror #10's face twisted. "Oh, spare me," he spat. "You think you're the conscience of the room now? You left kids in a river."

Juror #11 didn't flinch. The steadiness in him was still there, but it had become brittle. "And I said it," he replied. "That is the difference."

Juror #10 took a step, not toward Juror #11, but toward Juror #8, as if the only way to stop feeling small was to make someone else smaller in front of witnesses. His hands hung at his sides, flexing. "If you're not part of this," he said, voice rising, "then prove it. Tell us what you did. Say the sentence."

Juror #8 met his eyes. "You don't want my truth," he said. "You want a lever."

"A lever?" Juror #10 barked a laugh. "I want a door to open."

Juror #5's chair scraped suddenly as he shifted, not standing, but angling his body toward Juror #10 with a street-ready alertness. "Back off," he said, low.

Juror #10 turned on him, sneer returning because it was familiar. "Or what?" he challenged. "You'll leave me bleeding like you left your friend?"

Juror #5's face tightened, and for a second the room leaned toward violence. It was there in the way shoulders squared and hands curled, in the way old instincts returned because words had failed too many times.

Juror #6's voice cut through it. "Enough," he said, louder now. He looked at Juror #10. "Sit down."

Juror #10 stared at him, chest heaving. He looked like he might keep going out of spite alone. Then his gaze flicked to the knife near the chalkboard, and something in him faltered. Not morality. Calculation. The recognition that this room didn't need help escalating.

He didn't sit, but he stopped moving.

Juror #1 finally found his voice again, thin and strained. "We are not doing that," he said. "We're not putting hands on anyone. That's not—" He swallowed, the old language of rules breaking under the weight of what had already happened. "That's not what we are."

Juror #7 murmured, almost to himself, "You sure?"

Juror #2's eyes filled, but she blinked the tears back hard, as if crying would be another kind of confession. "Please," she whispered, looking at Juror #8. "Just… just tell us something. Anything. If the room wants symmetry, give it symmetry."

Juror #8 looked at her for a long moment. When he spoke, his voice was calm, but it had an edge now, not sharpness, something like finality. "Symmetry is how you justify cruelty," he said. "You make it fair on paper and call it clean."

Juror #4's mouth tightened. "This isn't philosophy," he said. "This is a practical impasse. The room escalates when it doesn't get what it wants. It has escalated every time. So we need to decide: do we force him, do we wait, or do we change the frame."

"What frame?" Juror #12 asked, voice cracking. "There's no frame. It's a nightmare."

Juror #9's gaze drifted to the chalkboard. FINAL STATEMENTS. SAY IT WITHOUT THE STORY. The tally marks beneath JUROR. He spoke slowly. "The frame is always judgment," he said. "Only the target changes."

Juror #3's voice came rough. "Then change it back," he said. "Back to the boy. That's what started this."

Juror #1 seized on that like a drowning man grabbing rope. "Yes," he said quickly. "Yes, we should return to the case. We should reexamine the evidence again, systematically. If the room is feeding on our confessions, we stop feeding it."

Juror #5 snorted. "We already fed it," he said. "It's full. It's not letting us out because it's hungry. It's letting us out when it's done."

"And who decides when it's done?" Juror #10 snapped. "Him?"

The accusation hung there and spread like a stain because no one could scrub it off with logic. Juror #8's missing folder was a hole in the pattern, and patterns were all they had left to cling to.

Juror #4 leaned back slightly, eyes narrowing as if the answer might be found in an administrative detail. "The selection list," he said suddenly.

Juror #1 turned toward him. "What?"

"The jury roster," Juror #4 clarified, tapping the tabletop with two fingers. "The paperwork. Names. Numbers. Alternates. If he's not on it, that's meaningful. If he is, then the absence of a folder is meaningful in a different way."

Juror #10's mouth curled. "Finally," he said, voice sharp with satisfaction. "Check the list. Prove it."

Juror #11's gaze tightened, wary. "We do not have access to that," he said.

Juror #1 stared at the locked door as if it might produce a clerk on command. Then his eyes drifted to the stack of trial materials they'd barely touched since the room turned itself inside out. The exhibits. The notes. The envelope with the verdict slips. The packet he'd carried like a badge of office.

His throat worked. "I might," he said.

Everyone looked at him.

Juror #1 swallowed hard, and the corporate manager in him tried to sound certain. "The bailiff gave me a folder when we came in," he said. "Administrative. Instructions. The list of jurors. I…" His hand trembled as it moved toward his briefcase. "I didn't think it mattered after everything else."

Juror #12's voice came urgent. "It matters," he said. "It matters if he wasn't supposed to be here."

Juror #2 shook her head quickly, panic rising. "What if he was?" she whispered. "What if we're just— what if we're losing it?"

Juror #9's voice came soft. "We are losing something," he said. "Not our minds. Our excuses."

Juror #1 hesitated with his hand on the briefcase clasp, as if opening it would be another kind of confession. Not of killing, but of incompetence. Of failing at the only job he'd been given in this room: keep track.

Juror #6 leaned forward, eyes hard. "Open it," he said.

Juror #1's fingers worked the clasp. The small metallic click sounded indecently loud. He pulled the briefcase toward him and opened it with careful hands, as if the room might punish sudden movement.

Juror #10 leaned in, hungry.

Juror #4's gaze sharpened, the analyst drawn to a document like a priest to scripture.

Juror #11 sat still, but his eyes did not leave Juror #8, as if the paper might confirm what his instincts had already begun to believe.

Juror #8 did not move. He watched the foreman's hands with the same patient attention he'd given every folder, every tally mark, every forced sentence. But there was something different now, something almost like anticipation, carefully contained.

Juror #1 rummaged through the contents: a pen, a folded instruction sheet, a sealed envelope, the edges of notes. His hands shook as he dug deeper, and the shaking wasn't fear of paper. It was fear of what paper could prove. Because if the list did not include Juror #8, then everything they'd been telling themselves about fairness and civic duty and accidental participation would collapse. And if the list did include him, then the room had still chosen not to call him, which meant the rules were not rules at all. They were a game designed to make them break each other.

Juror #1's fingers closed around a stapled packet. He pulled it out slowly, like removing a weapon he wasn't sure was loaded.

The group leaned toward him as one organism, twelve heads angling, twelve breaths tightening.

The room, too, seemed to lean in. The fluorescent hum deepened a fraction. The murmur behind the walls stilled, as if even the unseen gallery wanted to hear what was written.

Juror #1 stared down at the top page.

His face drained of color.

"What?" Juror #12 demanded, the word sharp with terror.

Juror #1 didn't answer immediately. His eyes moved across the page as if rereading could change what it said. His lips parted, then closed. He swallowed hard. Then, in a voice that sounded too small for a man who'd tried to run this room, he said, "This is the roster."

Juror #10 leaned closer, almost smiling. "Read it."

Juror #1's hand trembled so badly the paper rustled. "Juror one," he said, voice cracking. "Two. Three. Four…" His eyes flicked up briefly, then back down, counting with dread. "Five. Six. Seven. Nine. Ten. Eleven. Twelve."

The omission hit the table like a dropped body.

Juror #2 made a sound like she couldn't find enough air.

Juror #4 went very still, as if his mind had finally found the anomaly that broke the system.

Juror #10's mouth opened in a grin that wasn't joy, only vindication sharpened into something ugly. "There it is," he whispered. "There it is."

Juror #6's chair scraped back a fraction, instinctively creating distance.

Juror #9's eyes closed slowly, not in surprise, but in recognition, like a man who has seen this kind of thing before and knows what it means when a name is missing.

Juror #11 didn't move, but his voice came out low and tight. "Eight," he said.

Juror #1 nodded faintly, staring at the paper as if it might start bleeding. "There is no eight," he whispered.

In the silence that followed, the group fractured in a way that couldn't be repaired by shouting or procedure or pleading.

Because now the question was no longer what they had done. It was who had been sitting with them the entire time, listening, guiding, refusing to confess. And what the room had been built to do once they finally noticed.

Chapter 14

The Revelation

Juror #1 kept staring at the stapled packet as if the ink might rearrange itself out of pity.

The roster lay open in his hands; top sheet slightly bowed from the tremor in his fingers. The paper was ordinary court stock, the kind that smelled faintly of toner and stale air-conditioning. It should have been the most dependable thing in the room. A list. A record. A solid object that belonged to the world outside the locked door.

"There is no eight," he whispered again, and this time it sounded less like discovery and more like a plea for someone to correct him.

Juror #4 leaned closer, his chair making a soft scrape that felt too loud in the hush. "Let me see it," he said.

Juror #1 didn't hand it over. His foreman instincts flared uselessly, protective of procedure even now, protective of the last scrap of authority he could still pretend to have. He lowered the packet to the table instead, flattening it with both palms like he could pin the truth in place.

Juror #4 bent over it. His eyes moved fast, taking in the header, the case number, the department designation. He read the list of names and juror numbers, then read them again in reverse, as if the omission might be a trick of sequence.

Juror #2 leaned in from the side, breathing shallowly. Her gaze darted from the paper to Juror #8 and back. She looked as if she'd stepped too close to a ledge and now couldn't remember how far the drop was.

Juror #10's face had changed. Vindication had lit him for a moment, sharp and ugly, but it didn't sustain. When it faded, what remained was a kind of animal fear. He didn't like being right if being right meant the room had been compromised from the beginning.

Juror #6 held himself rigid, shoulders squared, like the posture could keep panic from reaching his hands. "Check the alternates," he said, voice low. "There's always alternates."

Juror #1 nodded too quickly, grateful for anything that sounded practical. He flipped the page with fumbling care. The paper rasped, loud in the sealed room.

The second sheet listed alternates, witness acknowledgments, the standard boilerplate about sequestration. Juror numbers again. Names again. The neatness of it felt obscene.

Juror #1 scanned, then looked up, eyes wide. “They’re listed,” he said. “Alternates are here.”

“And?” Juror #10 demanded.

Juror #1’s throat worked. “No eight,” he said. The sentence came out as if it physically hurt.

Juror #4’s finger traced the columns with precise, almost clinical movements. “It’s consistent,” he murmured. “No gap. No placeholder. It goes from seven to nine as if eight never existed.”

Juror #7 made a thin sound that might once have become a joke. It died before it could form. “Maybe they misnumbered,” he said, but his voice didn’t carry belief. He was offering a possibility the way a drowning man offers a prayer.

Juror #9’s gaze stayed on the paper without leaning forward. He looked tired enough to have lived through multiple versions of this moment. “Misnumbered is not how a court behaves,” he said softly. “Not with something as sacred as a headcount.”

Juror #2 shook her head rapidly. “But we saw him come in,” she whispered. “He was with us. He sat down. He… he voted.” Her eyes flicked to Juror #8.

He sat in the same posture he always had, hands resting on the tabletop, palms neither up nor down now, simply present. His face was calm in a way that felt increasingly unnatural, like a photograph that refused to blur.

Juror #12's voice came tight and brittle. "What if the list is wrong?" he said. "What if this is an old sheet? A draft? Paperwork gets messed up all the time."

Juror #1 seized on that, desperate. "It's possible," he said. He flipped back to the first page, searching for a date, a stamp, anything that could turn this into an administrative error instead of a nightmare. "There's a date," he murmured. "Selection date. It's from this morning."

Juror #4 pointed at the bottom corner. "Clerk's initials," he said. "Bailiff's sign-out. It's not a draft."

Juror #12's face tightened. "Then maybe he's a substitute," he insisted, voice rising. "Like, someone got sick. Someone didn't show. They brought in a replacement."

Juror #6 stared at him. "You don't just bring in a replacement and skip the number," he said. "Not in a place that worships forms."

Juror #11 hadn't moved much since Juror #1 read the list aloud. Now he leaned forward a fraction, eyes dark and steady. "Read the full panel," he said to Juror #1. "Not just the numbers. The names."

Juror #1 hesitated. Something about speaking names felt more intimate than speaking numbers, like it would make the paper less abstract and more like a ledger of the living. But he obeyed, because obeying was the only thing he still knew how to do in a room that had rewritten authority. He cleared his throat, voice hoarse. "Juror one," he said, and his own name followed, too ordinary to belong to a horror story. Then two, three, four. He spoke them in order, each name turning into a face around the table. Five, six, seven. Each name made the absence more concrete, like stepping on stairs and finding a missing tread. "Juror nine," he continued, and Juror #9's eyes didn't change. He was listening the way he'd listened to the chalkboard, the way he'd listened to the murmur behind the walls. Ten. Eleven. Twelve.

When Juror #1 finished, the silence that followed was not empty. It was full of the shape that should have been between seven and nine.

Juror #10 exhaled sharply, then pointed at the paper with a shaking hand. "So who is he?" he demanded, the question sharp enough to cut. "Because he's sitting right there."

Juror #2 flinched at the word he, as if it had become dangerous to even use pronouns.

Juror #5's gaze stayed on Juror #8, unblinking. "Could be an alternate they forgot to list," he said, but the words had no conviction. He sounded like a man offering a street explanation for something that didn't belong to the street.

Juror #4 lifted his head, eyes narrowed. "This is not forgetfulness," he said. "This is absence by design."

Juror #1 swallowed. His hands, still splayed on the roster, felt suddenly foreign. He remembered the chalkboard: IF YOU WANT A VERDICT, LOOK AT YOUR HANDS. His fingers pressed into the paper as if trying to anchor himself in something real.

"How," he whispered, and then had to try again because his throat didn't want to form the sound. "How did we not notice?"

Juror #9 answered him without looking away from Juror #8. "Because we wanted the room to be ordinary," he said. "We wanted the day to be routine. Twelve chairs. Twelve strangers. Twelve votes. We accepted the shape because the shape was familiar."

Juror #7's voice cracked. "I remember him in the hallway," he said. He glanced around quickly, searching for confirmation, for someone to tell him memory could still be trusted. "Don't you? We were all standing there. He was there. He had the same badge sticker."

Juror #2 nodded too fast. “Yes,” she whispered. “Yes, he did. He did.”

Juror #4’s jaw tightened. “Did you see him receive it?” he asked.

Juror #2 went still. Her eyes searched her own recollection, and her face pinched with confusion. “I… I don’t know,” she admitted.

Juror #6’s brow furrowed. “I remember him at the water fountain,” he muttered. “Or maybe I remember somebody at the water fountain.”

Juror #12 rubbed his forehead hard, as if he could scrub away the last few hours. “This is what isolation does,” he said, voice brittle. “We’re mixing things up. We’re—”

“Don’t,” Juror #3 said suddenly, voice low and harsh. The furious father’s gaze was locked on Juror #8, and there was something in it that hadn’t been there earlier: not just suspicion, but recognition of a certain kind of presence. “Don’t tell me I’m mixing things up. I know who I’ve been listening to.”

Juror #10’s laugh came out short and wrong. “Oh, you do? You want to tell us?” He gestured at Juror #8, the movement sharp. “Because I’ve been listening too, and he’s been steering us like we’re cattle.”

Juror #11's voice cut in, controlled but tight. "You were eager to be steered," he said. "All of you were, at the start. You wanted to go home."

Juror #10 whipped toward him. "Shut up," he snapped, then looked back at Juror #8. "Answer," he demanded. "Who are you?"

Juror #8 didn't move. He didn't shift in his chair, didn't glance at the roster. His calm was no longer reassuring. It was a refusal to join their panic, and that refusal made the panic sharper, like a scream in a room with no echo.

Juror #1 forced himself to look up from the paper. His foreman badge felt like a joke against his chest, a tiny piece of metal trying to insist he was in charge of anything. He looked at Juror #8, and his voice came out small.

"When we were sworn in," he said, "the clerk read the numbers. I heard them. I thought I heard them. Did she skip eight?"

Juror #4's eyes flicked to him. "We don't have the transcript," he said, but his voice lacked its usual certainty. Because he could not summon a clean data point from memory either.

Juror #9's mouth trembled slightly. "I remember the rhythm," he murmured. "I remember expecting a pause at eight and not hearing one. But I did not think about it. Why would I?"

Juror #2 began to shake her head again, but the motion slowed, as if the truth was catching up to her muscles. "It… it felt normal," she whispered. "Everything felt normal until it didn't."

Juror #5 leaned back a fraction, eyes still on Juror #8. "So either the paper's wrong," he said, "or our heads are wrong."

Juror #6's voice came heavy. "Or he ain't supposed to be here," he said.

The sentence sat in the air, plain and brutal.

Juror #1 looked down at the roster again, and suddenly it wasn't just an omission. It was a confirmation that the room had been lying to them long before the door locked, long before the clocks stopped, long before the chalk moved by itself. He flipped through the packet again, faster now, as if speed could uncover a hidden addendum. His fingers caught on a page and tore a corner slightly. The small rip sounded like damage to something sacred.

Juror #12 flinched. "Careful," he said automatically, then swallowed the absurdity of it. Careful with paper. In a room where truth wrote itself on slate.

Juror #1 ignored him. He kept turning pages, scanning for any mention of Juror #8: a note, a correction, a handwritten change. Nothing. Only the same clean certainty repeated across forms that had no room for ghosts.

At the back of the packet he found the juror information sheet. Standard instructions. Emergency contact protocols. The paragraph about not discussing the case. The paragraph about how deliberations must remain confidential.

He stared at the final line where the foreman was meant to sign for receipt.

His signature was there, shaky but unmistakable.

His own hand had certified the count.

Juror #1's breath hitched, and he realized with sudden clarity that the room had not only trapped them physically. It had made him complicit in the trap with ink and habit and the blind comfort of routine. He pressed a finger to the line and spoke without meaning to, voice breaking. "I signed for twelve."

Juror #4 looked at the signature, then at Juror #8. "But the court selected eleven," he said, as if saying it precisely might make it less insane.

Juror #10's voice went hoarse. "Then he's not a juror," he said. "He's something else."

Juror #2's hands rose to her mouth again. "What something else?" she whispered, eyes wide and wet. "A bailiff? A clerk? A—"

Juror #9 answered, and the softness of his voice made the words more terrifying. "A thirteenth," he said.

The phrase slid into the room like smoke.

Thirteen. An extra seat that wasn't supposed to exist. A number that didn't belong to their civic story. A number that belonged to superstition and bad luck and verdicts that never made it into records.

Juror #1 stared at the roster until the lines blurred. His stomach turned, not from nausea but from the sensation that the floor of reality had tilted. He looked up again, and this time his eyes didn't go to Juror #8's face. They went to his hands. Ordinary hands. Calm hands. Hands that had never touched a folder.

Juror #1's voice came out thin. "You've been here the whole time," he said, and it wasn't accusation yet. It was the last attempt at sanity. "You sat with us. You argued. You made us talk."

Juror #8 met his gaze.

"Yes," he said quietly.

The simplicity of the answer did something to the room. It didn't resolve anything. It made their uncertainty feel childish, as if the truth had been sitting in plain sight and they had only now developed the courage to look directly at it.

Juror #6's hands flexed on the table. "Then tell us what you are," he said, voice hard. "Because you ain't Juror Eight."

Juror #8 remained still. His gaze moved slowly across them, as if measuring the distance between where they thought they were and where they actually stood.

Behind them, the chalkboard did not write. The room did not murmur. Even the fluorescent hum seemed to steady, as if the building itself had been waiting for this administrative proof, this tiny, devastating confirmation.

The foreman's paper lay open like an indictment, and in its clean omission the jurors finally understood: the room had never been asking whether a boy deserved to die.

It had been counting them.

And it had brought someone in to do the counting who was not supposed to exist.

Juror #8 remained still. His gaze moved slowly across them, as if measuring the distance between where they thought they were and where they actually stood.

Behind them, the chalkboard stayed unchanged: FINAL STATEMENTS. SAY IT WITHOUT THE STORY. The boy's sentences still haunted the slate like bruises that would not fade. The tally marks beneath JUROR sat in their crooked stack, indifferent to titles, intent, and the fragile distinctions they kept trying to rescue.

Juror #6 pushed his chair back a fraction, not to stand, but to make room around his fear. "Then tell us what you are," he said again. "Because you ain't Juror Eight."

Juror #8 did not answer right away.

Juror #10 made a ragged, disbelieving sound. "He's going to do it again," he muttered. "The quiet thing. Let us fill the silence until we choke on it."

Juror #2's voice came out thin and childlike. "Please," she said, looking at Juror #8 as if pleading could turn him back into something ordinary. "Just… explain. If you're not on the list, then how are you here? How did you get in?"

Juror #4's eyes were fixed on Juror #8's hands. He'd been trained by years of spreadsheets to watch what moved and what didn't. Nothing about Juror #8 moved. No fidget. No tell. The stillness was a strategy.

"You didn't sign in," Juror #4 said, tone clipped, testing. "You didn't receive a folder. You didn't get called by the board. Yet you speak as if you belong in the process. So tell us, plainly. Are you court staff? Law enforcement? Someone planted here?"

Juror #7 let out a short breath. "Or is he the room," he murmured, and immediately looked away, ashamed of how the thought sounded and unable to stop having it.

Juror #11 leaned forward slightly, a posture that felt like readiness. "In my country," he said, voice controlled, "men like you came with lists too. Names. Numbers. Categories. They did not always wear uniforms." His eyes tightened. "Sometimes they wore civility."

Juror #8 finally lowered his gaze to the roster on the table. Not with interest, but with the faint regard one gives a document that has already served its purpose.

"That paper is real," he said.

Juror #1 flinched at the calm certainty. The foreman's fingers were still splayed over the packet as if he could keep it from rewriting itself. "Then answer," he said, voice cracking. "Who are you?"

Juror #8 lifted his eyes. "You already know what I am," he said.

Juror #5's laugh was sharp and humorless. "No we don't," he replied. "We know what you've been doing. That ain't the same thing."

Juror #9's voice came soft, almost respectful, and that respect made it unsettling. "Say it without the story," he murmured, nodding toward the chalkboard. "That is what the room asked of us."

For the first time, something shifted in Juror #8's expression. Not fear. Not guilt. A faint recognition, as if Juror #9 had finally used the correct key.

"You want a sentence," Juror #8 said quietly.

No one answered, because the room had trained them that sometimes silence was the only way to keep from making things worse. But their faces said yes. Their posture said yes. Their raw, exposed hands on the table said yes.

Juror #8 nodded once, almost imperceptibly, as if agreeing to a formality.

Then he spoke.

"I am not a juror," he said.

The words did not echo. The room absorbed them the way it absorbed confessions: without reaction, without comfort, without relief.

Juror #2's breath caught, sharp. Juror #12 made a small sound like a whimper and pressed his palms to the table as if to keep it from tilting. Juror #6's jaw tightened so hard a muscle jumped in his cheek.

Juror #10's eyes widened, then narrowed, fury trying to rise and finding nowhere to land. "Not a juror," he repeated hoarsely. "Then what the hell are you doing here?"

Juror #8's gaze swept the table. "The same thing you've been doing," he said.

Juror #4 snapped, "Don't do that. Don't speak in riddles."

Juror #8 looked at him, and his voice remained even. "You came to decide whether a boy should die," he said. "You were prepared to make it quick. Clean. Efficient." His eyes flicked, briefly, toward Juror #1's badge, toward the neatness Juror #4 always clung to. "You brought your own definitions of guilt into the room and called them standards."

Juror #1 swallowed hard. "We were doing our duty," he said, and the sentence sounded stale the moment it left him.

Juror #8 did not argue with the words. He let them hang, then spoke as if addressing something older than any of them.

"You thought you were judging a boy," he said.

Juror #2's eyes filled, and she shook her head as if refusing the premise could change what had already happened. "No," she whispered. "No, we were. That was… that was why we were here."

Juror #8 met her gaze with a steadiness that felt like an answer and a refusal at once.

"The world has been judging you for years," he said.

The sentence landed like a verdict. Juror #12's mouth opened, and no sound came out. Juror #7's hands curled into fists and then relaxed, as if his body couldn't decide whether to fight or to surrender.

Juror #10 leaned forward, voice rising. "What are you, then? Some kind of… angel?" The word came out as a sneer, but it wobbled with fear. "A demon? Is that what you want?"

Juror #8's expression did not change. "I don't want anything," he said. "Want is your language. Want is how you defend choices."

Juror #6's voice went low, dangerous. "You locked the door," he said.

Juror #8's eyes moved to the door, then back. "Did I?" he asked.

Juror #5's stare hardened. "The chalk," he said. "The folders. The voices. You gonna tell me you didn't do any of that either?"

Juror #8 paused, and the pause felt deliberate, like choosing a precise tool.

"I didn't have to," he said.

The temperature in the room seemed to drop, not physically, but in the way hope leaves a body and takes warmth with it.

Juror #9 whispered, "A thirteenth."

Juror #8's eyes flicked to Juror #9, and for the first time he looked almost approving. Not pleased. Accurate.

"Yes," Juror #8 said. "That's the number you keep circling without wanting to say it. The extra. The one that shouldn't be there."

Juror #1's voice cracked. "Why?" he demanded, and it came out raw. "Why us?"

Juror #8 looked at him. "Because you were willing," he said. "Because you walked into a room to decide death and you told yourself you were clean enough to do it."

Juror #2 shook her head, tears breaking free now and sliding down her cheeks. "We didn't know," she whispered. "We didn't know about each other. We didn't know we were… like this."

Juror #8's gaze moved to her hands, then back to her face. "You didn't need to know about each other," he said. "You only needed to believe your own story."

Juror #4's voice sharpened, grasping for one last foothold. "What are you, then?" he asked again, as if repetition could force an honest label. "A person? A concept? A mechanism? If you're not on the roster, you still have a name. Give it."

Juror #8 held the question for a moment. His eyes drifted to the chalkboard. FINAL STATEMENTS. SAY IT WITHOUT THE STORY.

When he spoke again, his voice remained calm, but something in it carried the weight of the room itself.

"You can call me whatever makes you feel less helpless," he said. "Investigator. Judge. Conscience. Punishment."

Juror #10 barked, "Which is it?"

Juror #8's gaze moved across them one by one, as if taking attendance in a different ledger than the roster could hold.

"I am the question you tried to keep outside," he said. "The one you pushed onto a boy and called it justice."

Juror #11's jaw tightened. "So the boy is a symbol," he said, and his voice was controlled but edged with pain. "A vessel."

Juror #8 did not deny it. "He is real," he said. "And so is what happened to him. That's why it works." His eyes went to the words on the chalkboard: I DIDN'T WANT HIM DEAD. I WANTED HIM TO STOP. "You were ready to kill a living person because it was easier than listening."

Juror #3's voice came low, scraped raw. "Don't you talk about listening," he said, eyes burning. "You sat here and made us tear ourselves open."

Juror #8 met his gaze. "No," he said softly. "You did that. You said the sentences. You supplied the details. You brought the dead into the room all on your own."

Juror #6's hands spread on the table again, palms up now without intending to, the posture of someone being made to show what he carried. "So what happens now?" he asked.

Juror #8's eyes moved to the tally marks beneath JUROR. Then to the roster. Then to the empty space where eight should have been.

"What happens," he said, "is what always happens."

Juror #1's voice was a whisper. "A verdict."

Juror #8 nodded once. "A verdict," he agreed. "But not the one you came in certain about."

Juror #2's breath trembled. "Are you going to kill us?" she asked, and the question was so simple it made everyone freeze.

Juror #8 looked at her for a long moment. When he answered, his tone held no comfort. "I'm not the one who decides what you deserve," he said. "I'm the one who stops you from pretending you don't decide it every day."

Juror #12 shook his head, eyes wide and wet. "That doesn't mean anything," he whispered. "It doesn't mean anything if we can't leave."

Juror #8's gaze slid to the door again, then back to them. "You've been leaving for years," he said. "You left factories. Hospitals. Homes. Streets. Rivers. Courtrooms. You left and you called it moving on." His eyes settled on Juror #1, and then the rest of them, as if pinning a final exhibit to the table. "You want to know why I'm here," he said. "Because you thought judgment was something you did for one afternoon, in one room, to one boy you could forget."

He paused, letting the words press into their ribs.

"This room," Juror #8 said, "is what happens when the verdict follows you back." The silence after Juror #8's last sentence did not feel like peace. It felt like the moment in court when everyone rises because the judge has entered, even if the judge hasn't been seen yet.

Juror #1 kept one hand on the roster packet, as if the paper could still prove there were rules in the world. His other hand hovered near the verdict envelope, the one he'd carried in like a formality. The official slip inside had been meant for a boy.

Across from him, Juror #2's tears had slowed, but her breathing was uneven, like she'd been running for hours. Juror #3 stared at the tabletop as if he expected to find a porch there, a door, glass with breath fogged on the wrong side. Juror #4's eyes moved between the chalkboard and Juror #8 the way they moved between columns of numbers: searching for an error that would turn this into something solvable. Juror #5 sat forward, shoulders tight, anger tamped down into vigilance. Juror #6 looked like a man holding himself still to keep from doing something he would regret. Juror #7's face had gone strangely blank, as if his mind had shut a door to keep the room out. Juror #9 watched with the tired attention of someone who had lived long enough to recognize the shape of judgment. Juror #10's posture was coiled, half outrage, half fear. Juror #11 sat upright, hands folded, eyes dark with a discipline that had survived worse rooms than this. Juror #12 kept rubbing his palms against his trousers as if he could erase the last hour.

The chalkboard remained crowded with the boy's words and the room's commands. FINAL STATEMENTS. SAY IT WITHOUT THE STORY. The tally marks beneath JUROR looked like a staircase drawn by someone who wanted them to climb and fall at the same time.

Juror #10 broke first, because he couldn't stand quiet unless it belonged to him.

"So that's it?" he demanded, voice rough. "We're supposed to just accept some… some thing sitting in our jury box telling us we've been judged? By who? By what?"

Juror #8 looked at him as if the question had been asked in every room that ever held a frightened person. "You still think judgment needs a face," he said.

"It does," Juror #4 snapped, and the analyst in him surged forward on instinct, reaching for structure like a drowning man reaches for a railing. "In any system that calls itself justice, it does. There's an authority. A process. A framework. Otherwise it's arbitrary power."

Juror #9's voice came soft, almost kind. "And that is what frightens you," he murmured. "Not guilt. Not consequence. The idea that the framework you trusted might have always been decoration."

Juror #1 swallowed. "We can't—" he began, then stopped. He had no sentence that didn't sound childish now. We can't be here. We can't be doing this. We can't be judged by chalk and locked doors.

Juror #8's gaze went to the verdict envelope under Juror #1's hand. "You brought a piece of paper into this room," he said quietly, "that you believed could decide life and death."

Juror #1's hand tightened, defensive. "That's not— it's a legal verdict," he said, the words automatic. "It's what the law—"

"The law is another piece of paper," Juror #8 replied. "Signed by people who needed the world to behave as if ink could make morality clean."

Juror #2 flinched as if the word clean had struck her. She stared at the chalkboard again, at IF YOU WANT A VERDICT, LOOK AT YOUR HANDS, and her fingers curled inward as if she was trying to hide her palms.

Juror #6 leaned forward, forearms heavy on the table. "Enough talking in circles," he said. His voice was blunt, but it shook slightly, not with fear of Juror #8 so much as fear of what the room might do next. "You said verdict follows you back. Fine. So, what's the verdict? What's it want?"

Juror #8 did not answer immediately. He looked around the table, meeting eyes one at a time, and the way he did it felt like a roll call in a place where names didn't matter as much as admissions.

Then the chalk on the tray clicked.

Every head turned.

The piece of chalk lifted with the same calm inevitability it always had, floated to the board, and began to erase.

Not everything. Not the boy's words. It left those intact, as if they were the foundation. But it scrubbed away FINAL STATEMENTS. SAY IT WITHOUT THE STORY. It rubbed out the neat headings and the sense that this was still a sequence they could track, still a process with steps.

A low, dry rasp filled the room. It sounded like teeth on stone.

Juror #12 squeezed his eyes shut. "I can't listen to that," he whispered.

When the chalk stopped, a cleared rectangle of slate remained beneath the boy's sentences, black and waiting like an open mouth.

The chalk wrote one word.

VERDICT.

Juror #1's throat tightened. A reflex rose in him, an old training: verdict means paper, means signatures, means an end.

Beneath VERDICT the chalk drew two lines, simple as a child's choice.

GUILTY. NOT GUILTY.

Juror #2 made a small sound of disbelief. "That's the boy," she whispered, clutching at the last ordinary thread. "That's what we were supposed to—"

The chalk wrote again, and the letters came slower, more deliberate, like a judge dictating a question that would be entered into record.

WHO?

The word sat there, stark and ugly in its simplicity.

Juror #4 stared. "It's ambiguous," he said, and even that sounded like a prayer. "It could still mean the defendant."

Juror #9 didn't look away from the board. "It has never been ambiguous," he said softly. "Not since the first folder landed."

Juror #10 barked a laugh that broke apart before it could become mockery. "Oh, come on," he said, but his eyes were wide now, flicking from the board to the tally marks. "No. No, that's not how this works. We're the jury."

Juror #8's voice came quiet, almost conversational. "You were," he said.

Juror #3 lifted his head, eyes bloodshot and hard. "You want us to vote on ourselves," he said, and the sentence came out like accusation. Like disgust. Like recognition.

Juror #8 held his gaze. "The boy's verdict was always going to be a way for you to decide what you deserve," he said. "To tell yourselves you're the kind of people who punish violence, the kind of people who protect society, the kind of people who can look at a teenager and call death reasonable." He paused. "The real question was never whether he was guilty. The real question was what you do with guilt when it belongs to you."

Juror #6's hands flexed on the table. "So that's it," he muttered. "We say guilty and we… what? We get out?"

Juror #8's gaze slid to him. "You still hear bargaining in everything," he said. "Confession as a key. Verdict as a door."

Juror #12's voice cracked. "Isn't that what this is?" he demanded, and the desperation in him was bare now, stripped of polish. "You keep saying we've been leaving for years. Fine. We can't leave now. So, tell us. Does voting do something?"

Juror #11 spoke before Juror #8 could. His voice was controlled, but there was a roughness in it, like sand under tongue. "We want an action that will make this meaningful," he said. "A lever. A mechanism. Because if there is no mechanism, then this is only suffering."

Juror #2 looked at him, eyes shining. "Isn't it?" she whispered.

Juror #11 held her gaze without flinching. "Maybe," he said. "But people cannot live inside maybe forever. That is why we invent courts. That is why we invent endings."

Juror #9's hands trembled on the table. "And that," he murmured, "is why the room has given us a verdict. An ending we can perform."

Juror #1 stared at the board, then down at the verdict envelope beneath his hand. His foreman badge felt like it weighed a hundred pounds. "We can't legally vote on ourselves," he said, and even as he spoke he knew how absurd it sounded in a room that had never cared about legality.

Juror #8's eyes settled on him. "You have been voting on yourselves your entire lives," he said. "Every time you decided what you could live with."

Juror #10 pushed back from the table, chair legs scraping tile. "No," he said, voice rising. "No. This is insane. This is some sick morality play. You think you get to make us say we deserve—"

The chalk snapped.

Not the board. The chalk itself. A clean, sharp crack.

The broken piece fell onto the tray with a small tap.

Juror #10 froze, mid-breath, as if the room had slapped him without touching him.

Juror #8 didn't look at the tray. "You can shout," he said, "but you can't un-say what you already said."

Juror #10's mouth opened, then closed. His eyes flicked toward the door, toward the seams, toward any place authority might leak in. There was nothing. Only the dead clock, the hum of the lights, the board with its two choices.

Juror #5 leaned forward, voice low, not friendly. "So, who goes first?" he asked, and the question landed like a knife because it meant he believed the room's question was real.

Juror #6 stared at the board. "It wrote verdict," he said slowly. "Not testimony. Not confession. Verdict." He looked around at the others, face hardening with a grim kind of acceptance. "We know how to do a verdict."

Juror #2 shook her head quickly, panic flashing. "I don't want to," she whispered. "I can't— if I say it, it makes it true in a different way."

Juror #9's voice came very soft. "It has been true," he said. "The only difference is whether you will finally speak as if it matters."

Juror #1's hand slid toward the envelope again, then stopped. He looked at Juror #8, eyes wide with a last, childish hope. "If we do this," he whispered, "what happens to the boy?"

Juror #8's gaze moved to the boy's words still on the board. I DIDN'T WANT HIM DEAD. I WANTED HIM TO STOP.

"What happens to him," Juror #8 said, "is what always happens to the person you used as a container." He looked back at the table. "Unless you stop using him."

Juror #4's voice cut in, tight. "You're saying the only way to be just is to refuse the easy verdict," he said. "To refuse death."

Juror #8 didn't correct him. He let the implication hang, because it was heavier that way.

Juror #3's voice came rough. "We already refused," he said, bitter. "We refused him. We refused to listen."

Juror #11's jaw tightened. "Then listen now," he said, and there was something like command in it. Not authority. Necessity.

Juror #12 swallowed hard and stared at the board. "WHO?" he whispered, reading the chalked word like it might change if he looked away. He glanced at Juror #8. "You want an answer."

Juror #8's face remained calm, but his eyes felt closer now, like the room itself had moved them inward. "Not my answer," he said. "Yours."

The chalkboard did not move. It did not need to. It had reduced the room to the oldest, simplest decision a human being can make about themselves: denial or ownership.

GUILTY. NOT GUILTY.

WHO?

And as the jurors stared at those words, the true judgment settled over them with a weight that had nothing to do with the locked door or the stopped clock. They understood, finally, what had been happening since the first vote. The boy's case was not the trial. It was the invitation.

The real judgment was whether they would keep doing what they had always done when confronted with the cost of their choices. Whether they would choose a story that let them go home clean. Or whether they would finally render a verdict that could not be filed away, could not be appealed, could not be forgotten.

A verdict on the only defendants still in the room.

Chapter 15

Verdict of Thirteen

For a long moment none of them moved, as if motion itself would count as a vote. The chalkboard waited with its crude, child-simple options. GUILTY. NOT GUILTY. WHO?

Juror #1's fingers remained near the verdict envelope, but he didn't touch it. The last time he had clung to procedure it had betrayed him. The roster had betrayed him. The numbers had betrayed him. Even the badge on his chest felt like an accusation now: a symbol of authority on a day he hadn't been able to keep a door unlocked or a headcount true.

Juror #6's voice came low. "We vote like normal?" he asked. "Hands? Paper? What?"

Juror #8 didn't answer. He didn't need to. The room had already taught them that if you waited long enough, the only instructions you got were the ones you gave yourself.

Juror #9 watched the board and spoke softly, the way he had spoken when the chalk first started writing like a mouth. "The foreman has the slips," he said.

Juror #1 flinched at the word foreman. It felt like a title that belonged to someone else, someone who still believed the world outside mattered. But he nodded once, as if nodding could keep him from unraveling. He reached for the envelope with a careful slowness that made his hand look guilty by itself.

Juror #2's breath hitched. "If we do it," she whispered, "then it's real."

"It's already real," Juror #3 said, staring at the table. His voice was rough, scraped down to something without ornament. "We already said it. This is just… signing it."

Juror #4's eyes moved from the board to the envelope with the hungry precision of a man who needed structure even if structure was a trap. "A verdict is a formal declaration," he said, as if reciting from memory could hold him upright. "If this room is asking for it, it wants the form."

Juror #7 let out a dry breath. "Of course it does," he murmured. "It loves forms. Folders. Lists. Tallies. Like we're paperwork."

Juror #10 shifted, still coiled with refusal, but the refusal had changed shape. It wasn't loud anymore. It was cornered. His eyes kept flicking to Juror #8, as if he expected him to announce the rules of the game at any moment, to make it explicit enough to fight.

Juror #11's voice came steady. "We should vote," he said. "Because if we do not, we will keep tearing at each other until there is nothing left but noise."

Juror #12's hands trembled on his thighs. "And if we do vote?" he asked, voice thin. "What then? We just… condemn ourselves?"

Juror #9 didn't look at him. "You already did," he said. "In private. This is only the first time you will do it with witnesses."

Juror #1 slid the envelope open. Inside were the standard slips, blank squares meant for the boy's fate. He tipped them onto the table. The paper fanned out like a deck of cards in a game none of them had agreed to play.

Juror #1's voice cracked. "Write what?" he asked, and he hated how small he sounded. "Just… guilty?"

Juror #4 answered without looking away from the board. "Guilty or not guilty," he said. "And who."

Juror #6 frowned. "Who meaning ourselves," he muttered, like he still wanted the room to say it out loud, to remove the last shred of doubt.

Juror #8's gaze lifted to the board. Then, finally, to them. "You've said who," he replied quietly. "Every time you said I killed." The air felt tighter after that, as if the room had pulled the walls in by an inch.

Juror #2's voice broke. "I can't write not guilty," she whispered. "I can't. Not after… after hearing myself say it."

Juror #10 snapped, not quite a shout, but sharp enough to cut. "So you're just going to give it what it wants?"

Juror #2 jerked as if struck. Tears shone at her lashes. "What do you want me to do?" she pleaded. "Lie again? That's what got me here."

Juror #10's mouth worked. "No," he said, but he didn't offer an alternative. His fury had always been built on opposition, not on answers.

Juror #1 looked down at the slips. His hands hovered over them, uncertain, and that uncertainty made him furious at himself. He had been trained to sign things. Approvals. Waivers. Reports. He had believed the act of signing was separate from the act of killing.

Now the paper in front of him felt heavier than any factory report ever had.

Juror #9 spoke gently. "We can vote in order," he suggested. "Like we did at the start. Like a jury."

Juror #7 made a small sound. "Except we're the defendant."

Juror #9's eyes stayed on the chalkboard. "Yes," he said. "That is why it matters."

Juror #6 rubbed a hand over his face. "Fine," he muttered. "Do it. One by one. Get it done."

Get it done. The phrase belonged to the world outside. It belonged to assembly lines and hospital forms and marketing decks. It belonged to every moment any of them had chosen speed over conscience and called it necessity.

Juror #8 didn't react, but Juror #11's jaw tightened slightly, as if he heard the phrase for what it was: the same engine that had carried all their secrets.

Juror #1 cleared his throat, and it came out like a failing engine. "All right," he said. "We… we'll go around."

He pushed a pen to the center of the table. No one reached for it immediately. The pen sat there like an object from a more normal universe, absurdly simple.

Juror #9 reached first. His fingers trembled as they closed around it, but his movement was careful, almost reverent. He pulled one slip toward him, bent over it, and began to write.

The scratch of ink on paper sounded too intimate in the sealed room.

When he finished, he didn't fold the slip. He placed it face down in the center, as if giving it privacy. "Guilty," he said quietly. "Me." The word guilty did not echo the way confessions had. It landed with a heavier finality. A verdict was not a story. It was an end you declared.

Juror #2 made a small sound and reached for the pen. Her hands shook so badly she had to steady her wrist with her other hand. She wrote for longer than seemed necessary, then slid her slip to the pile. "Guilty," she whispered, and then, as if the room demanded precision, "Me."

Juror #3's turn came next, and he didn't hesitate. He wrote with brutal speed, the way a man rips off a bandage because slowing down would make him scream. "Guilty," he said, voice flat. "Me."

Juror #4 took the pen and held it for a moment without writing, as if waiting for logic to save him at the last second. His eyes flicked to Juror #8, not pleading, but measuring. Then he looked down and wrote. When he placed the slip down, his mouth tightened around the word like it tasted wrong. "Guilty," he said. "Me."

Juror #5's hand closed around the pen with a street-quick decisiveness that looked like anger, but his eyes were wet. He wrote hard enough to leave an impression in the table beneath the slip, then shoved it into the pile. "Guilty," he said, voice low. "Me."

Juror #6 wrote with the heavy practicality he brought to everything, but his shoulders were tense, as if his body still believed there might be a way to blame someone else. When he finished, he stared at the slip for a second too long, then set it down. “Guilty,” he said. “Me.”

Juror #7 took the pen and held it with a strange delicacy, like it didn’t belong in his hands. His usual grin was gone; even the muscle memory of humor looked exhausted. He wrote slowly, carefully, as if neatness could make him a different kind of man. “Guilty,” he said, and he swallowed hard before he added, “Me.”

The pile of slips in the center of the table looked like a small, quiet grave.

Juror #1 took the pen next. The foreman. The man who had started the day thinking twelve chairs meant safety. He stared at the blank slip, and in his mind he saw three men in a factory, the ventilation report he had signed, the widow he hadn’t spoken to because he had a meeting. He wrote. His hand shook. When he placed the slip down, his voice came out hoarse, stripped of corporate language at last. “Guilty,” he said. “Me.”

Only a few remained.

Juror #10 sat rigid, staring at the pile like it offended him, like it tempted him, like it proved he was surrounded by weakness. “This is insane,” he muttered again, but the mutter didn't stop his breathing from quickening.

Juror #11 reached for the pen. He wrote without elaboration, without shaking, with the steady discipline of someone who had lived through the consequences of refusing to name reality. When he placed his slip down, his voice was quiet but unambiguous. "Guilty," he said. "Me."

Juror #12 took the pen last among them, and his hands looked wrong holding it, the way his hands had looked wrong when he admitted what words could do. He wrote, paused, wrote again, as if wanting to add something that might soften the verdict and finding there was no space for softness. He slid the slip into the pile. "Guilty," he whispered. "Me."

All eyes turned, slowly, toward Juror #10.

He stared back, jaw clenched, hate and fear wrestling behind his eyes. "What," he snapped, "you want me to join the club? You want me to say it so the door opens?"

No one answered immediately. The room itself seemed to wait, not for a confession this time, but for the last holdout to decide what kind of man he was when no audience could be fooled.

Juror #9 spoke, voice tired. "This isn't for the door," he said. "It's for the truth."

Juror #10's laugh came out jagged. "Truth," he spat, as if the word had betrayed him first. His gaze flicked to Juror #8. "And what about him? He doesn't vote?"

Juror #8 remained still. "I'm not on the roster," he said calmly. "Remember?"

Juror #10's face twisted. "So you get to watch," he said, voice rising. "You get to sit there and collect our guilt like trophies."

Juror #11's voice cut in, controlled. "Write your verdict," he said. "Or don't. But do not pretend this is about him."

Juror #10's breathing grew rough. He stared at the pen as if it were a weapon pointed at him. Then, with a violent motion, he snatched it up and yanked a slip toward himself. For a second it looked like he might write NOT GUILTY out of spite alone.

His hand hovered. Trembled.

His eyes darted to the chalkboard, to the boy's words still scabbed into slate: IF YOU SEND ME TO DIE, DO YOU THINK YOU GET TO GO HOME CLEAN?

His mouth opened, and the sound that came out wasn't rage. It was something smaller, uglier. Fear of being the only one left lying. He bent over the slip and wrote. Hard. Fast. As if carving. When he shoved it into the pile, he didn't look at anyone. "Guilty," he said hoarsely. "Me."

The room held that final word like it had been waiting to close its fist around it.

A full set of verdicts sat in the center of the table, face down, each one a tiny piece of paper that said what their mouths had already said, but with the cold authority of ink.

Juror #1's throat worked. He looked at the pile, then at the verdict line on the chalkboard, and for a moment he seemed to remember what his job had originally been.

"We have to read it," he whispered.

Juror #2 flinched. "Why?"

Because that's how verdicts become real, the part of him answered without speaking. Because silence is how you keep pretending.

Juror #1 reached for the pile.

Before his fingers touched it, Juror #8 spoke softly, and the softness forced them to lean toward him despite themselves.

"You understand," he said, "that this is the first time today you've treated guilt like it belongs to you."

Juror #1's hand hovered in the air.

Juror #3's voice came rough. "And the boy?" he asked, and the question sounded like a wound reopening. "What about the boy?"

Juror #8's gaze drifted to the chalkboard where the boy's sentences still clung to slate, unerasable. "He's still outside," he said. "Waiting for twelve strangers to decide if his life is convenient."

Juror #9 closed his eyes briefly. "Then we were right," he murmured. "The verdict follows you back."

Juror #8 looked at the pile of slips. "Count them," he said.

Juror #1 swallowed and began to gather the slips, one by one, stacking them carefully as if neatness could protect him. His fingers brushed the paper edges, and he felt an absurd urge to apologize to the dead for the bureaucracy of it.

He counted under his breath. "One. Two. Three…"

When he reached the end, his hand stopped. His lips parted slightly.

Juror #4 leaned forward. "What?"

Juror #1 stared at the stack as if it had changed shape. His voice came out thin, shocked into honesty.

"There are twelve," he said.

Juror #6 frowned. "There's supposed to be twelve."

Juror #1 shook his head, slow, horrified comprehension spreading across his face like ink in water. "No," he whispered. "No, I mean… there are twelve verdicts. Twelve guilty verdicts."

He looked up at Juror #8. "But there were only eleven selected."

The fluorescent hum deepened, just a fraction, enough to make their teeth ache.

Juror #8's eyes held the stack of paper with quiet attention, as if he had been waiting for the count all along.

Behind them, the chalkboard did not change.

It didn't need to.

The room had its answer now, not in chalk, not in murmurs, but in the simple arithmetic of a missing juror and an extra verdict.

Twelve slips. Eleven names.

And the thirteenth presence sitting among them, never called, never counted, yet somehow always included in the outcome.

Juror #9's voice was barely audible. "Verdict of thirteen," he murmured, and the phrase sounded less like a title and more like a sentence.

Juror #1 held the stack of verdicts with both hands, knuckles white, as if he could feel something moving through the paper.

Then, with a trembling inhale, he began to turn the top slip over to read what they had already said out loud.

And the lights, above them, flickered once.

Juror #1's thumb slid beneath the top slip.

The paper was thin and stiff, the kind designed to be handled without ceremony. His hands, though, treated it like something that could cut. Around the table, no one spoke. Even Juror #10, who had spent the day trying to bully sound back into existence, held his breath as if noise would draw attention from the wrong thing.

The fluorescent lights above them steadied after that first flicker, then hummed louder, as if compensating.

Juror #1 turned the first slip over.

Black ink, block letters, shaken into something almost illegible by the hand that had written it. GUILTY — ME.

He stared at it longer than he needed to, as if the ink might rearrange into a different word if he looked hard enough. Then he set it down on the table, face up. A small, obscene display of ownership.

Juror #2 made a sound in her throat. Not a sob, not speech. Recognition, like the way she'd recognized the chart she altered years ago, the way she'd recognized the allergy note and changed it anyway.

Juror #1 flipped the second slip. GUILTY — ME.

Then the third. GUILTY — ME.

The repetition began to do something to the room. Not comfort. Not closure. The sensation of a mechanism clicking forward, tooth by tooth, like a lock being turned from the outside.

Juror #4 leaned in slightly, his eyes tracking the slips like data points. His jaw flexed each time the ink repeated itself, as if his face wanted to insist on variance, on anomaly, on anything that would prove this wasn't simply a tally of sins.

Juror #1 kept going.

One after another, the slips became a line of identical admissions. Different handwriting. Different pressure. Different shakiness. But the same verdict.

GUILTY — ME.

Juror #7's slip had careful letters, as if neatness could make him less drunk, less selfish, less the man who hadn't stopped. Juror #5's was gouged hard enough to leave a dent. Juror #6's was blunt and heavy, written like a work order. Juror #12's looked like it had been rewritten mid-stroke, the pen hesitating, then digging in with finality.

Juror #3's slip was almost violent in its simplicity. No trembling. No flourish. The ink looked like a door slammed. GUILTY — ME.

Juror #11's was steady and spare, like a man used to writing his name on forms that meant survival. GUILTY — ME.

Juror #10's was angry, the letters biting into paper. GUILTY — ME.

When Juror #1 reached the eleventh slip, his throat tightened. Because eleven was the number that belonged to the roster. Eleven was the number that belonged to what the court had actually selected. Eleven was what reality had promised.

He turned it over.

GUILTY — ME.

He swallowed hard. His fingers hovered over the last slip, the twelfth one. The extra. The one that should not have existed.

Juror #2's eyes were wide, fixed on his hands. She looked as if she might speak, but the room had trained them all: speech did not stop the mechanism. Speech only fed it.

Juror #9 murmured, barely audible. "Read it."

Juror #1 looked up, eyes darting, and for a moment he looked like the corporate manager again, terrified of a number that didn't reconcile. "We didn't…" he began.

Juror #4 cut in, voice thin with strain. "We did. We wrote them. Whatever this is, it used our hands."

Juror #6's gaze flicked toward Juror #8. "Or his."

Juror #8 didn't move. He watched the final slip the way he'd watched the chalkboard, the folders, the thud of a new label appearing like fate.

Juror #1 took the last slip between his thumb and forefinger.

The lights flickered again, longer this time. The fluorescent tubes dimmed until the jurors' faces sank into gray. Then they brightened, stuttered, and steadied, leaving a faint afterimage in Juror #1's eyes.

He turned the final slip over.

The slip was blank.

No GUILTY. No NOT GUILTY. No ME.

Just clean, empty paper.

For a second, Juror #1 couldn't understand what he was seeing. The blankness felt louder than ink. It felt like a refusal, and in this room refusal was the one thing that never went unpunished.

Juror #12 leaned forward, voice cracking. "What does it say?"

Juror #1's mouth opened. Closed. He held the blank slip up slightly, as if showing it to the room might make it fill itself out of shame.

"It's empty," he whispered.

Juror #10 let out a short, sharp breath, half laugh, half relief. "There you go," he said, voice rising as if he'd found the argument that would save him. "There you go. That's his. The quiet guy. The saint. He didn't vote."

Juror #6's hands curled on the table. "Or it's yours," he said to Juror #8, low and dangerous. "Or it's the room's."

Juror #4 stared at the blank slip as if trying to calculate it into meaning. "A null value," he muttered, then stopped, because calling it that made him sound insane.

Juror #2's breathing went shallow. She shook her head, small and fast, as if her body could reject the blankness the way it would reject poison. "No," she whispered. "No, no, no. It wants completion. It wants a full set. It… it won't leave a space."

Juror #9 watched the blank slip with old eyes. "A space is the point," he said softly. "The missing tread. The missing name. The part that makes you fall."

Juror #3's voice came rough, and it carried no theatrics, only the blunt instinct of a man who had finally learned what absence could do. "Whose is it?" he asked.

No one answered.

Because the room had already taught them that the moment you tried to assign blame, the blame came back sharper.

Juror #1 lowered the blank slip onto the table, face up. It sat among the others like a dead eye.

Juror #8's gaze moved to it. Then to the chalkboard, where the boy's words still clung like a bruise that wouldn't fade. IF YOU SEND ME TO DIE, DO YOU THINK YOU GET TO GO HOME CLEAN?

Juror #8 spoke quietly. "You want the thirteenth to be me," he said. "You want the extra verdict to belong to a person you can point at."

Juror #10 snapped, "Because you're sitting here like you own the room."

Juror #8 looked at him. "I don't own it," he said. "You do. You built it. Piece by piece. Signature by signature. Lie by lie. You brought it with you."

Juror #12's voice rose, brittle with panic. "Then what is that?" He jabbed a trembling finger toward the blank slip. "What is that supposed to mean?"

The fluorescent hum deepened. Not louder, exactly. Lower, like a throat clearing before speech.

Juror #2 flinched and pressed her palms to the table, as if the wood could keep her grounded.

The lights dimmed a fraction, and the corners of the room thickened with shadow. It was subtle at first, like a cloud passing over a window. But there were no windows. The dimness came from inside the room itself, from the building deciding it no longer needed to pretend.

Juror #1 stared up at the ceiling. “No,” he whispered, not as a command but as a prayer to procedure. “No, don’t do that.”

The lights flickered again. This time the stutter was uneven, like a heartbeat skipping. Bright. Dim. Bright. Dim.

Juror #7’s chair scraped as he shifted, not standing, just trying to put distance between his body and the sensation that the air had turned thick. “It’s going out,” he said, and the words sounded childish because the fear was.

Juror #6’s voice went hard. “Everyone stay where you are.”

“Why?” Juror #12 snapped, almost hysterical. “So we can watch it swallow us?”

Juror #11's gaze moved to the locked door, then to the dead clock, then back to the table. "This is what happens when the verdict is returned," he said quietly.

Juror #4's eyes flashed. "Returned to who?" he demanded.

Juror #9 answered without looking at him. "Returned to the only court that never adjourns," he murmured. "The one that follows you."

The hum became a vibration. Juror #1 could feel it in his teeth. The light above the chalkboard flared suddenly, bleaching the slate for a heartbeat. The boy's words flashed stark and white.

Then the flare collapsed.

The room plunged into a dim half-light, emergency lighting without the emergency, a sickly gray that made everyone's face look like paper.

Juror #2 let out a small, strangled sound. "I can't see," she whispered, though she could. It was not darkness yet. It was the onset of it, the way night comes before it arrives.

Juror #5's voice came low. "Don't look away," he said, and it wasn't advice. It was instinct. The street in him knew that the moment you broke eye contact with the threat was the moment you lost track of where it was.

Juror #3's hands flattened on the table again, fingers splayed, as if he could hold the world in place through sheer will. "Stop," he muttered, and the word had no audience, no target. It was the same word his son used to say, the same word the boy on the chalkboard had begged for in another shape.

Juror #10's breathing grew loud. "This is bullshit," he said, but his voice shook. "This is—"

The lights went out.

Not a fade. Not a flicker. A clean severing, like a cord cut.

The hum died with them, sudden and total. The silence that followed was not quiet. It was pressure.

For a fraction of a second, there was the sound of bodies reacting at once: a chair leg scraping, a sharp inhale, someone's hand slapping the table to orient themselves.

Then, in the absolute dark, a different sound arrived.

Paper whispering.

Not the slips. Something larger. A single sheet being lifted, straightened, set down with deliberate care.

Juror #1's voice came thin and high, stripped of all authority. "Who's there?" he called, though they were all there. They had to be. Twelve chairs. Twelve breaths.

In the darkness, Juror #8's voice came from the same place it had always come from, calm and close enough to feel like it belonged inside Juror #1's head.

"You returned a verdict," he said softly.

Juror #2 began to cry, the sound small and broken.

Juror #12 whispered, "Open the door. Please. Please, I'll do anything."

No one answered him. Not the room. Not the building. Not the court outside that might as well have been a different universe.

Juror #9 spoke into the darkness, his voice trembling but deliberate. "Is this the part where we leave?" he asked.

Juror #8 did not reply immediately.

In the dark, time felt like it had stopped again, even without a clock to prove it.

Then, quietly, with the same measured certainty the chalk had used when it wrote the boy's words, Juror #8 said, "This is the part where you understand what leaving costs."

And somewhere in the blackness, so close it might have been inside their own chests, the boy's voice echoed one last time, not angry now, not pleading.

"Look at your hands."

But there was no light to see them.

Only the sensation of their palms against wood, and the certainty that the room could still see everything.

In the darkness the room was no longer a room.

It was a held breath.

Juror #1 kept his hands on the table because it was the only thing he could prove was still there. The wood was cool under his palms, the grain familiar, a cheap laminate meant to survive coffee rings and impatient knuckles. It felt indecent that something so ordinary could remain when everything else had been cut away.

Somewhere to his left someone's chair scraped, then stopped abruptly, as if the person who'd moved remembered they were not supposed to.

"Don't," Juror #6 said, voice close and harsh. "Nobody move."

"As if that matters," Juror #10 muttered. The sound of his breathing was loud. It had been loud for a while now, ever since he'd written guilty with his teeth clenched and his hand shaking. In the dark, bravado couldn't hide respiration.

Juror #2's crying came in small pulls, like she was afraid even sobs would count as evidence.

Juror #12 whispered, "There was paper."

No one answered him, but the sentence landed anyway. They had all heard it. The soft slide, the careful straightening. Something placed with intention. An act performed in the dark as if darkness were privacy instead of terror.

Juror #1 forced his throat to work. "Where?" he asked.

No one could point.

Then the boy's voice, or the room's imitation of it, came again, close enough to feel like it was standing between their chairs.

"Look at your hands."

Juror #3 made a sound in his throat. Not a word. Not a sob. Something raw that might have been the beginning of prayer if he still believed in that kind of mercy.

"I can't see them," Juror #7 said, and for once his voice had no attempt at humor. It was naked, almost childlike.

"You don't need to," Juror #8 replied from the dark, calm as ever. "You know where they've been."

Juror #10 snapped, "Shut up."

The silence after that was thick, waiting to see if the room would punish defiance. Nothing happened.

That was worse. In the absence of immediate consequence, Juror #10's fear had room to expand.

Juror #9 spoke softly, careful. "You said leaving costs," he said, his old-man voice steady only through effort. "So tell us. What does it cost?"

Juror #8 didn't answer right away. In the dark, seconds didn't feel like seconds. They felt like being held under water. Juror #1 realized he was clenching his jaw so hard his teeth hurt.

Then Juror #8 spoke, and his voice seemed to come from everywhere and nowhere at once. "It costs the story you use to live," he said. "The one where you walk out of a room and the harm stays behind you. The one where consequences belong to other people."

Juror #1 swallowed. "We voted," he said, as if naming the action might stabilize it. "We did what it asked."

Juror #8's voice remained quiet. "You did what you know how to do," he said. "You returned a verdict and hoped it would be the end."

Juror #2 whispered, "Is it not the end?"

Something shifted in the dark. Not air, not light. The sensation that the room had turned its attention. That whatever had been listening behind the walls had leaned closer.

Juror #12's voice rose, brittle with panic. "I don't want to pay," he said. "I don't want some… some spiritual bill. I did what it wanted. I said it. I wrote it. What else is there?"

Juror #11 answered him, not Juror #8. His voice came from across the table, measured, resigned. "There is always the part you think doesn't count," he said. "The part you did not mean. The part you did not touch. The part you thought was just words. Just signatures. Just following."

Juror #12 made a strangled sound. "Stop," he pleaded.

Juror #6 exhaled hard through his nose. "We're talking like it's a person," he said. "Like it's bargaining."

"It isn't bargaining," Juror #8 said. "It's recording."

Juror #4's voice cut in, sharp even in the dark. "Recording what?" he demanded. "We already confessed. We already rendered verdicts. What is left to record?"

Juror #8 answered him with a calm that made Juror #4's insistence feel childish. "The only thing you haven't given," he said.

Juror #4's breath hitched. "Which is what?"

A pause. Then, from the darkness, Juror #8 said, "A collective."

The word sat in the black like a new rule.

Juror #1 felt the table under his hands and remembered his factory. Reports. Risk profiles. Probability of fatalities. Everyone had known. Everyone had let it be normal because it was easier when the guilt was spread thin. When no single hand could be blamed without implicating the rest.

Juror #9 murmured, as if speaking to himself, "All of us."

Juror #10 laughed once, short and ugly. "No," he said. "No. Don't you start that. Don't you make it some group confession. I didn't kill with him. I didn't kill with her. That's not how responsibility works."

"It is how you survived it," Juror #8 said. "You broke it into pieces small enough to swallow."

Juror #3's voice came low. "My son didn't die in pieces," he said. In the dark, the sentence felt like a hand reaching for something it couldn't hold anymore.

The room stayed black.

Then a sound arrived that was not a voice and not the lights: the faint scrape of paper being drawn across wood, slow and deliberate, like a clerk aligning a document to the edge of a desk.

Juror #1's fingers twitched. "That's on the table," he whispered.

"Whose table?" Juror #7 asked, and the question made no sense until Juror #1 realized what he meant: whose authority, whose court, whose judgment.

Juror #2's crying stopped abruptly. She was listening so hard her breath barely moved.

Then there was another sound: a pen cap clicking off.

Juror #1's stomach turned. "No," he whispered. "No, we already wrote."

The scratch of ink began.

It did not sound like the jurors' earlier writing, hurried and shaking. This was steady. Patient. The way a hand writes when it knows it will not be contradicted.

Juror #10's voice rose. "Who's writing?" he demanded. "Who's got a pen?"

No one answered. No one could prove their hands were empty in the dark, and that was the point. The room had taken away sight and left them with nothing but their own certainty, which had never been enough.

The writing continued, a few strokes, then a pause, then a longer line, as if the writer were choosing words carefully.

Juror #12 whispered, "Is it... is it our verdict slip?"

Juror #1 remembered the envelope. He had tipped the slips onto the table, fanned them out. He had watched them pile up like a small grave. He could not remember gathering the official verdict form itself, the one the court expected, the one meant to be carried back out into the hallway with a foreman's signature. It should have been on the table. It should have been blank.

In the dark, he heard the last stroke of ink.

Then paper was lifted, straightened, and set down again with that same deliberate care.

Juror #8 spoke softly. "Now," he said.

Juror #6 swallowed. "Now what?"

The lights did not return gradually. They did not flicker. They snapped back into existence in a clean, brutal instant, as if someone had flipped a switch.

For a fraction of a second the brightness hurt. Juror #1 blinked hard, eyes watering. His hands were still flat on the table, exactly where he had kept them, as if he'd been afraid the room would accuse him of moving.

He opened his eyes.

The room was empty.

No chairs scraped. No bodies shifted. No breaths. No sobbing. No muttering. No furious laughter. No steady immigrant voice. No old man's whisper.

Twelve chairs sat around the table in their proper places, pushed in neatly, as if no one had ever sat in them. The air was too still, the kind of stillness that follows a building after hours. The fluorescent hum was back, ordinary and indifferent. The dead clock still read two twenty-six.

The chalkboard still held the boy's words, crowded and ugly in their permanence. But the headings, the tally marks, the mess of their process felt like artifacts from another room entirely.

Juror #1's heart hammered once, then twice, then seemed to stumble. He looked down at his hands because he had been told to, because the command had lodged in him like a splinter.

His hands were there.

But no one else's were.

On the table, centered where the pile of slips had been, lay a single sheet of paper. Larger than the individual juror slips. Clean court stock. The official verdict form.

It had been filled out.

In firm, steady letters that did not match anyone's shaking hand, the line read:

GUILTY — ALL OF US.

Juror #1's mouth opened. Nothing came out.

His gaze darted around the room, searching for any sign of prank, of hidden doors, of bodies slumped beneath the table. There was nothing. No movement. No warmth of human presence.

Only paper.

Only ink.

Only the verdict that had never been an option in the court outside.

Juror #1's knees weakened. He grabbed the table edge, fingers digging into laminate. The verdict slip did not move. It lay flat, perfectly aligned, like it had always belonged there.

He forced himself to look again at the empty chairs, counting without meaning to.

One. Two. Three. Four. Five. Six. Seven.

Eight.

There were twelve chairs. There had always been twelve chairs.

He swallowed, throat burning.

The chair in the eighth position sat as blank and ordinary as the rest.

No imprint. No jacket. No warmth. Nothing to prove anyone had ever occupied it except the memory of a calm voice and a missing number.

On the chalkboard, the boy's words watched him in silence.

IF YOU SEND ME TO DIE, DO YOU THINK YOU GET TO GO HOME CLEAN?

Juror #1 stared at the verdict slip again.

GUILTY — ALL OF US.

His foreman badge caught the light when he shook, a tiny flash against a suit that suddenly felt like costume. He thought of the court clerk outside, waiting for a verdict about a boy, unaware of the other trial that had just concluded in a room the building now pretended had never been used.

The door remained shut.

The clock remained stopped.

The room remained sealed.

And the only thing left of twelve people who had spoken the simplest sentence of their lives was a single piece of paper that made the simplest sentence impossible to misunderstand.

Chapter 16

A New Deliberation

Juror #1 stared at the verdict form until the words stopped looking like letters and started looking like a bruise.

GUILTY — ALL OF US.

It lay centered on the table as if someone had measured the distance to every edge. The paper was too clean, too formal, too much like the world outside. A world where verdicts were read aloud and recorded, where a foreman's job ended when he handed the slip to the bailiff and watched the defendant's face change.

His hands clamped the table harder. He expected the laminate to feel warm from twelve bodies leaning over it for hours. It was cool. The kind of cool a room had when it hadn't been used. He looked up again, scanning for any sign that he was simply missing them in the brightness. A jacket on the back of a chair. A half-finished cup of water. The edge of Juror #12's glossy folder. Juror #2's twisted hands. Juror

#6's heavy forearms. Juror #10's clenched jaw. Anything.

Nothing.

Twelve chairs. Pushed in.

The knife sat where it had sat, near the chalkboard, clean and patient, the blade catching a small line of fluorescent glare. The chalk tray held the broken pieces of chalk, undisturbed. The board still carried the boy's words like scabs you couldn't pick off without bleeding.

IF YOU SEND ME TO DIE, DO YOU THINK YOU GET TO GO HOME CLEAN?

The dead clock still read two twenty-six.

Juror #1's throat tightened so hard it felt like his body was trying to swallow the room.

"Hello?" he said, and his voice sounded wrong in the space, too loud and too alone.

The room did not answer with a murmur. The unseen gallery was gone. The pressure behind the walls was gone. Even the hum of the lights sounded like it belonged to a different building entirely.

He pushed back his chair.

The legs did not squeal.

He waited for the sound to arrive late, like the room had delayed it on purpose. It never came. It was as if the chair hadn't moved at all, though he could see it had.

His foreman badge flashed faintly when he stood. A ridiculous little piece of metal on a suit that suddenly felt like it had been dressed onto him by mistake.

He took one step toward the door.

Another.

The carpet muffled his shoes in that bland courthouse way, but even that seemed staged, too neat. He had a sick thought that if he turned around, the chair would be back under the table, the way it had been when the lights snapped on, as if the room could rewind him while he was still inside it.

He reached the door and stared at the handle. The memory of it refusing to turn was so vivid his hand hesitated just short of contact, like touching it would burn him.

"Bailiff?" he called, and hated how pleading it sounded.

His fingers closed around the handle.

It turned smoothly.

For a second his mind refused to accept what his hand felt. He turned it again, harder, waiting for the catch to clamp down, waiting for the metal to go stubborn and dead.

It didn't.

His stomach lurched with a different kind of fear. The door had not changed because the world had returned to normal. It had changed because the room had decided he was allowed to test it now. Allowed to learn, on his own, what freedom meant in a place like this.

He pulled.

The door opened.

Beyond it lay the hallway. Pale institutional walls. A strip of ceiling lights. The corner of a drinking fountain. Nothing supernatural. Nothing bent. A soundless corridor that felt like it had been drained of people.

He leaned out, looking left and right.

The courthouse should have been alive with small noises: footsteps, distant phones, the soft mutter of lawyers, the squeak of carts. Even after hours there were always clerks and bailiffs and someone pushing paper.

This corridor was empty.

Not abandoned in the ordinary sense. Empty in a deliberate sense, like a set after the actors had gone home and the props department had cleaned too well.

He stepped out.

The door swung wider without complaint.

The jury room behind him remained brightly lit, the chalkboard visible through the opening like a mouth that had already spoken.

He looked back at the table, at the verdict slip centered like an offering. The sight of it from the doorway made the whole thing feel staged for him alone. A final image to carry until it rotted him from the inside.

He turned back to the hallway.

“Is anyone there?” he called again.

His voice traveled down the corridor and died without echo. Not absorbed by carpet and drywall. Simply ended, like the building refused to return it.

Juror #1 took a few steps away from the room, slow, testing. His pulse beat in his throat. He glanced down and realized his hands were still trembling. The same hands that had signed the ventilation approval. The same hands that had counted slips and found a number that didn’t belong.

His mind reached for procedure out of reflex. Find the bailiff. Report an incident. Request security. Document the event. There had to be a form for this. There had to be someone whose job it was to respond.

But the courthouse held no one.

He tried to picture the courtroom where the boy waited. The judge. The lawyers. The defendant sitting too young in a suit that didn't fit. The bench and the flags and the seal. He tried to make the image solid enough to walk toward.

The corridor offered nothing but empty doors.

He walked to the nearest one and tried the handle.

Locked.

He tried another.

Locked.

Every door he tested yielded the same result: sealed, unresponsive, the building suddenly full of boundaries again, but not the ones he expected.

He returned his gaze to the jury room door standing open behind him.

That door was the only door that opened.

Of course it was.

He stood in the hallway for a long moment, breathing, listening for anything that would prove other people existed. A footstep. A cough. The squeak of a cart. The distant drone of courtroom voices.

Nothing came.

He backed toward the jury room as if pulled, not by force, but by inevitability. The building did not feel hostile now. It felt concluded. Like it had reached a decision and was waiting for him to catch up.

When he stepped back inside, the air changed. Not temperature. Not scent. Something less physical: the sensation of being observed returning, not like eyes, but like record-keeping. Like the room knew he was back where the accounting happened.

He looked at the verdict slip again.

GUILTY — ALL OF US.

His first irrational impulse was to destroy it. Tear it in half, crumple it, smear the ink, deny the room its neatness. He could imagine the relief of ripping it like it was a contract signed under duress.

But his hands did not move.

Because even if he tore it, the words were already in him. He had heard them. He had watched them appear. He had watched his own pen scratch guilty onto paper. Destroying the form wouldn't destroy the verdict. It would only be another act of control. Another attempt to make the consequences go away because he didn't like the evidence.

He sat down slowly.

The chair made no sound. The chair might not have been there until the moment he needed it.

His eyes drifted to the eighth position at the table. The chair looked identical to the others. Empty, ordinary, clean. If he hadn't lived the last hours, he would never have noticed it as anything but furniture.

He whispered, "Who are you?"

The room did not answer.

And yet he could not shake the feeling that if he turned his head quickly enough he would catch a glimpse of a calm face, hands flat on laminate, eyes steady with a patience that felt older than any courthouse.

He stared at the chalkboard again, at the boy's words.

I DIDN'T WANT HIM DEAD. I WANTED HIM TO STOP.

The boy's voice had been reduced to sentences on slate. That was what they did to people. They made them statements. Exhibits. Quotes. They turned a living person into material for deliberation.

Juror #1 swallowed and forced himself to speak into the empty room, because silence had been the room's favorite weapon and he was tired of feeding it.

"We were supposed to decide his case," he said, voice rough. "We were supposed to decide if he did it. If he killed his father."

The room remained still.

Juror #1's eyes dropped to his own hands on the table edge. He flexed his fingers, as if checking they still belonged to him.

Then, without warning, the verdict slip slid a fraction of an inch across the tabletop.

It did not drift. It did not flutter. It moved with the precise, measured motion of something being squared.

Juror #1 froze.

He did not reach for it. He did not pull back. His breath turned shallow, and his body braced for a sound to follow, for the chalk to lift, for the fluorescent lights to stutter again.

Instead, the paper stopped.

Centered more perfectly than before.

A tiny adjustment made by an unseen hand that cared about alignment.

Juror #1's throat burned.

"Is that what you are?" he whispered. "A clerk?"

No answer came. But the absence of an answer felt deliberate now, not mysterious. Not a trick. A refusal to give him a story.

The cost is what the words do to you once they're said.

He understood then that he was waiting for a final instruction, a final ritual, something that would make the room open like an exit wound and spit him back into his life.

The room offered nothing.

Only the verdict.

Only the board.

Only the stopped time.

He looked at the clock again. Two twenty-six. Fixed. As if the day had been pinned there, as if everything that happened after that moment belonged to a separate ledger.

He blinked, long and slow, the way a man does when he is trying to clear grit from his eyes.

When he opened them, the room looked sharper, not blurrier. Too sharp. The edges of the table, the corners of the chalkboard, the straight lines of the tile. All of it had the clean, dead clarity of a photograph.

And Juror #1 felt, with sudden sick certainty, that he was no longer moving through time. He was being arranged.

He tried to stand again, to prove he could. But his legs responded a half-beat late, as if the decision had to be approved somewhere before his muscles could obey.

He sat back down, breathing fast.

The verdict slip did not move.

The chalkboard did not change.

The door remained open now, but the hallway beyond still held no people, no sound, no life.

He stared at the empty chairs, and for the first time it occurred to him that he might be the last thing in the room that did not belong.

The room had already cleaned away eleven jurors and one impossible thirteenth presence as if they'd never been there. It had reset the chairs, steadied the lights, left the boy's words like permanent graffiti, and placed a single completed verdict at the center like a seal.

A record.

Juror #1 swallowed hard and looked down at his hands again.

They were still there, but the skin looked strangely pale under the fluorescent glare, like paper left too long in the sun.

He pressed his fingertips into the laminate until they hurt, needing sensation, needing proof.

The pain came, thin but real.

He exhaled shakily.

Then the room did something so small it might have been nothing: the air shifted, the way it shifts when a door opens behind you and someone steps in.

Juror #1 turned his head toward the open doorway.

No one stood there.

But the jury room, for all its brightness, for all its ordinary objects, felt suddenly unoccupied in a deeper way. Not empty of people.

Empty of event.

Empty as if it had never held twelve strangers deciding death, never heard confessions, never watched paper stack like a grave.

Juror #1's mouth opened to call out again, to resist being erased by insisting on witness.

No sound came.

Not because his throat failed.

Because the room, in its quiet, meticulous way, had begun to remove him too.

The last thing he saw clearly was the verdict slip, perfectly centered, the ink dry and final.

GUILTY — ALL OF US.

And then even his awareness of seeing it thinned, as if his mind were being filed away with the rest.

As if the room were finishing its work.

As if, when someone finally came to check on the jury, they would find what the room wanted found.

Twelve chairs.

A chalkboard with the boy's words.

A dead clock.

A table untouched by panic.

And a verdict waiting to be carried out into the world like nothing unusual had happened at all.

The first sound in the corridor the next morning was a cart wheel complaining softly against tile. It was an ordinary courthouse sound, the kind that belonged to coffee cups and paper stacks and men in wrinkled suits moving too quickly because time was billable. It arrived like a correction, as if the building itself had decided it was done pretending to be empty.

Court Clerk Marisol Vance kept her eyes on the docket sheet clipped to her folder as she walked. Department 12. People v. Keene. The same case number she'd been staring at for days. The same teenage defendant. The same judge who hated delays and acted as if the calendar were a moral authority.

She turned the corner toward the jury deliberation room with the practiced briskness of someone who'd done this a hundred times.

Then she slowed.

The hallway light was on. The water fountain bubbled when she pressed it, clear and cold. The air smelled like lemon cleanser and the faint bitter edge of burnt coffee. Everything was normal in the way normal can feel almost aggressive.

But the door to the jury room was ajar.

That was wrong. It was never left open, not after a jury went in. It was a rule that lived in muscle memory. Shut the door. Seal the process. Guard the sanctity of deliberation like it was a religious act.

Marisol reached the door and hesitated with her hand on the edge of it. For a second she had a ridiculous, fleeting thought that she was about to interrupt something private and violent. A fight. A breakdown. Someone on the floor.

She pushed the door open.

Light spilled out. Fluorescents. Bright, indifferent.

The room was empty.

Not empty in the way a room can be empty when everyone is at lunch. Empty in the way a room is empty when it has never been used. Chairs pushed in. Table clear. No jackets. No cups. No stray notepads. No crumpled verdict slips. The air didn't have that stale warmth of twelve bodies breathing and sweating and shifting.

Her eyes went immediately to the wall clock.

Two twenty-six.

It had stopped.

Marisol stood in the doorway and waited for the sense in her body to catch up to what her eyes were reporting. It didn't. Her pulse rose anyway, as if her body recognized a problem her mind refused to name.

Then she saw the chalkboard.

The board wasn't clean. It should have been wiped after the jury left. It always was. Someone always did it. Someone always erased the day's mess, because leaving it was like leaving fingerprints at a crime scene.

But the board still carried writing.

Large, uneven sentences that didn't look like anything the judge had ordered written up for reference.

IF YOU SEND ME TO DIE, DO YOU THINK YOU GET TO GO HOME CLEAN?

Below it, in a different line, the kind of line that looked like it had been pressed out of someone rather than written for legal clarity:

I DIDN'T WANT HIM DEAD. I WANTED HIM TO STOP.

Marisol stared at the words until they stopped being legible and became only shapes. Her mind tried to fit them into context. A juror must have written them. Someone must have been dramatic. Someone must have been reprimanded for it.

But she could not explain why the writing looked so deliberate, so centered, so final.

Her gaze dropped to the table.

A single sheet of paper lay perfectly centered, aligned as if someone had taken time to square it with the edge.

The official verdict form.

Filled out.

Marisol stepped into the room. Her shoes made almost no sound on the carpet, and that, too, felt wrong. The silence had a texture to it, a pressure that didn't belong to an ordinary morning.

She reached the table and read the form.

GUILTY — ALL OF US.

A cold wave moved through her, so physical it made her fingertips go numb.

"All of us," she whispered, and hated the way the words sounded in her own voice, like she was reading aloud in a place where sound counted.

Her eyes flicked around the room, searching for a joke, a prank, a camera. There was nothing but the fluorescent glare and the stopped clock and the chalkboard's sentences that did not look like the handwriting of anyone who expected to be laughed at later.

Her gaze snagged on something near the chalk tray.

A knife.

Not a butter knife from a lunch bag. A long kitchen knife, clean and placed with the same careful intentionality as the verdict form. It sat there like a prop that had been handled by someone who didn't worry about leaving prints.

Marisol's throat tightened.

She backed away from the table and stepped back into the hallway, moving faster now, her professional rhythm cracking into something sharp and urgent.

"Bailiff," she called, and the sound of her voice in the corridor made her feel briefly sane. "Bailiff!"

The bailiff appeared from around the corner a moment later, coffee in hand, keys at his belt, expression already annoyed by whatever disruption was about to land on his morning.

"What is it?" he asked.

Marisol pointed into the room without going back in. “The jury room,” she said. “They’re not… it’s empty.”

His annoyance flickered into confusion. He stepped past her and looked in. His face changed in stages: a quick inventory, then the frown, then the subtle stiffening of a man who understands that ordinary problems have become something else.

He entered, taking in the chalkboard, the verdict form, the stopped clock. His gaze lingered on the knife. He didn’t touch anything.

“Where are they?” he asked, but his tone already contained the knowledge that there wasn’t a simple answer.

“I don’t know,” Marisol said. “They’re not here. And this…” She nodded toward the verdict form, still centered like an offering. “This isn’t the defendant’s verdict.”

The bailiff took a step closer to the table, read the words, then looked back at Marisol with an expression that made her stomach drop.

“Don’t say anything yet,” he told her, voice low. “Go to the courtroom. Tell the judge we have a problem with the jury. Tell him we need a recess before we do anything on the record.”

"A problem," Marisol echoed, her voice thin. It felt obscene to call it that. It felt like calling a fire a temperature issue.

The bailiff's eyes stayed on the room. "Go," he repeated. His hand had drifted, unconsciously, toward his radio.

Marisol turned and walked quickly down the hallway. As she moved, the courthouse sounds returned in fragments: a door opening, a laugh from somewhere, the clack of heels, the distant murmur of attorneys warming up their voices.

Normal life. Normal noise.

Behind it, the image of that empty room followed her like a shadow.

In Department 12, the courtroom was already filling. The prosecutor stood at counsel table arranging exhibits with the neatness of someone who trusted objects. Defense counsel sat close to the boy, leaning in to speak low and steady. The defendant, Jonah Keene, wore the same ill-fitting suit he'd worn throughout the trial. He looked smaller than his age, as if the courtroom air pressed him down.

Jonah's eyes lifted when Marisol entered. They were tired. Not just from sleeplessness, but from the kind of exhaustion that comes from being discussed like a concept.

The judge sat on the bench, reading over notes, jaw set with the morning's impatience.

Marisol crossed to the clerk's desk and leaned in toward the judge as he looked up.

"Your Honor," she said quietly, "we need a brief recess. There's an issue with the jury."

The judge's eyes narrowed. "An issue how?"

Marisol kept her voice even with effort. "The deliberation room is open. The jury is not inside."

A beat of silence.

Then the judge straightened slightly. "What do you mean they're not inside?"

"I mean it's empty," Marisol said. She did not mention the chalkboard. She did not mention the verdict form. She did not mention the knife. She could not make those words behave in a courtroom that still believed in procedure.

The judge's expression tightened into anger, then shifted into something more cautious. He looked past Marisol to the bailiff, who had entered behind her and now stood near the door with his radio in hand.

"Recess," the judge said abruptly, more sharply than necessary. His gavel struck once, hard. "Everyone remain in the courtroom. Counsel, approach."

A low murmur rose from the gallery. The prosecutor looked irritated. Defense counsel looked suddenly alert, sensing the advantage that chaos sometimes brings.

Jonah didn't speak. He sat very still, watching. Marisol couldn't tell if he was afraid or simply accustomed to adults panicking around him.

At sidebar, voices dropped. The judge's face reddened. The bailiff spoke in quick, controlled sentences that Marisol could not hear. The prosecutor's brows climbed. Defense counsel's mouth tightened as he listened, then he glanced back at Jonah as if checking that his client was still real.

After a tense few minutes, the judge returned to the bench. His posture was rigid now, official in a way that suggested the courtroom itself was a shield.

"Ladies and gentlemen," he said to the room, "there has been an unexpected circumstance regarding the jury. We are going to take a longer recess. No one is to discuss the case. Counsel will remain available."

The prosecutor started to rise. "Your Honor, the People—"

"Counsel," the judge snapped, cutting him off. "Not now."

Defense counsel stood as well. "Your Honor, my client has been waiting. He's been waiting while twelve strangers decide whether he lives or dies. If there is a problem with the jury, we need to address—"

"You will address it when I tell you to," the judge said, voice controlled but sharp. He struck the gavel again. "Recess."

The bailiff moved toward the jury door at the side of the courtroom as if out of habit, as if the missing jurors might file in at any moment looking embarrassed and apologetic.

They didn't.

Marisol watched Jonah as the courtroom stirred, confused voices rising, attorneys clustering in low conversations. Jonah sat still, hands folded, gaze fixed on the empty space where a jury should have been.

He looked, for a brief moment, like someone listening to a room no one else could hear.

Then his eyes shifted slightly, almost involuntarily, toward the jury box where the next jury would eventually sit.

A line from the chalkboard, the one that had made Marisol's hands go cold, surfaced in her mind with ugly clarity.

Do you think you get to go home clean?

Marisol swallowed and forced herself to keep moving, to keep doing her job, because jobs were what kept panic from turning into prophecy.

Outside the courtroom, the judge's voice was low and furious behind closed doors. The bailiff's radio crackled. Someone mentioned contacting security. Someone mentioned calling the police. Someone used the word "missing" as if it were an administrative category.

But in the courtroom, the trial remained on the calendar.

Jonah remained at the defense table.

And the bench, the seal on the wall, the flags, the rows of hard wooden seats all kept their shape, insisting that whatever had happened in the deliberation room was an interruption, not a verdict.

By mid-morning, the judge returned to the bench with a face carved into resolve.

"We will proceed," he said, as if saying it could force reality to comply. "The prior jury has been discharged due to circumstances beyond the court's control. We will seat a new jury."

A wave of reaction moved through the room. The prosecutor looked relieved in the way an institution looks relieved when it can avoid explaining itself. Defense counsel looked furious, then calculated, already pivoting toward motions and objections.

Jonah's expression did not change much, but his eyes flickered, quick and unreadable. Not hope. Not despair. Something like recognition, as if he had seen this pattern before: adults deciding, resetting, continuing.

Marisol sat at her desk and placed a fresh stack of forms in front of her with hands that still didn't feel fully like her own. The paper was crisp, white, obedient. It did not tremble. It did not confess.

The clerk's script began again. Names called. Numbers assigned. The machinery of justice reassembled itself piece by piece, pretending nothing had happened in a locked room at two twenty-six.

The courtroom filled with new faces.

Twelve chairs in the jury box waited to be occupied.

And as the first of the new jurors stood to be sworn, Marisol caught herself glancing, once, toward the empty space where Juror Eight would have been.

As if her mind, against all sense, was still counting.

Marisol Branch read the oath again with the steadiness of someone who had learned, in one night, that steadiness was a costume you wore so the room didn't see your hands shake.

The new jurors stood in a line that looked too clean, too well arranged. They were strangers in ordinary clothing, faces already trying on the blank neutrality people believed the system required. A woman in a gray cardigan held her purse straps as if she might be asked to surrender them. A man with a sunburned neck blinked too often under the fluorescent lights. Another juror kept glancing toward the defendant like he couldn't decide whether to meet his eyes or avoid them.

Twelve bodies.

Twelve chairs.

The judge watched them with the hard patience of a man forcing the calendar to behave. The prosecutor's shoulders had loosened, relief disguised as professionalism. Defense counsel kept one hand on the table near Jonah Keene, as if touch could anchor a boy who looked like he'd been waiting his whole life to be told what he was.

Jonah did not look at the jurors as a group. He looked past them, through them, as if the people in the box were only a shape the courtroom needed to complete.

Marisol felt her gaze drift, against her will, to the side door that led to the deliberation room corridor. She could still see the chalkboard in her mind. The stopped clock. The knife placed like punctuation.

The verdict form centered as if a ruler had measured it.

GUILTY — ALL OF US.

She swallowed and kept her voice even.

"Do you solemnly swear or affirm that you will well and truly try the matter now pending before this court," she recited, "and that you will render a true verdict according to the evidence and the instructions of the court?"

The line of jurors answered in overlapping voices. "I do."

The sound was ordinary. That was the worst part. The building had not cracked. The lights had not flickered. The seal behind the judge remained a flat emblem of authority, untroubled by the idea that authority could be staged.

They filed into the jury box and sat down in a ripple of movement, fabric and shifting weight and knees turning under the wooden rail. Marisol listened for something else behind it, a second sound that didn't belong. Nothing came.

The judge began the instructions again, summary and clipped, the same language he had used yesterday, as if repetition could erase whatever had happened off the record. There were a few changes, a few added cautions that felt like tiny bandages on a broken bone. Don't speak to anyone. Don't do outside research. Don't discuss the case until deliberations begin.

Don't.

The word sat in Marisol's mind with a strange weight. She had heard it too many times now, spoken by people who believed a command could stop what was already moving.

The judge turned to counsel and asked if either side had anything further before the case was submitted.

Defense counsel rose. "Your Honor, in light of the court's decision to discharge the prior jury—"

The judge cut him off with the practiced sharpness of a man keeping a lid on something boiling. "The matter has been addressed. Your objection is noted. Sit down, counsel."

Defense counsel sat, jaw tight, eyes flicking to Jonah and then back to the judge like he was measuring how much damage had been done and how much could still be used.

The prosecutor rose next. "Nothing further, Your Honor."

The judge nodded once, satisfied. He looked toward the jury box, his expression shifting into the solemn performance of consequence.

"Ladies and gentlemen of the jury," he said, "you have heard the evidence and the arguments. It is now your duty to retire and deliberate. Select a foreperson. Review the exhibits. Follow the law as I have instructed you. Your verdict must be unanimous."

Unanimous.

Marisol's fingers tightened around her pen. The word had a different taste now. Yesterday it had been a technical requirement. Today it sounded like a demand for sameness, for conformity, for the comfort of everyone agreeing so no single person had to carry the full weight of being wrong.

The bailiff opened the side door. The new jurors filed out in a line, moving with the subdued alertness of people who had been told something serious was about to happen and didn't yet understand how serious.

As they passed, Jonah's eyes followed them. His face remained still, but something in his gaze sharpened, like he was listening for a particular footstep among twelve.

Marisol kept her eyes on the paperwork in front of her. She told herself she was not counting. She told herself she was only watching her job proceed, a set of duties moving forward because courts moved forward.

She told herself that, and then one juror stepped past the rail and her breath caught anyway.

He wasn't remarkable at first glance. Mid-thirties, maybe early forties. A plain jacket. A posture too calm for a man about to decide whether a teenager lived or died. His face held no obvious arrogance, no open fear. He did not scan the room the way the others did, searching for guidance in the judge's expression, searching for cues in the lawyers' body language.

He simply walked as if he already knew where he was going.

Marisol's pen paused mid-stroke. A small, involuntary halt that made a dot of ink bloom on the page.

The man did not look at her as he passed. Not directly. But she felt, with a sick certainty, that if he did look at her she would recognize something in his eyes she did not have language for.

The bailiff closed the side door behind the last juror.

The courtroom settled into the waiting shape it always took when the jury left. Murmurs. Papers shuffling. The judge retreating into his chambers. Lawyers beginning their quiet calculations.

And under it all, in Marisol's mind, the image of that empty deliberation room remained like a bruise.

The way it had been cleaned too thoroughly. The way the clock had stopped at two twenty-six as if time itself had been pinned to a board.

She forced herself to inhale and keep writing. She was the clerk. She recorded what happened. She did not interpret. She did not imagine.

In the corridor outside the deliberation room, the bailiff walked the new panel to the door with the same routine movements he'd used yesterday, keys at his belt, coffee now gone cold. He reached for the handle, opened it, and gestured them inside.

The room looked normal again.

That was the lie it told best.

The table sat centered under the fluorescent lights. The chairs were pushed in. The chalkboard had been wiped clean sometime between Marisol's discovery and the judge's decision to proceed. The boy's words were gone. The ledger marks were gone. Only a faint ghost of chalk dust remained in the tray, ordinary residue the way any used board would have.

The wall clock now ran again. Its second hand moved with a steady, indifferent tick.

If you didn't know what had happened, it was just a room.

If you did know, the normalcy felt like a threat.

The jurors sat down one by one. They introduced themselves in the awkward, polite way people did when pretending they weren't terrified of making a mistake in front of strangers. Someone mentioned the heat. Someone mentioned missing work. Someone laughed in the wrong place, then coughed to cover it.

The bailiff gave the usual instructions, voice flat. "You can request exhibits through me. You can request readbacks through the court. Let me know if you need anything."

He stepped out and pulled the door shut.

The latch clicked.

Several jurors glanced at it, then back at each other, as if the sound of the latch had startled something old in their bodies. But no one said anything. They had no reason to, not yet.

A man in a blue shirt cleared his throat. "All right," he said. "So, we pick a foreperson?"

A woman with neatly braided hair nodded. "Yes. We should. Get organized."

A few heads turned, appraising, looking for someone who seemed capable of being the adult in the room.

The calm man who had walked in without scanning the courtroom sat with his hands on the table. Flat. Not clasped. Not fidgeting. The gesture looked casual until you noticed how deliberate it was, like he wanted the table to feel the weight of his palms.

A juror near him spoke. "Sir, would you be willing to—"

Before the sentence could finish, another juror cut in with nervous energy. "Maybe we should just do a quick vote first. See where we're at. It seems pretty straightforward."

A few nods. A few murmurs of agreement. Straightforward was a word people loved because it promised an easy ending.

The calm man's head turned slightly. Not fast. Not dramatic. Just enough to bring his gaze across the table.

"Before we vote," he said.

The room stilled by degrees, as if the sound of his voice had lowered the temperature. It wasn't loud. It didn't force attention through volume. It forced attention through steadiness, through the odd sensation that he wasn't improvising.

He looked at the jurors one by one, his eyes resting briefly on each face as if taking attendance.

"I think we should talk," he finished.

For a moment, no one reacted. The sentence was too reasonable to argue with. That was what made it dangerous. Reasonable sentences were how rooms like this began to shift.

A woman near the end of the table let out a small laugh that didn't carry humor. "Sure," she said, as if agreeing quickly could keep the suggestion from turning into something else. "Yes. We can talk."

The man in the blue shirt frowned. "We can. I just don't see the point of dragging it out."

The calm man did not argue. He didn't challenge. He didn't even look offended. He only asked, quietly, with the same calm that made the question feel heavier than it should have been, "What's the hurry?"

A juror with glasses shrugged. "It's a murder case. We all sat through the evidence. The kid admitted he stabbed his father. The knife. The neighbors. The motive. I mean…"

His voice trailed off because the room had gone too quiet. He had expected agreement and found attention instead.

The calm man nodded once, as if acknowledging the list. "And the father," he said, gently. "What did you think of him?"

The juror blinked. "The father? He's dead."

“Yes,” the calm man replied. “But he was alive in the evidence. In the testimony. In the photos. In what people said about him. What did you think of him?”

The question shifted something, small but real. It pulled the case out of the category of straightforward and into the category of human. Into the part that required thought.

A woman with a gray cardigan hesitated. “He was… cruel,” she admitted. “From what they said.”

Someone else muttered, “Alcoholic.” Another juror said, “Abusive.”

The calm man let the words hang without correcting them, without using them as ammunition. He simply looked at them as if he was waiting for the room to become honest enough to notice what it was already saying.

Then he asked, softly, “So what are we judging? The act, or the life it came from?”

No one answered right away.

In the hall outside, the bailiff leaned against the wall near the door, listening out of habit for raised voices, for trouble. He heard only the faint, indistinct murmur of conversation.

Inside the room, the clock ticked steadily.

The door stayed shut.

And twelve ordinary jurors, unaware of what the room had done yesterday and how neatly it had erased the record, began to talk as if talking could save them.

The calm man sat with his palms flat on the table, his posture easy, his voice quiet, guiding nothing and yet shaping everything.

And somewhere, deep in the building's bones, the old question stirred again, patient as a blade laid carefully on a chalk tray.

www.ingramcontent.com/pod-product-compliance
Lightning Source LLC
LaVergne TN
LVHW050910080826
845145LV00001B/35

* 9 7 8 1 9 6 9 7 7 0 1 4 2 *